W9-CBD-516

Praise for *Mollie Peer*

"Thoroughly easygoing and entertaining . . . Mollie Peer is great fun set in Victorian New England." —*The New York Times Book Review*

"A wonderful successor to Reid's *Cordelia Underwood* . . . sparkles with neo-Dickensian comedy, romance and melodrama."
  —*Kirkus Reviews*, starred review

"[Reid] extracts humor from nearly every detail, writing with a gleeful vigor, evoking—nay, escaping to—a time when men trembled at the sight of a lovely woman, baseball and newspapers had just begun to flourish, and adventures seemed to await all comers at every boarding-house, tavern, railway station and wharf."
  —*Publishers Weekly*, starred review

"Reid continues to deliver stories that delight, encouraging readers to put up their feet for a while and enjoy a good old-fashioned yarn."
  —*The Christian Science Monitor*

"This is wonderful storytelling and simple kindness expertly combined."
  —*Salt Lake City Desert News*

"Reid's plot and style are a delightful departure from the dark corners of human existence illuminated in the majority of fiction."
  —*Bangor Daily News*

"It is the suspense of what the plot has in store, combined with the well-written and humorous buffoonery of the Moosepath League and their antics that keeps the reader turning pages."
  —*The Times Record*

"The Moosepathians are back in their second hilarious adventure, intertwined with more legendary stories of Maine and new eccentric characters . . . read *Cordelia Underwood* first and then enjoy this second volume in a promised trilogy." —*Library Journal*

"Reid is a born storyteller with a solid grounding in the history of Maine." —*Booklist*

"This is old-fashioned storytelling at its finest."
  —*The A List*

PENGUIN BOOKS

MOLLIE PEER

Van Reid, whose family has lived in Maine since
the eighteenth century, has for the last eight years
been assistant manager of the Maine Coast Book
Shop in Damariscotta. He lives with his wife and
two children in Edgecomb, Maine.

To access penguin Readers Guides on-line,
visit our Web site at www.penguinputnam.com
and click on Club PPI.

The Van Reid Readers Guide is
also available in *Cordelia Underwood*.

VAN REID

Mollie Peer

⛬ OR ⛬

The Underground Adventure

of

THE MOOSEPATH LEAGUE

PENGUIN BOOKS

PENGUIN BOOKS
Published by the Penguin Group
Penguin Putnam Inc., 375 Hudson Street,
New York, New York 10014, U.S.A.
Penguin Books Ltd, 27 Wrights Lane, London W8 5TZ, England
Penguin Books Australia Ltd, Ringwood, Victoria, Australia
Penguin Books Canada Ltd, 10 Alcorn Avenue,
Toronto, Ontario, Canada M4V 3B2
Penguin Books (N.Z.) Ltd, 182–190 Wairau Road,
Auckland 10, New Zealand

Penguin Books Ltd, Registered Offices:
Harmondsworth, Middlesex, England

First published in the United States of America by Viking Penguin,
a member of Penguin Putnam Inc. 1999
Published in Penguin Books 2000

1   3   5   7   9   10   8   6   4   2

Copyright © Van Reid, 1999
All rights reserved

Map by James Sinclair

THE LIBRARY OF CONGRESS HAS CATALOGED
THE HARDCOVER EDITION AS FOLLOWS:
Reid, Van.
Mollie Peer, or, the underground adventure of the Moosepath League/Van Reid.
p.   cm.
ISBN 0-670-88633-5 (hc.)
ISBN 0 14 02.9185 7 (pbk.)
I. Title.   II. Title: Mollie Peer.   III. Title:
Underground adventure of the Moosepath League.
PS3568.E4769M65   1999
813'.54—dc21   99–17375

Printed in the United States of America
Set in Electra
Designed by Francesca Belanger

Except in the United States of America, this book is sold subject to the condition
that it shall not, by way of trade or otherwise, be lent, re-sold, hired out, or otherwise
circulated without the publisher's prior consent in any form of binding or cover other
than that in which it is published and without a similar condition including this
condition being imposed on the subsequent purchaser.

To Marjorie Stevenson Hunter,
the best of mothers-in-law,
and to the memory of
Col. Robert Davis Hunter,
whom I wish I had known.

CONTENTS

Book Eight
OCTOBER 16–30, 1896 · 311

Epilogue: Runners in the Night
HALLOWEEN, 1896 · 331

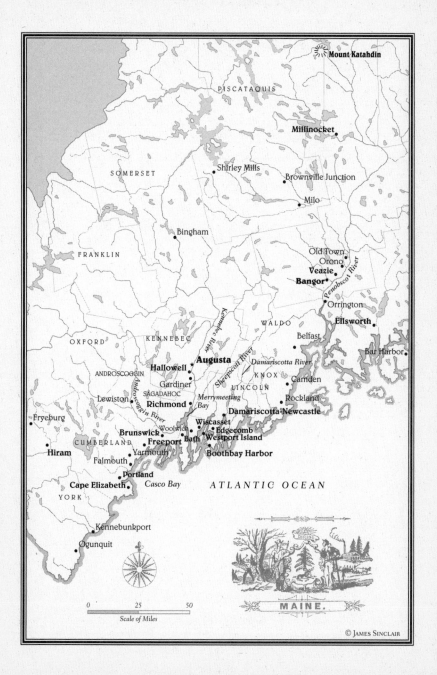

Mount Katahdin

PISCATAQUIS

Millinocket

SOMERSET

Shirley Mills

Brownville Junction

Milo

Bingham

FRANKLIN

Old Town
Orono
Veazie
Bangor

Penobscot River

Orrington

OXFORD

KENNEBEC

Kennebec River

WALDO

Ellsworth

Belfast

Bar Harbor

Hallowell

Augusta

Damariscotta River

ANDROSCOGGIN

Gardiner

Sheepscot River

KNOX

Camden

LINCOLN

Lewiston

SAGADAHOC

Richmond

Merrymeeting Bay

Rockland

Damariscotta-Newcastle

Freyburg

Androscoggin River

Wiscasset

Woolwich

Edgecomb

CUMBERLAND

Brunswick

Bath

Westport Island

Hiram

Freeport

Boothbay Harbor

Yarmouth

Falmouth

Portland

Cape Elizabeth

Casco Bay

ATLANTIC OCEAN

YORK

Kennebunkport

Ogunquit

0   25   50

Scale of Miles

DIRIGO

MAINE.

© James Sinclair

Mollie Peer

⊱ OR ⊰

The Underground Adventure

of

THE MOOSEPATH

LEAGUE

from the *Journal of Christopher Eagleton*
(September 24, 1896)

. . . *dinner at the Shipswood with the club. There was something in the day's fall-like weather that enkindled the recollection of past months. We delighted to hear Mister Walton and Sundry Moss tell again of their adventures last July. And how curious and diverse those adventures were!—from the search for the circus bear and Mr. Lofton's great anger when Mister Walton did not shoot the creature to the night watch with Sheriff Piper and Colonel Taverner for smugglers who escaped by river from the precincts of Fort Edgecomb.*

Mr. Moss, in particular, was affected by this retelling. He maintains that the little boy, named Bird, who was with the smugglers, could not have been more than four years old. Indeed, it was the next day—at Boothbay Harbor—that Mr. Moss rescued the child from bullies, and he greatly wishes that he might have rescued the little fellow from his present guardians.

Mister Walton expressed his own concern in this regard and hoped, in a prayerful way, that there might be others looking out for the little boy named Bird. . . .

Prologue: The Nightrunners
SEPTEMBER 28, 1896

❈

THE BLOCKHOUSE AT FORT EDGECOMB, on Davis Island, had presided over another summer of picnickers and squealing children. Young boys had fired at the ghosts of British invaders (who had never actually ventured so far upriver). Rusticators had paced the embankments, and lovers occasionally found an unescorted moment in which to steal a kiss in the cool shade of the wooden fort. Names were carved on the blockhouse walls and upon the benches that lined its upper story. Sometimes an old salt, living nearby, would climb to the lookout and watch an afternoon pass over the Sheepscott River.

But the warm, often humid days of summer proceeded into fall. Crickets filled the air with their chirr, and sometimes a screech owl could be heard at twilight from the few wooded acres on the southern end of the island. The nights cooled quickly, and the stars shined more brightly.

Two nights before the end of September, however, clouds quilted the sky, obscuring all but the most indirect light of the moon, and a north wind brought little squalls of rain that watered the meadows and rippled the river.

"Woke early this morning well before sunrise and worried over Caleb," wrote Sallie Davis in her journal on the twenty-ninth of September 1896. "Raining. Heard oars on the water, rubbing in the locks. I went to the window and caught the briefest glimpse of a lantern. Nightrunners, I suspect. . . ."

By night, the river was a fair highway for smugglers, and small crafts passed quietly in the dark, signaling the transportation of goods not bearing the Custom House stamp. But only recently had a boat disturbed the shore of the island once the sun was down. A vessel had come several times in the past few months—an odd little novelty, hardly twenty-five feet from stem to stern but supporting the fuming stack of a steam engine—and as on this night, a dinghy would venture forth, and the creak of its oars would round the southern tip of the island as the boat entered the small backwater known as the Eddy.

"What are you at?" rasped one of the dinghy's occupants on this particular night. "Get me closer to the fort, you imbecile!" They were several yards from shore, the oars, like the stiff legs of a water bug, radiating dark ripples that touched the near bank and disappeared in the current of the river. Then the boat chuckled against the strand as a broad-shouldered man shipped the oars and clambered to his feet.

"You *are* an idiot!" hissed the still-seated man. "Is this as close as you can get us? Well, you're lugging him, not me. Haul us up further! I'm not catching my death because you can't master a pair of oars!"

The other man, who proved tall as well as broad when he straightened to his full height, splashed up to his calves in the cold water, grasped the gunwale of the boat, and leaned into the shore. The boat came easily, scraping lightly on the pebbly beach.

A third figure—a child of no more than four or five years—was lifted onto dry land, and the seated man, small and narrow in his voluminous coat, looked up at the banks rising to either side of the little cove. "Well, tie it off!" he insisted. "We haven't got all night! Now get his head. I'll help you get him out of the boat, but you're lugging him the rest of the way."

The larger man waded back to the floating end of the boat and raised from it the head and shoulders of a stiff form. The other lifted the feet into view, and with the child looking on, they carried the still shape to land. A sound came from the nearby woods, a long, vowelly yowl that was not completely distinguishable from a human wail. Residents hereabouts would recognize the voice of a bobcat—one lived on the island—but it seemed that nobody in the small group had ever heard such a sound, for all talk and movement came to a halt.

"Quick, quick!" demanded the smaller man in a strangled whisper, and in a moment they were climbing over the bank, in the direction of the fort, the largest member of this strange band laboring beneath the weight of the unmoving figure. They crossed the parade ground, glancing up at the old blockhouse and over their shoulders in this exposed place. They might have imagined that the octagonal walls, looming in the dark, opened a shuttered eye to watch them pass. Crossing a corner of the island, they came to a steep bank where brick and stone embankments rose above granite ledge. The larger man laid down his burden, and the smaller man leaned over the banquette to look for a shelf of rock. He let the larger man dangle him down over the side till he had his footing there.

Then the man at the top of the bank (a great bull of a man, really) took up the stiff figure and climbed over, leaving the child to crouch in the intermittent rain and cool air of the predawn. The wind rippled and tugged along the edge of the parade ground.

In her journal, Sallie Davis wrote, "*Lay awake till dawn. October coming.*" Perhaps she was superstitious, for she added in the margin of the page, "*Soon I suspect other things will be wandering the night.*"

Book One
OCTOBER 8, 1896

1. Out of the Fog

It was difficult to say no to Mollie Peer, especially knowing she had spent an entire day at her typewriter, working on her columns for the *Eastern Argus*. It had been a lovely afternoon, despite prognostications, and Hilda hated to deny her friend and fellow boarder a few minutes' walk before the sun went down. Besides, Mollie was never so ready to listen as when she had just finished her society column, and Hilda, as always, had much to say.

Stepping onto the porch of Makepeace's Boarding House, they were taken by how dark it had grown so early in the day. Signs of last night's storm spotted the lawn—leaves and twigs and smaller limbs strewn beneath the maples on either side of the walk.

The newspapers had warned against a hurricane, reporting telegraph messages of death and damage up the eastern seaboard (a ship was missing off the coast of Virginia), though later editions predicted merely a gale. From Portsmouth to the Maritimes, the coaster fleet sought shelter, and many of them had come into Portland the day before, so that the harbor was a thicket of masts and spars, and there was concern that the ships and schooners—so densely anchored in a high wind—might do damage to one another. But the storm that arrived on the seventh of October, though strong enough to warrant caution, had mostly blown itself out by the time it reached the Portland waterfront, and the eighth had come off cool and clear.

Mollie was glad that the trees had held on to their foliage; the maples and oaks along the street were red and yellow—looking purple and brown now in the gloaming. The air was colder than she had expected, and she considered going back for her wool cloak; but fearing to discourage Hilda, who had not been so keen for a stroll, she pulled her shawl closer about the shoulders of her jacket and led the way down the walk.

Hilda chatted, as she always did, discussing the private lives of her fellow workers at the rope factory and her flirtation with a packer who worked near her station. Mollie made the perfect companion for such talk; Hilda thought her friend overly secretive about her own affairs, but she knew from experience that Mollie would hear every word she said. Arm in arm, kicking at the fallen twigs, they let the path of least resistance draw them downhill in the direction of the harbor.

It was well past five o'clock and the streets were strangely quiet, as if an autumnal stillness had arrested the movements of homecoming shop-keepers and businessmen. Mr. Duncan, Plum Street's lamplighter, was mounting the hill, raising his long staff and fiery wick to the gas lamps as he approached them. He recognized Mollie and Hilda and tipped his hat when they passed, then turned and looked after them.

Hilda, with her light brown hair and plump figure, was an attractive enough girl, but the lamplighter's eyes lingered on Mollie before he turned back to his evening's chore.

Mollie was tall and moved with an assurance that one might suspect was developed through physical (even athletic) activity. She had strong shoulders and was considered large-boned for a woman. Though only twenty-two years old, she seemed, at first glance, more matronly than youthful. A second glance, however, often merited a third one—and the third, a fourth. Some men's heads would rise and fall as their attention grew increasingly distracted by what they saw, like a person who slowly be-gins to realize that he has misread an entire page of text.

As for her features, they were somehow more than the sum of their parts: Her nose had an Irish lilt (like her father's) and may have been a shade too small, and surrounding it her mouth and eyes (taken after her Italian mother's) seemed exaggerated and overprominent; and yet to-gether with the intelligence in those eyes and the wry set of that wide mouth, those strangely matched features conspired to make her beautiful the more one considered them.

Hilda chatted. They breathed in the crisp air, spiced with the scent of dry earth and leaves and wood smoke. Mollie kept her friend to a brisk pace, arms swinging with pleasure—not the picture of demure femininity but of glowing suffrage.

Then Mollie saw the boy walking uncertainly in their direction; a waif, a ragamuffin, four or five years old, his clothes barely holding to-gether. *He must be cold*, she thought. When he was within a few yards of them, he looked as if he might cross the street, and so she said hello to him.

He stopped, looking more uncertain still. Hilda ceased her gossip for a moment to consider the child, considered him of little interest, and recommenced her story.

"What's your name?" asked Mollie.

Hilda came to a second halt and looked put out. "What is it?"

"It's a little boy," said Mollie, approaching him.

"I can see that, but why are you talking to him?"

"Because he interests me." Mollie leaned down with her hands on her knees. "What's your name?" she asked again.

"Everything interests you," said Hilda with some irritation.

"It's my business."

"I dare say *he* won't make the society pages."

"I don't know. There have been millionaires who started with only a penny." She addressed this to the boy with an encouraging smile. "My name is Mollie." She held out her hand.

He put his hand in hers, as if he were giving her something rather than shaking it. He said something in a small voice.

"Bert?" said Mollie.

Only slightly louder, he said, "Bird."

"Bird!" she said, as if the word gave her great pleasure. "What a fine and unusual name! Where do you live?"

This was more problematic. Confusion and possibly even guilt swept past his face. "With Mr. Pembleton."

"Bird!" came a harsh croak, and the boy's eyes went wide. Hilda jumped with a little shout.

Mollie had seen the man coming in the periphery of her vision. She looked up and smiled, saying, "Mr. Pembleton," as one would greet a friendly neighbor.

The man gave her a sharp look. He was a scarecrow; ragged, thin, and dirty. He wore an ancient hat and a long, pockety coat, and even his blond hair—long and thin and hanging at all angles from under his hat—lent him the appearance of something standing in a field. He dropped his gaze to the little boy and swung an arm. "Come here! Where were you going?"

The boy had no answer but obeyed the command quickly, shoulders hunched as if in expectation of a blow.

The blow was aimed—the girls saw the man's muscles tense—but he shot a glance backward and lowered his hand to the boy's shoulder. His grip went white. "Come, come. We've been looking for you. Did you get lost?"

Behind the two young women, past the houses and through the trees on the street above them, the clouds glowed with a last purplish grandeur.

Ahead of them, in the direction the raggedy man and the raggedy boy disappeared, murk and shadow rose like an incoming tide.

Mollie took Hilda's arm and tugged; there was only a moment's resistance before Hilda fell in. "Goodness, he frightened me!" said Hilda.

"He likes to frighten, is my guess."

"Well, he can frighten someone else, thank you." Hilda was beginning to take note of the gathering gloom. They were alone on the street. "Haven't we come far enough? It's getting dark."

"So, what did Mr. Court say to you when you remarked how strong he was?" asked Mollie, looking avid to know the answer.

"Oh, he blushed!" Hilda laughed. "I like a man who can blush, don't you?"

"A man who can't blush has no shame, my mother used to say."

Hilda's chatter filled the air once more as they descended the hill with more of a fast walk than a leisurely stroll. Bits of lamplight appeared ahead of them, glowing bowls in islands of gathering fog through which the silhouettes of Mr. Pembleton and Bird rose and disappeared.

Hilda was still extolling Mr. Court's virtues, as well as the virtue of young men in general, when it occurred to her that Mollie was tiring her out. "What is the hurry, dear?" she asked.

"No hurry," answered Mollie. "I'm feeling energetic."

"*That* can't be healthy. Let's go home. It's getting dark."

"The lamps are lit."

"We have to walk *up* this hill?" exclaimed Hilda, as if suddenly realizing that what went down must go up.

"We're nearly to the foot of it. We might as well say we went the entire way."

"Mollie, what are you about?"

"About? I'm about nothing. I'm going for a stroll, is all."

"You're following that man and that boy, aren't you."

"Now, why would you think that?"

"You said yourself, it's your business."

"And you said yourself, they won't make the society pages."

"Then let's go back."

Mollie glanced anxiously down the street. The shadows of the two ahead of them were hardly discernible near the bottom of the hill. "Oh, come! Where's your sense of adventure?" She pulled at Hilda's arm with sudden urgency, her voice lowered to a whisper.

"Sitting next to my bed, in Mrs. Randolph's latest novel!" Hilda was hurrying with her despite her protestations.

"But aren't you concerned for that boy?"

"He's with his father."

"He wouldn't call his father *Mr.* Pembleton."

"Mollie!"

Mollie Peer stopped to look at Hilda standing just above her on the sidewalk. "I am going alone, then," she said simply, and hurried off.

"You most certainly will not!" exclaimed Hilda, and hurried after.

They slowed their pace near the bottom of the hill, where Plum Street emptied onto Commercial Street. At the brick building there, they stopped to creep up to the lamp-lit corner. There were no shadows to hide in, but Mollie stayed close to the cold brick as they peered out at the wide street and the warehouses and waterfront beyond.

Fog rolled in from the harbor, billowing about the bows of great ships that loomed above the cobblestones and shifted between the buildings with the movement of water like stirring creatures in their berths. There were footsteps in the gathering atmosphere, ringing on the pavement in the dampness; hoofbeats and wheels railing out of the dark beyond the limits of the lamplight. Hilda held her breath. Mollie leaned away from the corner of the building, searching for the figures of the man and the boy.

A hand gripped her wrist with sudden ferocity; Mr. Pembleton was dragging her from her cover. "Feeling interest, are we?" snarled the man as he drew her close, and though she was as tall as he, he seemed to tower over Mollie with his dark anger.

Hilda let out a frightened wail.

"Let go of me!" demanded Mollie, doing her best to sound unafraid, though his clutch on her wrist was painful.

He focused a hard eye upon her, gritting his teeth as he bore down. Mollie cried out, and when Hilda stepped closer to the struggle, he stopped her with a single glance. "You must have something you care to ask me!" he was saying. "You've taken such care to follow me!" The night mist rose up from around their feet.

"Let me go!" Mollie said again.

Hilda had only gotten hold of the man's ragged coat when some dark force lifted her into the air and dragged her several feet away. A great bull of a man held her as she would the smallest child, and in his unyielding clench Mollie could see no sign of her struggling against him. For a moment Hilda and the large, silent man disappeared as the fog blew past in an unexpected gust of wind and a man's voice from around the corner shouted out a surprised "Whoops!"

A homburg hat floated into Mollie's view, spiraling on its own axis to land not six feet away.

"Where did it go?" came the voice.

"I think it went round the corner," came another.

Mollie feared that Pembleton and his associate would make short, nasty work of her and Hilda, but then they were gone, vanished in the gloom and haze.

A tall, young man hurried onto the side street and found the hat. "It's here, Mister Walton," he called. The women were still frozen against the brick wall, and when he straightened up with the hat, he caught sight of them with a small start. "Hello," he said in such a friendly, straightforward manner that, conversely, tears came to Mollie's eyes. He tipped his own hat.

"Hello," she said with surprising conviction.

There was laughter again and a jolly voice declaring that hats sometimes showed as much a mind of their own as the heads on which they sat. Then a portly gentleman wearing spectacles and without a hat (or hair to speak of) appeared. "Have you found it, then? Sundry, thank you! I am reminded of the day I came back to Portland and met Cordelia Underwood. . . ." He caught sight of the two young women then, paused, and reached to tip his hat before realizing that his friend was in possession of it. "Good evening, ladies," he said with a cordial smile.

"Sir," said Mollie, standing straight now.

It was clear that the portly fellow thought they had surprised two women of the night and was politely ready to allow them to go their way; but then a look of concern fell across his face, and having retrieved his hat from his friend, he stepped closer. "Is everything all right?" he asked, directing his question toward Mollie.

"Well, to tell the truth," she said, feeling an unaccountable sense of security with this man, "to tell the truth, we've had a bit of a fright."

Hilda let out a sob, and Mollie took her under one arm.

"How can we help you?" asked the bespectacled man, hat in hand as he stepped forward. "My name is Tobias Walton." The young man who had retrieved Mister Walton's hat was at his side with the readiness of a squire. "This is my good friend Sundry Moss," said Mister Walton.

Mollie stepped forward, albeit shakily, and offered her hand. Mister Walton's grip was firm, but it conveyed a gentleness that worked like a salve on her rattled nerves. He did not ask what had happened, demonstrating a degree of circumspection that she herself would not have possessed. The young Mr. Moss peered into the rolling mist, up Plum Street, looking for the who or what that had frightened the young ladies.

"May we take you somewhere?" Mister Walton was asking.

Mollie thought of Mr. Pembleton and his large associate waiting above them in the fog. "Yes, that would be very kind of you."

"Our carriage is just down the street."

"We would be sorry to inconvenience you."

"Not at all," said Mister Walton as he led the way. "We were just going to the Shipswood to meet friends—a weekly sort of thing we do—and they will forgive us for being a few minutes late." The horse, then the vehicle itself, loomed out of the fog, and a driver dropped down from his seat to turn up the lanterns and open the door. "Mr. Griggs," said Mister Walton.

"Mister Walton," answered the driver, surprised to see his recent fare so quickly again. He glanced at the women curiously.

"Good heavens, child!" Mister Walton said as he handed Hilda into the carriage. "You're shivering." He insisted that she take his coat.

Mollie explained where she and Hilda lived. "It's only straight up on Plum Street," she said, "but if you could take a round way about—" She was thinking of Mr. Pembleton watching from somewhere on the hill.

Mister Walton caught a raised eyebrow from Sundry Moss, then looked up and down Commercial Street. "Of course, dear. We'll go to Middle Street by way of Market and circle around."

Mollie rested a hand on his. "Thank you."

There was silence between the two parties as the carriage got under way, during which they attempted, in those darkened confines, to size one another up without appearing to do so.

"If there is anything else we can do . . . ," Mister Walton began, his expression composed but his eyes filled with what Mollie had long ago termed (in her own father) an *unassuming concern.*

"Thank you," said Mollie. "We will be fine." Hilda, who had not said a single word since the attack, looked ready to belie this, and Mollie laid a hand on her friend's lap.

"The fog is quite thick tonight," said Mister Walton.

He did remind Mollie of her father—not physically (her father was large and muscular; Mister Walton, barely of medium height and portly), but there was a gentle vitality to both men. Watching Mister Walton, who smiled placidly as he peered out the window, she realized that he was not as old as she had first imagined.

The younger man wore a bemused expression, his arms crossed, his legs stretched where he could find room for them. He was not handsome, exactly, but pleasant enough to look at, with a wide nose and a square jaw. He was long and wiry, his manner courteous, if reserved. "I always thought a thick fog more like chowder than pea soup," he said to no one in particular. He seemed gratified by an expression of mystification on Hilda's face and a small smile from Mollie.

"There were two men," said Hilda suddenly.

Mister Walton glanced from one to the other of the young women. "Are you sure you're all right?" he asked.

"Yes," said Mollie. "You came just in time." She felt it necessary to say as little about the incident as possible; her landlady already thought her more adventurous than was becoming to a young woman. Mister Walton, she was sure, sensed (in a general way) the reason for her reticence and was debating how far he could, in good conscience, honor it. "I write for the *Eastern Argus*," she said, as if this would clear the matter.

"Really," he said, then, to the younger man, "Mr. Ephram will be very pleased. A fellow club member," he explained to Mollie, and she could see a delighted amusement enliven his eye. "Mr. Ephram is a great reader of the *Eastern Argus*."

"How nice," said Mollie, at a loss for further response. "A fellow member, you say."

"Yes," said Mister Walton, and this, too, seemed to amuse him. "You may have heard of us—the Moosepath League. Several members were in the newspapers last summer."

Mollie had heard of them. "Was that the buried treasure?" she asked, and sat forward, curiosity overcoming her recent fright.

"It seems very *much* buried at the moment," said the man. "But my friend, here, came very close to recovering it."

"A miss is as good as a mile," said Sundry Moss with good-natured self-deprecation. It was clear, however, that he was still thinking about Hilda's single comment.

"And there was a woman kidnapped," continued Mollie.

This was a subject about which Mister Walton could not jest. "There was indeed," he said, his expression serious again. "Though it all turned out well, I fear she had a very frightening experience." And this train of thought led (quite unintentionally) back to the two young women and their own recent fright.

"Did these men . . . accost you somehow?" asked the younger man.

Hilda only looked to Mollie, who said, "The fog makes everything so much more frightening, of course."

They were pulling up to the address Mollie had indicated, and she quickly took advantage of the distraction, opening the door before Sundry could reach it and expressing her gratitude.

She stepped onto the street, and Mister Walton appeared from around the horses. "Are you sure there is nothing else we can do for you?" he asked, his hat in hand, his balding head shining beneath the streetlight.

"Thank you, but we're really fine now," said Mollie, though Hilda did not look so sure of this. "It's been so nice to meet you." But by the time she had given her hand to both men, the door to the boardinghouse had opened, and Mrs. Makepeace was peering out at the assemblage. "Oh, dear," said Mollie. "This will take some explaining. Hilda, you'll never walk with me again."

"Would it ease matters if I went in with you?" asked Mister Walton.

"Oh, Mister Walton," said Mollie, "we've kept you away from your friends far too long already." She was shaking again, suddenly, and needed to use the distance between the street and the boardinghouse porch to gather herself for the inevitable round of questions from an inquisitive, if well-meaning, landlady. "Thank you so much," she said again, putting off any further offers on the part of Mister Walton, and taking Hilda's arm, she deliberately led them away from the carriage.

2. At the Shipswood

SMOKE AND VIOLIN MUSIC similarly drifted through the atmosphere of the Shipswood Restaurant, and if the members of the Moosepath League did not indulge in the Luciferian practice (any more than they played the stringed instrument), yet they were accustomed, here in their weekly meeting place, to the smoke of other men's cigars and pipes and felt invigorated, in a manly way, by the blue haze, even if they did not contribute to it. The violin music was nice, too.

The Shipswood was a fine establishment, with pleasant round tables and brightly lit chandeliers. The tablecloths were always clean, the service was friendly, and the tall, many-paned windows gave view during the hours of light to the business and hurry of Commercial Street and the better section of the waterfront.

Mr. Matthew Ephram, Mr. Christopher Eagleton, and Mr. Joseph Thump (of the Exeter Thumps) were old hands at this sort of thing. They had been meeting weekly at the Shipswood for more than twelve years, but that was before the fateful night when they were inspired to form a club. That was, in fact, before they had met and admired Mister Tobias Walton, whom they elected as their chairman; and it was well before they experienced several exploits in several other parts of the state while forming the Moosepath League!

During the past weeks they had had a succession of breathless escapades, taking tours about the city and even dining at Mister Walton's home. They had celebrated Eagleton's fortieth birthday, on which occasion Mister Walton had introduced them to the glories of baseball. They had observed a bicycle race at Deering Oaks and become subscribers to Portland's telephone service. They had made several telephone calls to one another.

Despite these wild sprees, Ephram, Eagleton, and Thump had not lost their sense of wonder; in fact, they continued to wonder a good deal, and on the evening of October the eighth they were wondering very specifically as to the whereabouts of their chairman.

"I do not recall," said Ephram, "that he has ever been late to one of our gatherings."

Eagleton, the club's self-appointed historian, gazed into the middle distance and considered this. "I myself have no recollection of any such tardiness and in fact rather consider him a man of admirable promptitude." It was well said, and Eagleton was feeling the effect of his own words when he realized that the particular middle distance in his direct line of sight consisted of a striking young woman who was returning his gaze with a good deal of interest. Thinking that he had collected more than was his share, Eagleton averted his eyes, sat straight in his seat, and raised his menu.

Ephram glanced toward the entrance of the Shipswood Restaurant. "What do you think, Thump?" he asked.

Thump looked up from his own menu and said, "Hmm?"

Ephram did not repeat his question, for it was then that a general hale-and-hearty welcome arose from the fore of the restaurant, and the three Moosepathians knew, from recent practice, that their chairman had arrived.

Other folk dined at the Shipswood of a Thursday night, and in the past several weeks they had come to recognize Mister Walton, who was able to spread cheer simply by passing their tables. His face beamed with sincere interest and pleasure in his surroundings as he entered, his manner was gracious as he stopped at one table to say hello, and his sense of humor was ever ready to appreciate a quip from this group or further a running jest with that.

Ephram, Eagleton, and Thump watched with pride as their chairman found his way to their table, followed by Sundry Moss. (A trusted companion and something of a gentleman's gentleman to Mister Walton, Sundry had been inducted as the fifth member of their society.) "Gentlemen, gentlemen," said Mister Walton when he arrived. "Forgive our tardiness."

"Good heavens!" said Ephram. "Never tardy! I would never say tardy! Would you, Eagleton?"

"Certainly not tardy!" agreed Eagleton. "What do you say, Thump?"

"I'm sure we were early," insisted Thump.

"You are very kind," said the portly fellow as he found his seat. "Sundry and I came upon two young women who had had a recent, if unspecified, fright, and we were pleased that they accepted an offer of a ride home."

"A fright?" said Ephram. The chairman was always in the middle of things, it seemed, and they greatly admired him for it.

"Young women?" said Eagleton.

"Hmm?" said Thump.

What had amounted to a slight digression in Mister Walton and Sundry's evening was viewed by their friends as a full-scale adventure. The members of the club were not a little taken with the description of the young women (Sundry's memory was especially glowing), and Ephram was very much amazed to hear that one of these ladies was a columnist for the *Eastern Argus*.

"Good heavens!" he said again. "And I a subscriber!" as if this were the most astonishing coincidence.

The conversation continued while dinner was ordered, waited on, and served, but Ephram found it difficult to immediately separate himself from thoughts of attractive young women and the *Eastern Argus*. Eventually, however, he rejoined the flow of discourse just as Sundry was informing them about his father's uncle, who had predicted the weather with great accuracy for twelve years, claiming all the while that he garnered his prophetic powers by milking a particular belted Galloway named Temperance. Certain anatomic features of the cow (which Sundry delicately left to the imagination of his listeners) were alleged to represent the four winds, and the difficulty or ease with which the milk came was given to foretell the corresponding variations of oncoming weather.

Ephram pulled at his fine mustaches.

Thump stroked his prodigious beard.

"I hope I do not sound precipitous," said Eagleton, who was fascinated with the weather, "when I say that I would like to look at this cow."

"I fear it is unlikely," said Sundry. "Both uncle and cow have long since departed." He raised his hands to stem the condolences; it had all happened long before he was born. "She lost her oracular powers, at any rate, before her demise. As a prank, one Halloween, some boys—or, rather, a crew of men behaving like boys—kidnapped her and bought her a ticket on the night train from Wiscasset. It wasn't till the train had nearly reached Bath that the conductor discovered her, but she was never the same again."

This seemed a sad end to a noteworthy career. Ephram, Eagleton, and Thump looked solemn. Mister Walton could not suppress a chuckle.

"But for ten years," added Sundry by way of consolation, "the village of Sheepscott hayed without fear of rain and canceled long trips before any blizzards hit."

"Ten years?" asked Mister Walton. "I thought your uncle predicted the weather for *twelve* years."

"Yes, but for two years nobody believed him."

"Ah!" Delight twinkled in Mister Walton's eyes.

"The Portland Bantams are playing an exhibition game against Lewiston tomorrow morning," said Eagleton, who had stolen a glance at the newspaper beside his place at the table. Mister Walton's enthusiasms were of great moment to the members of the club, and through him the local baseball team had garnered their fierce loyalty, though the game itself was still something of a mystery to them. "The paper looks to Mr. O'Hearn for some feat by which the year, if not the season, might be made memorable."

Ephram made a sound of interest and leaned over to see the headline indicated by Eagleton's index finger. Thump frowned down at his hands, which were open before him. He was considering the mysteries of bovine anatomy.

"I'm sorry to miss that," said Sundry. "But I think we will be preparing a way north tomorrow morning."

"My word, yes!" said Ephram. "The Hallowell Harvest Ball!"

"We have been forgetting your impending rendezvous with Miss McCannon!" said Eagleton to Mister Walton.

"Hmm," said Thump. He seemed to be counting something on his fingers.

Mister Walton smiled. "The ball isn't till Monday night," he announced happily, "but Sundry and I will be leaving tomorrow."

Several weeks before, Mister Walton had received a letter (which even now resided in his breast pocket) from Phileda McCannon, whom he had met during the previous adventurous summer. Though he had been forced by circumstance to leave her side more quickly than he would have wished, they had kept in communication ever since by post.

His friends, all of whom had been greatly impressed with Miss McCannon, could not have been happier if they themselves had been invited. Sundry, who had detected a bit of loneliness in his employer of late, was perhaps the happiest of all.

"Wonderful!" said Eagleton.

"Bravo!" said Ephram.

"Hmm," said Thump.

"Twenty past nine," said Ephram, consulting one of the three or four watches that he always carried about his person. They had stopped outside the Shipswood to take stock of the night and those noises intrinsic to the waterfront.

"High tide at eleven forty-eight," announced Thump, though he was somewhat distracted. He was musing again over the anatomic structure of cows. He had never been very close to one.

"Some chance of ground fog this evening," assured Eagleton. "Though this should be cleared by a wind changing to the southwest and brief showers before dawn." The ground fog was, in fact, all about them, and their carriage, some lengths down the glistening street, was nearly obscured by the mists that slunk from the alleys and drifted along the cobbles.

"The fog does make things *sound* very much closer, doesn't it?" said Ephram, adding, "Or perhaps I am mistaken. Perhaps the things we hear actually *are* near at hand and it is the fog that makes us think they are distant." He deferred in this question to Eagleton, whose great love, if not métier, was meteorography.

"I hadn't considered," said Eagleton carefully. "But it is a very remarkable effect."

Thump was looked to next, but he was still thinking about cows. "Hmm?" he said.

"I know that when my room is dark," said Sundry, "the foot of my bed is often not where I think it should be."

Ephram petitioned Mister Walton for his opinion on the subject of fog and its effects upon human perception. Eagleton attempted to explain to Thump the two theories that had already been expounded. Thump realized, with a start, what portion of the cow Sundry had been speaking of.

"I trust you will be back in time for next Thursday's meeting?" ventured Ephram.

"Oh, yes, surely," said Mister Walton.

Sundry, who had less confidence in human design, simply said, "Barring unforeseen incident," which comment they would all remember when next they met, at another time, in another place.

Mister Walton's late aunt August had always said, "Young Toby has a traveling bee," and it was perhaps not far from the truth, since he had spent many years away from the state of Maine. Recently, however, he had, with the help of Sundry (and his family's elderly retainers, Mr. and Mrs. Baffin), settled nicely into his family home and had remained more or less a constant inhabitant of Portland since the end of July. He had reacquainted himself with his neighbors, looked up old friends, and attended two or three concerts and a play.

He had, in fact, resituated himself from the outside in, spending his first month back in Maine traveling the state. August brought greater introspection, and he was seen less outside his house as he explored the family treasures and heirlooms from attic to cellar, reading old letters and much-beloved books, growing misty-eyed over brown photographs and silvered tintypes, tenderly brushing his father's suit or refolding his mother's wedding dress before putting them back into their trunks.

One day he took inspection of his parents' room and came across a small, stoppered vial of his mother's perfume. Sitting on the edge of the bed, he lifted the opened vial to his nose; the lily-of-the-valley scent had lost some of its vigor, but the ghostlike fragrance was all the more potent for its subtlety. Mister Walton felt as if his mother had walked into the room, and he was filled with an astonishing assemblage of emotions, wrapped up in affection and warmth. He was almost shocked to see his own face reflected in the mirror; he had not realized that he looked so much like her.

It was then that he forgot, for a moment, that he had made friends everywhere he went, that somewhere in the house Sundry was mending an old chair, Mr. Baffin was polishing the banister, and Mrs. Baffin was cooking supper. He forgot the members of the Moosepath League, who would have come running at the merest hint of his melancholy. He could only think of his parents and his brother, who were not here anymore, and of his sister, who was (the last he knew) in Africa. Sunlight fell through the window beside the bed and struck the waving shadows of an oak tree in the boundary of a skewed rectangle upon the carpet.

He was thinking of that patch of sunlight as the carriage rolled home that night. Ephram, Eagleton, and Thump had gotten off before their respective doors (with many a lifted hat and hearty handshake). "Miss Greenwood was wearing lily of the valley," he said, so quietly that Sundry had to think a moment before realizing what had been said. Sundry was attempting a reply to this when the older gentleman looked up and smiled. "My mother wore lily of the valley," he explained.

Sundry nodded his understanding. "She made me think of my sister."

"They are lovely girls," said Mister Walton.

This fact had not escaped Sundry. Hilda had reminded him a little *too* much of his sister, but Mollie had struck him as a very handsome young woman.

Oh, Aunt August was saying in Mister Walton's mind, *young Toby has a traveling bee.* He could see the trapezoid of light on the carpet, the shadows of leaves and limbs waving.

"It will be good to see Miss McCannon," said Sundry.

Mister Walton nodded and smiled.

When they had paid the driver, bid him good night, and walked through the gate, the old house rose up before them—a welcoming presence in the evening air. A breeze ruffled the trees on either side of the house; crickets sounded a slow cadence. They mounted the steps, opened the door, and stepped into the hall. The smell of something baked filled the house, and they followed it to the kitchen, where one of Mrs. Baffin's apple pies awaited them in the warming oven.

Book Two

OCTOBER 9, 1896

❈

3. What the Cigar Revealed

A SMALL CROWD WAS GATHERED the next morning on Portland's Western Promenade to view what would prove to be the local baseball team's final game of the year. The wind off the Fore River shook the pennants and favored the left-handed hitters, which was of little comfort to the Bantams' right-handed lineup. The *Portland Courier* would take note of this subtle complication, saying in the next day's edition that *"the wind did not blow in favor of the local nine during their contest against Lewiston yesterday, but this does not excuse their playing as if they were facing directly into a gale. . . ."*

It had not been a good year for the Portland Bantams. One day, late in the season, the *Eastern Argus* had run the baseball standings upside down, just so the readers could see their local team at the top of the column. The next day, the Bantams had returned to the field, filled with indignation at this sting, and lost to the New Bedford Harpoons, 12–2.

The season had been charged with frustration and injury; the fortunes of the team declined, and the gate receipts fell off accordingly. The semi-professional players had reached the end of the summer with their pockets pretty thinly lined, so the Bantams' manager organized several postseason matches in hopes of augmenting their dwindled pay with a few extra dollars. A Friday morning game, however, had brought out only a few delinquent students, baseball-loving mothers, and professional gamblers.

It was October. Baseball would soon be only memory and talk till the month of May saw fit to dry the fields. Now was the time to hope for one last heroic catch or legendary crack of the bat that could be discussed around the fire through the winter months.

To the core of his being, Angus McAngus was a sports reporter, a strange journalistic alloy of athletic events and newspapers that had only recently, in human terms, been mixed and tested upon the public.

It was during the War Between the States that American newspapers had come into their own, and no surprise. The country had echoed with gunfire on the battlefields of the South, rung with the chaos of draft riots in the streets of New York, and shivered with expectation at the quiet thunder of the Emancipation Proclamation. The prose might be purple, and the print might rub off on your hands, but the plot was second to none. By the time of Lincoln's assassination, most of the reading public needed their newspapers each morning, if only to convince themselves that they still had a country. By 1896 necessity had metamorphosed into obsession.

Baseball, it is presumed, was born during the war; indeed, late-nineteenth-century memory imagined that the sport had sprung full grown from the broken skull of the country, like Athena from Zeus's split head. There was a wisdom to baseball; its battles were fought on bloodless fields, men performed epic poetry, and a duck-billed cap replaced military regalia.

With no war being fought, certain wordsmiths turned to the baseball diamonds and bare-knuckled rings for their inspiration. The ring, of course, was an obvious sort of battleground, but most great reporters looked for a little subtlety with their conflict; baseball, created for the mind as much as the body, mixed a nearly subversive form of subtlety with the breath-catching surprise of the strikeout and the towering magnificence of the home run.

Angus McAngus loved baseball. Angus loved baseball so much that he would actually admit to it when in his cups. (Children and dogs he was closemouthed about.) Standing behind the ropes along the first-base line, a cigar tucked into one corner of his mouth and a camel-hair coat draped over one arm, he was a familiar sight to fans and players in the Portland district. With his silver hair, crisp bowler, and tailored suits, he would have cut a dandified, if portly, figure were it not for a measure of grit evident in his straight posture and unconvinced expression.

That expression was especially evident on this day, when Wyckford Cormac O'Hearn, dubbed by the press (perhaps by Angus himself) as the Hibernian Titan, took the bat in the seventh inning of play between the Portland Bantams and the Lewiston Bears. Angus had watched the Bantams practice the day before, and Wyckford had put in a miserable performance—chasing the ball at the plate and losing it in the field.

Angus looked up the right-field line, where the more motley spectators (including himself, it would seem) stood behind a rude waist-high rail. At a post not far away leaned the short, wiry frame of Horace McQuinn, his face weathered, his eyes bright as he waited O'Hearn's turn at the plate. O'Hearn was an occasional companion of McQuinn's, which was mysterious to some people, but standing with McQuinn now was another of his odd friends, Maven Flyce, whose extraordinary cowlick and perpetually astonished expression made him the image of a newspaper caricature.

Dotty Brass appeared beside Angus just as O'Hearn approached the batter's box, and she watched the redheaded giant with the eye of someone who knows her ballplayers. Dotty and Angus were an item as far as anyone could tell—an item, that is, in the fashion usually associated with younger people. Angus was nearing fifty; Dotty was a few years older than that (by most people's guess), and yet there was an air of courtship between them, and had been for most of a decade. That Dotty was proprietress of a "house" did nothing to facilitate people's understanding of their relationship. Some thought it scandalous, whatever it was.

The blunt remainder of a cigar migrated, without benefit of hands, from one corner of Angus's mouth to the other. "Watch this," he said when he felt Dotty take his arm.

The Lewiston pitcher, who was still up to speed as the seventh inning commenced, looked down the alley at Wyckford O'Hearn. He had faced the mammoth player before and knew that O'Hearn had developed a sharp eye at the plate to compensate for a certain bulky inflexibility. O'Hearn had difficulty finessing a marginal pitch and stayed away from them.

The perimeter of the playing field on the Western Promenade was noisy today, the sound of the crowd punctuated by the occasional blast from a bugle in the grandstand. Wyckford O'Hearn, known to be kind to dogs and children, was a favorite among the fans, and a certain concentration upon his at bat was apparent as he and the pitcher fell into their respective roles.

The man on the mound threw the first pitch down the pike, and O'Hearn's swing was so obviously ill timed and so laden with effort that the pitcher knew with an unfamiliar certainty that he had his man.

"You didn't hurt yourself, there, did you?" asked the catcher.

O'Hearn said nothing. He shook out his muscles, tapped his shoes, and raised his bat. Anyone who knew O'Hearn, who had observed him in game after game at the plate, could see that he was as taut as a guyline. He took a deep breath as the pitcher wound up. The ball shot past him in a straight line above the knees, and he looked at it as if he had never seen such a pitch before. There was an astonished silence from one section of the crowd, for the Hibernian Titan was not known for letting two fat pitches get past him. The portion of the crowd from Lewiston, however, roared with approval, and the bugle gave out a blast to indicate its allegiance.

The pitcher hid his own astonishment. He had not meant to send in such a square pitch, but having gotten away with it, he looked (as he scuffed the mound) like he had purposely challenged the huge man at the plate.

In the early innings, the game had meandered quietly, like a wide river on a pleasant day, even if the current were going predictably against the home team. Now, in the course of two pitches, a classic duel had formed. More mental English and side bets were levied against this particular face-off than on the eventual outcome of the game itself. The river had approached a swift and precarious narrows.

An encouraging chatter from their respective teams rose up behind the contestants. The pitcher wanted no delay; the count, and the attendant emotion, were in his favor. It might have behooved O'Hearn to step out of the batter's box at this moment and realign his concentration, but a certain pride, which he should have known better than to obey, kept his feet firmly planted at the plate.

Once the ball was in his glove, the pitcher found his place on the mound, made eye contact with the catcher in a tense pause, and drew back into his windup. The crowd held its collective breath. The sun had disappeared behind a cloud. The slightest breeze touched O'Hearn's back. The pitcher's arm was a blur in the immediate periphery of his vision, and the crowd gasped at the sound of a terrific snap.

The catcher jumped into the air, took his hand from his glove, and wagged it before him. The pitcher was frozen upon the mound, and O'Hearn was twisted onto one knee, his bat propping his poised bulk from tipping into the dirt. It was a moment before the crowd understood that O'Hearn had struck out on three pitches and that the catcher had stopped such a fireball that his hand was numb.

The cheer from the Lewiston side was deafening, as was the disappointed silence from the Portland fans. O'Hearn stood almost to his true height and walked to the Bantams' bench with as much grace as he could muster. The captain of the team, Francis Magoon, made brief eye contact with O'Hearn but said nothing.

"Happens to the best of us," said blue-blooded Charles Althinate Kilfelder, which was almost high praise coming from "the Prince," as the press had dubbed him.

If Angus McAngus had gambled (and he was one of the few sportswriters who did not), he would have lost on that last pitch. Angus liked Wyckford O'Hearn, and though the newspaper reporter knew that hitting a hard-pitched ball was difficult in the best of circumstances, his sense of hope always overshadowed his judgment.

To anyone in the crowd (anyone except Dotty, perhaps), Angus's expression had not altered. The stub of his cigar, though, had been bitten in half.

4. Between Piling and Post

WHEN MOLLIE REACHED MIDDLE STREET, she was encompassed by the sidewalk commotion of Friday morning, which was heightened today by the *fallish* hurry in people's movements, a willingness toward brisk activity against the season yet to come. The year's final harvests trundled past in carts and wagons toward the Exchange, piles of late squash and dark turnips and jolly mounds of pumpkins bumping by behind frisky horses and mules tensed with mischief. Carriages for hire drove past, but Mollie much preferred to walk, which she did with an energetic attention toward everything and everyone she met.

She waited with an elderly gentleman by the curb and crossed Middle Street with him when the traffic allowed. A dog and a boy bounded by, weaving among the pedestrians, followed by a scowling policeman and a man shouting, "Let him go, let him go! I'll know him if he comes again."

Mollie stopped to watch this small drama disappear down a side street. She had errands to do and had been doing her best not to think about the unpleasant incident of the night before.

Passing the City Hotel, she peered sideways through the windows of the dining room, then crossed Exchange Street to the post office. The elderly man hurried to hold the door for her. The interior of the building seemed masculine and brawny to Mollie; the lobby of wood and brass was dark and smelled of wax and business. At the far wall she stopped to find her key.

Her post-office box produced a single envelope.

On her way to Federal Street and the Printers' Exchange, a man fell in step with her. He touched the brim of his top hat, which showed a bit of wear about the edges, and spoke a deep good morning.

"Amos," she said simply.

Together they walked along Exchange Street, which was, if anything, busier than Middle Street, and certainly noisier where the markets added their own hectic rhythms. Here there were all too many people and too many things to see, too many obstacles to avoid (animate and otherwise) for anyone to notice Mollie pass the envelope to the tall, thin fellow who walked beside her. By the time she reached Federal Street, the man had tipped his hat again and fallen out of pace, disappearing into a tobacconist's.

The first floor of the Printers' Exchange was as rough-and-tumble as a wharf swarming with longshoremen; the great presses thumping and banging, the men running them dark with ink and sweat. There was a side entrance by which the intense heart of the newspaper could be avoided, but Mollie chose to walk among the machines and men, thrilled by the commotion, as if she walked beside a stormy surf.

Putting the presses behind her, if not altogether their noise, she became aware of the chatter and clack of the typesetters. She passed among them, working like spiders, peering at the copy, their hands darting blindly from the rows and racks of type.

The inner stairs were rickety, and there was no railing, but she mounted them without hesitation and followed the hall above to a door that shivered to the noise of the presses. She did not knock; this amenity was considered a nuisance by the editor in chief of the *Eastern Argus*, who worked at a large desk among a heap of books and papers that leaned like the last moment of Jericho's walls. Wreaths of smoke rose from behind the debris.

Mr. Corbel was not visible till she approached the desk, when his white hair, then his ruddy face, came into view. He was smoking a cigar. "You're always on time," he growled, like an accusation.

"Thank you," she said without expression.

"What is it today? Mrs. Whackit's annual charitable dinner for wandering minstrels?"

"Mrs. Armitage's soiree, actually, for her fourth daughter's coming-out." She handed him a sheaf of papers from her bag.

"Good God!" he swore. "Use last year's column and change the daughter's name!"

"How do you know I didn't?"

He eyed the papers she had handed him, a great billow of smoke forming about his face; then he tossed the papers with a hundred others on his desk. "People want to read it," he said.

"I am gratified. I sometimes wonder that anyone does when you put my items beside those of that Peter Mall."

Mr. Corbel grunted. He looked about himself, then on the floor beside him, and took up a copy of the morning edition. He snapped through the paper till he found the object of his search, then tossed the open page on the desk. " '*The Degeneration of a Rum Drinker; Officer Skillings de-*

scribes the last days of an imbiber.' It's a temperance piece. Does Mrs. Armitage have something against teetotaling?"

"He has a crude way of putting things," said Mollie. This was one of her favorite pastimes, criticizing Peter Mall.

Mr. Corbel leaned forward and took the cigar from his mouth to punctuate what he had to say. "I hate to tell you, Miss Peer, but Peter Mall is the best writer I have."

Mollie raised an eyebrow in doubt.

"You know," said the editor. "You speak so poorly of the man, I might wonder that you harbor an affection for him."

"I have never met him," she replied coldly.

"You're not alone. I've only met him twice. Once when he came here with some of his work, and another time, by chance, at the baseball field. Acted like he didn't know who I was, then fell over himself shaking my hand." The cigar returned to his mouth. "He's an odd duck, make no mistake."

"I don't think I will as far as he is concerned."

"He's not much to look at, it's true."

"I am duly warned."

Mr. Corbel took a deep breath and frowned. "It surprises me that you don't care for his work."

"And why is that?"

"You're for the women's vote, aren't you?"

"Yes, but I don't see how that—"

"I thought all you *sufferers* liked plain talk."

"We like the truth, Mr. Corbel."

"Yes . . . well, it's much the same thing, isn't it."

"Perhaps."

He returned to the papers on his desk, tossing the copy of the *Argus* onto the floor. "You're always on time," he said again.

"Have a good day, Mr. Corbel," she said at the door.

She could hear him chuckle past his cigar as she went into the hall. She laughed as well. She especially loved to scold Mr. Corbel about Peter Mall, even if she did have to agree privately that he was the best writer on the paper.

Back on Exchange Street, she walked the way she had come, toward the harbor. The thin man with the worn top hat fell in step with her once again, and this time the transaction went the other way.

"Miss Peer," he said with a note of urgency. He hurried alongside her and was quickly winded by the pace she set, nearly colliding with several people as he followed her path through the crowd. "Miss Peer," he said again when she did not immediately respond.

"What is it, Amos?" she said, barely looking at him.

"I would greatly admire the opportunity of a tête-à-tête," he said, touching the brim of his hat.

"I would greatly admire seeing you when business dictates," said Mollie.

"My purpose in seeking you out is *in* the nature of business, Miss Peer."

Mollie halted on the sidewalk. There was nothing particularly threatening about Amos Guernsey, but small troubles followed him everywhere, which was why she had been able to make him part of her plans in the first place and also why she often regretted that she had.

"I am in a bit of a situation, Miss Peer," he said when he realized that he had been given leave to speak. "A pickle, you might say. A difficulty, certainly."

It would have been crass to signify her absolute lack of interest in Amos's difficulties, so she only waited for him to continue, moving to the edge of the sidewalk to avoid a collision with a man who was looking down at his feet while he walked.

"You are not unaware, Miss Peer, I know," he began, "of the circuitous fortunes which are the conventional probability and common lot of those adherent to my chosen trade." Amos was, in fact, a jobless actor, and he took his hat off for this speech. Mollie was taken by how much the man had aged since she first approached him more than a year ago. "I have not, as you know, proved anomalous in this shared destiny and in fact rather have tended toward the less propitious arc of that proverbial circumference—"

"I have just paid you, Amos," said Mollie.

"It is true," he replied, his bony hands raised in a practiced gesture. "But it is not what a man might thrive on by itself."

"It is all out of proportion to the task, Mr. Guernsey."

"I am very grateful."

"And that notwithstanding, it never occurred to me that it would answer for a livelihood."

"Fortune has not smiled on me as of late," he sighed.

"Do you drink it, Amos, or gamble it away?"

"Dear me!" he intoned, as if he had never heard of such things. He cast a horrified glance at nearby pedestrians.

"Have you even *looked* for employment?" asked Mollie.

"My particular specialties are not in the current vogue, Miss Peer."

"I can't believe that."

"Your disbelief is an honor to me," he said with a small bow.

Mollie might have found his conversation droll if she hadn't felt the need for haste. "If you're asking for money, Amos, I have just paid the month's room and board. Not that I would be inclined to throw the good after the bad."

"But Miss Peer—"

"Next week, Amos." Mollie was already crossing to the next corner, thinking that she could skip ahead of a carriage coming her way and therefore put some traffic between herself and Amos. But Amos said something barely audible, and the surprise she felt from what she *thought* she heard brought her up short so that the driver of the carriage had to pull up quickly. She did not hear the shouts that ensued but returned to the corner where Amos stood. He looked like a boy braving it before the town bully. "I beg your pardon," she said.

He cleared his throat, held his hat with both hands before him, and said very clearly: "There are those who might be *interested* in our little exchange, Miss Peer."

This was both a road she had foreseen and one she refused to travel. "Have you ever heard the tale of the goose that laid the golden egg, Mr. Guernsey?"

"I am familiar with that fable, yes."

"Then we need not squander any more of each other's time. Next week, Amos." Mollie did not look back as she crossed the street. The carriage she had brought to a halt pulled onto Congress Street, and the driver cast irate looks back at her. She turned down Pearl Street in the direction of the harbor. The day was, if anything, warmer than yesterday, and she soon regretted her fall jacket.

When she was some distance down the sidewalk, Amos Guernsey began to follow a parallel track from across the street. Few took notice of such a scarecrow; many, in fact, avoided his eyes as, stepping past him, they turned their shoulders away. Amos took off his tall, worn hat and collapsed it with a clap of his hands to a size that fit neatly into an oversized pocket on the inside of his threadbare coat. Then, as if he were growing warm from the exertions of his walk, he took off his coat and looked almost presentable in a pressed shirt and starched collar.

5. Saving the Blue Hubbard

IN THE SCHEME OF THINGS—that is, the fate and history of the world—
it would not appear that a mishap involving runaway vegetables merits
the same study as, say, accepting an invitation to the Borgias for lunch or
underestimating the number of Indians you plan to meet at Little Big
Horn, and yet large issues might pivot upon a single grain of incident. It is
difficult to imagine how things would have fallen out for the Moosepath
League had they *not* walked the Exchange that day, but certainly the delay they experienced on that avenue had its unforeseen consequences.

It had been decided the previous evening, among the charter members of the Moosepath League (all three of them), that their chairman
should be presented some token to commemorate his trip to Hallowell.
Thump, known for his perspicacious nature, suggested they shop for this
gift at Exchange Street, where he knew of a bookseller whom he liked to
patronize.

When Christopher Eagleton arrived at Exchange Street on the afternoon of October 9, 1896, he had his driver stop at the top of the hill so that
he might have the pleasure of taking in the sights of the market. Tall,
blond, and clean-shaven, Eagleton walked head up, ever watchful of the
weather, which held an endless fascination for him. He strode among the
crowd, smiling, tipping his hat to the ladies, looking dapper in his tan suit,
the city's Republican journal—the *Portland Daily Advertiser*—tucked beneath one arm.

The Exchange was milling with buyers and sellers; barrels and kegs
and boxes of comestibles lined the way; shop windows were filled with
signs and bargains. Eagleton gave wide berth to the pyramids and leaning
carts of fruits and vegetables; he was never very sure how they stayed together upon the slope of the street, though they seemed as stable as stone
walls.

The sign of the bookseller had actually come into Eagleton's purview
when he apprehended an uncommon phenomenon. Outside one shop,
several people were considering a blue Hubbard squash that was propped
atop a heap of its brethren against an upended cart. Girdling this item like
a starched collar was a strip of pasteboard on which were the words
"William Jennings Bryan—Not for Sale!" It seemed an odd declaration to
attach to a squash, and Eagleton invested some concentration upon it before realizing that the plant bore a remarkable likeness to the famous ora-
tor and Democratic candidate.

"My goodness sakes!" he said, not knowing whether to be delighted or indignant. It was his fellow member, Matthew Ephram, who championed the Democratic cause, and though himself a Republican, Eagleton wondered if the display wasn't a little indelicate. Then perhaps it was only meant to indicate the original Bryan, who was expected in Portland soon. The owner of the shop appeared on the stoop, wiping his hands on his apron and asserting great pride in the object. "I paid three times the going rate for that squash!" he said. "You've never seen anything like it!"

"It is true, I haven't," admitted Eagleton, though he had once seen a potato that he thought looked like Sir Arthur Conan Doyle. He leaned closer to the display, and while he gazed upon the blue Hubbard that bore such a strong resemblance to the presidential candidate, a hand reached beneath his elbow and actually pulled another squash from the base of the mound.

The result of this action startled everyone within shouting distance. The store owner did shout, in fact, and as sort of a reaction, Eagleton let out such a whoop that people twenty feet away jumped. Eagleton was sure that he had triggered this falling out, and he stood back, hardly able to breathe as the great hillock of squashes tumbled out from under one another and proceeded to roll and bounce down the street.

The more personable among these vegetables was the last to go, hovering for a moment in balance at the back end of the tilted cart before it rolled to the street, bobbled over Eagleton's shoes, and followed its fellow flora in the general direction of the waterfront.

The effect of this rolling vegetation was immediate. The blue Hubbard is an irregularly shaped squash, and so its course in such a descent is difficult to predict. The pedestrian traffic below grew particularly active, and it was admirable how even the elderly rose to the occasion.

Further down the street, other fruit and vegetables—turnips and pumpkins, apples, and even a stand of walnuts—seemed inspired by the fleeing squash, and several joined in, so that people further down the slope had greater quantities of these objects to avoid and less prospect of doing so. Store owners and customers appeared in doorways to see what the commotion was. Horses reared at the bounding edibles, and carriage wheels laid several of them out in the midst of the street. There was a great barking of dogs.

Eagleton, convinced of his culpability in the matter, knew that if he saved one article of produce that day, it must be that Democratic squash, and thus galvanized, he sped after it, following the blue Hubbard's serpentine path down the sidewalk.

Matthew Ephram was a little amazed when he stepped out of his carriage at the corner of Exchange and Middle Streets. An avalanche of fruit and vegetables careered past him, and the crowded sidewalk was alive with leaping pedestrians. Fast behind this tumbling harvest came his good friend and fellow member Christopher Eagleton, holding his hat and shouting for everyone to make way for William Jennings Bryan.

Never having seen a political candidate preceded by vegetables, Ephram was intrigued. The *Eastern Argus*, which he held beneath one arm, had reported Bryan's imminent visit, and being a member of the Democratic Party, Ephram was interested in seeing the man. He marked the moment by consulting one of his three or four watches. He was greatly enamored of time (his house was filled with clocks and watches and gonging chronometers) and was often seen comparing the tales told by his own and other timepieces. Ephram pulled at his fine mustaches, straightened his gray herringbone suit, and proceeded on to the Exchange.

What he saw there was Joseph Thump—third Moosepathian, inveterate watcher of the tides, and a Green Back Silver Standard Bearer (though that party was for the past ten years officially defunct). Thump was lifting his short, solid self a little groggily from the pavement. There was in his lap a large blue Hubbard squash. The day's edition of the *Portland Courier* was scattered all about him, and Eagleton was ecstatically shaking his hand.

"Ever in the fore!" declared Eagleton.

Thump's immediate response has not been recorded, and his exceptional growth of beard and mustaches made it difficult to see his expression.

"It was a remarkable capture!" cried Eagleton. "I have never seen anything like it!"

Thump hadn't actually tried to capture anything. "Is it a squash?" he asked, blinking at the object in his lap. This was just the sort of perceptive thinking they had come to expect from him and one of the meritorious traits for which he was admired.

"Indeed!" declared Eagleton.

"A squash," said Ephram. He did not fully understand what had occurred, though he suspected, knowing his friends, that it was momentous.

Once on his feet, Thump looked at the squash by which he had been struck, and he was startled by how much it looked like his uncle Crispin.

"Good heavens!" said Eagleton, for in the thrill of the chase he had quite forgotten the larger mishap surrounding them. The general effects of the "Great Exchange Street Vegetable Tumble" (as the *Eastern Argus* would dub it in the next day's edition) were only then subsiding, and all about, pedestrians were jabbering, carriage drivers veered their horses around the larger bits of mashed plant stuff, and store owners pursued their produce.

"What excitement!" said Ephram.

"I fear that I have precipitated an unfortunate misadventure," confessed Eagleton. "There was this squash—" He hesitated to describe the peculiar characteristic of the vegetable. Clearly he must make amends by helping retrieve the wayward harvest, and though the owner of the "Bryan Squash" (as it was dubbed by the *Portland Courier* in the next edition) insisted that Eagleton was not at fault, the three friends spent a good measure of the afternoon scouring the gutters and adjacent alleys for delinquent vegetables. Ephram, in the course of his searching, had a nice conversation with a man who had only piano stools around his dining table.

Thump was disconcerted to find that *several* of the blue Hubbards resembled his uncle Crispin.

6. Second Sight

"THE NEXT TIME, MOLLIE, I won't chase after you!" Hilda had warned the night before, once they had run the gauntlet of Mrs. Makepeace's curiosity and retreated upstairs. As it happened, Hilda forgave Mollie for what had happened, her anger perhaps set aside to make room for consternation when Mollie professed a continued interest in the little boy named Bird.

What Mollie did not admit to Hilda was that she *had* seen the child before—several times, in fact—and had even caught sight of Mr. Pembleton down at the waterfront the previous summer. It had been while working for the *Eastern Argus*, observing the society crowd at the arrival of the British steamer *Henrietta*, that she had first seen Bird watching from around the corner of a holding shed. There had been such a contrast between the gala on the dockside and this dirty face peering from the shadows that she had straightaway seen in it (or so she told herself) a dramatic tale.

The incident with Pembleton and his thug had infuriated Mollie, however, and there was enough of the contrary in her nature that she decided now to press the issue (by day, at any rate, among the crowds) and look for the boy.

Pembleton had stunk of rum, and Mollie was willing to bet he was full of the stuff before the night was very old. It occurred to her, when she got up this morning, that dipsomaniacs were always looking for an excuse to open another bottle, and she was sure that (in his mind) he had been given one last night. *He'll be asleep or incapacitated*, she said to herself as she neared Commercial Street and the docks, *and Bird will be free to roam as he pleases*. Or Pembleton might be suffering from his excess; and as everyone knew, a nip of what made you ill is the best cure. He would send Bird off to procure him another bottle!

It was past noon, and she had been wandering for an hour among the stalls at the street end of the Custom House Wharf before she spotted him. The crowds had turned out again, with nearly as many people on the wharves as one would expect at the height of August.

Maine does have its exquisite summer afternoons, its bright July mornings when the fog is rolled back by a western breeze and the warmth of the sun melts the dew before breakfast. But no season in the state is so commonly uncommon in its perfection as the fall—the harvest, the changing foliage, the sun throughout the day like the gold of summer's late afternoon, the cool nights, the poignancy of an autumn rain. The humidity of summer passes with relief, the knowledge of winter gilds every warm moment, makes the grass seem greener, the ocean bluer, and the year's final flowers more lush.

But Mollie was not in a sensitive frame of mind. She did her best to look interested in the day, smiling at an occasionally familiar face and buying herself another bag of peanuts, but she was intent on her mission. After an hour or so she was rewarded by the sight of a ragged creature walking along the periphery of the wharf. And what did he have clutched in the crook of his arm but an empty bottle ready for refilling!

When Bird turned the corner and headed west on Commercial Street, she followed him. She had not gone far, however, when a voice spoke inside her: *And what about Mr. Pembleton's big friend? What if he was not incapacitated?* Already she had reached a place where the crowds had thinned. An old man sat on a stoop across the street, watching her with indifference.

A group of mariners, walking toward her, chortled among themselves; one of them winked as he passed. Bird dwindled in the distance, unhurried, hardly looking from side to side as he crossed an alley. A horse and wagon pulled out from one of these and blocked her view of him, then pulled onto Commercial Street, and he was smaller still.

She was disappointed in herself and discouraged with the world in general. It was all well and good to act the Nellie Bly, but Nellie Bly was a reporter with an entourage of reporters reporting on her; she was able to frequent dangerous places and meet strange people by becoming the story.

Mollie turned back to the stalls again, weaving through the crowd unseeingly, all the while coaxing a particular thought from the back of her mind. On the wharf, she considered the faces of the sightseers and sailors. She passed the armless Lyman Peabody, tying knots with his tongue and his toes and his stumps. She saw an old white-bearded salt spinning verbal yarn about a small crowd. The further she walked, the more apparent became the harbor; masts loomed in the sky, gulls banked overhead, the sense—perhaps even the sound—of water thrummed beneath the crowd.

Across the width of the wharf she caught sight of a short, wiry fellow of indeterminate age, his hair a yellow gray, his clothes old but tidy. She had seen him before when she had been here during the summer, *and* his companion, unmistakable with his great cowlick.

There was a third man whom she did not recognize—a redheaded hulk of a young fellow with a cigar over his ear and wearing a derby.

Bird would be coming back with that bottle filled, she knew. She moved among the stalls, where she had first sighted the little boy. She watched Lyman Peabody from a distance and ate some peanuts. From this vantage point, she could see the red-haired giant on the other side of the wharf. She waited till she saw the little fellow walking with that same unhurried, dreamlike pace, then handed her bag of peanuts to a boy passing by and strode purposefully down the wharf.

"Gory, Hod!" piped Maven Flyce. "It sure is a choice afternoon!"

Horace McQuinn rarely looked at Maven when he spoke to him, and even now his sharp gray eyes were taking in the nimble movements of a two-master as it picked its way past the crowd of ships anchored near the wharf. "It's a good thing," he said deliberately. "Since there is little choice about it."

"My word!" said Maven, as if considering the immutability of the weather for the first time. "You're absolutely right!" He regarded Horace's bony form as if he had never seen the man before.

"You'd be the first to say so." Horace gave out a laugh that sounded like the wheeze before a cough. He passed a tobacco-stained hand over his yellow-gray hair.

Maven's amazement did not dwindle with this communication; indeed, his normal state of mind was that of unending surprise, his identity embodied by the remarkable cowlick that stood, as if in complete astonishment, from the crown of his head. Maven had been on the Custom House

Wharf a thousand times, but he stared about himself, mouth open, as if it had grown there overnight. Then a cloud drifted before the sun, and he stared at it, mouth open, as if clouds were unknown to him.

No one was better known on the Portland waterfront than Horace McQuinn, a man of many and varied experiences who was content in his later years with observing the passing tide of humanity from a particular post on the Custom House Wharf. Occasionally, when monetary needs arose, he facilitated the transport of certain spirituous goods. Put straightforwardly, he ran rum.

It was usual to see Maven beside Horace McQuinn, but at Horace's *other* elbow this afternoon—while the traffic on the quay increased—was a great pylon of a fellow. Barrel-chested, long-limbed, and mighty-thewed (the circumference of one thigh appeared nearly as large as Horace's waist), he wore a brown derby over his red hair, a cigar cradled over one ear, and a gold watch in his vest pocket—the latter engraved with the gratitude of the city for a home run hit in the ninth inning (August 11, 1888) against Portsmouth, New Hampshire.

Wyckford Cormac O'Hearn—dubbed the Hibernian Titan by the sporting press—stood head and shoulders above his companions, and Wyck (as the giant was known to his friends) was slouching. "A horde of people out," declared Wyck with mild approval.

"The storm dragged some southern weather behind it," said Horace sagely.

"I do like to see the people out," said Wyck.

"Half of them, anyway," returned Horace, thinking that the young man liked seeing the women a good deal more than he liked seeing the men.

What both of them said was true. Wyckford had experienced a dismal morning, which was the final blow in a poor season at the plate and only a passable one in left field. But fall had arrived, and the cold, dry air and the mysteries of the season filled him so that he weathered the day with increasing optimism. He felt like doing somebody good, especially if that somebody were female, young, and pretty. He was not stingy with his smile, however, and any female, old or young, plain or pretty, received a tip of his hat. "Ma'am," he said to a passing matron, then, "Ma'am," in a slower drawl, to the daughter in her wake.

The daughter, though taken aback by his red hair and his size, wished him a pleasant day in a sweet tone. The older woman, less impressed by Wyckford and the company he kept, sensed her daughter lagging and stopped to size up the seriousness of the situation. Wyck, for all his bulk, held no terrors for a mother of practical bent; he looked, indeed, like easy prey, and she thought she did him a favor by calling her flirtatious daughter away just as he was succumbing to a pair of trembling eyelashes.

"Come along, dear," came the word of command.

Wyck tipped his hat three times before the young woman had disappeared in the crowd. "Wasn't she pretty," he said, feeling brighter for having seen her, however briefly.

"I was so amazed!" said Maven, looking after her with admiration.

Horace recited:

> "Men will steer clear of a blowey gale,
>   And curse a hurricane utterly;
>   Yet be drawn without fail,
>   Over mountain and dale,
>   To the breeze from the lash that is fluttery.
>
> "The gale is a terror to sailor and salt,
>   And the hurricane something to fear;
>   But the lash's assault,
>   Brings a man to a halt,
>   And keeps him from thinking of beer!"

"How does he do it?" asked Maven, in awe of Horace's poetic prowess.

Wyckford O'Hearn's chuckle was heartfelt. "I have often wondered."

Horace had amused even himself this time and looked gleeful, packing the pipe he had got from his pocket. "Well," he said with the moderate air of a man who has lived and learned. "It is true."

"I must admit," said Wyck, "beer was not uppermost in my mind."

"Young women are precarious," said Horace with mock severity; he was warming to his supposition now and continued as if speaking in the Rostrum. "You wait, and experience will bear me out. That little girl was dangerous, in a downy sort of way, but another will come along and—"

Then he saw her, and not for the first time. She appeared from the street end of the wharf, for all the world like a teacher ferreting out the party responsible for a schoolhouse prank. This impression may have conjured up some long-forgotten incident in Horace's memory, for he looked wide-eyed and whistled, or it might have been the woman herself. "You remarked that it was a choice afternoon, Maven," he said.

"Good heavens!" said Maven, catching sight of the woman. She was approaching them.

"Something choice right there," suggested Horace with a sly look in Wyck's direction.

Wyck straightened to his considerable height, took off his hat, and brushed the hair off his forehead.

"She's tall, isn't she!" declared Maven.

"Safe to say," said Horace, who was himself barely above five feet. "But you know what the bear said about the honey tree."

Wyck was ready to dole out the greater part of his charm when she turned, as if looking for something, and locked eyes with him.

"No, I don't," Maven was saying. "What *did* the bear say?"

"Stand by for a broadside," Horace said dryly. Maven took this as an answer to his question and found it baffling.

Wyck's deliberate bearing dropped from him as the young woman approached, and suddenly he was just an uncertain hulk, wondering what to say when a woman looked as if she actually had something to say to him.

7. Pawn to Queen Four

WHEN MOLLIE TURNED and fastened her eyes upon the redhead, she caught him looking with great interest at her; and though she addressed all three men, she poured the lion's share of her distress onto Wyckford O'Hearn. "Oh, please!" she said. "I am looking for a little boy! I promised my mother I would find him!"

The man with the cowlick gaped at her, and the redheaded fellow said, "Pardon me, ma'am?" The older fellow appeared to have a ready quip, but he only rubbed the stubble on his chin and asked, "What sort of boy?"

"He's been living somewhere nearby. There's a terrible man, Mr. Pembleton—"

"Pembleton?" said Horace McQuinn. "Sir Eustace Pembleton?" His voice wavered between amusement and disdain.

"Is that his name?"

"Pembleton, with the toy steamer?" asked Wyckford O'Hearn. He felt he was one behind in this conversation. Maven, from the look on his face, hadn't got up to bat.

"You'll know him—the little boy, I mean; he's only four, and he's dressed in rags!" She was quite surprised to find tears in her eyes.

Wyckford O'Hearn felt weak as a wet towel, just to look at her in such a state. Her eyes were tearing, she caught a sob in her throat, and Wyck reached for his handkerchief, trying to remember if he had used it.

"You mean one of the wharf kids," said Horace. He had an odd look on his face, as if looking for the answer to a question other than the one he had asked. He put his pipe in his mouth and drew on it, though there was no fire left in the bowl.

Wyck had ascertained that his handkerchief was safe to pass on, and he handed it to Mollie. "You say he's nearby?"

Mollie took it and dabbed at her face, casting her eyes to the opposite side of the wharf for a glimpse of Bird. "He's all I have left, and I promised I'd take care of him."

Horace cleared his throat. "He and mother, of course," he said.

"My, that's sad!" Maven was saying. "Who's she looking for, Hod?"

"Is that him?" asked Wyck, looking over her head.

Mollie saw the little waif moving down the midst of the wharf, his cargo safely wrapped in a cloth bag. *He's barefoot,* she thought, and wondered why she hadn't noticed before. "Yes!" she said in a stage whisper. "That's my brother! Oh, get him please!"

"Why don't you get him, Wyck?" said Horace.

Wyckford glanced from Horace, who looked as if he suspected a good joke, to Maven, who was too astounded to be of any help. Then he turned to Mollie, and his heart went out to her. "Hey, little fellow!" he shouted across the wharf. "You come here now!" He took a step or two in the boy's direction just as Bird turned to catch a glimpse of the Hibernian Titan in all his bearlike stature. The child's jaw dropped, and his eyes widened; then he was gone, pell-mell, into the crowd, and Wyck charged after him with as much speed as he could manage without knocking someone down.

"Hod, I'm so amazed!" said Maven.

"Does remind me of a chase you had just this summer," said Horace with a delighted gleam in his eye.

"I *am* astounded!"

Mollie hurried after Wyck, planning what she would do when Bird was caught, but she had neither Bird's mouselike ability to dart among the crowd nor the redheaded man's mass to part it. When she got to the other side of the wharf, neither was to be seen. She glanced from face to face, turning about on one high-heeled boot. Lyman Peabody caught her glance and winked at her.

"If it isn't like last summer!" said Maven, who had chased after a young thief the previous July with mixed success.

Horace let out one of his wheezing laughs. "Now if we could snag old Tobias Walton into this somehow," he said, "it would be *just* like last summer."

8. Old John Neptune

ONLY THE SELFLESS ARE VERY LIKELY TO WORRY if they have been selfish, and thus it was with Mister Walton, on the morning of October ninth, when he wondered if the members of the Moosepath League should have been invited to accompany him and Sundry Moss on their trip to Hallowell. Miss McCannon had only been able to invite Mister Walton to the Harvest Ball, it was true, but there must be other diversions (Sundry was counting on it), and "the more the merrier" was a maxim to which both these men subscribed.

"I have allowed my anticipation of Miss McCannon's company to cloud the sight of my friends!" said the portly fellow when the Moosepathians did not show up to see them off. In the middle of the afternoon, Sundry volunteered to make the requisite calls upon the telephone, which lately had been installed beneath the front-hall stairs at the house on Spring Street.

But the gentlemen were not home; not a one could be reached, and Sundry's inquiries were answered only by an apologetic servant or no one at all. It seemed strange that all three members of the club would be away; presumably, something important was keeping them.

The Walton family's elderly retainers, Mr. and Mrs. Baffin, saw Mister Walton and Sundry off with good wishes and a large hamper of food for the trip, and soon a hired carriage was taking the travelers in the direction of the Grand Trunk Depot. Mister Walton was still a little concerned that he had not thought of Ephram, Eagleton, and Thump soon enough. "Perhaps we should send them a telegram," he suggested to Sundry, "and ask them to meet us somewhere." This solution seemed to answer, and having thought of it, the portly fellow felt a good deal better.

It was more than two hours after Mister Walton and Sundry had left that Mr. Baffin answered the front door and was greeted by Ephram, Eagleton, and Thump. The gentlemen looked a little harried and were very sorry to have missed their chairman.

"We brought a gift for him," said Eagleton. They had purchased a copy of *Where Would She Turn*, by Mrs. Acton Tendergarten, which Thump had read and considered gripping.

"Toby was looking for you, actually," said Mr. Baffin.

"How considerate of him," said Ephram.

"We were retrieving vegetables," Eagleton explained.

"I see," said Mr. Baffin. He had noticed that Thump had a large squash under his arm.

"We met a man," said Ephram, "with a very interesting philosophy regarding the adjustment of proper dining height to the individual."

"Perhaps we should forward the book to the hotel in Hallowell," Eagleton suggested.

Thump looked as if he wasn't sure why he was carrying a large squash.

"I am sure he would be very glad to hear from you," said the elderly retainer with a gentle smile.

"It's a very good idea, Eagleton," said Ephram.

"Thank you, Ephram."

Mr. Baffin waved good-bye as they moved down the walk. Ephram was wondering where he might find a piano stool.

The day was as fine an example of fall along the coast of Maine as Mister Walton had ever known, a perception no doubt influenced by his destination. The foliage had not yet reached its peak in that section of the coast, and only those colors (which the trees would provide as the days progressed or the traveler progressed north) could have improved the view from their carriage window.

Only those colors might improve the day, thought Mister Walton, *or another reading* (was it the hundredth?) *of Phileda's letter.* The letter survives still, and as it speaks nothing but well of the writer and the person whose eyes for which it was originally designed, we feel no misgivings in revealing it these hundred years later.

Dear Toby,

I was wonderfully pleased to find your letter when I arrived this morning. I had so enjoyed my stay with Jared at Harvard that coming back to Hallowell seemed a mixed blessing. Though I have many dear friends here, I live alone in a house once peopled by my family, and returning to it—now empty—always fills me with sad ideas.

So imagine my great relief to find your letter when I stopped at the post before going home. It was like having a friend come through the door with me to fill the cool atmosphere with his sunny conversation. I could almost believe that you predicted both my melancholy and the effect of your letter.

And now that I have confessed the good offices of your friendship, I will be bold to ask of you a further favor still, knowing that true friendship is not reliant upon such service.

On Monday, the twelfth of October, there will be a Harvest Ball at the home of Mrs. Capt. Ledland Blythe, and since it is the leap year, the conceit of the affair is that the ladies invite the gentlemen, and a great deal of talk it is causing, I promise you! All manner of conjecture is bandied about

*concerning those of us who are unmarried, and everyone is "keeping mum,"
so it would be doubly pleasurable to make my appearance on the arm of a
mysterious stranger if that stranger were yourself.*

*I hope that a leap-year invitation is not deemed improper in Portland,
but I rely on your good nature to respond kindly, even though circumstance
or inclination cause you to turn it down. I assure you that your declining
would only darken my regard for a day or two.*

*To make your decision easier (I hope), I have made arrangements for
you at the Worster House. I may only invite the one person to the ball, but
I trust (if you come) that I will also see Mr. Moss, whose company I so enjoyed last summer, and have accordingly made arrangements at the hostelry
for two.*

*I am glad to read that you and your friends of the Moosepath League
are well, and whether or not my inducements can have their intended effects, I hope to see you in the near future. I will tell you of my latest excite-
ments on Monday if I see you then or write to you of them if such is not the
case.*

Thank you again for greeting me on my return.

*With fond regard,
Phileda*

Sundry took note of several chuckles and at least a single sigh while
his portly friend read this letter again, but the young man thoughtfully
kept his eye upon the passing scene.

Mister Walton was thinking that leap year was a very interesting and
likable phenomenon when he finished the letter and tucked it carefully
into his vest pocket.

On the other side of the station house, a waiting engine gave off a blow of
steam, and a sudden hurry was manifest among the people passing by,
which is common when an outgoing train chuffs like a straining beast of
burden.

Only one figure seemed unresponsive to, and perhaps unaware of, the
train's impatience—a dark-complected man with neatly trimmed coal-
black hair and lined features more closely associated with gray age. He
carried, over his shoulder, a drawstring sack about the size, if not the
shape, of a woman's hatbox. He moved at a brisk enough pace, but his
progress was unrelated to anyone or anything else's timetable.

While Sundry was lifting their bags down from the top of the carriage
and enlisting the services of a porter, Mister Walton took note of this man,
a faint recollection niggling at the back of his mind. It was not strange,

then, given Mister Walton's interest in people, that he watched as the older man boarded and no more than a factor of his natural curiosity when he led Sundry to that same car.

Sundry was mildly surprised when his employer indicated a particular seat that he wanted to occupy; Mister Walton was more apt to wave away any preference with an "Anywhere is fine with me." "Whatever is easiest" and "Whatever you would like" were common answers, so that Sundry was actually pleased when the decision was made for him.

The Maine Central Railroad carried spacious cars, and the seats alternated front to back so that groups of people could observe and talk with one another as if sitting two on either side of a table. The old man with the black hair sat with his back to the front of the train, his sack on the seat beside him, and Mister Walton and Sundry sat themselves down, facing him. By now, Mister Walton was beginning to recall where he had met this man before.

The black-haired man sat straight, a hat in his lap. He was of one of those tribes that had greeted Europeans to these shores, and when Mister Walton exchanged nods with him and looked directly into his brown eyes, he knew who he was. "You are John Neptune, aren't you, sir?" asked Mister Walton. He held out his hand.

"I am," said the Indian, reaching out to shake hands with Mister Walton. He searched the round face above the offered hand and the bright, dark eyes behind round spectacles, but registered no recognition.

"You will not remember me, sir," said Mister Walton. "You had more on your mind when we met than a sixteen-year-old boy filled with questions, though you were very kind to answer what you could."

With a quick estimation of Mister Walton's age, the old man was able to venture a guess. "It was after the great war with the South," he said simply.

"It was."

"If it had been during the war, you would have been with us, and you would have had no questions."

"You are very right," said Mister Walton. "I am Tobias Walton. I was a drummer boy in the Twelfth Maine during the last months before Appomattox. You were with Sherman's army, I believe. We met in Washington."

The old man nodded.

"This is my friend and aide-de-camp, Sundry Moss."

John Neptune shook the young man's hand, and Sundry was conscious of a firm grip and dry, callused skin.

"It has been more than thirty years, but you have changed very little," said Mister Walton, which was perhaps more gracious than true.

"You have grown some," said John Neptune. There was the light of humor in his eyes.

Mister Walton patted his stomach. "I would make several of my former selves," he agreed.

"It is good to go into winter with a little extra," said the old man.

Mister Walton chuckled. The train jostled forward, and its first short movements seemed almost to propel his humor. Sundry stretched his legs into the aisle, folded his arms, and watched the old fellow. Though the Indian's hair was jet black, Sundry guessed, as much from the man's manner as from the extraordinary map of wrinkles on his face, that Mr. Neptune must be past his seventieth birthday.

"I am surprised that you remember," said John Neptune. "The city was filled with soldiers after the war."

"There were several of your tribe in your regiment, as I remember."

"We were the Penobscots," said the man.

Mister Walton had resisted guessing, knowing that a certain amount of tribal rivalry still existed among the Penobscot, the Passamaquoddy, and the Micmac and that a wrong speculation regarding someone's affiliation might result in hurt feelings or even anger.

The train was chugging out of the Grand Trunk Depot now, picking up the rhythm of the rails as the great station and the surrounding buildings fell away, revealing the harbor on one side and Munjoy Hill on the other. Sundry caught sight of the Portland Observatory above them as they passed.

"I should remind you," said Mister Walton, "that you were very kind."

The old man shrugged.

"I had considered not returning to my family," continued Mister Walton. "I had run away to join the war, and it was my first, and perhaps my only, great act of disobedience to my parents."

"I gave you a stone," said John Neptune. The memory was returning to him, and again the light of humor entered his face.

"You did," said Mister Walton. "I told you how worried I was that my parents would not have me back after I had run away, and you assured me that the sins of the prodigal are forgotten in the joy of his return."

"It is an old Indian tale," agreed the old man. "But you did not accept it. So I gave you a stone."

"Yes," said Mister Walton delightedly. "You told me that it was a magic stone that would make my parents greet me with open arms."

"And did it work?"

"I am pleased to say it did."

"I am sorry to say I lied," intoned John Neptune. He closed his eyes for a moment, and for a moment he looked as if he might have gone to sleep. Then he took a single deep breath and looked at Mister Walton again. "The stone did not open your parents' arms," he said. "They were already open, as I told you. But the stone gave you the courage to go home."

"It did indeed. Where did you find it?"

"On the ground beside your feet. I was able to distract you by pointing to something and asking you about it." Here John Neptune peered out the window. They were just rounding the Eastern Promenade, the engine already steaming onto the trestle that would take them across the mouth of Back Cove. "Is that a cow or a bull?" he wondered.

Sundry leaned closer to the window and gazed up at the back side of Munjoy Hill, where some people still kept the occasional milking cow, though he had never seen a live bull within the city limits of Portland. When he turned back, the old Indian was holding a card out to him. Sundry could see the phone exchanges of the club members on the card, and he realized that it had come from his inside jacket pocket. "Are you a magician?" asked Sundry.

"It is an old shaman technique," said John Neptune.

Sundry realized, then, that he had been used to demonstrate how easy it was to distract someone. "It was a cow," he said.

They had reached full steam by now and were trundling past the wide opening of the Presumpscot River. On the opposite bank, long slopes of browning grass reached up to barns and farmhouses, which looked tiny with distance. Beneath the red mound of a great maple, a cow grazed, and not far away a horse kicked up its heels. There was quiet as they contemplated either the scene before them or the past behind. Then John Neptune closed his eyes, and before long Mister Walton was also resting.

Sundry stretched his legs, and after some miles the rhythm of the tracks lulled him not into a nap but into that half-waking state in which something like a dream might obscure the outer world.

Passing by, the conductor took note of Sundry's brow, which was knit into an expression of deep concentration. An odd sound had entered the young man's ear, and he opened one eye. He searched for the source of the noise, which (for lack of a better description) he would have called a singsong whir, and he considered the drawstring sack that lay beside John Neptune.

Sundry's other eye opened as something moved in the bag. He was then encouraged to sit up when that something attempted egress from the sack. He leaned forward, not without trepidation, and was startled when a hand—a very tiny, seemingly black-gloved hand—pushed its way between the tightened noose of the drawn strings.

Leaning closer still, Sundry was able to ascertain that it was not a hand (however human it first appeared) but a paw, black and smooth, with five digits and rather sharp-looking, needlelike claws. The paw withdrew for a moment, then reached back out of the sack and explored its immediate surroundings.

Sundry tapped Mister Walton's shoulder. The man stirred, sighed inarticulately, and remained asleep. "Mister Walton," said Sundry.

"Hmm?"

"Mister Walton." Sundry gave his employer a more forceful nudge.

"What? Yes? Sundry?" Mister Walton sat up, blinking, looked to Sundry for explanation, then traced the direction of the young man's forefinger. The paw had retreated once more, and in its place a single eye peered at the bald fellow. Mister Walton adjusted his spectacles and leaned forward. The eye blinked at him. Mister Walton blinked at the eye. "Is it a cat?" he asked.

"Not from what I saw of it," said Sundry.

John Neptune slept quietly, upright in his seat.

"Oh!" said Mister Walton, for a snout protruded from the bag; then a pair of eyes emerged, peering from a banditlike mask; and finally, the two triangular ears of a baby raccoon. "My word!" said Mister Walton with something of a laugh. Nearby passengers looked up from sleep, scenery, or conversation to level inquiring expressions.

The raccoon bared its teeth (which seemed a weak attempt at an ingratiating smile), and Sundry thought that if he had ever witnessed a scoundrel, this was one.

Mister Walton nodded to the people looking at them and spoke next in a quieter tone. "Sir," he said, and he touched John Neptune's arm.

The Indian came awake all at once, without a start or a yawn; his eyes opened as if he had only blinked. "Yes?" he said.

"Your—" Mister Walton leaned closer and indicated the bag. "Your friend is attempting to escape, I fear."

The Indian looked down at the bag at his side. The tiny raccoon looked up at him and made the whirring sound that Sundry had first heard—something between a growl and a purr. The creature smiled at the Indian. "Where did he come from?" asked John Neptune.

Sundry was astonished, and Mister Walton's eyes looked as round as saucers behind his spectacles.

"Just a joke," said John Neptune.

Mister Walton could not suppress a laugh, and even Sundry, whose form of humor tended toward the dry, let out a delighted "Ha!"

"Is that part of your shaman magic?" asked Mister Walton.

"My friend Isherwood Tolly discovered him crossing the railroad tracks, just ahead of a train, and grabbed him up before he was run over. The raccoon caused some confusion in a dining car when he took him on board the Portland and Rochester. Knowing that the raccoon is my family totem, he left him with my friend Jack Bogwood. Isherwood named him Shotgun, but I call him Eugene, after my grandfather."

The raccoon looked from one to the other of them as if carefully following the conversation.

"Eugene!" said Mister Walton with a delighted chortle. "My word! It's a fine name!" Eugene blinked at him with a great show of innocence, and Mister Walton chuckled with every glance from the creature. "Aren't you afraid he might get out of that bag?" he asked.

"No. I don't think he can escape," said John Neptune. He reached a hand out and tickled the inquisitive snout, pulling away just in time to avoid an experimental nip.

"Are you returning to Old Town, then, sir?" asked Mister Walton.

"No. My home is in Brewer, not on the reservation. But I am stopping first in Bath. I have another friend there who has a strange difficulty."

"I am sorry," said Mister Walton.

"Perhaps you would care to meet him," said John Neptune. He was watching Mister Walton with renewed interest.

"Another time I would like that very much," said Mister Walton.

"I believe you might be of some help," said the Indian.

A look of concern crossed Mister Walton's face, and he turned to Sundry, who appeared merely curious.

"A *strange* difficulty?" Sundry asked.

"I think it is not usual," said John Neptune.

"I don't know how I can help your friend . . ." Mister Walton began.

Sundry had no idea what a *strange* difficulty might prove to be, but he shared John Neptune's faith in Mister Walton. He also knew that they had left a day or so early not so they could dawdle but so that Mister Walton might see Miss McCannon the sooner.

"We will come with you, sir," said Mister Walton before more thought could be put into the matter.

"Thank you," said John Neptune.

"Well, then," said Mister Walton. "That settles that! Let's break open the hamper, Sundry." He asked the old man, "Are you fond of apple pie?"

"If it is a little tart and the apples are somewhat firm."

Mister Walton let out a great laugh. "You *are* a magician, sir. You describe Mrs. Baffin's recipe exactly."

"I know good pie."

Sundry was searching for the item in question but was thinking of the magic stone. "Do shamans often reveal their tricks?"

"Sometimes the trick," said the Indian, "is better than the illusion." His eyes were bright and cheerful, perhaps with the prospect of apple pie. "When one grows old, one feels the need to pass such things on." Nodding toward Mister Walton, he added, "One shaman to another."

Sundry looked up from his search in the hamper to glance at his friend and employer. This last statement had not been lightly uttered, and Mister Walton looked down at his knees, bemused and even embarrassed. There was a compliment in John Neptune's words that Sundry felt his friend greatly deserved. He glanced then to the old man, who was looking at him solemnly.

"Do you have any rat cheese to go with that?" asked John Neptune.

9. Below the Wharf . . .

WYCKFORD O'HEARN HAD NEARLY REACHED the other side of the wharf when he lost sight of the little boy. The frightened child fled into the thick of the crowd, and it was duck and sight the entire way. Wyck was tall enough to see over most people, but the boy must have found a large crate or a wide skirt to hide behind; perhaps he had slipped away in another direction.

Wyck looked over the hats and heads, feeling the unseasonable heat of the day rankle under his collar, which was a little too stiff and a little too tight. His generous mood was evaporating, and irritability rose with the flush on his face and the beads of sweat on his brow.

Lyman Peabody caught Wyck's attention with a raised eyebrow. Wyck politely nodded, noticing that Lyman seemed to have developed an odd tick; the old fellow's head jerked to one side as though he were tightening a knot, like a dog pulling at the end of a leash.

Slowly, Wyck recognized Lyman's expression and wove his way toward the old man, frowning at the spot that Lyman indicated. Peering over the side, he saw an ancient ladder nailed to the side of the wharf. Wyck caught his cigar just as it was slipping from his ear and tucked it into a vest pocket. "He went down there?" he asked Lyman.

"Like a rat abandoning ship," said Lyman, adding, "He lost his bottle."

Wyck considered the drop. The harbor water sloshed against the pilings. The thought of the young woman's distress prodded him, and he backed up to the edge of the wharf. Lowering a leg, he caught the first rung of the ladder with the arch of his boot.

"Watch yourself, now," said Lyman. "It's not the first time I've seen him take that route, and he's not the only one. They use it mostly at night. They run along down there like squirrels."

Wyck didn't ask who *they* were, but eased himself down three more rungs, testing them as he went. He could feel the tremor of the crowd upon the wharf and sense the swirl of water below. A gull swooped by him. The fifth rung creaked ominously beneath his weight, and he took a strain with his arms till he had reached the next.

Now he could look below the wharf; slowly, his eyes adjusted to the shadowy cat's cradle of timbers and pilings. Wyck was appraising a rude walk of planks that he could reach with one step from the ladder when a rumor of movement, toward the street end of the wharf, caught the periphery of his vision. He tested the plank nearest him with most of his weight before committing himself, then let go of the ladder, hunkered his tall self beneath the surface of the wharf, and scuttled as best he could toward the shore.

The relative coolness beneath the quay was welcome at first, till the sweat became a chilly presence beneath his shirt. The smell of salt and tar and damp things, coupled with his height above the water, made him feel light-headed, but another movement, some yards ahead of him, encouraged him to further his pursuit.

At the land end of the wharf, he expected another ladder leading to the surface or down to the thin lip of shore beneath the commercial piers; what he found was another plank that reached to an opening about four feet in width and dug into the bank of the shore itself. Irregularly shaped but nearly six feet at its highest, it was, perhaps, part of a drainage system, fashioned when the waterfront was built out years ago and Commercial Street was constructed. From somewhere above him Wyck heard the tone, if not the detail, of a vendor hawking his wares over the murmur of the crowd. Wyck looked back through the length of the wharf, squinting at the triangle of light piercing the furthest complex of beams and pilings.

A man, dirty and ragged, sat some yards away, on a side path of the plank walkway, watching the red-haired giant with only vague interest. The man was without hat or coat, leaning against a truss with no evident purpose or occupation. He did not acknowledge Wyck, but only stared back without expression. Wyck was not a little apprehensive—Lyman Peabody's cryptic advice to "watch himself" suddenly remembered.

Turning to the dark opening in the man-made shoreline, curiosity rubbed shoulders with his original intentions, and Wyckford O'Hearn, with a sharp glance back at his seemingly apathetic observer, balanced his way across this last plank.

In the rock-lined opening he did not have to duck down, and he paused a moment to arch his back. When his eyes had adjusted to this new level of darkness, he shuffled two or three steps into the man-made cave. The presence of several oil lanterns on a small shelf of rock near the mouth of the hole gave him fresh pause. Wyck retrieved one of the lamps, shaking it to hear the slosh of oil in its base, then lit it with a wooden match from his pocket.

The yellow glow through the lantern's smoky glass was hardly noticeable till Wyck moved further into the passageway. A cold breeze, as light as a breath, met his face as he picked his way past loose stones and debris.

"Hello," he said into the darkness beyond the effect of his lamp. "I'm not here to harm you. Your sister asked me to bring you back to her. She seems very nice." His voice sounded strangely flat in this narrow place, and he had the intuition it had gone unheard. "Hello!" he said in a louder tone.

Wyckford counted his steps now and reckoned that he was below Commercial Street when he came to a second passage, perpendicular to the first. This was more obviously part of a drainage system; it was narrower, its floor a four-foot drop from where he stood, its ceiling higher. He could hear water trickling, and the light of his lamp caught the glisten of a small stream in the ditch below. The lantern held little sway at any distance, however, and fear of close places spoke quietly in his chest. He looked, without the lamp, up and down the conduit.

To his right, a faint orange glow, not unlike the light of his own lamp, shone nebulously in the distance. With a grunt of satisfaction, he set down his lantern and lowered himself to the trench below, which trickled with about four inches of cold water that seeped, almost immediately, into his boots. He gave a look back to be sure that nobody was following him, then took the lamp and splashed as quietly as he could toward the glow in the distance.

10. . . . and Above

MOLLIE FELT A RUSH OF UNCERTAINTY as she followed the redheaded man across the wharf. His willingness to help her made her dread more the moment when she would be forced to admit that Bird was no relation. It had not been an original deception; she had read of Nancy doing the same in *Oliver Twist*. She told herself that her motives were more honorable than those of the hapless woman in Dickens's novel, but this did not ease her discomfort, and she was angry with herself for feeling timid about the man's inevitable reaction when he discovered the truth.

She was confounded, then, when she got to the other side of the wharf and could see neither boy nor man. She turned on her heel and scanned the crowd. Then she saw Lyman Peabody, who winked as if he knew something.

"Looking for someone?" asked the man.

"There was a little boy, and a man, quite tall—" A sailor brushed past her, a little more closely than was dictated by the immediate crowd, and she gave him a good whack in the head with her purse.

"The baseball player?" Lyman Peabody was asking.

"Watch yourself!" she demanded. The sailor never looked back, and she would have berated him further if there weren't more pressing concerns. "Is that who he is?" she said to Lyman.

"Redheaded?"

"Yes, that's him." Another man smiled as he approached Mollie. She caught sight of him from the corner of her eye and shot him a dangerous glance. The man, possibly innocent of anything but admiration, raised a startled hand to his hat and stepped well around her.

"Wyckford O'Hearn," said Lyman Peabody.

"Is that his name?" she said. "Where did he go?"

"I didn't see him," said Lyman.

Mollie was vexed with the man. She took a few steps along the wharf, peering through the crowd. She even looked over the side, half-expecting to see someone floundering in the harbor.

"The kid could dart anywhere," said Horace when she returned, "but a man like Wyck is troublesome to lose."

Maven's mouth hung open. "Gory, Hod!" he exclaimed. "Where'd he go?"

Horace swung his gray-eyed gaze briefly in Maven's direction. He smiled (more on one side of his mouth than the other), and the tip of his tongue rode on his lower lip. "You say this boy is your brother?"

Mollie looked less distraught, suddenly, and more irritated. "Yes," she replied snappishly, which caused Horace's smile to broaden. "Where could they have gone?" she said again.

"I am dumbfounded," declared Maven.

"Oh, they just moved quick, is all," assured Horace.

The young woman turned sharply and regarded Horace's smile. "Is this some sort of trick?"

"Trick?" piped the old man. "We went after the boy, didn't we?"

"*You* didn't do anything. It was the other man who went after him."

"*I* sent him off," explained Horace. She heard a snicker from the man and a sound of astonishment from Maven as she walked away.

It is true that the person quick to play someone for a fool, for whatever reason, is often quick to accuse another of the same, and Mollie felt her face reddening. Perhaps they all knew each other, these layabouts and Bird and Pembleton; or perhaps Pembleton alone was acquainted with these men. She glanced over her shoulder, half-expecting to see *both* the redheaded man and Pembleton's bull of an accomplice coming for her.

Then she looked at Horace and Maven. The man with the cowlick didn't look capable of fooling anyone, and the old man had already turned his attention to other interests.

She was only gone for fifteen minutes or so when she walked back down the wharf to see if Wyckford O'Hearn had returned; Horace McQuinn caught sight of her and waved, but she spoke before Maven had even realized she was near. "What was that man's name?" she asked.

"Oh, my!" said a startled Maven Flyce.

"You mean Wyck?" said Horace. Mollie was distracted by something she had seen, and he followed her gaze. "Do you see them?" he asked.

"No," she said with a note of uncertainty. But she *was* sure that she had seen Amos Guernsey. The man had changed his dress somewhat and seemed to be wearing a mustache—indeed, it had taken her a moment to realize who he was and why that particular face would trouble her—but once Amos's name came to mind, she was sure that she had seen him. After his threat earlier in the day, the sight of him among the crowd on the wharf gave her an uneasy turn. "I am afraid I have to go," she said.

"Goodness sakes!" said Maven.

"Do you want me to tell Wyck where you're going in case he comes back with the boy?" asked Horace.

"No," she said. "I'll be away from home this afternoon, and it would be too much of a shock to my poor mother, who is ill, if they just showed up at her door without warning."

Horace's eyes widened, and he made a long face. "We'll send him to the police station," he said. "You can inquire there."

"Thank you." She wondered what events she might have set into motion, but Amos's presence made things more complex. For a moment, she considered going after the man and confronting him where he stood, but instead she backed away, glancing at Maven, whose mouth continued to hang open. "Good-bye."

"I like your society page," said Horace, his expression serious. "I catch up on it whenever the weather turns bad."

Mollie was startled by Horace's knowledge of her. "Thank you," she said quietly. Horace shrugged. Trying to hide her anger, Mollie turned about and walked away.

"My word, Hod!" said Maven. "People are something!"

"Oh, they are, Maven," said Horace. "They're something, all right."

"I sure hope she finds her brother," said Maven.

11. Beneath the Streets

THE TUNNEL WAS SO NARROW IN PLACES that Wyckford had to move with one shoulder forward to squeeze past. It was fortunate that the drain was well vented, or the sense of claustrophobia might have been overwhelming; a variety of scents, not all unpleasant, wafted by him on a current of cold air. Rats squeaked from small niches in either wall, occasionally scuttling past him or over his boots, and bodiless voices echoed down drainpipes and seeped through ancient foundations, so ghostlike that the hair at the back of Wyck's neck prickled. The rumble of a trolley sounded overhead, and he looked with misgivings at the ceiling until it passed.

The orange glow emanated from a breach in the left-hand wall, and a pile of rubble, partially damming the water in the drain, littered the breach itself. The walls of the tunnel had been slabs of black rock, backed, he guessed, with gravel and fill. Now ancient masonry appeared as he drew near the hole, which proved to be a doorway—the surrounding brickwork the lower section of a timeworn foundation.

Wyck heard a human murmur. He peered inside and saw a debris-filled room lit by a fire in a small hearth and a single lamp on a crude table. A great heap of ancient rags lay in the corner to his immediate right.

By the table was a wild-haired scarecrow of a man, Eustace Pembleton, and standing in his voluminous coat and looming in the room like a goblin, Pembleton was shaking the little boy by the shoulders and barking at him for having dropped the bottle of rum. Their two shadows shivered upon the ceiling and walls like forms beneath a depth of water. Wyck did his best to step quietly over the rubble in the doorway, but the man turned the moment the redheaded giant moved.

Wyck cut a formidable figure, standing to his full height in the shifting light; but he was surprised, and not a little unsettled, to see an absence of fear in Pembleton's expression (though, admittedly, little besides the man's eyes could be seen behind the dirt and the tangled beard). The boy, hardly four years old and as dirty as the man, was astonished, his eyes and mouth forming perfectly horrified circles. "You can let the boy go," said Wyck. "I'm taking him back to his family."

"Inviting people in now?" said the man, and he cut the boy such a blow on the side of the face that the child was thrown onto his back. Not content with this, the madman drew his foot back with the object of kicking the still figure, and Wyck stepped forward. "You strike him again," shouted Wyck, "and I will break your neck!"

Something heavy shattered across Wyck's back, and pieces of rotting wood scattered past him in wet shards as he dropped the lantern and fell to his knees. A single grunt exploded from him as he landed, and there was a terrible moment when he feared he wouldn't be able to breathe. Then he dragged a great gulp of air into his lungs, shifted his weight to one side, and watched the makeshift club fly past his nose. Wyck swung his great torso about, saw the man behind him—a heap of dirty rags that had been invisible among the pile in the corner—and, from his knees, caught his attacker in the stomach with one ham-sized fist.

Wyckford had been in more than one melee in his day, but he had never struck anything so large and solid, and if the truth be known, the great bull of a man who had attacked him had never been struck by anything so large and solid. The blow took the assailant square in the breadbasket, and for the first time in Tom Bull's life, the wind was knocked from him.

Wyck drew in a second breath, the sound of which was like the warning of an angry bear. Pembleton backed away, and Tom Bull groaned, bent double, the whites of his eyes glowing in his dirty face. Wyck stood; his attacker gave a start, faltered on the debris underfoot, and went down on one knee.

Left on its side, the ballplayer's lantern had gone out, its wick still glowing an angry red. Half-stunned by the blow to his back, Wyck looked past Pembleton and saw a stairwell rising from the corner of the room behind the table. "Where does that go?" he demanded.

"Nowhere," said the man. "It's walled up."

"Is it?" Wyck scooped the little boy from the floor.

"You leave him be!" snapped the wild-haired man. "You just . . . put him down! Do you hear?"

At the foot of the stairs, the Hibernian Titan turned and eyed the man dangerously. "I bet if you were dead, no one would miss you," he said. With the boy over one shoulder, he snatched the remaining lamp from the table and ascended the ancient stairs. The way was dark and clammy, walled in brick; the treads were of wood, and he feared they might not hold beneath him. He moved softly and swiftly till the stairs had turned ninety degrees and ended at a landing and a bricked-up arch.

He set down the lamp and eased the boy to the floor. The child was unconscious, but he detected a heartbeat and felt a small breath when he held a forefinger to his nostrils. Wyck had half a mind to go back and break Pembleton's neck, anyway.

Facing the bricks, he picked at some flakes of mortar. When not playing baseball for small pay in the warmer months, he was a part-time railway jack, replacing ties and rebedding rails. Once, though, he had torn down old buildings for a living, and he had carried from that job a certain talent for finding the weak point in any structure he wished to bring down—baseball pitchers, he had once hoped, included.

Here he was pleased to find an ancient and less than admirable job of masonry. He tested the bricks with a moderate shove of his shoulder, and after three solid charges, the plug fell out in almost one piece. The noise it made when it hit the ground was like a cannon shot. Dust blew up and briefly clouded the sudden view.

He was in an alley, at the rear of a conglomeration of run-down tenements and abandoned warehouses. With the boy cradled against one shoulder, Wyck bent his head back and tried to guess which chimney was connected to the wretched hearth below. Thin sprills of smoke rose from several of the pots above. He caught sight of a dog running off in the direction of Fore Street. A face looked out at him from a dirty window.

He was suddenly astounded at what he had done, and for a woman he didn't even know, however pretty she was. Well, he had gotten up this morning wanting to do a good deed.

Gently, he carried the stirring child from the alley.

12. The Man with the Strange Difficulty

MISTER WALTON HAD BEEN THROUGH BATH BEFORE; he had even looked back at it from the rail ferry that crossed the Kennebec, but he had never lingered in the city itself. The train pulled into the station, not far from the famous iron works, where battleships and yachts had been launched since the end of the Civil War. The great ways, the skeletal staging and ramps that circumscribed the unfinished vessels, gave the riverfront the look of a city under construction.

Opposite was Front Street, a stalwart and brickish business district, and Washington Street, rising up a long slope and graced by handsome churches and grand homes that reflected the city's prosperous maritime legacy.

There was a moment, not so many years before, when forty-four vessels were under construction at the same time and nearly as many—recently christened and launched into the dark waters of the Kennebec—were being rigged and equipped for their maiden voyages. At this historic place in time, the city of Bath, Maine, was the preeminent shipbuilder of the United States, perhaps the world.

Mister Walton knew the fame of the city, and was awed, not so much by what he saw but by what he sensed about it as the train pulled out of the station and revealed the other half of Bath.

John Neptune led them up High Street, a walk that provided some pleasant exercise on this bright fall day. From High Street they turned down a lane, the name of which Mister Walton did not catch, then another, and finally they passed through an alley between two houses and came out onto another street, where stood an old house.

After the Indian knocked several times, an elderly woman came to the door; she looked at him with suspicion, as if a hundred years and more had not passed since the region's last Indian war. "What do you want?" came her short query. A small dog barked at her heels. Eugene climbed up the old man's shoulder and stared balefully at the woman.

"We are here to see Mr. Echo," said John Neptune. He lifted his hat in deference to her gender, if not her conviviality.

"Are you," she said. "Well, he's up in his rooms. I've never seen a man in such a state! He'll kill *himself* if he doesn't stop it! Are you Mr. Neptune, then?"

"I am," said the man.

He was not what she had expected, and she showed it plainly. "Come in," she said grudgingly. She eyed the raccoon on John Neptune's shoulder. "I hope you've got a good line on that thing," she said. She looked as uncertainly upon Mister Walton and Sundry, both of whom doffed their hats.

They were led through the hall toward the back of the house, and on one side of a pantry was a door, behind which ascended a narrow staircase. "He's waiting for you," said the woman, standing with the door open. "Mr. Echo!" she called up the stairs. "Your friend is here!"

"Oh!" came a startled voice. "Send him up, send him up!"

The woman rolled her eyes, though it was difficult to say if this was meant to be taken as a comment upon the man above or as an instruction to the visitors to hurry along.

"Thank you, ma'am," said Mister Walton as he passed her, hat in hand.

The stair treads were shallow and steep, and Sundry, in particular, found them unaccommodating to his long feet. Their boots clumped loudly. When they reached the upper floor, Mister Walton and Sundry were surprised, after the paucity of staircase, to discover an apartment of several large rooms, every wall of which (from where they stood) seemed to be lined with shelves jammed with books and periodicals (the single exception being a topmost shelf on the other side of the room where an ancient clock held court). Presumably, all other shelves were filled to their capacity, since the perimeters of the floors were also thick with leaning stacks of books and piles of papers.

A man stood near the middle of the parlor—a small, very nervous-looking man, his sparse hair in disarray, his jacket wrinkled, the knot of his tie loose. He was not very prepossessing, average in every imaginable way, and even his thin mustache had a wan quality about it. He was hunched over, as if expecting a blow, and there was a frightened look in his eyes; one might have wondered that his visitors didn't pose some sort of physical threat. "Is that you, John?" he asked.

"Yes, Henry," said the Indian. "It's John Neptune."

"You have someone with you," said the man.

"Yes, I have brought some friends."

"What is that on your shoulder?"

"It is a raccoon," said John Neptune.

"A raccoon? What does that mean?"

The old man raised a calming hand. "They are very good fortune—raccoons. Isn't a raccoon a sign of good fortune, Mister Walton?"

This was more than Mister Walton honestly knew, but it seemed prudent to agree. Eugene was, at the moment, gnawing on a piece of hair behind John Neptune's ear.

"My mother told me of a raccoon once," said Sundry, "that led a fellow to two hundred dollars."

"This is Mister Tobias Walton," said John Neptune. "Mister Walton, may I introduce to you Mr. Henry Echo."

"Sir," said Mister Walton. He stepped over a collection of Bulwer-Lytton (he read the title, *Paul Clifford*, in transit) and extended his hand.

Henry Echo flinched, as if the expected blow had arrived. Mister Walton halted his advance, but the nervous man put out his own hand, so

Mister Walton recommenced his movement, upon which Henry Echo flinched again. This series of stops, starts, and flinches repeated themselves several times before they had properly greeted one another.

"This is Sundry Moss," said John Neptune. "Mr. Moss, Henry Echo."

"Very glad to meet you," said Sundry, staying where he was.

"I hope, sir," said the man, "that you can say the same to me when the sun rises next."

With a characteristic smile, Mister Walton said, "I am sure, Mr. Echo, that any friend of Mr. Neptune's—" He deliberately left the sentence unfinished.

"I should not have said, Mister Walton, 'I hope you can say the same,' but, truly, 'I hope that I am alive to hear anything you say at all.' "

13. Bird

"THAT'S A GOOD BOY," said Wyck, as if the little fellow had rallied only to please him; but when Wyck looked at the boy, there was such a disoriented expression on the child's face that his apprehensions returned.

Having discovered what street he was on, Wyck realized he was walking in the wrong direction, and turning himself around, he carried the little boy past the Custom House and back to the Custom House Wharf. Along the way, they garnered curious glances; the huge man was, after all, in some visible distress, and there was such a motionless quality about the boy.

The crowds had thinned on the quay. Horace was amused to see them, and Maven perplexed. "Now, where have you come from?" asked Horace. Wyck's clothes were damp and filthy, and his boots were wringing wet.

"Believe me, Horace, you wouldn't believe me." Wyckford lowered the boy from his shoulder but found that the child didn't want to (or perhaps couldn't) stand by himself. The kid's legs wobbled. "Where's his sister?" wondered Wyck, looking around for the handsome dark-haired woman.

"She's gone off," explained Horace. "You only just missed her."

"Gone off? But I've got her brother! What do you mean, she's gone off? I nearly had my back broke down there!"

"Good heavens, Wyck!" declared Maven. "How did it happen?"

Even Horace showed interest. "Did you get into a scrape?"

Wyck stopped himself in mid-curse and glanced down at the boy. "I think he's really hurt, Horace." The old man leaned forward, and his hand shook slightly as, with tobacco-stained fingers, he searched through the boy's dirty hair. "He's had a knock on the head."

"It was Pembleton," growled Wyckford. "I should've broke his neck for him! Is he all right? Pembleton hit him, but I didn't think it was that hard. He must have hit his head when he fell back. My God, Horace, is he all right?" Wyck realized that they were drawing attention from passersby; some had stopped to see what was happening, and more gathered while the three men discussed what to do.

"Hey, little fellow," Wyck was saying. He propped the child like a puppet on one knee. "Are you awake?" The little boy blinked but still seemed dazed.

"He's stunned, maybe," said Horace. "I'd get him someplace where he can rest."

"But where? Where's his sister?"

"She left," Maven said. "I was so amazed."

"I'm not sure she had the right kid," said Horace.

"Is he drunk?" asked someone.

"The right kid?" asked Wyck. "What do you mean, the right kid?"

"I'm not all that sure she was his sister."

"Gory, Hod!" said Maven.

"She writes for the paper, you know."

"Where does she live?" asked Wyck. The boy was stirring in his arms.

"It can't be too hard to find out," assured Horace. "I'll tell you what. You take him home—"

"Home?"

"—and I'll see if I can't find where she is."

"Home? Take her to Mrs. Barter's?"

"Or to the police—"

"I couldn't take him *there*. He hasn't done anything wrong."

Horace made a face. "Maybe he should go to the hospital."

"No," said Wyck emphatically. "I'll take him home for now. Mrs. Barter will know what to do, if she doesn't throw us both out. He isn't much to look at." Wyck felt himself choke up every time he looked down at the boy. "I guess I'll have to carry him."

"Let's get a carriage for you," Horace said.

"Horace, I don't think I have the price of a beer in my pocket. I just paid my rent by the skin of my teeth."

"I think I've got something," said Horace with a knowing grin. He reached into a pocket. "Old Hod's got it. Don't you worry."

"That's awful decent of you, Horace," Wyck said.

The older man crossed Wyck's palm with a bill. "Get that kid somewhere where he can lie down."

"Is there anything I can do?" asked an older woman, standing a few feet away; other people registered concern with her. A police officer was making his way through the crowd.

"It's all right, thank you, ma'am," said Wyck. He avoided eye contact with the cop. "I've just got to get him home, is all."

"Let me hail a cab for you," said a thin man who had approached the scene.

"When did you grow a mustache, Amos?" asked Horace to the newcomer.

Wyckford was carrying the child toward the street, and the actor only pivoted on one heel, tipped his missing hat, and said, "Why, just this morning, Mr. McQuinn," before following the redheaded man.

"What could happen next, Hod!" exclaimed Maven when the two men and the boy were gone. "Circumstances can be puzzling!"

"It's his little brother," explained Horace to the older woman and the cop, who watched Amos Guernsey lead Wyck and his burden toward the street.

Wyck settled the child beside him in the carriage that Amos hailed and thanked the skinny fellow.

"Very much my pleasure, sir," said the man. "I hope matters turn out in a congenial manner."

Wyck frowned at the man's mustache; it moved so strangely when Amos spoke. "He hit his head," said Wyck to the driver.

"To the hospital, then?" inquired the cabby.

"No, to Pine Street," answered Wyck. "My landlady will know how to look after him." He waved to Amos.

The boy stirred when the cab jerked into motion. Wyck stared down at the little boy, and horror filled his breast as it occurred to him that what he had done amounted to nothing less than kidnapping. *Oh, Lord,* he thought, *Ma always said a pretty face would get me hung quicker than robbery!* He caught a glimmer of watchfulness from beneath the child's seemingly closed lids. "My brother's boy," said Wyck for no apparent reason.

"I see the resemblance," said the driver without looking back. Clearly, it was of little moment to him, and soon the carriage pulled up beside a neat white-picket fence and a white-clapboarded house.

Not at all sure of what he was doing, Wyck spoke to the boy. "Come on, now. We'll look after that bump." He held his hands out, palms up, but the child did not respond. Wyck lifted the boy into his arms. When he had paid the driver, he opened the gate and hurried up the flagstone walk to Mrs. Barter's front door.

There were two hospitals in the vicinity of Portland in those days—the Mariners' Hospital, on Martin's Point, and the state hospital, which Wyck could see from the north-facing window of his room at Mrs. Barter's—both as forward-looking establishments as probably existed in 1896.

It was not strange, however, that Wyck avoided taking his unexpected charge to any hospital. A community was fortunate to have such an institution, but no one was ever considered fortunate to go to one. In Wyck's mind and in the minds of many of his contemporaries, the word *hospital* had the ring of hopelessness. The ratio of success to failure in the practice of medicine throughout the country had improved since the Conflict Between the States, but reputation had not risen accordingly.

Wyck did not know what a concussion was, though the medical profession had recognized the symptoms since the sixteenth century. Certainly trauma, whether physical or mental, was an *idea* to which he had never been exposed, though the physical reality had visited him more than once. He'd been hit on the head and even knocked cold for nearly ten minutes by a wild pitch two years before. Harold Duncan, the catcher on their team, swore that Wyck's batting average had improved because of it.

Furthermore, Wyck had been raised on a farm, north of Bangor in a town called Veazie. There were few sorts of injuries that he had not seen his mother deal with—some with unqualified success—and he associated the healing process with the presence of a no-nonsense matron, to which species both his mother and Mrs. Barter belonged.

It is a tribute to Mrs. Barter's lack of nonsense that Wyck—after considering a good story to cover his sudden role as guardian—spilled the truth in less time than it took the landlady to lead them to the parlor.

"You knocked down a wall," she said matter-of-factly.

"It was *part* of a wall."

"And you just took him?" She waved a hand to indicate a certain type of negligence abhorred by meticulous mothers and strict business accountants. "You never inquired who he was or how he might be related to this man?"

"I wasn't exactly on speaking terms with him. I had just offered to twist off his head."

This was about as uncivil a set of words as Mrs. Barter would allow in her parlor, and Wyck knew from her expression that he had *muddied the air*. The landlady, with her graying hair wound tight in a bun and her gaze shot critically down her nose, had a severe aspect that was not entirely indicative of her character.

Although a busy person, she produced enough of what was pleasant through her labor to convince those benefiting by it of good intentions and therefore a good heart. She was skeptical of most things and downright dismissive of many others. She was a small person, with a sharp nose, gray eyes, and thin lips. Wyck could not imagine that she had ever been handsome, and yet her occasional smiles, small as they were, had softened his impression of her, as her concern for others had raised his regard.

"What's his name?" she asked. When Wyck's mouth had hung open long enough, she raised an eyebrow in the child's direction.

It was difficult to tell much about the boy. Wyck thought that he couldn't be any more than four years old. His hair was long and matted, but it looked to be, by nature, a dark brown. His face was black with dirt, his brown eyes wide with uncertainty. There was a scar visible beneath the grime on his forehead—about four inches long. His clothes, gaping with holes and shiny with filth and long wear, were too large for him. To Wyck's relief, the boy's expression seemed less confused, and his eyes darted about the cozy room with interest and trepidation.

"You do have a name. I am sure of it," said Mrs. Barter, not unkindly. There was another silence in which the boy blinked at her and Wyck. "But you're sure to be famous for the state of your clothes *and* the dirt on your face if we don't do something about them. Wyckford?"

"Yes, Mrs. Barter?"

"Bring the big washtub from the cellar and take it to the kitchen."

"Yes, ma'am." The big fellow lumbered out of the parlor and into the hall with only one backward glance.

"I don't suppose, by the look of you, that you have eaten very recently," she said to the little boy, and she thought there was just the flash of a reaction. "Well, I won't have you eating in my kitchen in this state. Come along." She held out a hand. "I could carry you, but I'm sure you would like to spare my old back. Come, come."

For the first time since Wyck found him, the child moved under his own power, standing uncertainly by the couch and taking in the relative splendor of Mrs. Barter's parlor. It was not an elaborate room by the standards of the day, but there were ancestors on the wall, chintzes on the overstuffed furniture, and doilies on every available flat surface. There was a piano against one wall, and the windows were draped to the floor with curtains.

There was something in the honest wonder of the little fellow's expression that struck Mrs. Barter, and her voice caught slightly when she spoke again. "Come," she said, and it was perhaps that unintended emotion that encouraged him to walk to the kitchen beneath her guiding hand.

By the time Wyck had dumped the blackened water from the washtub in the backyard and returned to the kitchen, Mrs. Barter had dried the boy with a towel and covered him with a flannel nightshirt of her late husband's. He looked more respectable but not any healthier once they were able to see beneath the layers of filth he had been inhabiting. The landlady declared his hair too long, but that would keep for another time, and she had it combed back away from his face, which showed several small marks from disease and more scars, the origin of which they did not like to think about.

His skin was pink now from her industrious cleaning, and they had found the bump at the back of his head where he had hit the floor of the cellar. The child only flinched once throughout, in Wyckford's words, *"a vigorous annihilation of dirt,"* and that was when the landlady inspected this recent bruise. When she was done, however, he glowed with a high polish, and she was satisfied with her labor. Feeding him was the next item of business.

Mr. Peevis, her other roomer, was not home from the glass factory, but she wasn't going to put off dinner and deprive the child of food any longer. Wyck and the landlady watched with satisfaction while the little fellow gravely dipped great hunks of bread into his stew and chewed it noisily. Wyck wondered how many times the boy would be allowed to dip his bread with impunity, but Mrs. Barter—who, under any other circumstances, would have forbidden such actions at her table—said nothing. Wyck was amused but knew better than to show it.

As the stew dwindled in his bowl, the little boy slowed the pace of his eating. Wyck thought that he was probably full by now, but his momentum increased again once he was confronted by a thick slice of Mrs. Barter's pumpkin bread.

"And you don't know his name?" Mrs. Barter asked again. Wyck shook his head, and it looked, from his landlady's expression, that she thought he didn't know much.

"Bird," said the little boy. They turned at the sound of his voice, but he did not look at them. He stared down at what was left of his pumpkin bread, a short hunk of it gripped in one small hand.

"Bert?" asked Wyckford. He shifted forward in his chair and rested his elbows on the table.

"Is that your name, child?" asked Mrs. Barter.

The little fellow shook his head gravely. "Bird," he whispered.

"You don't suppose he means *Bird?*" Wyck wondered aloud.

"It seems he might, since that is what he is saying," returned Mrs. Barter. "Bird," she said. "That is a fine name."

Bird did not seem to think so. He looked down at his plate as if he had lost his appetite.

"Now, who gave you such a name?" asked Wyck. It didn't seem a proper sort of name to him at all, and his tone of voice did nothing to disguise his feelings. Mrs. Barter shot him a hard glance, and Wyck realized his error. "Well," he said quickly, gaining the floor without knowing what to say. "Well," he said again, and finally: "It is. It's a fine name. Beats the he — Beats the brass out of Wyckford."

"You eat the rest of your bread now, Bird," said Mrs. Barter with a comforting firmness. "Dinner will be ready as soon as I set the table," she told Wyck, who was beginning to feel hungry himself. He realized that he had been eyeing the remainder of the pumpkin bread with undisguised interest and felt himself blush.

"Mr. Pembleton called me that," said the little boy. His shoulders were lifted in a protective hunch, and his chin was buried in his chest.

"Is that the man he was with when you found him?" asked Mrs. Barter.

Wyck nodded.

"Was he your father?" asked the landlady. This engendered a shake of Bird's head. There was a long silence then, in the midst of which Wyckford's stomach could be heard to growl. "Now, Wyckford," said Mrs. Barter. "What do you intend to do —" She stopped in mid-sentence. Wyck, who had inched himself close enough to the stove to smell the stew, looked at the little boy, who was asleep, his head on the kitchen table.

14. Second Thoughts

It had been a warm day for October, but the air was clear, the sky cloudless, and the temperature plummeted quickly once the sun was down. There was something bracing about the gloaming of a fall night, and Mollie had hoped it would be more conducive to clear thinking.

Leaning against a post on Mrs. Makepeace's porch, she heard Hilda coming up the walk from her day at the rope factory. Hilda had a green wool shawl that became her complexion and her blond curls, and this was wrapped tightly about her as she mounted the steps. "Oh!" she said, surprised to look up and find Mollie on the porch. "I'm very glad to see *you* in good health!"

"Have *you* been feeling poorly?" asked Mollie, hiding her true state of mind with a flippant reply.

"*You* know what I mean."

"I know there seems to be an especial emphasis whenever the second person singular is employed."

Hilda responded with an exasperated gasp. "I wish you were *all* talk, Mollie Peer," she said. "That will get you into trouble enough, but when you go wandering into places you shouldn't be—! Come in before you catch cold."

Mollie followed her inside. Mrs. Makepeace did not stint on the fuel, and the house was cozy warm. They could hear the landlady in the kitchen, readying dinner.

"I haven't forgotten last night, you know," Hilda was saying in a low voice as she mounted the stairs.

"I don't imagine you have" was Mollie's reply, delivered with more volume so that she might be heard above the rustle of their skirts against the treads.

Hilda stopped at the top of the steps and turned, her pretty, round features wide with wonder. "It scares me worse the more I think of it."

"I *am* sorry," said Mollie. She had been thinking about it, too, when she wasn't mulling over her afternoon and the incident on the wharf.

Hilda put a hand on Mollie's arm; she felt so bad about scolding people that Mollie thought she would make a good mother someday. They had grown up not so far apart, in time or place, and in similar conditions, with large families among the workers on Munjoy Hill. But aside from this, they had little else in common except friendship. Mollie, whose Italian mother had contributed something of the patrician to her daughter's face, blended easily with the society crowd about which she had come to write. Hilda looked the picture of a healthy milkmaid in an old man's dreams.

Mollie's father had encouraged even his daughter toward education. Hilda's family respected schooling as long as there was food on the table; consequently, Hilda had not finished her fifth year at Munjoy Hill but had gone to work at the rope factory. There was no going back, of course, when she went out on her own, and from that point onward there would be little or no change in her life till she found the proper beau and married. There were her rooms at Mrs. Makepeace's Boarding House, her circle of friends at the factory, and the factory itself. There was the work, and there was Mollie.

Hilda was a little awed by Mollie—despite her motherly perspective toward the tall young woman—and not the least bit envious, though she believed Mollie was moving toward better things.

But there was something hard in Mollie's childhood that Hilda sensed at times (though she had never found it out), some failure that Mollie had never learned to accept, and if the truth be known, it may have been some seemingly insignificant event that made Mollie what she was. "Am I so mysterious to you?" Mollie had said once to Hilda, and Hilda had answered, "You're a mystery to yourself, Mollie Peer."

Mollie expressed love and sometimes admiration for her family, but there were no pictures of her people on the walls of her room or cherished mementos on her dresser. Hilda's room was a museum of her earlier life upon the Hill, and even moments that had made her angry or sad might be remembered by a length of ribbon or a pressed flower.

"Was someone knocking?" asked Hilda at Mollie's door. There were several more raps and the sound of Mrs. Makepeace moving in the hall below. They heard voices, and in a few moments there were footsteps on the stairs and a light knock at Mollie's door.

Mrs. Makepeace leaned into the room. "Your policeman is here to see you. He was concerned that you got home safely."

"Home safely?" said Hilda.

"He's not *my* policeman, Mrs. Makepeace."

"Well, he seems very attentive. He heard you were on the wharves today," said the landlady with a frown.

Officer Skillings was a tall and not altogether unhandsome lad whom Mollie had used as a source for one of her "prospective stories." He had been to the house more than once lately, however, and impressed both Mrs. Makepeace and Hilda as a marriage prospect. In their half-teasing way of speaking, he had become *Mollie's* policeman.

"Please tell Officer Skillings," informed Mollie, "that I am quite safe and that I am not able to see anyone just now."

"I've cooked plenty for supper," said Mrs. Makepeace, her voice lilting with insinuation. "He's more than welcome."

"I am sure that somebody has dinner waiting for him, Mrs. Makepeace."

"If you say," whispered the landlady, and she disappeared.

"He's a nice-looking fellow," said Hilda, a little disappointed to be missing male company at the table. Just the rumor of a man in the house had sent her scurrying for her brush.

"I think he is using me to get to you," said Mollie flippantly.

"Stranger things have happened," said Hilda.

Mollie searched for a means by which to change the subject. "You should wear your hair back and exhibit that wonderful complexion of yours," she said as she sat at her desk.

Hilda was amenable to this; she stood at the mirror on Mollie's dressing table and pulled her hair back. "Do you think?" She pulled a sigh. "I think he's good-looking. And a policeman—very *braw*. It was nice of him to ask after you." A thought occurred to Hilda. "But *what* were you doing on the wharf, Mollie Peer?"

"I was following a story."

"Following that little boy!"

"Don't jump to conclusions."

"Well, if he thought it necessary to ask after you—"

"Good heavens!" exclaimed Mollie, her arms waving in exasperation. "How are we women to prove anything about ourselves if we can't *do* anything out of the protective custody of some . . . ardent male?"

"It's simply the natural order of things, Mollie!" Hilda looked like a mother again, explaining something to a particularly dense child.

"Well, the lioness drives the hunt, so *there's* the natural order for you!" said Mollie. She folded her arms and nodded emphatically once.

Hilda was almost laughing now. "Is he ardent, then?"

"Who?"

"Officer Skillings!"

"Never mind. I used the wrong word." Mollie caught sight of some stray locks in the mirror and made a show of tending to them. When Hilda went to her own room, Mollie sat and considered her reflection, and somehow the business on the wharf echoed in her mind with increasing seriousness.

What was I thinking? she wondered to herself.

15. Forge Light

THE WIND INCREASED as Mollie climbed Munjoy Hill. She stopped briefly to visit her mother's grave, to brush the few leaves away and think for a bit. The twilight gathered, and the wind came about, so that when she stepped outside the cemetery, she felt as if it were chasing her up the steep slope of Congress Street. The western sky was deepening to purple, the east already taken by night. Below her she could see a light in the observatory. Beyond, there was the harbor, dark with the hulls of vessels and dotted with lantern light. People often wondered why this marvelous view was left to Portland's laboring class till they felt the fall wind brisk off Back Cove or walked once upon the hill in the teeth of a winter squall.

Her father's house and forge stood almost alone several yards down the northern slope of the hill. The doors to the furnace were open, and his tall shape stood dark against it. The sky to the west sent out a flash of brilliant red, and it was easy to imagine that the light in the sky and the light in the forge emanated from the same source.

Despite the roar of the furnace and the metallic drag and clank of his tools, he sensed her approach and looked over his shoulder, catching sight of her before she was close enough to speak. Though he turned back to his work, she could tell he was pleased to see her. His hammer rang. Sparks flew like fireworks, as he fell into a rhythm, and Mollie was put in mind of the presses at the Printers' Exchange.

While he worked, she leaned against the corner of the smithy and looked in the direction of her home and the newspaper, then the water-front, though they were each effectively barred from her view by the brow of the hill and the houses occupying it. She wasn't sure, really, if she were feeling guilt or repentance, or just a little fear that she would be altogether caught out. What was Amos up to, following her? Nothing, probably, but satisfying his own curiosity. Well, he had forced her hand, however know-ingly, and she had left the business unfinished. She considered the sly parting words of Horace McQuinn, who had known from the start that she wasn't the boy's sister.

The image of the boy brought back the memory of his little bare feet; she hoped she had done nothing to make things harder for him. And then there was the big Irishman; she had felt a certain disdain for the man when she first saw him, imagining that he wasn't very bright and also that he could be convinced to do anything for her simply because she was a young woman. One does not admire an unthinking servant.

But he had not seemed so unthinking in the end, and Mollie won-dered if he wouldn't have done the same for an old woman or even an-other man. His quick determination troubled her, as did the likelihood that he would find out about her deception.

"For Mrs. Feeney's outhouse," said her father. He held a hinge up by his blacksmith's tongs; the end of the tongs and the hinge changed slowly, before her eyes, from a dull red to black. He was a big man, tall and broad at the shoulder. Her height came from him; certainly not from her mother, who had been a small woman. "Did you walk up?" he asked, turning back to his anvil. "You shouldn't be walking this time of night. The coaches can't see you"—he looked at her over his shoulder—"and you never know who's lurking about these days. They still haven't caught that fellow who was shooting at people down on Vaughan Bridge."

"People only lurk in books, Dad."

"Don't you believe it! Lurk in books," he said to himself as he returned to his work.

"How are you?" she asked.

"I'm working still," he said, which meant that things were as they had been most of his life, not counting that he lived alone now.

Even by the corner of the building she could feel the heat from the furnace. It seared on one side as the chill fall air nipped at the other. "I stopped by to see Mother," she said.

"Yes, I was by this morning." Mollie knew that he went down to the cemetery every morning. He said again, "Shouldn't be out walking alone this time of night."

"Dad, I think I did something poorly." It was something she had said once, as a child, that amused him.

It seemed to amuse him still. He chuckled. "What! You, Mollie? What have you been up to this time, dear? It wasn't the paper?"

"No, no. It wasn't the paper."

"I've been reading your pieces, and they're fine. You must see some choice places at those galas."

"Mother wouldn't have approved."

"Your mother would have been proud, though she might not have said so."

Mollie didn't pursue this. He was damping down the furnace now, closing the forge doors and shutting the vents after using a long-handled scuttle to bank the coals. She wandered into the smithy, absently helping him pick up, hanging things on their proper pegs. She touched the inside of one of the wide doors, annealed to a smooth, hard finish by the constant exposure to the forge.

"What was it this time, Mollie, my dear?" he asked again. She shrugged and pulled a face; he chuckled again—the not unkind humor of experience, the parent's almost sad laugh. His hair, which wanted cutting, was wild in the breeze. He never wore a hat, maintaining that he needed to let off steam whenever he was away from the forge. It was near dark, almost night, but clouds above them shone dimly with reflected light from around the curve of the earth. "A storm is coming," he said. "I think it may be worse than the last one. Got time for a cup of something hot?"

"No, thank you, Dad. I should be getting back. Mrs. Makepeace will be looking for me."

"And well she should." He had been kicked by a horse years ago (an injury that nearly crippled him), and he still had a pronounced limp. "You can't walk back," he said as he came out. "I'll drive you down." Mollie protested, but her father would hear none of it. He went to the stable and harnessed up his horse to the wagon that carried his movable forge.

Mollie stood in the space between buildings and looked at her father's house, where he had lived with his wife for nineteen years and raised his six children, four of whom still lived. The wind rattled the first fallen leaves among the dying vines of the small garden. A storm was coming, and she was glad, if the truth be known, to have her father drive her back to the boardinghouse. A small anxiety caught at her heart whenever she remembered how mad and how dangerous Eustace Pembleton had seemed, with his huge companion.

What if the big Irishman had caught the little boy? What if someone had seen her speaking with the ballplayer? What if Pembleton connected her to it all? Certainly Horace McQuinn had no reason to keep what he knew a secret. She had walked up to her father's just to prove to herself that she *wasn't* afraid, but she had been nervous the entire way, which made her angry.

It had been a silly scheme, of course, sending the redheaded man after the little boy, and no doubt nothing had come of it. No one would be the worse or the wiser. *It'll blow over*, her father would say if she had told him—as might the storm.

She could hear the horse whinny as it was led out of the stable in harness, pulling the cart behind it.

16. At the Sign of the Crooked Cat

"BIG DOINGS OVER THE WHARVES TODAY, HOD," said Percy Beal, the proprietor of the waterfront's dimmest tavern. He peered after Horace, who had situated himself in one of the darker corners of the room.

"Is there?" said Horace, as if surprised.

"Well, there was," said Percy, disappointed that Horace could not, or would not, elucidate.

"Wouldn't know a thing about it," said Horace.

Percy seemed to think this was far-fetched. "Adam was looking for you."

"He will find me, I guess."

"I guess he will. Turkey pie?"

"And a nurse."

The *nurse* Percy brought back to Horace sloshed in the confines of a pewter tankard. Horace nodded his thanks for a prompt delivery, then watched with amusement as Percy lumbered off to another customer.

Percy had never been to sea, but his gait was not unlike that of a mariner who is unused to the immutability of firm ground. He was a medium-sized man from the floor to the top of his head, but his stomach was large, and he navigated the tables with the careful maneuvering of an overladen ship.

Anyone searching for atmosphere would certainly have found plenty of it at the sign of *the Crooked Cat*. Tucked between a net-mending yard and a small warehouse, the business had been known for half a century as *the Governor Danforth*, and an imaginative portrait of that worthy had hung above the door, surviving both British entanglements and the great fire of 1866.

But close proximity to the wharfs, along with the smell and gurry associated with fishing nets and the ample hiding places offered by the warehouse, drew rats. Percy's solution was to acquire a cat—a monstrous gray cat, in fact—to which, in the spirit of his enterprise, he gave the name Governor Danforth.

Governor Danforth (the cat) was a fierce and tireless hunter and quite single-handedly improved the living conditions of the tavern and thus improved business. He further ingratiated himself by keeping Percy's feet warm on winter nights. When Governor Danforth (the cat again) came to an untimely end chasing the grandfather of all rodents across the nearby railroad tracks, Percy honored his companion and displayed his own grief by replacing the portrait of the first Governor Danforth with that of his feline namesake.

The artist of this new work was an itinerant sign painter whose ability to render living creatures left something to be desired. The picture resembled several creatures, none of them remotely catlike, but there was something admirable about the painting—it was so honest in its awfulness—and patrons took to calling it, affectionately, *the Crooked Cat*. The popular name for the tavern itself followed suit.

Raising his tankard, Horace saluted the Governor Danforth that currently presided over the establishment and drank with a smack of his lips. The tavern door opened, and Maven Flyce straddled the threshold, cowlick waving in the air, mouth hanging open as if he hadn't trod these floorboards a hundred times. Maven gaped about several times before seeing Horace; then he let out a whistle of amazement and joined his grizzled friend.

"Goodness sakes, Horace! I have never!" exclaimed Maven.

"I don't suppose you have, Maven," replied Horace, who hadn't the slightest notion of what the man was referring to.

"You mean, you know already?"

"Word does get around."

"It's hard to believe!"

"I bet it came as a shock."

"Nothing gets by you, Hod!"

"I keep my ears open."

"I thought I was a goner!"

"It was a close call. Have one on me."

Something had startled Maven considerably, and Horace might have garnered the entire story from the astonished fellow, without once admitting to his complete ignorance of it, if Maven hadn't suddenly remembered the affair on the wharf. "What do you suppose Wyckford did with the little fellow, Horace?"

Horace put a finger to his lip.

"I've never seen the like of it, the way he carried that boy off!"

"Keep it down, Maven," said Horace.

"Keep what down, Hod?" Maven's cowlick, for a moment, was all Horace could see; Maven was looking under the table. "What is it, Horace?"

Percy might have caught some of what Maven had said, and he sailed near them, but Horace waved two fingers in the air, and the tavern keeper veered off for the back room.

"Hot work, McQuinn?" came a voice from the other side of the room. A stout man, impeccably dressed, with silver hair to his shoulders, leaned back on a bench, his feet stretched before him, his hand on the brace of a tankard.

"Not if I can help it, McAngus," returned Horace.

"You are a wise man," said Angus McAngus. He straightened his posture, stood, and clapped a coin upon his table.

Horace extemporized:

> "Work, they say, is fearsome hard,
> And labor can produce a frown;
> But merely watching others toil
> Is quite enough to wear me down."

Maven clucked his tongue in wonder.

"May I quote you?" asked Angus. He settled his customary bowler on his head and made for the door, which opened before he could reach it. Adam Tweed, who had been looking for Horace earlier, slouched for a moment in Angus's path. Dirty and desultory in appearance, Adam gave the writer an expression that, on the surface, appeared bland and impassive. Beneath the dull eyes, though, lay banked fires of potential hazard, the glow of which barely touched Angus, whose own expression was undaunted, even patient.

After a moment, Tweed stepped aside, flashing an unhealthy smile. Once Angus was past, the unkempt man walked over to Horace's table. *There's a gun beneath his coat*, thought Angus, briefly catching Horace's eye, before leaving the tavern.

"I've been looking for you," said Adam Tweed to Horace, and there was a vague sense of menace in his voice. He was a man of only medium size, somewhere below middle age, and less than prepossessing in his habits; he was unshaven (which is not to say that he wore a beard), his clothes were shiny with dirt, and his teeth were stained with tobacco.

Horace was not overwhelmed. "Percy said."

"You're usually easier to find," said Tweed.

"I wasn't lost, if that was worrying you," answered Horace.

Tweed glanced at Maven, who stared back openmouthed. He had seen Maven with Horace a hundred times but had never spoken a word to the fellow. "Do I know you?" asked Tweed.

"I don't think so," said Maven quietly.

"Then what are you looking at me for?"

"You're looking at him, and he doesn't know you," said Horace, which was as much as to say: *Leave the fellow alone.* The truth was that there was nothing very intimidating about Horace McQuinn except for his steel-gray eyes when the humor left his face. He was old—in fact, old beyond his years—and somewhat used up; and though he had been hard and wiry in his youth, he looked—in his *age*—narrow and brittle. But there was something odd and unsettling in Horace's steel-gray eyes when the humor left his face.

Tweed's gaze lingered on Maven for an uncomfortable moment, but he was aware of Horace's scrutiny. "Your friend O'Hearn is pretty bold."

"Oh, Wyckford can take care of himself," Horace drawled.

Tweed grunted. "Well, he might want to *think* about taking care of himself."

"I'll pass along your concern."

There were questions that Tweed wanted to ask—that was obvious— but he knew Horace well enough not to bother. Horace worked for Adam

Tweed on occasion, running questionable goods (most of which were conveyed in a barrel) through the city; but it was "a job done and money paid" and nothing more. Horace was nobody's minion.

Tweed had several others in his employ, all of whom made Horace appear genteel in comparison, and one of them stepped into the tavern. Tweed made a signal, and the man went back out. Tweed turned back to Horace and asked, "What is it about this kid, McQuinn?"

Percy came up with Horace's turkey pie, glancing from Horace to Tweed for permission to step in and serve it. Steam rose from the plate. Neither Horace nor Tweed acknowledged his presence. Maven eyed the pie hungrily.

"I wouldn't have the slightest," said Horace. Without glancing at Percy, he reached up for the plate.

"O'Hearn had better be careful," said Tweed. "There are some who do."

Tweed only graced Percy with a quick glance before walking to the back of the tavern and through a door to a back room.

"I said there were big doings," said Percy.

"Wouldn't know it by me," insisted Horace.

"My word, Hod!" said Maven. "What was that all about?"

"Tweed just has an odd way of seeing things," said Horace after a good gulp of ale to start his meal. It wasn't surprising that Adam Tweed knew about Wyckford O'Hearn's taking the boy; he knew everything that happened along the waterfront, especially everything that wasn't supposed to happen. "He just doesn't understand people, is all."

"You don't say!"

A moment later, the door to the tavern opened again, and Amos Guernsey stepped inside, followed by Tweed's henchman. The two of them walked straight for the back of the room, but Amos stopped when he caught sight of Horace. He was missing his mustache but had regained his hat, which he lifted from his head with a bow. "Mr. McQuinn," he said grandly.

"Amos," said Horace. "What are you about?"

"It has been a day of high adventure and quiet intrigue," stated the man bluntly. He seemed very cheerful.

"I'm not sure your mother would approve of the company you're keeping," said Horace. He took Tweed's henchman in with a glance.

"Alas," said Amos, "that dear lady has passed from this tearful vale, lo these many years ago, and I am clean broke."

"Guernsey," came a voice from the back of the room. Tweed stood in the doorway and said nothing else, but with the urging of Tweed's henchman, Amos strode to the back room. As the door was shut behind them, Horace caught a glimpse of Eustace Pembleton.

"Goodness sakes, Horace!" said Maven. "I've never been so amazed! What does it all mean?"

"I couldn't say," replied Horace, but the gears were turning behind those gray orbs.

"Gosh, Hod!" said Maven. "You sure do know some people!"

"That's about all I do know, Maven," replied Horace.

Outside, Angus McAngus, who had been watching from the shadows through the tavern window, turned away and disappeared up the street.

17. Echo Till Midnight

"WHAT DO YOU EXPECT OF ME, GENTLEMEN?" asked Henry Echo when his guests had navigated the stacks of volumes and seated themselves. He sat in a tall wing-backed chair. "I suppose you think that I am mad!" he said.

"What would lead us to such a conclusion?" said Mister Walton.

"What indeed, for it may be that I am, sir."

"A man seldom knows himself so well," said John Neptune, not without humor.

"You, perhaps, recommend your sanity by questioning it," agreed Mister Walton affably.

The short man spoke heatedly. "I can tell, however, by your manner, sir, that you are put upon your guard."

Mister Walton took a moment to reply, and though he might not be on his guard, Sundry Moss, who moved a mound of *Blackwood* magazines to accommodate his long legs, most assuredly was. "I would take pains, Mr. Echo," said Mister Walton, "not to say or do anything that would cause you greater distress than that which you are already obviously suffering."

Henry's upper lip twitched, and the life this lent to his mustache gave him the appearance of an anxious mouse. There was a book on the table beside his chair, face down and open, and his hand rested upon it the way someone might touch the head of a favorite dog. "John has told you of my situation, then," he said.

"He has only said that you have a *strange* difficulty."

"That sounds like John. You know him well?"

"Save for a brief meeting thirty-one years ago, hardly at all. We met today on the train at Portland."

"Do you live there?" asked Henry, and upon Mister Walton's nod, he said, "You *should* know of him. Your city would not be the place that it is if not for John Neptune and Isherwood Tolly. Theirs was a piece of work to merit a statue in their honor, I assure you."

"I would love to hear of it!" declared Mister Walton.

"There is a history of Portland on the shelf behind your head, Mister Walton, but sadly our friend is not mentioned there. You must have *him* tell you once this night is done."

"You should tell Mister Walton *your* story, Henry," said John Neptune, looking patient, with Eugene, on the back of the sofa, half-sitting on his head.

"There's not much to tell," said Echo. "But I very much fear that I will die at midnight."

"Good heavens!" said Mister Walton again.

"Would *you* believe in a curse, Mister Walton, if it had already struck with frightening accuracy on two occasions?"

"Without further details, sir, I would reserve opinion, but two events, however similar they appear, might easily fall under the name of coincidence."

"And if those two events *coincided* with prophecy?"

Mister Walton raised his eyebrows and gave the man every assurance of his attention. There was a span of silence during which it was obvious that Echo was debating whether to tell the story at all; then, without any indication that he had reached a decision, he spoke.

"There are few, here in Bath, Mister Walton, who remember the name of Zebulon Echo, and yet there were many, more than half a century ago, who had reason to hate it. He was my grandfather, though I never knew him. If you go to the cemetery at Maple Grove, you will find a poorly tended plot and a stone with his name upon it bearing the birth date of 1798 and a day of reckoning in the year of 1840." Henry sat once more and seemed for the moment to have some control of himself. "My grandfather," he continued, "was ambitious; by the time he was nineteen, he had secured himself a position in a prosperous mercantile firm, ingratiating himself with the owner, who was childless, by his hard work and seeming loyalty.

"The owner of the firm, Henry Stableford, for whom I was named, is buried not far from my grandfather; and though he was without direct heirs, *his* place is well kept. There are no weeds upon his grave or mosses upon his stone, and it is my family that has tended it for nearly eight decades. So you see, Mister Walton, where my story might be going."

"I sense a *sad* story, Mr. Echo." Mister Walton glanced in the direction of Sundry Moss, who appeared tense himself and perhaps a little sorry that they had come.

"It is a story that may end tonight," replied Henry. "My grandfather was nineteen when Henry Stableford fell ill. Henry was not old by any means, as you will see, and had been the definition of health; but he contracted the consumption, according to the doctors. His condition deteriorated with extraordinary speed, and while he still could wield a pen, he had a will drafted up in the interest of my grandfather, who was ever at his side and who managed the business during these dark days.

"But weeks later, when his death was imminent, Henry Stableford called the doctor to his side and pronounced his belief that he was being poisoned."

The speaker left off his story for a moment while this communication was given time to make its mark. "And was he?" asked Sundry, his voice sounding strange and inappropriate in that suddenly quiet space.

"To the very instant of his death, he believed it. The doctor feared the man was tormented by delusions, but he stayed by his side for three days, till the end came. My grandfather was there, and Henry said to him, 'I have had a lucid moment when I saw you for what you are, and I can only wonder if God will allow you or your sons more days than you have allowed me.'

"And he died. And though the doctor could detect no foul deed on the part of my grandfather, he went away a troubled man.

"For his part, Zebulon was thought to have proved his accuser out by an avaricious nature and by the meanness with which he treated his debtors. Henry Stableford was perhaps not the last to die, however indirectly, for want of some spark of human kindness from my grandfather, my grandmother included."

"And how old was Henry Stableford when he died?" asked Mister Walton.

"He was forty-two, sir."

"The very age, according to the dates upon your grandfather's stone, that *he* died as well."

"Alone, and under the greatest weight of fear, it appeared, by the condition of his remains. His face was twisted into a mask of complete terror. And though my father sold the business that he inherited and gave all he acquired from it to charity, though he proved as good a man as *his* father was mean, he succumbed to a similar fate twenty-three years later."

"At the age of forty-two," conjectured Mister Walton.

"At the very age I gained this morning," said Henry Echo. His hand shook as he reached into a jacket pocket. He did not find what he was searching for, and as he grew more jittery still, he tried another.

"It's on the table, I think," said John Neptune, who had not opened his eyes. Henry turned to the table beside his chair and shuffled through the several books till he found a piece of paper, which he passed to Mister Walton. It was a clipping from a newspaper:

Local Shipping Partner
Dead at Forty-Two

The friends and associates of Henry Ward Echo regret to announce his untimely demise. Mr. Echo had been a partner in the Butterworth-Echo shipping firm for twelve years. The firm, located on Front Street, currently handles some dozen ships, including the *Irma V.*, which sailed for Glasgow last Saturday.

News of Mr. Echo's death was a great shock to those who knew him. He had appeared in fine health when he was last seen by his associates at the firm.

Mr. Echo died exactly on the stroke of midnight, as Friday the ninth of October was giving over to Saturday the tenth. The cause of his death remains unknown.

Mr. Echo is survived by a sister, who lives in Kingston, N.H. His grandfather came to Bath in the last century, and his father was once celebrated for an immense act of charity. . . .

The remainder of the death notice listed the man's accomplishments, as well as those of his family, and indicated the plans for his funeral.

"Good heavens!" said Mister Walton for a third, then a fourth and a fifth time. Sundry sat close enough to lean over and take in the gist of the clipping. "Friday the ninth," said Mister Walton. "That is today!"

"It is."

"And this . . ." Mister Walton held out the item. "This was published when?"

"Three weeks ago."

"But surely," said Mister Walton, "you must look to some mortal agent for such a threat; someone known to possess a very poor sense of humor or who has purposes similar even to your grandfather's!"

"Who would know of this curse?" Sundry asked, more interested than fearful now.

"What is whispered in my family, I believe, is at least rumored elsewhere," said Henry.

"It is disconcerting," said Mister Walton, "but I doubt that it should cause you any fear for your life. It is too . . . obvious somehow. What did the newspaper say when you showed them their error?"

"They apologized, of course," said Henry, growing more agitated. "But there was no record of the obituary having been tendered to them. No one remembered seeing it come in. No one remembered setting the type. No one seems to have been aware of it till my partner, Hugo Butter-worth, came out of his office that day, looking shocked and amazed, and showed it to me."

"It is a mystery," said Mister Walton. "But perhaps no one wanted to take the responsibility."

"It was a prophecy, Mister Walton! A dire warning!"

"Not at all, Mr. Echo!" insisted the bespectacled fellow. "This is a poor joke, I fear, but nothing more."

"There are things in there that not everybody knows about me," said the man, pointing at the clipping as at a false accusation.

"But certainly nothing that a person couldn't find out."

"I thought the same, sir, when I first read it. My heart *did* falter a bit, I admit. Anyone would be offended to find such an item before him; offended and a little horrified. But I asked myself, Who could have perpetrated this hoax, and why? I am not a man of many friends, Mister Walton, besides this company in print you see about us, but enemies I have none; certainly not the spiteful sort it would take to do such a thing."

Henry wrung his hands and breathed as if a weight were pressing upon his chest. "The very strange thing was that the item was predated. If a simple joke, one would have expected my death to have been described as already having occurred. This spoke of my demise in the past tense but having happened on a day, in an hour, yet to come. And it is in there that the peculiar seed of inevitability was planted.

"My colleagues were appalled. My partner was enraged and demanded satisfaction from the newspaper. He threatened to bring suit against them. I calmed him down. *I* calmed *him* down. There was no real damage done; a retraction could be easily printed.

"But if the offense I took dissipated, the small thrill of horror grew. Without realizing it, I began to count the days; I took notice of every calendar, heard every clock, was troubled by the advancing date upon the newspaper's masthead. A week went by, during which the retraction was printed, and yet there was something in the retraction, some indefinable sense of hesitancy, that troubled me more. It was as if, having printed a notice of death so bluntly and with such surety, the paper itself—not the people but the organism that is made up of people and machinery and print and ink—could not be so sure that I was indeed, would indeed be, alive after Friday midnight.

"Another week passed, and I became aware of my own distraction. Even among my books, my mind would wander: I would ask myself, *Who could have done such a thing?* and *How many ways could a man die unexpectedly?* By night I had vague dreams of missed appointments, barely remembered when I woke. Then there were *vivid* dreams of an unseen horror hunting for me in a maze of rooms or the thick of a forest. And finally, any dream at all seemed a luxury as I lay awake at night, my forehead damp, my breath shallow and panicked.

"I was embarrassed by my growing fears, ashamed of them. I hid them from my associates for those first two weeks, but then the tension in my face, the nervousness of my posture, and the shaking of my hands—" Henry held these up before him, and they were indeed trembling. "I was obsessed with the notion that I would die . . . tonight . . . at midnight. I could think of—can think of—nothing else. Last week, I took a leave of absence from the firm.

"I have not slept for three days," he said, looking every bit of it. Indeed, the others wondered how he managed to speak or do anything after such a siege. "Well," he said with a sort of forced calm, "in a little more than seven and a half hours, we will know. Or *you* will know." He shivered to hear himself. The clock on the shelf called out the half hour. "Seven and a half hours," he said, and excusing himself, he nervously went into another room. The tick of the clock seemed loud.

"I had an uncle who thought he was going to die," said Sundry, whose voice was a welcome interruption from listening to the clock. He picked a book from the floor beside him and perused its spine.

"Yes?" said John Neptune. "And did he?"

"No, he got married instead."

"Ahem," said Mister Walton.

"She was a nurse," explained Sundry.

When Henry Echo returned, he did not sit, but proceeded to pace the floor. "You seem a man of reasonable health," said Mister Walton, "*and* even from your own words a man of healthy reason. We are here, and will remain with you, but you must calm yourself somehow or the prophecy will become self-fulfilling!"

"You are right, of course. And you, Mister Walton, seem a fortunate man. I am glad you came. Thank you."

"We must carry on as if it were any other night," said the bespectacled man. He looked to John Neptune, who nodded. The Indian scratched Eugene behind the ear, and the raccoon responded like a cat, though he let out a low growl rather than a purr. "Do you play cards, sir?" asked Mister Walton.

There was little food in Henry's larder (although there was a set of encyclopedias in the pantry cupboards), and no one was courageous enough to ask the landlady for a meal, so Sundry was sent into town. With directions from their host, he found a tavern, where he was able to procure a hamper of cider and sandwiches. It was dark when he returned. John Neptune made coffee in the kitchen. Piles of books and *Strand* magazines were shifted so that a card table could be erected, and among the cups and plates and silverware a game of cribbage was embarked upon.

Sundry was the life of the evening, once he was fed, and there were times when Henry was almost distracted by the young man's litany of eccentric relatives. Mister Walton was glad for Sundry's company, the more so since his own reserves of humor and energy seemed drained.

John Neptune, with a raccoon on his shoulder instead of a parrot, looked like some strange form of pirate. Eugene watched the old Indian's cards intently.

Henry Echo played like a man awaiting execution who cannot help wondering if he is wasting his last hours on earth. But he played, hesitating only when the clock struck and reminded him of the passing hours. When seven strokes rang out, he took a deep breath and closed his eyes. They could not interest him in any food or drink, which led Sundry to wonder, silently, if he might die of starvation before the night was out.

Eight o'clock came, and the plates and cups were cleared from the table. Outside, the wind had increased; they could hear it reeding against some corner of the house. The lights seemed to dim of their own volition, and Sundry got up to adjust them twice.

At nine o'clock, Mister Walton asked to be excused; a call to nature and a stretch was in order. Henry considered the raccoon and thought aloud that it was a strange thing for his friend to bring on such a night.

"The raccoon is my family totem," the old man said. "I thought it bode good fortune when Isherwood gave it to me."

By ten o'clock, Mister Walton had begun to sincerely suffer for the man. "I fear I have wasted my life," said Echo, as if answering a question heard by no one else.

"Surely not," said Mister Walton.

"I have always prided myself," said the man, "that I have avoided the family fear of my grandfather's curse, but perhaps I have hidden myself away, with my books and my papers, without understanding the real reason why." He looked so fatigued that they wondered he didn't collapse in front of them. "I have never felt so sad," he said aloud.

"Mr. Echo," said Mister Walton. "A single kindness might justify an entire life."

"You are kind to say so, but . . ." He shook his head.

"Certainly a friend such as John Neptune, here, signals merit in your soul." The old Indian, faithfully seated with them, was sound asleep. Eugene was standing in his guardian's lap and helping himself to the remains of a sandwich on his plate. Mister Walton smiled and put a hand on Sundry's shoulder. "I would be pleased to think that a man's friends might be read like tea leaves to describe his heart."

"If that is true, Mister Walton," said Henry Echo, "then I would hope to count you among my own." And then, exhausted beyond further endurance, the little man laid his head upon the table and fell into a death-like slumber.

Mister Walton stood up, startled by the man's sudden collapse. He glanced at the clock behind Echo's chair. It was only just past ten. "Sundry," he said, almost afraid to ask. "Is he—?"

"He's only dead tired," said Sundry, who lifted the man from the table and laid him back into his chair. Echo's chest barely rose and fell; his feet splayed out and kicked over a set of Dumas. "But if he *does* get through tonight," added Sundry, "he still has the rest of the year to dread."

"If he gets through tonight, Sundry, I believe he will dread no more." Mister Walton lifted the spectacles from his nose and rubbed his eyes.

"You need some rest yourself," said Sundry. "Why don't you take the sofa and close your eyes for a bit."

"Oh, I couldn't. I would feel as if I had abandoned him."

"Of course not," said Sundry. "I'll stay up. If he stirs, I'll speak to you."

Mister Walton felt so weary that he could not resist Sundry's logic, so with a last glance in the direction of the clock on the wall, he turned to the sofa, moved a volume of Scott, and lay down. *It is a tale for October*, he thought as he closed his eyes and fell asleep. The last thing of which he was conscious was Sundry lowering the lights and the wind sounding like something trying to get in.

Book Three

OCTOBER 10, 1896

18. Right Chapter, Wrong Book

"Mister Walton."

"Yes?"

"Mister Walton!"

"Yes!" He almost leaped from the sofa. "My gracious! I didn't think I would sleep so soundly!" He blinked his eyes. "Mr. Echo?"

"He is still asleep," said Sundry. "But look at the clock."

The clock on the shelf said half past twelve. "And he is—?"

"He was muttering to himself a moment ago."

"Sundry!" said Mister Walton, a hand to his heart. "I couldn't help but worry!"

"Of course you couldn't. *I've* been watching him like a hawk. And I was particularly tense when the clock struck twelve!"

"It's amazing that we all didn't wake up."

"Well, you *were* snoring, if I may say so."

"Did I drown the hour?" asked Mister Walton.

Sundry smiled. "If there was a chance of his dying of fright simply from hearing the clock strike midnight, then you may have saved his life. Perhaps we should wake him, though, and let him know he survived the hour of his death."

"You stood the watch, Sundry," said Mister Walton. "You should give the call that all is well."

Stepping past several stacks, Sundry went to the wing-backed chair and shook Mr. Echo gently by the shoulder. "Sir," he said. "Mr. Echo." Those haunted eyes flickered open, and they were filled, respectively, with confusion, fear, and sadness. "Look at the clock, Mr. Echo," said Sundry.

There was astonishment on the man's face before he ever stood from his chair and turned around—Sundry's meaning was that clear to him.

"Thank God and all the angels!" he said in a hoarse voice. His knees buckled, and Sundry caught him beneath the arms.

"Easy now!" said Sundry. "Let's prove the paper wrong by more than half an hour."

"But it *was* wrong, Mr. Moss! It *was* wrong!"

John Neptune roused himself, took in the turn of events, and was ready to fall back to sleep. Then the old man realized that Eugene was missing, and he sat up and looked around.

"Gentlemen!" Henry was shouting. "How can I ever repay you?"

"Repay us?" said Mister Walton. He chuckled happily.

"I know it seemed absurd! I know my fears sounded wild and unimaginable! But I promise you, my friends, they felt real as rock. Every hour was a lonely two in the morning. I was chilled to my soul, grieving for a squandered existence. Alone, I might have killed myself with fear. But you three have seen me through the darkest hours of my life."

"I think we should celebrate," said Sundry.

"You?" said Mister Walton. "You are the one who hasn't slept."

"I feel invigorated!"

"Well, *I'm* awake and ready," said the bespectacled fellow. "How about you, Mr. Echo?"

"I feel as if I could outrun a train!"

"I think you've been cooped in here long enough," said Sundry. "Let's get out and take some air. Will you come with us?" he asked John Neptune.

"No, thank you," said the old man. "I will sleep some more, and perhaps that scoundrel will come out of hiding." He leaned from his chair and cast about for the raccoon.

Henry returned to the parlor, ready to leave. "I certainly can benefit from a dose of new air, though I hope we don't wake Mrs. Thorpe. Her bedroom is just below the stairs."

"There's not another way down, is there?" Sundry asked.

"Actually, yes, though it isn't used very often. There is a small door in my kitchen that opens into a chamber above the ell and from there a door that leads to the upper story of the barn."

"Then by all means," said Sundry, "let us avoid disturbing the woman."

Mr. Echo took a lantern and led them to the kitchen, where he pulled a curtain aside to reveal a short door, the room beyond which was low enough to necessitate Sundry's ducking his head. A second door gave onto the barn, where the smells of hay and dust yet prevailed. This ancient home had once been a working farm when it was alone in the midst of several tens of acres.

It seemed strange to Mister Walton that Mr. Echo's landlady would hold any real terror for Sundry, but the young man was adamant that they take every precaution to keep from waking her. He *put a strain* upon the door of the barn as he pushed it aside so that it didn't creak or groan. "Leave it open," he proposed, "and we'll come back this way."

It was a cool night, and they were glad for their coats and hats. A wind rattled in the old trees of the neighborhood, and somewhere a shutter or a sign or an outhouse door was squeaking. The moon had not risen, and there were few streetlights about, so the stars appeared bright from behind a progression of unhurried clouds.

"Let's shut down the lantern so we can see the stars better," suggested Sundry, and when Mr. Echo had done so, they stood in the barnyard while their eyesight adjusted to the near blackness. The buildings about them were only shapes where the Milky Way was not visible; the smells of wood and coal smoke carried on the wind.

"It's beautiful," said Mr. Echo, his eyes reflecting the light of the stars as he looked up at them with renewed wonder.

Mister Walton could just see Sundry ahead of him as the young man led the way toward the front of the house, almost tiptoeing on the lawn. They paused beneath a maple tree and considered the night from this new situation.

Mr. Echo was surprised when Sundry whispered into his ear; the young man spoke twice before he was heard. "Don't be startled," he was saying, "but what is that up on your roof?" He tapped Mister Walton's shoulder and made a large, silent gesture to indicate that they should be looking up at the house.

The human eye can demonstrate an imagination of its own when there is little for it to focus upon. Waking in a pitch-black room or gazing into a night-bound forest, the mind lends movement to a chair beneath the window or a face against the shadow of the wood.

There was the sound of something scraping above them. From beneath the dark end of Henry Echo's rooms, the slates and gables were barely defined in the starlight; but upon them there was formed the impression of shadow upon shadow, a silhouette shifting like a spider.

Henry experienced a sense of the shadow upon the roof that transcended simple vision; almost *feeling* the shape, as if he had his arms around it, as if he gripped it close enough to hear breath and comprehend a heart beating. He started at the *shush* of a window sash rising in its casement. Mister Walton stepped forward, ready to speak out or run back into the house, but Sundry stopped him with a hand upon his shoulder.

A low glow touched the windowpanes, and Henry let out a groan. "It's the light from the parlor," whispered Sundry. "The door to the parlor has been opened."

"Sundry!" said Mister Walton, his own voice hushed, if not the emotion contained in it.

"Don't be alarmed," said Sundry. "I think you're going to hear—"

A series of low thuds seemed to indicate that someone had come into unexpected contact with the clutter in Henry Echo's apartment. Sundry seemed to expect this, but even he jumped when a terrific shout came from the house. He gripped Henry by one shoulder, and Echo grimaced with fright, his face partly turned away, as if shying from a blow. For a moment he looked as he had when Mister Walton and Sundry first saw him; then a second cry rang out, this one a shriek of horror.

"Good heavens!" declared Mister Walton. "Mr. Neptune is up there!"

"I had forgotten that," said Sundry, a little shocked.

Another terrified cry shot into the night, much louder than the first, and the glow from Henry's parlor was fleetingly obscured by the shadow of a man climbing from the window. There was a clatter upon the slates and the sound of sliding; then the figure regained control of its descent and launched itself into the maple. There was the sound of ragged breathing, a moan of fright, and the shadowy form—plainer now that their eyes were adjusted to the night—clambered down the tree.

Mister Walton and Henry were rooted where they stood, but Sundry stepped up to the trunk of the maple, and when the figure was within six or seven feet of the ground, Sundry reached up and said very cheerfully, "Can I lend you a hand there?"

The figure in the tree let out another cry and fell, landing on one foot a yard or so away. Sundry caught hold of the figure, only to be stunned by the sight of a death's-head with a small raccoon gripping its bald pate with all four taloned paws. Sundry let the man go before he saw the mask start to come away. Then Eugene fell from the man's head, and the man got to his feet and ran away with a pronounced limp.

Henry Echo let out an angry cry and charged after the figure, but Sundry stopped him. "No, no!" Sundry was saying.

"I have to catch him!" shouted Echo. "I have to find out who he is!"

"All you have to do is wait, Mr. Echo. Find out who is limping around town or who leaves it."

"Should we get the police?" asked Mister Walton.

"We had better go inside and see what happened," Sundry reminded them.

"Oh, my goodness, John Neptune!" said Echo, and he charged up the lawn to the front door. A light had come on in the lower part of the house, and they could see the glow of a lantern at one of the windows.

"Is Eugene down there?" came the Indian's voice from above.

"I'll look for him, sir," called Sundry. He found the lantern where Echo had dropped it and with a little searching caught sight of two red eyes glowing from the lower branches.

"Could you hold this light for me, Mister Walton?" asked Sundry.

The portly fellow came over and took the lantern while Sundry pulled himself up into the limbs of the tree and retrieved the raccoon.

"My word, Sundry!" Mister Walton was saying. "How did you know?"

"I didn't, really. But I thought it was possible." Sundry eased himself back to the ground, with Eugene gripping him a little painfully by his upper arm. "It's not to wonder that the fellow gave out a holler or two with this hanging on to his head."

A church clock tolled the hour, and Mister Walton was confused when the bell did not stop at one or two or three. He counted the strokes till he reached twelve and the great clock, somewhere in the October night, fell silent once more.

"That said twelve o'clock," said the bespectacled fellow.

"I know," said Sundry. "While everyone was asleep, I set Mr. Echo's clock ahead an hour."

19. Panic and Pancakes

Wyckford O'Hearn gazed at a crack in the ceiling that he was not accustomed to seeing from his bed, then remembered that he was not *in* his bed but in a cot that had been fetched from the attic. When Bird had fallen asleep at the kitchen table, Mrs. Barter had insisted he be put to bed immediately. Wyck had carried the boy, who hardly stirred, to his room, and they tucked the little fellow into the four-poster bed that stood against the eave.

They stood for several minutes watching Bird sleep. "What are you going to do with him?" asked Mrs. Barter, her arms crossed before her.

"Do with him?" said Wyck. "I'll bring him to his sister, first of all—if she *is* his sister. Horace seemed to think he could find her."

"Horace *McQuinn*?" asked Mrs. Barter with an expression of distaste. "I wouldn't want that old scoundrel finding *me*!"

"Horace is all right. He's the one who told me to bring him here."

"I doubt your mother would approve of his company."

Wyck did not undertake a reply. Bird turned in his sleep, his mouth open, his hair disarrayed.

"He ought to have a haircut," said Mrs. Barter.

"Where do you suppose I should sleep?" asked Wyck.

"Sleep? What's wrong with your bed? He doesn't take up much of it. And he's just had a bath."

"The size of him," said Wyck. "I'm sort of afraid I'll turn over in my sleep and smother him."

After looking first at the man and then the tiny boy, Mrs. Barter concluded that Wyck's fears were not wholly unfounded. "I have a cot in the attic," she said, and led the way out of the room.

Wyck closed his eyes and shifted in the cot, which was too short for him. Mrs. Barter had demanded to hear the entire story again over dinner. Wyck thought it embarrassing, somehow, and looked it. Mrs. Barter couldn't get over that he had knocked down a wall, or even (as Wyck continued to insist) part of one. Rescuing waifs was all very well, but dismantling pieces of standing architecture without proper warrant seemed hasty.

Looking up from the cot, Wyck knew he must get up and find Horace, which should be easy enough, though thinking about it made him feel worn out. It occurred to Wyck to ask Mrs. Barter to help, but she certainly wouldn't enter into any endeavor that included Horace McQuinn; and besides, he knew without asking that she would adhere to a *"you start it, you finish it"* philosophy.

Details had always been Wyckford's downfall, and he knew it. He could work day in and day out at hard labor (and had, at his family's farm, on the railroad), but situations demanding an attention to detail plain wore him down. There was only one element in his life under the *details* of which he flourished, and that was baseball.

But, unlike so much of life, baseball made perfect sense—redolent with familiarity every time a batter stood at the plate, and fraught with random possibility every time the ball left the pitcher's hand. There were rules and statistics and expectations sometimes fulfilled; and on certain afternoons, when the gears of the world momentarily turned in unison, your glove found a deep fly ball, your arm found home plate an instant before the tying run, or your bat met with the perfect pitch and barked with joy.

Wyck wondered what time it was; early, he supposed. He could hear movement in the kitchen below, so Mrs. Barter must be fixing breakfast.

He stretched, swung his legs out from under the covers, and sat up on the cot. "Ready to get up?" he asked, then realized that the bed beside him was empty.

The bedcovers were tossed aside, and Bird was gone. A stray thought—that he wouldn't have to *do something* with the little fellow after all—flitted past Wyck like the shadow of a gull, then was gone. Distress followed in its wake, and a cold fingertip touched him in the chest. A moment later, he charged from his room with his shirt untucked and his shoes in his hand and plummeted with such speed down the stairs that he had to carom from the front door with one hand in order to make the turn down the hall.

"Mrs. Barter!" he shouted. "Mrs. Barter! He's gone!"

She appeared at the kitchen door with a large wooden spoon in her hand, and Wyck barely brought himself to a halt before colliding with her. "What in heaven's name is the matter, Wyckford?" she demanded.

"He's gone," he said.

"*Who* is gone?" she asked, which, in retrospect, must be considered a disingenuous question.

"The kid! Bird! He's not in his bed!"

"Well, of course not. He's having breakfast, and quite sensible, too, not sleeping the day away." She turned back into the kitchen, and when Wyck looked after her, he could see Bird at the table, peering over a tall, though half-demolished, stack of pancakes. Wyck blew a sigh of relief but wondered at the feeling he had experienced when he thought the boy gone. "I thought you'd up and left us," he said.

Bird shook his head, his eyes wide. Absently, he took a forkful of pancake and chewed it. Mrs. Barter had been busy this morning; Bird was wearing presentable clothes—hand-me-downs, as it turned out, from the children next door.

"Of course, he wouldn't go when I was cooking breakfast," said the landlady. "I was ready to send him up to wake you. Wasn't I, Bird?" This appeared to be new information to the child. The woman laid a great plateload of coddled egg and bacon and hotcakes at Wyck's place.

Wyck realized that he was famished. He sat down with a wordless expression of gratitude and reached for the jar of maple syrup.

Mrs. Barter poured herself a cup of coffee and sat herself between them. "This young woman who claimed to be his sister—Horace McQuinn thought she wrote for a newspaper?"

Wyck paused over his plate. "I think that's what he said."

"Well, Bird is not aware that he has a sister, but you had better find her to be sure."

"I will." It dawned on the man that he had not heard the boy voice anything other than his name, but the landlady had evidently gleaned something from him.

"Bird had better stay with me," she was saying, "if you are going any-place frequented by Horace McQuinn."

She invoked Horace's name with such doubt that Wyck felt honor-bound to speak up for the man. "Horace is not such a bad sort," he said, but with the qualifying adjective, he knew it seemed a little backhanded.

"If this young woman can't supply us with some answers," she continued in a quieter tone, "I shall go to the police station."

"The police station? They'll put him in one of those awful orphan-ages!" It occurred to Wyck that he was speaking carelessly, and he glanced at Bird's stricken face with wincing regret.

"That is not necessarily so, Wyckford. I just want to find out if there have been any reports of missing children in the past five years."

"Past five years?"

"Well?" she asked. "How old does he seem to you?" She turned to Bird and gave him a look that was both firm and warm. Wyck wondered where she found a look like that, quite sure that he had nothing of the sort in his own expressionary arsenal. "Do you know how old you are, Bird?" she inquired.

The little boy thought for a moment, then shook his head gravely.

Mrs. Barter patted his hand. "It's nothing to be concerned about," she said. "I know how old I am, and I wish I didn't. Now, finish up your break-fast." This seemed to make the little fellow feel better; the ghost of a smile hovered briefly within the more complex emotions in his eyes. Mrs. Barter turned back to her place and addressed her coffee, as if every issue in the world were soon to be resolved. "Wyckford," she said.

Wyck realized that his plate was growing cold. "Oh, yes," he said, and tucked in. "I had better hurry so I can find Horace, first thing."

"I wouldn't choke myself hurrying to see Horace McQuinn," said Mrs. Barter.

20. The Lilac Station

MRS. BARTER SAW HIM when she stepped from her back door to shake out a rug. The man stood on the corner of Carleton Street with his back to her, looking down the short slope in the direction that Wyckford had walked. An intuition, sudden and unpleasant, told her the stranger was as-suring himself that Wyck was not returning soon. She gave the rug a few good snaps, then hurried back to the parlor, where she had left Bird with a feather duster, daubing at a hassock as if he were painting it. "Bird?" she said. "Come with me."

The little boy looked as if he hated to part with the duster.

"You can bring it," she assured him, and urged him down the hall to the kitchen. "Come here, to the window. Have you ever seen that man?"

Bird was just able to peer over the sill, toward the southeast and the center of Portland, and he seemed to be taken with the venue for a moment before he located the man at the corner.

"Have you ever seen him?" Mrs. Barter asked again.

Bird nodded slowly, giving the question his full attention.

"Do you know him?" This generated a negative response. The landlady got herself down on one knee. "That isn't Mr. Pembleton?"

"No," said Bird, his brown eyes wide at the thought.

She was relieved for a moment, and considered her previous intuition to be idle and foolish. Then she saw that the man was walking toward the house and that a second man had joined him. Neither of them looked reputable to her; she felt the hair on her arm prickling. She looked up and down the road and thought she caught a glimpse of a third man standing up by West Street.

"Bird," she said; still on one knee, she took hold of his shoulders and spoke to him deliberately. "I want to show you a very secret place, and I want you to be very quiet and still there while I talk to these men." The little boy looked uncertain, and she wrinkled her nose, which had once been her own little boy's version of a wink. "Come, quick."

With an economy of motion that years of household chores had refined, she took up a lantern from the hall on their way back to the parlor. Here she lifted a corner of the heavy braided rug and folded it over with a little work. Beneath the rug were floorboards painted gray, and from one of these she popped a large knot. With a finger in the hole, she was able to pull up a small, craftily hidden trap door and reveal a short ladder. She did not wait for Bird to climb down, but took him beneath the arms and handed him down. Then she hopped down after him, using only a couple of the ladder's rungs.

"Years ago, my parents used to hide people here who were going to Canada," she said, more to fill the cold, dark atmosphere than with any expectation that he would understand what she meant. In the first few feet of the space below she had to bend over, almost double; but then the hard-packed floor dropped again, and they came into a tiny room of relative comfort. She lit the lantern and set it on a low table. "Bird, you are to stay down here while I see what those men want. You be still, do you hear? If I don't come and get you, you wait till you hear Wyck come back; then you shout for him. And if you have to, there is a hall back there and a little passage that will take you out into the middle of that stand of lilac bushes."

She paused for a moment to take stock of his expression, which was brave. His shoulders were hunched, and his face was tense. He looked as if he were holding his breath. Mrs. Barter reached out and touched his cheek, then climbed the ladder, dropped the trap door, and kicked the rug back over.

She let them knock three times. *Only strangers and drummers come to the front door*, she thought to herself as she reached for the knob — it was an old New England dictum. She opened the door with a broom in her hand and a certain amount of irritation evident in her bearing. "Yes?" she demanded.

Four men stood there, three loitering behind the one on the step, like comic foils, unshaved and unwashed, in a bucolic play. They held their hats before them as if they might break out into four-part harmony, but there was no hiding their crude natures — either in their bearing, their eyes, or their voices. "You will pardon us, ma'am," said the man on the step, who attempted a genteel manner, "but we have come for the boy."

"The boy?" she snapped.

"Yes, ma'am," said the man with only a slight darkening of his expression. "We've been sent by his uncle Eustace to get him. You will be glad, I guess, to have him off your hands."

"If I had him on my hands, what makes you think I would pass him over to someone I had never laid eyes on? Why, the ridiculousness of it!" She was angry now rather than frightened, and she shook the broom without realizing how much like a weapon it appeared.

The man eyed the stick the way one might a wasp and said, "We passed O'Hearn as we come up, and he said to tell you it was all right."

"You are a liar, young man!" she declared.

The man on the steps was astonished. "A liar?" he growled. "A liar?" The other men looked to see if the neighbors might be watching. "Well, I don't have to take that from anybody!"

There was not a lot of traffic on these streets on the western end of Portland in the middle of a Sunday morning, so Mrs. Barter noticed when a wagon, with two men on its bench and pulled by a gray swaybacked horse, appeared around the corner and up the slope of Pine Street.

"You don't have to take it; you're right!" she said with the sort of calm severity she would have exercised on a naughty child. "You can make yourself scarce from my doorstep! Why would Mr. O'Hearn tell you that you could come for the boy when the boy isn't here anymore?"

The man on the step gaped past Mrs. Barter, leaning one way, then the other, as if he might catch sight of the boy. "Are you sure?" he asked. "I was told to come and get him."

The horse and wagon came to a halt in front of the house, and a small, wiry old man hopped down to the sidewalk.

"Do you suppose I don't know who's in my own house?" she said sharply.

The man on the step gave a glance to one of the men behind him, then said, "I'll take a look inside," and had almost shouldered Mrs. Barter out of the way when a new voice called up from the front walk.

"Well, boys, how are things? What brings you off the waterfront, Jack?" asked Horace McQuinn of the man on the step.

"Horace," said the man.

"Oh, Mrs. Barter," said Horace, as if remembering why he was there, "I dropped that kid off at the station."

"Thank you, Mr. McQuinn," said the landlady without a blink or hesitation.

Horace waved to indicate how little it was.

"What station?" demanded Jack.

"Down on Center Street." Horace hooked a thumb over his shoulder.

"The cops?"

"I think they prefer to be called policemen," intoned Horace. His gray eyes danced with amusement.

"Well," muttered Jack, "why didn't you say so." He stepped down, though not before he threw a glance at Mrs. Barter, and beyond her to the hall.

When she spoke, there was a harsh, almost strangled sound to her voice. "Don't you ever try to push your way into my house!"

Jack eyed her like a dog that wavers between uncertainty and attack.

"If you don't think I can't knock your head in with a broomstick," she promised him, "you just try it!" The four men slunk away, slowly, and only looked back once or twice before disappearing in the direction of the harbor. "I will be very honest, Horace McQuinn," said Mrs. Barter when they were gone. "I never expected to be glad to see you."

"I couldn't have predicted it myself," Horace admitted.

Mrs. Barter looked over the man's head at the wagon. She had never met Maven Flyce, but Wyckford had described him many times to her, and she could see Maven's famous cowlick from where she stood. "Who were they?" she asked, watching the last of the men disappear down Pine Street.

"They are part of Adam Tweed's gang, down by the waterfront."

"Tweed? I don't know him."

"That's just as well."

"Why were they looking for him?"

Horace gave one of his elaborate shrugs and pulled a frown. "Pemble-ton went and asked Tweed for help finding him, I guess. It seems odd, though. Tweed doesn't often offer help if there isn't some profit in it."

"Perhaps I had *better* speak to the police."

"Pembleton's beat you to it. They're looking for the boy, too. Matter of fact, you might be seeing them before the day is out."

This held no fear for her. "How could he dare?" she asked. "He went to the police after the way he treated that boy?"

"He has as clear a title to the kid as anyone," Horace opined.

Mrs. Barter bristled. "He's not going back to that monster!" she stated simply. "What will they do now?" she asked. "That gang."

"They'll send someone to inquire after the boy at the station."

"And then they'll be back."

"More than likely."

"Wyckford's looking for you," she said.

"I saw him. Gave him Miss Peer's address and sent him on his way."

"Is that the boy's sister?"

"I wouldn't place my last dollar on it."

Mrs. Barter thought on this for a moment. "You had better come in."

Mrs. Barter felt weary when she returned to the parlor; the braided rug was suddenly heavier and the trap door less wieldy than before. Horace didn't offer to help, but leaned in the doorway.

"Your folks were good abolitionists," he said.

"Some people find things other than rum to smuggle," she said.

"I know," he said, and added enigmatically, "I have myself."

The landlady called for Bird, and after a moment, two eyes blinked up from the darkness beneath the floor. The little boy looked from Mrs. Barter to Horace. "Perhaps we *should* take him to the police," she said.

"That'd be drastic," thought Horace aloud. "He'll just end up in some orphanage, or more than likely they'll just give him back to Pembleton if he comes and claims him."

She didn't like the idea herself but didn't know what else to do.

"He can come with me," suggested Horace. "I'll take him over to Miss Peer's, and she and Wyck can cipher it out. He'll be safer with the big fellow."

Mrs. Barter didn't know that the child would be safe traveling with Horace. "Perhaps I should take him, then."

"You don't imagine all those men have gone, do you?" asked Horace.

"Do you know Mr. McQuinn?" she asked Bird.

The little boy looked at the old man and nodded almost imperceptibly.

"He's seen me around," said Horace McQuinn.

"They can follow you just as well as they can follow me," she said.

Horace looked down at the hole in the floor. "This cubbyhole of yours must go somewheres."

"Out to the lilacs," she said before stopping to realize that she had just revealed to Horace McQuinn a very precious family secret.

"You take him out there, just out of sight, and when I drive by, he can scoot out and hop up between Maven and me."

"What if they see him?"

Horace walked to the front door as if everything were decided and agreed upon. "You get a sheet and carry it out as if you were hiding something behind it. Take it around t'other side of the house and that'll distract anybody watching you." He didn't even wait to hear her reply, but went out the door and down the walk.

Mrs. Barter hurried down the ladder beneath the floor, where Bird stood throughout the conversation, listening to others decide his fate. He stiffened slightly when she took hold of his shoulder and pulled him along, through the little room with the low table to the narrow passage beyond. "Now, Bird," she said. "You know Mr. McQuinn, who I was just talking with?"

"Yes," came the little voice.

The woman felt her heart in her throat. "Mr. McQuinn is going to take you to see Mr. O'Hearn."

"Wyck," said the boy.

"Yes, Wyckford. I want you to go to the end of this passage and wait for Mr. McQuinn's wagon to come alongside the lilacs. Do you understand? Then you hurry out as quietly as you can and jump up with Horace and his friend and scooch right out of sight beside them. Do you understand?"

Bird nodded gravely, eyes wide in the dark. Abruptly, she put her arms around him and hugged him. Slowly, he raised his own arms and astonished her by patting her on the back, as if *she* were in need of reassurance. When she let go of him, he turned and felt his way down the passage toward the gray light that filtered through the thicket of lilacs.

Well! thought Mrs. Barter. *Someone must have shown him some gentleness for him to know how to do that.* She shook herself and proceeded calmly; she took up the lantern on the table as she passed, blew it out, climbed the ladder, hid the place beneath the floor once again, and snatched the tasseled throw from the parlor sofa.

From the small windows at the side of the front door she watched as Horace shook the reins and urged the horse forward. The old nag barely seemed to rouse herself from a nap before lumbering down the street. When they neared the lilacs, she burst out of the house, holding the throw before her, as if she *might* be hiding something behind it. She took it around to the other side of the house and hung it on her laundry line, praying that she had caused enough of a distraction. Then she hurried back to the front of the house, allowing herself only the merest glance after the wagon.

The figures of Horace and cowlicked Maven Flyce sat alone (presumably), already well past the lilac bushes. Mrs. Barter went inside and sat on the stairs in the hall. Tears stole from beneath her closed eyes, but she was still, her breathing quiet and even. She thought of her own son, who had left for a life at sea more than twenty years ago.

21. More Pieces in Play

MOLLIE DAYDREAMED OVER HER TYPEWRITER, a vertical black monstrosity she had bought at a pawnshop and with which she had an ambivalent relationship. The sticking *E* key, once an irritation, had become a way of life; the bent *J* and the *A* with the missing leg were now her notion of those letters, so that a proper *J* or *A* looked wrong to her.

Sitting with her chin in her hands, her elbows on the desk, the scents of metal and machine oil in her nostrils, she gazed unseeingly out the window, over Mrs. Makepeace's lawn and Plum Street, to the trees and lawns and houses opposite. A squirrel did catch her attention finally, running up an oak across the street, and she roused, as if waking, straightening her posture and stretching with a groan. "This will never do," she said to herself.

She considered the stack of social announcements sent to her in care of the newspaper.

> Mrs. Henrietta Fothcart expresses gratitude that her home has been selected as the sight of the eleventh annual Conclave for Women's Suffrage, which will be held nightly during the week preceding the election. . . .

> Mrs. Samuel Riverille of Cape Elizabeth is expecting a full house on October 31st when she once again hosts what is thought

to be unique in the county and possibly the state—a Halloween masquerade. Residents from the Cape and surrounding boroughs will remember the gay time that was had in past . . .

Mr. and Mrs. James Underwood of Spring and High Streets are pleased to announce the engagement of their daughter Cordelia Elizabeth to Mr. Dresden Ebuelon Scott of Millinocket. James Underwood is the son of . . .

Simultaneous balls in the state's three major cities will be held in honor of the expected victory of William Jennings Bryan and Arthur E. Sewell on the night of election, November 4th. The Falmouth Hotel on Middle Street will be the site of Portland's celebration. . . .

With one dark eyebrow raised, Mollie turned back to the engagement and the name of the prospective groom; she had read so many of these announcements that they sounded trite to her. She might even have formed some ironic picture of Cordelia Elizabeth Underwood, but she had met the woman even before Cordelia had become a name in the newspapers for having been kidnapped and rescued and had liked her.

"Good heavens!" said Mollie, reading the end of the item.

The future Mr. and Mrs. Scott plan to live in one of the unorganized territories northwest of Millinocket.

"They must enjoy one another's company," she said aloud. She couldn't think of a person with whom she would spend a week in the woods. *More's the pity*, she admitted silently to herself. *Or perhaps not.*

That dark eyebrow lifted again as movement below her window caught her eye. She leaned forward but was not in time to see who had approached the front door. She heard the knock, three rapping knuckle beats, then silence, and realized that she was holding her breath.

The three knocks came again, then a "Yes, yes" from Mrs. Makepeace. The door was opened, and conversation flowed audibly but not intelligibly upstairs. Mollie thought she recognized the voice of the caller. She felt a queasy sense of panic for a moment before Mrs. Makepeace rapped her own knuckles on Mollie's door. "Yes, Mrs. Makepeace?" she called.

"There is a . . . young man to see you," said the landlady.

"Yes?"

"Mr. O'Hearn, he tells me."

"Yes, I'll be right down."

She came out on the landing with her coat and hat and looked down at him. Peering at a framed portrait in the hall, he was not immediately aware of her presence. He looked outsized and awkward, his red hair slightly askew, his bowler hat in his hand. Mrs. Makepeace was explaining to him, politely, who was represented in the picture, and he was doing his best, politely, to appear interested.

Mollie assumed an expression that she hoped conveyed both gratitude and apology as she came down the stairs with a rustle of petticoats. Wyckford O'Hearn turned and watched her descent with only partially concealed appreciation. He looked exactly what he was, a tall and brawny member of the laboring class who would not have been out of place at her father's forge. His dark red hair was a little too long in the back, but he was cleanly shaven, and his blue eyes were innocent of guile. His strong jaw was raised with the moderate self-assurance of a man entering the batter's box.

"Mr. O'Hearn!" said Mollie before the man could speak. She tossed a glance in the landlady's direction. "I am so glad you came by! I was hoping to talk with you and even went to Mr. Corbel's office to see if anyone knew where you lived."

The name of the *Eastern Argus*'s editor gave Mrs. Makepeace the intended impression that here was another subject for interview (though certainly not for the society page!), and the landlady offered the use of her parlor.

"Oh, it's such a lovely day!" declared Mollie, passing the man her hat while she put on her coat. "I've been upstairs writing all morning, and I just hate to miss it all. Perhaps we could walk for a bit."

Wyckford O'Hearn had not arrived in the best of humors. After talking with Horace McQuinn, he was anxious for the little boy and Mrs. Barter, though the old rascal had assured him there was no reason to fret. What Horace had told him about Miss Peer—that she was a newspaper writer and possibly interested in Bird only for his value in print—had brought him to the leading edge of anger as he walked. And he didn't know who Mr. Corbel was.

But he was a little confounded. The woman was candidly offering him occasion to speak his mind by suggesting a stroll, and he couldn't help be a little glad of it simply because she was so dashed handsome.

"Would you mind awfully?" she asked with a smile.

"Not at all," he said with the same chivalrous deference that he had demonstrated when he took after Bird the day before. He would have tipped his hat if it had been on his head; instead, he nodded and shrugged and nodded again, all the while shuffling on the carpet like an uneasy horse.

"Don't be gone long," said Mrs. Makepeace. She gave Wyck a solemn stare, and he nodded and shrugged again before Mollie had them both out the door.

"I can't tell you how embarrassed I am!" said Mollie as they moved down the walk. "To mistake that poor little boy for my brother! I was so up-set after speaking to my mother—"

"So he *isn't* your brother," stated Wyck.

"No, and I am sorry for the trouble you must have—"

"How do you know he isn't? You thought so pretty certainly when you saw him at a distance. What told you he wasn't?"

"Someone else found my brother last night and brought him home, and my mother was almost beside herself."

Wyck had thought that he would have to moderate his long stride, walking alongside the young woman, but she kept up, perhaps even drew him along as they went down the hill. The wind was rising, coming around to the east, and certain gusts tugged at the trees. Clouds had been gathering all day as the looked-for storm collected like an eddy above the coast.

"It must have been frustrating for you not to catch him, then to come back and find me gone."

"But I did catch him," said Wyck. "Or I found him, actually, in pretty bad straits."

"Oh?"

"Pembleton knocked him down, and the kid's head hit a rock."

"Oh!"

"Put the kid out for half an hour, and I got a piece of lumber broke across my back for my troubles."

"I'm so sorry!"

"Your brother, is his name Sean?"

Mollie was caught off guard, anxious to hear the details of the big man's tale. "Yes," she said, not sensing danger when he named one of her real brothers.

"Horace tells me that your brother Sean is dead," said Wyck flatly. He stopped short, and she took a step or two before turning.

"I'm sorry. Not Sean. What could I be thinking?"

"Horace says your mother is dead, too."

Mollie was at a loss. She had not expected such a canny trap from this fellow. It was a mistake she was liable to, misjudging a person because of their class, possibly because it *was* the class to which she had been born.

Add to that a desire to outwit members of the opposite gender, with a dash of disdain for men who labored with brute strength (despite her love for her father) and she discovered that she had been fairly caught. "*Horace,*" she said, "would make a good policeman."

"Or a newspaper writer," said Wyckford.

"Well, Mr. O'Hearn," she said, squaring her shoulders. "Think of me what you will, but I am honestly sorry to have led you on a wild-goose chase, and I apologize."

"It *wasn't* a wild-goose chase. I found the boy, and I'm glad of it. I just don't know what's to become of him." Wyck's face indicated distaste. "But calling upon your dead mother—!" He did not finish, his lips tight with disgust.

Mollie felt a little dizzy; she hadn't considered very deeply the moral implications, only charging along, as was her wont, and devil take the hindmost. Now the shabbiness of her deception came home to her. She did her best to match gazes with him, but her eyes dropped involuntarily, and she was enraged to find tears blurring her sight.

"I better walk you home," he said quietly. He was embarrassed, now that his anger was dispelled.

"Thank you; I can find my way."

"I'm going back that way, at any rate," he said, and she fell in with him as they moved much more slowly up the hill.

Mollie's curiosity began to master her other emotions, and still feeling small for the use of her poor deceased mother, she yet began to wonder how to satisfy her interest gracefully. Where had he found the boy? Who had broken a piece of lumber over this giant's back? She thought of the little barefoot child with a sudden, unaccustomed pang.

The sensation brought her to a halt. "The little boy, how is he?"

Quite by accident, and quite honestly, she had asked the question that Wyck had been waiting to hear. "I think he's going to be all right." He stopped a few steps above her and considered her expression—the hand above her breast, the look of confusion. "He has an awful egg on his head." Though drilled by Horace in the technique of tricking Mollie, he was out of his realm once more and feeling more uncomfortable with every passing minute.

And it was in this tableau that they were discovered by the three on the buckboard—Horace McQuinn, Maven Flyce, and Bird. "By the looks, I think we gave Wyckford enough time to say his piece," said Horace with dark humor glinting in his gray eyes.

"Goodness sakes, Hod!" said Maven, almost in a shout. "Isn't that the lady from down on the wharf?" Bird recognized Mollie as well and seemed puzzled to find her and Wyck together, neither of them looking very happy.

"Is there a telephone here?" Horace asked as they pulled up.

"What is it, Horace?" asked Wyck. "What's happened?"

"Some of Adam Tweed's bunch came by your landlady's."

"*Tweed's* bunch?"

"If you've got a telephone, go call a carriage," said Horace to Mollie.

He did not seem ready to explain, so after trading looks with the little boy, she turned down the walk and hurried, without running, into the house.

It was difficult to explain to Mrs. Makepeace who the strange men were, but Mollie invoked her job, the newspaper in particular, and societal crimes against children in general so that the woman was partly mollified. This state was quickly changed, however, when Mollie announced that she was leaving with these people and Mrs. Makepeace advised solemnly against it.

"The young man seemed decent enough," said the landlady, "though not enough to warrant riding off with him unescorted, but these other fellows do not look reputable." Mrs. Makepeace came close to insisting that Mollie stay, almost to the point of threatening the young woman's removal from the house if she didn't, but Mollie called upon their shared faith in suffrage and promised she was in safe company.

By the time the cab arrived, Mollie was hurrying down the walk. Maven was given the reins of the buckboard and sent back up the hill with orders to head for the observatory in a roundabout manner. "Probably if I had told him to get there straightway, it *would* have been roundabout," said Horace.

Wyck and Bird were in the carriage when Horace climbed in from one side and Mollie opened the door on the other. There were several looks exchanged, but Horace only grinned. "What are you doing?" asked Wyckford.

"I'm coming with you," she said.

He gave her a searching look that stopped her from climbing in. The driver leaned over to get a glance at her. Horace settled himself into the seat opposite Wyck and Bird.

"Yes," she said. "I *am* curious. I want to know what it's all about. But I'm responsible as well, and perhaps I can be of some help." She looked Wyck square in the eye. "I'd like to make up for it if I can."

Wyckford might have met this last statement with more approbation if Mollie had appeared more certain of it herself. Instead, he turned to Horace, who put out a hand and pulled Mollie into the cab, saying, "Get in!"

22. The Best Revenge

HENRY ECHO STOOD IN THE BACK HALLWAY of his apartments with a book in his hand. He had picked it from a stack against the wall and opened it to some middle chapter that called him as he passed. Mister Walton and John Neptune were talking in the parlor. Sundry, who had brewed some coffee in the kitchen, stopped with the tray when he came in line with the hall and watched for a moment as Henry stood absorbed by the words before him.

The man had risen that morning in a grand state of elation. He felt freer than he had in weeks, he told them, perhaps in years! What could he do to repay them? How he would remember last night! Even Eugene came under these sunny declarations, and the raccoon was feted with sugar from the pantry.

Profoundly moved by the simple expedient of an altered clock, he could not have been more grateful to Sundry, or more impressed with his powers, if the young man had turned back time itself. Sundry, in turn, was of the opinion that the greatest work had been done by Mister Walton, whose calming influence had allowed Henry to fall asleep. "You might have slept through midnight *without* my hurrying it along," said Sundry.

"When one reaches my age, one comes to understand the importance of proper delegation," said John Neptune. "I can read clocks, but their purpose has always seemed a little troublesome." Then he amended himself somewhat by saying, "I am sure they are useful to the people who schedule trains."

As far as they could ascertain, the prowler discovered John Neptune sleeping in the chair and mistook him, in the dark and from behind, for Henry. Peering around the chair, his death's-head mask glowing in the light of the fire, the figure in black gave out a shout but was frightened himself by the unexpected face of the Indian, whose eyes started open with a fierce glare rather than with shock.

Eugene, who *had* been frightened, sprang on the prowler's head and dug in his claws. After the astonishment of John Neptune's face, this new sensation was enough to send the figure in black back where he had come from, vocalizing the very terror that he had expected to inspire.

After their great excitement, it had been difficult for some of them to sleep again. The old Indian had no trouble; once he knew the where-abouts of Eugene, he lay down on the sofa, closed his eyes, and soon was snoring. The host insisted that Sundry take his bed, and the young man, who had set the vigil, was soon sawing his own logs.

Mister Walton had gotten just enough sleep to give him a second wind; Henry, understandably, was alive with excitement; wakeful, they returned to the cribbage board and played till three in the morning.

"We should inform the police," Mister Walton had said during breakfast.

"Yes," said Henry, as if he hadn't thought of this. "I suppose we should." To begin with, he seemed the only one among them who wasn't interested in the identity of the intruder. Then, as the morning wore on, he exhibited increasing signs of agitation, and finally anger. He came out of the hallway when the coffee things were laid out and stood at the door, pulling absently with one hand at his thin mustache.

When the sheriff arrived, they led him through the previous night. The October sun was yet strong enough to raise the dew in smoky tendrils from the lawn, and as they stood beneath the maple from which the prowler had fallen, the mist whirled about their coattails like a low-lying fog.

"He made a very graceful leap from the roof," said Mister Walton.

With his hands in his pockets, the sheriff looked up to consider the maple. "With a raccoon on his head!" he marveled. His name was Edward Mulvaney, and he was known for appearing half-asleep when he was thinking the hardest. He had an unlit pipe between his teeth, and Sundry wondered why it didn't drop from his mouth when he spoke.

"I think he may have bitten the man's ear," said John Neptune. He had Eugene on his leash, and the raccoon was sniffing about the foot of the tree.

"I'd liked to have seen that," said the sheriff, still with his hands in his pockets. He frowned at the house. Henry's landlady, Mrs. Thorpe, was glaring at them from a front window. Henry waved to her, and she disappeared.

While Henry saw the sheriff to his carriage and John Neptune was wandering the grounds with his charge, Sundry spoke of Mister Walton's plans. "Do you think we should excuse ourselves and pick up the trail to Hallowell?"

"The Passamaquoddy contend that to save a person's life is to take responsibility for it," said Mister Walton, which seemed a little cryptic. "You had more to do with helping Mr. Echo than I, of course, but I understand the tenet better now than I have before. I feel some responsibility for the man," said Mister Walton with a sigh, "the more so since I fear that anyone who would go to such lengths to frighten him must look for some gain by it."

"Anyone who would gain by his death must necessarily be someone close to him," Sundry agreed. The sheriff's carriage was pulling away, and Henry was walking back from the road, looking more absent than ever. "It is perhaps," added Sundry, "a point he is coming to himself."

"I believe he has been coming to it all morning," said Mister Walton, "and I am sure that the sheriff has said something to confirm his doubts."

Henry came up to them, and he did look newly troubled. "The sheriff will be back this afternoon," he said quietly, "after making inquiries. I'm not sure that any of this is important now," he added, almost to himself.

"It may be best to know, in the end," said Mister Walton.

Henry seemed less and less a party to them as morning fell to afternoon. For brief moments, he might enter their conversation, but then lose himself in the pages of a magazine found beside his chair or disappear into another room in search of a particular volume on the wall. Once, while John Neptune was out walking Eugene, Sundry reminded Henry of the story regarding Portland's debt to the Indian and the man named Isherwood Tolly.

"There was also a man named John Poor," said Echo, briefly distracted.

"The railroad man?" Mister Walton reflected aloud.

"Yes, indeed. John Poor was responsible for the whole venture—the whole *ad*venture—in the first place."

"He was a lawyer from Bangor," Mister Walton explained to Sundry, "and contrary to his own name in all things, it seems. He prospered in his field, he was a figure of great energy, and he had a wealth of love for his state."

"It was in the zenith of the clipper days," said Henry, "when others hadn't the imagination to see anything flourish beyond the reach of a sail, but *he* had a vision that the future of commerce lay with the railroad. In the early forties Poor came to Portland with what some thought an absurd notion—that, with its wonderful harbor, the city could be linked by rail to Montreal and become Canada's winter port. He spent his own money having a route surveyed and was so enthusiastic that, despite certain naysayers, he was able to obtain a loan from the city for two million dollars."

Even fifty years later, it seemed a fantastic sum of money, and Sundry's eyes widened at the thought.

"But in December of '46," continued Henry, "Mr. Poor was apprised that the Montreal Board of Trade was meeting with agents from Boston who had made overtures on behalf of that city as a winter port. John Poor came rushing into the Portland Livery the day he learned about the meeting and demanded of old Skully Peaslee, 'Who is your swiftest driver?'

"Skully looked across the stables where Isherwood Tolly was handing over the harness to one of the boys; he had just come in from a late stage run. The snow was deep that season, and it was all sleighs till April. A nor'easter was brewing to boot, and he was more than a little glad to be in for the night. 'Ish is the quickest around here,' said Skully, 'but he's just in from a long haul, and he'll be asleep in ten minutes.'

"But John Poor wasn't listening. He marched up to Isherwood and told him the fate of the city was resting on *their* deeds! Those were the words, I've been told. '*Our* deeds,' he said actually. '*Our* deeds.'"

The story had just gained momentum when John Neptune came in with Eugene and announced that the sheriff had returned. Sundry was disappointed; Henry hadn't even touched upon the Indian's involvement. Henry met the sheriff outside, by the tree, and they spoke for a long while.

When the sheriff left, Henry relayed the policeman's regards. "He says that my presence is not necessary to his investigation, and I have decided to leave town for a while, till the effect of our adventure has passed away or some conclusion to the affair is reached by the law." He had a different manner about him, almost stoic, and Mister Walton put this off to a determination not to face up to the probability that someone close to him had attempted to speed his demise.

"We will stay with you, then," said Mister Walton, "till you are ready to leave. Then we may travel with you a bit if you are going in the same direction."

"I have already asked too much of you, gentlemen," insisted Henry. "I know you have destinations of your own, and I think I will be much better company to myself in the near future." It was an abrupt change both in his demeanor and their expectations. He did not possess the social grace to keep the moment from turning awkward, and they were surprised that he would seem so anxious to have them gone.

"I am going to visit my sister," he told them. "I will not eat myself up with this. There is every chance that the intruder, and therefore the person behind him, will never be apprehended, and I will not waste the remainder of my life, now that I *have* life that remains, in worrying about who did this or in contemplating revenge." It seemed an admirable position, but he voiced it with all the lack of confidence one might sense in a dipsomaniac who swears off drink after a rough night with the bottle.

Even John Neptune's presence was not required, and soon the three men (along with Eugene) were waving to Henry Echo from the windows of a hired carriage. He watched them go from the front door.

Mrs. Thorpe stood at the end of the hall, radiating her disapproval. Her small dog yapped in her arms. "They're gone, then, are they?" she growled.

"They are," he sighed. He heard her shuffle back to her rooms. Henry felt weary. He went back to his own apartments and waited for the sheriff. Mister Walton and Sundry were done with Henry Echo's story, but Henry Echo, unbeknownst to anyone (himself included), was not done with the Moosepath League.

23. Quentin's Charm

MOLLIE HAD SEVERAL LEGITIMATE QUESTIONS as the cab drove on—where they were going would have been a place to start—but Wyckford was as much in the dark as she, and he thought it inappropriate to say much about Bird or his intended fate in front of the child.

The little boy was absorbed by Mollie and watched her with frankly admiring eyes. The dirt had been washed from him, and his clothes were clean, so he seemed more human to her. Till now she had only seen the dirt and not considered the face behind it; his soft brown eyes, peering from that sooty mask, had not seemed real. Now she was looking at a small child who might have been one of her brothers. He had shoes on now, a little too big for him; she thought about his skinny little feet inside them and looked away.

He had his small, scarred hands in his lap, and when she looked back, he was looking down at them. Perhaps he had seen the change in her expression. Next to Wyckford O'Hearn, he was a doll, a stick figure, tucked in the corner of the swaying cab.

The waterfront flashed between city blocks as they crossed avenues. They were heading east, along a series of streets and drives, avoiding the larger thoroughfares. Then the carriage turned down an old alley and pulled up before a storefront.

Horace nodded to Wyck, who threw open the door, picked up Bird, and set him down on the street. There was no sidewalk, only a gutter on either side of the cobblestone paving. Mollie had no opportunity to glance at the sign above the door. Horace brought up the rear, and when she turned, the cab was already gone.

The room they entered was dark. Objects and piles of objects and shelves filled with objects lined the walls and obstructed the windows and made aisles and (in some cases) filled the aisles. To their left and toward the back of the wide, low room was a single electric light hovering over a countertop and a desk that stood at right angles to one another.

"A moment, a moment," came a voice. A white-haired, white-bearded man, barely taller than Horace, sat at the desk, hunched over his work, with a small tool in one hand. Mollie looked to Wyckford to see if he knew where they were, but he was mystified as well.

The man at the desk was contentedly speaking to himself, or, rather, to his work. "There you go, my little darling," he said, his voice deep and mellifluous. He held what appeared to be a watch to the light—a lady's watch that might depend from a gold necklace. "Aren't you lovely," he was saying. He held the piece to his ear and listened, for all his attitude, as if to beautiful music.

"Are you looking for business or not?" shouted Horace. The others flinched, for Horace's bark seemed out of place, even profane in that quiet room.

"What?" said the man. "What? Business? I'll give you the business. Who's asking for business?" He got to his feet and strode around the counter, shielding his eyes against the single light to look into the darkness beyond.

"Why, you couldn't *wind* a watch properly," said Horace. His head was lowered between his shoulders, as if expecting something to be thrown at him, but his eyes were merry, and he was grinning.

"What?" said the bearded man again. "Horace?"

"No, it's your grandmother," said Horace. "Look at you! You're all bent up like a crab-tree stick!" Horace walked through the center aisle, not very straight himself.

"Me?" said the other fellow. He peered over his spectacles, a grin akin to Horace's spreading across his face. "*You* look like a man in need of a physic! Why, you look like the dog they ran too hard!"

Horace was pointing now, almost in tears, he was so delighted with the other man's aging posture. "You old goat! You look like you got your hide thrashed and you can't sit down!"

The bearded fellow was fairly dancing. "If you don't get any handsomer, the least you could do is get yourself a little smarter!"

And the next thing the astonished people by the door knew, these two were thumping one another on the back and hooting and cackling with pleasure. Wyckford O'Hearn was more astonished than any of them, for he had known Horace for most of his adult life. But there was more akin between the two men than their grins. "It's his brother!" said Wyckford. "They're brothers!"

Mollie's eyes had adjusted to the dim room, and she was able to see what filled the shelves — clocks and watches, clockworks and watchworks, bins of wheels and cogs and springs, tiny boxes of tiny screws and pins, mechanical artifacts and pieces of mechanisms and wires and bolts.

"You might come by and see a body!" declared Horace's brother.

"I'm no further away from you than you from me!" replied Horace.

"Go on with you!" said the bearded fellow. "You're up to no good." Wyckford came out of the semidarkness, toward the light, and the bearded fellow considered him with an interested frown. "Well, there!" stated the old man. "Who do we have here?"

"This is Wyckford O'Hearn," said Horace.

"You're brothers," said Wyckford.

"Don't spread it around," said Horace.

"Like two peas in a pod," said Wyckford, almost laughing to look from one to the other.

"You sure know how to hurt a man," said Horace's brother.

"I'm glad to meet you," said Wyckford, and he held out his hand.

The older fellow's grip was like iron, and it was with honest pleasure that he shook the ballplayer's hand. "Quentin McQuinn," he said.

"I'm pleased to meet you, Mr. McQuinn. Horace, you never told me you had a brother!"

"You hear that," said Quentin. "You're *Horace*, but I'm *Mr. McQuinn*."

"Strangeness has its benefits," said Horace.

"What else do we have here," said Quentin. "Boys, howdy! You didn't tell me a lady was present. What's wrong with you? Come in, ma'am. Well, there! Is this your son?"

"No," said Mollie. "This is Bird. I am Mollie Peer."

Quentin looked up to Mollie's height, and he might have been the bear considering the honey tree. His eyes shone with pleasure, and his smile had a youthful appeal about it. "Well, there!" he said again. "You're traveling with some rough company, aren't you?"

"I shall put myself under your protection," said Mollie, reflecting some of Quentin's charm back at him.

"I wouldn't laugh," said Quentin to his brother. "She knows a gentleman when she sees one." He did laugh, though, at the snorting noise that rose from Horace. "What?" he said, grinning from ear to ear. "What?" He laughed again. "Well, there!" He looked down at Bird then. "What do you say, young fellow? Come have a look at old Quentin's workshop."

The workshop was itself like the inside of a clock, for there were great timepieces and measuring devices and objects mysterious upon the wall, humming and clicking with mechanical life. Everything was as neat as a pin, the lack of dust remarkable for a room with so many separate items and compartments. Wood glowed with aromatic polish, and metal shone in the yellow light of the single lamp. Quentin found something in a drawer and set it on the counter. He cranked a key several times and let the device go. A mechanical bear walked across the counter, paused to up-end itself, and stood on its hands. When it was done with this operation, the toy bear turned about-face and began again.

Bird was awestruck by the toy. The top of his head barely reached the counter, and he stood, chin in the air, eyes wide, mouth open. Horace laughed his sneezy laugh. "That's Maude," he pronounced. "I know a man who could *talk* a bear into standing on her head."

Behind the workshop were several cozy rooms in which Quentin lived. Everything was plain and utilitarian, with just enough room about the kitchen table for them all to have a cup of tea and some rather fine biscuits that the clockmaker had baked that morning. Perhaps the room looked a little more cozy than was usual with a woman seated among them, her hat hung on the chair behind her and her coat on a hook behind the door.

"I suppose, *Mr.* McQuinn," said Mollie to Horace, "that you will make everything apparent before long."

"If you'd like to take your brother home . . ." said Horace dryly.

Mollie had a retort fixed at the tip of her tongue but stopped herself.

"Let's be careful what we say," suggested Wyck.

Bird looked from one to the other of them as they spoke.

"I think you should all stay put right here," said Horace, "till I find someone to scurry the kid out of town."

"Out of town?" said Wyck.

"Here's Maven now," said Horace, and in fact that man's cowlick was visible passing by the window. "He must have shrunk some. Quentin, get him inside before someone sees him!"

"Whoa!" hollered Maven when the door swung open to reveal him crouched on the stoop. "I didn't even knock!"

"We knew you were here," said Horace.

"I *am* amazed!"

"What are you doing, Maven, hunkered down like that?"

"I was trying to be inconspicuous," said the man.

"Well, put a hat on, then," suggested Horace. "Get in before someone catches sight of that hair and finds us all."

"I left the horse and buckboard with the fellow at the observatory."

"Why don't you take the kid into Quentin's workshop and tour about some," said Horace to Maven. "Take a biscuit," he added, catching sight of Maven's hungry look. Maven took two, on Quentin's insistence, and led Bird back to the workshop, but before they went through the door, the little boy turned to look at Wyckford and Mollie.

"We'll be right here," Wyck assured him. But as soon as the door was shut, Wyck's attention was on Horace. "Now tell me," he said. "What was Adam Tweed's gang doing at Mrs. Barter's?"

Mollie had been wondering whether the redheaded man had an ounce of curiosity (which she equated with sense) about him. It was obvious now, from his voice and his manner, that he was as eager as she to know what was happening, and she was not sure if she admired him or was irritated that he could have hidden it so well. "Perhaps someone could tell *me* how the boy came into your hands," she said.

"Well, Wyckford?" said Horace. "Tell her how you found the boy."

"I found him, that's all."

"That's all," said Horace. "Except for scrambling around in the drains underneath the streets and having it out with Tom Bull and knocking down a brick wall. That's all."

The enumeration of these accomplishments did not have a quieting effect upon Mollie's inquisitive nature.

"Knocked down a brick wall?" said Quentin, standing by the kitchen stove with the teapot in hand.

"Last night, down at the Crooked Cat," said Horace to Wyck, "Tweed came in, sort of worried. He thought you had been a little reckless."

"What has he to do with Pembleton?" asked Wyck.

"Nothing till last night, when Pembleton showed up and offered Tweed in on something if he can help him get the boy."

"How do you know all this?" asked Mollie.

"You'll want to learn, in your sort of work, ma'am, that a little free beer can wobble a person's tongue. There was more than Tweed and Pembleton in the room while they talked."

"I don't understand why Pembleton is so set on the kid," said Wyckford. "He treated him worse than you'd treat a mule."

"Pembleton says the boy knows the whereabouts of everything they've stashed the last two years; if someone gets the kid near the place, he's sure he'll lose the whole of it."

"Stashed?" said Wyck. "You mean stolen."

"It is a fair assumption."

"Probably they think that's why I took him."

"They're sure of it, Wyckford," answered Horace.

"What did *you* know about this?" asked the ballplayer of Mollie.

"Nothing. I was interested in the little boy."

"For your newspaper writing."

"Now, now," said Quentin, who took the opportunity to dole out the tea he had been brewing. There is a calming influence to be had from the ceremony of tea, however it is served—the conviviality of the communal pot, the pace set by steam rising from the cups, and the flowery scent of the brew wafting past the nostrils as a person takes the first sip, which is inevitably too hot. Here the interruption of the tea itself had the effect of dulling the tension between Wyckford and Mollie.

"So, some of Adam's men came to Mrs. Barter's," prompted Wyckford.

"She handled them like a line boss," said Horace. "Had the boy hid away and was giving them what for when Maven and I came by."

"Well, it's a good thing you did," said Wyck. "I appreciate your help, Horace. But why does the kid need to leave town? He's safe enough with me."

"I suppose you're going to keep him tied to you day and night."

"Tweed would answer to me if anything happened to him."

"I don't think he's worried about it. You don't know the man, Wyck. He may not be crazy like Pembleton, but he's crazy. There's only one way to make the kid safe, from my point of view, and that's to keep him out of Tweed and Pembleton's way till they've recovered whatever Pembleton's hid. Then the kid isn't worth anything to them anymore."

"What if Pembleton doesn't want to recover it but just wants to keep the kid quiet. Maybe we should talk to the police, after all."

"Pembleton talked to them already. Claimed you kidnapped the boy."

"Kidnapped?"

"What do you call it?"

"Rescued is more like it!"

"You just sit tight and don't let anyone see you with him. They know who you are and where you live."

"Then *I* should take Bird somewhere," said Mollie.

"They have a very nice description of you, too," added Horace. "You put on a pretty good performance down at the wharf."

"We'll just explain it to the police," said Wyck finally.

"Maybe," said Horace. "But how anxious are you to keep the kid out of Pembleton's hands? You don't know whether they're related or what sort of claim the man has. Pembleton might not want to recover his stuff just now, but Tweed knows about it, and it won't be long before he'll have it, and Pembleton, out of the way, if I'm not very much mistaken."

Mollie shivered, partly with excitement—it was all such fodder for a raft of articles—and partly from the matter-of-fact manner in which Horace was suggesting Eustace Pembleton's imminent demise. Somewhere in the house a clock struck noon; then other gongs and bells followed, till the building vibrated with the hour.

Wyckford calculated something in his head. "I was hoping for a couple of pickup games this week," he said. He was in need of some ready cash. "But I guess I had better take him somewhere."

"*That'll* go unnoticed," said Horace ironically. "You're only about a head taller than everybody. Tweed'll have every station and dock covered."

"We'll go at night."

"The best thing you can do is throw them off by staying home. They're not convinced he isn't still there."

"I should get back, then. What about Mrs. Barter?"

"The cops are probably there already," said Horace. "Unfortunately, I found out this morning that the fellows I *would* have picked to take care of the kid have left town. But I think we can scare someone up."

"Scare someone, is right," said Mollie. "I don't know of anyone you could trust, who would trust *this* situation."

"Have faith, Miss Peer," said Horace, his eyes bright with continued good humor. "There is someone standing by for any job."

"Do you like clocks?" asked Quentin McQuinn of Bird. He had wandered back into his workshop and found the little boy and Maven waiting beneath a cuckoo clock for the resident spirit to make its reappearance. "I've always loved them," said Quentin. "Gears and springs and levers! Never ceases to amaze me when I open the back of a running clock. I didn't make that one. I bought it from a German fellow who moved out to Ohio. Thought I'd use it as a model to build more, but I'm not sure it's very accurate."

The clock's minute hand jigged toward the quarter hour, and they could hear gears buzzing to life. The little door opened, and the cuckoo shot out and announced fifteen minutes before one. Maven looked as if he hadn't seen it three times before. "I can't imagine it," he said. "I *am* astounded."

Bird looked up at some carvings that hung on the wall; one in particular, of a white-tailed deer, poised to dart away.

"Our uncle made those," said Quentin. "He was quite a hand with a piece of wood, or a bit of tin, for that matter. Do you like animals?" The child wasn't sure, and Quentin laughed in his deep tone. "Come here. Come here," he said. He led the way back around the counter. He pulled out and put back two or three drawers before he let out a noise of discovery and set a cigar box on the counter. "Look at these."

Quentin opened the box and took from it several oval-shaped badges. He held them before Bird like cards splayed out for a trick. The old man's uncle had used a metal punch to decorate the pieces of tin, cleverly articulating certain native creatures with the series of holes the punch had made. "Take one," he said to Bird. "It's all right."

Bird pulled one of the tin badges from the several held out to him.

"My uncle used to make these for the Indians up north. They all have totems, you know. Every clan and family is known by a spirit animal that they talk to in their dreams. Beavers, fox, frogs. They would sign their names with a little picture, and many of them were seen with my uncle's little emblems on their chest. Let's see what you picked."

Quentin held out his hand, and Bird passed him the badge reluctantly. Quentin laughed. "Oh, you can keep it. I just want to put it on you. A moose! Now that's a fortunate animal to have on your side. People will tell you a moose is dumb as a stump, but I don't think so. They are pretty noble, with that rack of antlers. They are not afraid of much, either. I'd say a moose for a totem was a superior thing."

He rubbed the badge on his trouser leg till he had produced a proper shine. There was a pin on the back of the badge, and Quentin attached it to Bird's shirt.

"Well, there! Look at you! You're part of the moose clan; have no doubt." He chuckled, then ruffled Bird's hair. Wyckford and Mollie, feeling awkward by themselves in the kitchen, had followed Quentin into the workshop, and neither of them could resist smiling in reaction to the little boy's obvious pleasure.

"Where's Horace?" asked Maven.

"He's gone after his mysterious agents," answered Mollie.

"Really?" said Maven. He whistled. "I never would have thought it!"

Wyckford knew that the cowlicked fellow *couldn't* have thought it, since he had absolutely no idea what Mollie meant. "He's gone off to recruit someone to take Bird out of town."

The little boy looked less happy now. "You don't want to go back to Mr. Pembleton, do you?" Wyck asked him. The child shook his head. Tears were in his eyes; not at this notion, thought Mollie, but at the idea of parting with Wyck. "I'm staying here," explained Wyck. "But you'll come back. Or I'll come and get you. Do you hear me?" Bird said nothing. He made no gestures, no motions of the head to indicate that he understood. "Do you hear me?"

But Bird seemed lost suddenly, as unresponsive as when Pembleton had struck him unconscious. Mollie turned away and studied the clocks on the near wall. Wyck said nothing more.

24. The Four Hinges of Happiness

BIRD HAD FALLEN ASLEEP, curled beneath a blanket in an overstuffed chair in Quentin's snug parlor. Maven sat in a corner by a window, gaping at an issue of *St. Nicholas* in his lap. He was reading a tale of talking rabbits and squirrels and was doing his best to imagine such a thing.

Mollie Peer and Wyckford O'Hearn sat across from one another, appearing about equally out of sorts. They had attempted conversation with less than successful results; there was yet enough bad feeling between them to stifle any "small talk" and too little in common to conjure anything worth saying. The attempted conversations were a degree more awkward than the silences they followed, and the silences following the attempted conversations were a degree more awkward still.

Quentin McQuinn was unaware of the relationship (or lack thereof) between these young people and was sure that any diffidence he sensed was a result of a lovers' quarrel. He very kindly returned to his shop, leaving them to work it out among themselves, though he was unable to pull Maven from his magazine.

So there was nearly as much silence in the parlor, while the afternoon wore on, as one would expect in the receiving room of an unpopular undertaker, this silence occasionally punctuated by Bird's quiet breathing or Maven's incredulous noises and always underscored by the sound of the oncoming storm.

It was Bird himself who presented some common ground on which to discourse. Wyckford was looking down at the boy in order to avoid looking at Mollie, whose eyes he had unintentionally met several times, and he remarked idly that "Mrs. Barter had intended to cut the little fellow's hair."

"It needs cutting," said Mollie.

"It's too bad," said Wyckford. "I hate to send him away looking so shaggy. She did wonders cleaning him up, though."

"His shoes are too big," said Mollie. She didn't know why this made her feel so sad. "I could cut his hair if I had a pair of scissors."

"Could you?" Wyck did like the idea of making Bird look proper.

"I used to cut my brothers' hair all the time."

Wyck thought of Mollie with brothers. Anxious for any excuse to move about, he volunteered to ask Quentin for the appropriate instruments and hurried out. In a few moments, he returned with the white-bearded fellow, who brought a pair of scissors. They rolled back the carpet and set a chair from the kitchen in the middle of the parlor. Bird was awakened by the activity. He sat up and rubbed his eyes, then looked apprehensive when Mollie explained to him what she intended to do.

"Come, come," she said, and Wyck urged him on. Bird sat with his head lowered and his shoulders hunched, as if expecting a blow. "I'm not going to cut your ears off!" she insisted.

"Easy!" said Wyck, who thought this a terrible thing to say.

But Mollie had decided upon her duty and was bound to fulfill it. She took Bird's head firmly and held it where she wanted it to stay, saying, "You're just like my brothers. I cut their hair a hundred times, and they never received so much as a scratch. But whenever I came near them with a pair of scissors, they flinched as if I made a practice of mauling them!"

Quentin stood to one side and observed Mollie's technique. "Maybe I should have you trim *me* up when you're done."

Bird touched his moose badge with one hand, as if it might give him courage, and Mollie went to work. "I have yet to meet a man who knows what a head of hair should look like." Wyck ran a hand through his own red mop, and she shot him a sharp glance. She grew red herself for some reason. "I'm not here to cut hair all day," she said, as if fearful that the big man might ask for similar treatment.

Long locks of light brown hair fell about Bird's shoulders and on the floor around his chair. Slowly, a presentable little boy was emerging from the disarray. Mollie's one hand ran through his hair with a comb, while the other snipped. Bird had relaxed, and he was looking up now, at her motherly figure and strong features. She glanced down, caught his expression, and something like a smile stole across her face.

Everyone was standing now, including Maven, who had torn himself away from his talking rabbits and squirrels, though a fox (who spoke in precise English) had just offered to eat them all. Wyckford stood back and watched with admiration Mollie's skill with the scissors, his hands clasped behind his back as he leaned forward.

"Well, there!" said Quentin. "You could make a living at that."

"Good heavens!" said Mollie. But once the sun had broken through her stern expression, it would not suffer another cloud to pass. Her dark eyes took on an amused light, and one eyebrow arched prettily as she reviewed her handiwork. "You *are* a handsome fellow," she declared, a small note in her voice indicating that she deserved a share of credit for the discovery.

"I wish Mrs. Barter could see you now," said Wyckford.

"Isn't it hard to believe, Wyck?" said Maven. "I wouldn't know him, I swear. Pardon me!" He leaned down to get a better look at Bird, who looked as if a weight had been taken off his head. Mollie appraised Maven's extraordinary cowlick, took hold of it, and offered it up to her scissors.

"Boys, howdy!" declared Quentin. Wyckford let out a gasp. Maven halted in place, paralyzed.

Mollie hesitated, one eye nearly closed, her mouth set with concentration. She might have been looking down the barrel of a gun. Then she relaxed and pulled the scissors away. "I don't have the heart," she said.

Maven straightened his posture, holding his head as if his entire noodle had been at risk. Wyck let out another breath, almost a whistle of relief.

"I wouldn't know you in a crowd without it, Mr. Flyce," said Mollie.

Maven was still holding his head when he sat down in the corner again.

But Mollie had returned to Bird, and her eyes shone as she took a brush and swept back his shortened hair. There seemed little need to groom him further, but she kept at it for a bit, smiling, and the effect of her expression spread throughout the room. Even Maven forgot to return to his story. She stood back again and considered her work, then looked up at Wyck. Her eyes darted back to the child, and she pulled a heavy sigh, as if she had been holding her breath. "There!" She playfully chucked the boy's chin.

"Thank you," said Bird quietly.

The smile fell from Mollie's face. "You're welcome," she said.

Wyck felt at sea, watching them, as if certain verities of his existence had suddenly been called into question. Quentin had gone to get a broom, and he came back to the parlor, singing softly in a rich baritone.

> "*Can she bake a cherry pie, Billie boy, Billie boy?*
> *Can she bake a cherry pie, charming Billie?*"

Mollie looked as if she had remembered something that did not please her, and the inscrutable expression returned to her face; her jaw took its characteristic set. Quentin swept Bird's hair from the floor.

"She can bake a cherry pie,
In a wink of her bright eye.
She's a young thing and cannot leave her mother."

Mollie directed Bird out of the chair and carried it into the kitchen. "When can we expect your brother, Mr. McQuinn?" she asked.

"I couldn't say," said Quentin. He kicked the carpet back into place. "Unless that's him now." The door from the workshop opened then, and Horace came in through the kitchen.

"Well?" said Mollie.

"They were quite willing," said Horace. "It took organization, is all."

"Who, Horace?" asked Wyck, growing impatient.

"They're coming," said the old fellow. He looked weary and sat down without invitation. "I could find a use for a beer, if you could stand to make a man content."

Quentin let out a grunt. If he *had* a bottle in the house, he was not going to break it out in front of Miss Peer and the boy.

"*Ahr!*" said Horace disgustedly. He reached into a coat pocket and pulled a bottle from it. He flipped the hasp and rolled off the stopper, leaned his head back, and took a long drink. "*Ahh!*" he said, and he wiped his mouth with the back of his hand. "Do you know, Wyckford, the Four Hinges of Happiness?" There was a familiar light in his eye, sly and amused.

"No, Horace," said Wyckford, partly amused and partly embarrassed by Horace's bold display.

"The Four Hinges of Happiness!" said Horace. "Swearing, stealing, lying, and drinking!"

"Very admirable, Mr. McQuinn," said Mollie.

Wyckford didn't think so. "Horace, is this—?"

"When you swear," stated Horace solemnly, "*swear* by God and your country."

Wyckford smiled.

"When you steal," informed Horace, "*steal* away from bad company."

Quentin seemed to know what was coming next, and he cleared his throat.

"When you lie," continued Horace, "*lie* with a beautiful woman."

"Horace!" said Wyck.

"And when you drink, drink with *me!*" Horace raised his bottle and took another long draft.

Mollie laughed. "May I quote you, Mr. McQuinn?"

"I look forward to reading the same in the *Eastern Argus*."

"We'll see if they print it." Mollie thought Mr. Corbel would like the Four Hinges of Happiness even if they got no further than his desk.

"Who have you recruited to take care of Bird?" asked Wyckford again.

"Here they are," said Horace, looking greatly revived. "Open the door. I told them to come this way so no one caught sight of them and me together." There was a knock, or rather a crash, against the door, then a silence, and finally a proper knock. Wyckford pulled at the knob. "The call has gone out!" said Horace gleefully. "The volunteers have answered!"

Three well-dressed gentlemen nearly fell into the kitchen, and a gust of wind followed them that rattled the calendar on the wall above the dry sink. One of them, the shortest, with a prodigious beard, was rubbing the top of his head. He looked as if the wind had blown something in his eyes.

"Unfortunate," said Christopher Eagleton. He shook his head.

"Thump's hat fell off in the wind," said Matthew Ephram. "He bent down to pick it up but continued moving forward."

"A man of constant motion," said Eagleton admiringly. "Ever forward!"

"Didn't see the door coming on," explained Ephram.

Joseph Thump caught sight of Mollie Peer standing before them in the cozy kitchen, and he straightened to his not considerable height. "A very meager blow, I assure you, ma'am," he said.

Eagleton's and Ephram's postures followed suit.

"Yes, ma'am," agreed Eagleton with great pride. "He's taken much worse."

"Good heavens, Hod!" said Maven Flyce. "It's the Moosepath League!"

"At your service," said Ephram.

25. That Other Great Society

"IT IS A BEAUTIFUL DAY," said Mister Walton to the man who settled himself beside John Neptune in the opposite seat, even as the train was leaving the Bath station. He was a tall, handsome fellow—somewhere between Mister Walton and Sundry in age—and he smiled quickly when the bespectacled gentleman spoke. He did more than agree with Mister Walton, however, saying:

> *Spring day, Summer day,*
> *Winter day and all;*
> *I will give you one of each,*
> *For a single day of Fall!"*

It was not a new observation, even a hundred years ago, that the Maine fall holds an almost mystical sway over those who have experienced it. Some will tell you that it is simply the mild, often warm days and cool nights. Some count the dry air after the humidity of summer, while others credit the theory of leaves—not just their obvious beauty to the eye but (and perhaps more importantly) the smell of spice and earth they lend to the cool, dry air.

The knowledge of winter coming, however beautiful it may be and however jolly the yuletide will prove, might make the fall more precious still.

Mister Walton felt all of this, even as he did his best to shake off the unresolved feelings brought on by their sudden departure from Henry Echo. He was not, however, ready to agree with the man completely. "I don't know if three days for one is good business," he said, "whatever the nature of the trade. But I will not quibble with you; for myself as well, fall is most certainly the queen of seasons."

There was an odd expression on the man's face when this was said that neither Sundry nor Mister Walton missed. Sundry gave the man a prefatory frown. Mister Walton's expression migrated in the other direction. "I have said something amiss," he guessed aloud.

"Not at all, sir," said the man. "Eli Wyatt," he said, and shook hands with both of them. "The reason for my indiscreet smile is your use of the word 'quibble.' I am, you see, a *Quibbler.*"

Unaware of any laudatory use of this word, Mister Walton thought it a strange admission and wondered if he should express his sympathies, as if the man had admitted a form of involuntary behavior. John Neptune was thinking about the word himself as he looked at the ceiling of the car.

Mr. Wyatt laughed then, and it was such a good-natured sound that his fellow travelers were put at their ease. "I might phrase it better by saying that I am a member of the *Quibbling Society.*" Now Mister Walton thought the man might be speaking in terms of his membership in the human race or perhaps his participation in *American* life. "To be specific," continued Mr. Wyatt, "I am a member of Brunswick's *Great Quibbling Society.*"

"Is there such an organization?" asked an amazed Mister Walton.

"I fear so, yes," said Mr. Wyatt, though, contrary to his words, he took a good deal of pleasure in confessing it. "I am surprised that you have not heard of us, for there can be few so practiced at quibbling nor many who have quibbled so much about so little."

"I bow to your mastery of this art, sir," said Mister Walton, inclining his head. They were passing the outskirts of Bath, though the unusual subject of conversation obstructed their interest in the scenery. "How did this great social order come to be?" asked Mister Walton.

"It all began," explained Mr. Wyatt, "with the 'Great Utensil War,' which was heartily waged in the columns of the *Brunswick Telegraph* some years ago. There was an editor of that newspaper by the name of Tenney who objected vociferously to the employment of a knife in the task of carrying food from the plate to the mouth."

"I see," said Mister Walton.

Mr. Wyatt was well versed in the history of local quibbling. "I quote," said the man. " *'One might as well use a shovel. Even the necessity of eating rapidly in a railroad restaurant justifies no departure from decorum.'* "

"Mr. Tenney was a man of conviction," Mister Walton suggested.

"A crusader, Mister Walton, I assure you."

"Did he have great influence on local eating habits?" asked Sundry.

"As it happened, he came up against serious conflict."

"It would needs be serious," Mister Walton said wryly.

"The paper was filled with the subject, and the tenor of the writing grew quite hot. No less a personage than Henry Ward Beecher himself weighed in, declaring in a powerful letter to the editor that he always ate pie with a knife. The four-tined fork, which was of recent invention, was brought into the argument, and soon the debate grew in scope to include those who did or did not cut up their food with a fork and those who did or did not adopt the European style of holding both fork and knife throughout the meal."

"I have seen this done," said John Neptune.

"As it happened," continued the man, "there were certain individuals who were so pleased with the uproar that they were not satisfied unless there was a similar uproar on an annual basis."

"I may have some relations in this tale," said Sundry.

"On October fourteenth of the next year—in fact, a year to the day after editor Tenney's initial column—a letter appeared in the *Brunswick Telegraph* that took to task many Brunswickians who raked their leaves in the fall. This writer asserted that they were depriving their natural surroundings of an exemplary cover from the ravages of winter, and he was a little rough with those who did not wait to rake their leaves in the spring.

"A new ruckus was raised, and as soon as the letters to the editor began to abate, one of the first writer's accomplices would send a new missive, on one side or the other of the controversy, in order to keep things stirred up. The success of this enterprise was impressive. The following year, when a letter appeared that championed the Lilliputian attitude toward an egg—"

"That is cracking it open from the small end," ventured Mister Walton.

"Yes," agreed Mr. Wyatt. "And when this subject was raised with as much emotion, there were those in Brunswick who suspected that their collective legs were being pulled."

"Nobody took this bait?" asked Sundry.

"I think one person did. But it seemed too bad to let such an art fade from disuse, and so Brunswick has been the site of great 'Quibbling' once a year, on the anniversary of that first historic column. There is a dinner and a baseball game; and we gather in the town hall and quibble in grand speeches over a subject picked in the aftermath of the previous quibble."

"If you only quibble once a year, then you are to be much admired," said Mister Walton.

"Is the entire city of Brunswick enrolled in the *Great Quibbling Society*, then?" Sundry asked.

"Heavens no!" said Mr. Wyatt. "I am a member of the *Great Quibbling Society*, but there are those who support the *Quibbletory Fellowship* and others who fraternize under the banner of the *Society of Great Quibblers*, among whom there has recently been such a schism that several have gone off to form the *Society for Great Quibblers*."

"I see no end," said a delighted Mister Walton.

"There will someday, no doubt, be as many societies and fellowships devoted to Quibbling as there are Quibblers."

"As it should be," said Sundry, not hiding his admiration.

"I live in Liberty these days," said Mr. Wyatt. "The town, that is, as well as, I hope, the state of being, but I return to my old haunts once a year to put to use my old skills."

"Have you come to quibble, then?" asked Mister Walton.

"Yes, indeed. We quibble on Tuesday night."

"Ah," said Mister Walton. "And what is the subject this year?"

"How high the lawn should be allowed to grow before it is cut. There are several stands one might take."

"And yours?"

"Two inches and three-eighths," stated Mr. Wyatt flatly.

"Perhaps you might contest the seasons someday," suggested Mister Walton. "You and I might care for fall, but others would surely patronize summer, or even spring."

"It would never do," said Mr. Wyatt very seriously.

"It wouldn't?"

"Much too poetic a subject, sir. You will never make a quibbler."

"Well," said Mister Walton, smiling with great satisfaction, "I will not quibble with you."

It was late in the day, and Mister Walton and Sundry decided to stay the night in Brunswick, which was a crossroad for the train system as well as the home of organized quibbling. Mr. Wyatt intimated that quibblers would already be gathering at the Tontine Hotel, and they decided to look for rooms there in hopes of seeing more of these happy disputants.

There was no way to know, of course, that in a later year, the *Great Annual Quibble* (or, as some would have it, the *Annual Great Quibble*; and then again there were those who held to the *Great Annual Quibblation*) would play a strange and momentous part in the history of that other great society, the *Moosepath League!*

John Neptune was interested as well and decided he would join them. "If you would like to follow me after dinner, I will take you to a place that will be much livelier than last night."

"I was hoping," said Sundry, "to hear more about John Poor and Isherwood Tolly."

John Neptune raised an eyebrow. "Henry must have been telling you."

"Yes," said Sundry, "and we had just gotten to the moment when the two men met, but he hadn't gotten round to telling us about your involvement."

"You will hear it in time, I think," said John Neptune.

26. Amos Buys In

WALKING INTO THE CROOKED CAT, Amos Guernsey was still considering how best to lie to Adam Tweed. He had spent the better part of the day and demonstrated a great deal of guile following Horace McQuinn without being seen, putting to use the practices of a sneaky lifetime. Horace was a wily old dodger—make no mistake—but some of his associates were not, and Amos had easily garnered what information was needed from one of these gentlemen after an "accidental" meeting on the street.

What he *didn't* know—what he *knew* he needed to know—was the reason for Adam Tweed's interest in Eustace Pembleton and the little boy known only as Bird. And so he stepped into the Crooked Cat late that afternoon, took direction to the back room from a nod by Percy Beal, and drafted the final touches of a specific lie even as he knocked on the door.

The back room was lit with a single lamp, and the shadowy corners were filled with Adam Tweed's hangers-on and henchmen. Bearded, un-scrubbed faces looked out from the perimeters of light like animal eyes in a darkened wood.

Adam Tweed was standing. He always stood; Amos had never seen the man sit. There was a pewter tankard on the table next to Tweed, and Amos gave it the look of a thirsty man. Tweed was picking at a tooth while he watched the actor without expression. "Where have you been?" he grunted.

Amos did not let the lowness of the venue alter his customary élan but bowed slightly and expressed in his most sonorous tones, "I have been studying the activities and movements of Mr. McQuinn, per your request."

"Where's the boy?" rumbled Tweed, who had a crude way of getting to the point.

"Well, that *is* the interesting thing," said Amos. "Quite unexpectedly, I came into possession of an address—"

"Where's the boy?" asked Tweed again.

Amos cleared his throat, only slightly, and said, "They have taken him out of town . . . as far as I can ascertain."

Tweed said nothing. Amos felt the room was growing warm. There was something about Tweed's stare that went through a man, and it didn't help that Amos was venturing upon the path of untruth.

Adam Tweed could not know this, however, Amos told himself, and he said, "There is a gentleman by the name of Tobias Walton, and his valet (it seems) who endures under the extraordinary sobriquet Sundry Moss; and it seems that they have taken the young boy to Hallowell with them."

"Hallowell!"

Amos again cleared his throat ever so slightly. "That is the name of the municipality to which he has been taken, yes."

"What's in Hallowell?" said Tweed. He was frowning now, unhappy. Amos thought that Tweed had been taken by surprise, but why? What had the man expected? Why *not* Hallowell? *Ah*, thought Amos, *there is some other specific place they expected the boy to be taken!*

"The address," Tweed said abruptly.

Amos was temporarily at a loss; then he said, "Oh, the address, of course!" and produced from his pocket a slip of paper. "Mister Walton and Mr. Moss expect to stay at the Worster House, in Hallowell." He glanced about the room, beaming a sudden smile at the men sitting against the walls and in the corners. "They have left already, so they may be there now."

Tweed thought about this, then went through the door at the rear of the room. As before, Amos could hear Tweed's voice as well as a second tone that he didn't recognize. It was not long before Tweed returned. He tossed Amos a small drawstring bag that jingled when the actor caught it.

"I am greatly appreciative," said the actor.

"Come back if you hear anything else."

"Most indubitably," said Amos. He gave another one of his graceful bows and left the room feeling much lighter for the weight of coins in his pocket.

"Sketchy," said Tweed, and a narrow-faced little man stepped forward. "Tell Percy to give you enough to get you up to Hallowell and watch this Walton and his friend at the Worster."

"What if I see the boy?" wondered Sketchy.

"Take Earnest with you," said Tweed, then growled, "Earnest!" when no one responded to this name.

A large man separated himself from the farthest corner, where he had been dozing. "Yes, boss?"

"Take him," said Tweed to Sketchy.

Back in the main section of the tavern, Amos was already seated before a large tankard, and as Sketchy and Earnest walked past, he very nicely offered to buy them a drink.

27. Off Widgery Wharf

WYCKFORD O'HEARN WAS NOT sure what the driver could see; many of the lamps along Commercial Street had flickered and died in the wind, so that only now and then pools of light beckoned through a halo of rain and glowed on the wet cobblestones. The wheels of the rig drove sheets of water from the small ponds that gathered at the foot of the steeper streets, and the horses' hooves splashed as if they were crossing shallow streams.

Up ahead a storm lamp swung crazily from a sign, and Wyck knew they were nearing the Shipswood Restaurant. Though an oilskin covered most of him as he hunkered on the upper seat and a sou'wester was crammed over his ears, he was wet and miserable. The driver pulled up and reached for his own lantern, the light of which cut a yellow swath through the rain and a broad expanse of wharf. He urged the horses onto the dock, where the clop of their hooves and the rumble of the carriage wheels took on the characteristics of far-off thunder. The carriage did not go far before it was pulled up and the driver vaulted down to open the door.

There was a hesitation as certain passengers jockeyed position so as not to appear eager to be the first out. Indeed, Ephram, Eagleton, and Thump, tense and electrified with their mission, deferred to one another, one *after* the other, their wet hats used as emphasis for their gestures as each insisted his friends precede him. This would not have proved a dilemma under normal circumstances (they had exited carriages before without significant difficulty), but the presence of Mollie Peer and the absence of their chairman attached an element of uncertainty to the protocol of the situation.

Two concerns contributed to this impasse. The first was the desire not to deny a friend the pleasure of assisting Miss Peer. The second, and by no means the least, was a certain lack of boldness to be the one to perform the feat. In the end, Mollie did not refuse help from the carriage; she was simply on the wharf and standing beneath an umbrella before they could untangle themselves from their quandary.

The driver watched the proceedings with curiosity. Horace had gotten out on the other side. Wyck jumped down and reached in for Bird. The rain came down in a persistent rush, rattling the slate roof of a warehouse that loomed behind them and drumming a high pitch upon the wharf.

"Stormy," pronounced Eagleton above the weather as he peered from the carriage. "Continued threatening weather and rain. Easterly gales. Expected clearing tomorrow." Not dressed for the situation, he flinched as he put on his hat and stepped out of the cab and into the wet atmosphere.

"Tide on the ebb," said Thump as he followed, peering up into the dark night and getting a fat raindrop in the eye for his troubles. "High tide at thirty-seven minutes past eight in the A.M." He staggered only slightly as he made the wharf, and Eagleton very solicitously took his friend by the elbow.

"Eighteen minutes before ten o'clock," said Ephram when he reached the surface of the dock. He looked up and down the wharf, vaguely disconcerted by the crouching shapes of crates and wagons covered in black tarpaulins.

Wyck and Mollie exchanged glances over Horace's head. Horace seemed greatly edified by these communications. "I told you they knew what was going on," he reminded them. A man appeared from the near end of the wharf and called to them through the rain.

In a heavy wind, there is something in common between the waterfront and the forest, and it is the speech of wood, which—if predictable in its creaks and groans—is varied enough in tone and interval to seem less like a consequence of natural events than the expression of a vague intelligence. It is no secret that forests are filled with goblins, for even the most experienced woodsman might wake in the dark of night to the wind in the trees and find himself listening uncertainly to the *grumphs* and *tree squeaks.*

At dockside in a high wind, the trees, fashioned into masts and spars and pilings, regain their powers of speech. The ships in harbor, rigged with shrouds and ratlines, boom and shudder like great instruments, and when storm winds rock and shiver the waterfront, these voices gather in a noisy cacophony.

The three-masted schooner *Loala* was anchored off Portland's Widgery Wharf, and from her deck Capt. Francis Amey watched, through the night and through the rain, for signs of the yawl-boat he had sent in; but he was hardly more conscious of the creaks and groans about him than a man is of the pulse that thrums in his ears. On land, contrarily, he would lie awake at night and think the silence noisy.

The captain of the *Loala* had been thought handsome in his youth, though age and weather had taken a pleasant aspect and replaced it with character of a sort; circumstance had underscored an already fractious nature and cultivated in him a disposition that was more pepper than salt. He was a dark man; his expressions were often dark; his dealings sometimes darker still. His favored locutions were picturesque and blasphemous.

The storm was the chief subject of his phraseology as he paced the rainy deck. The wind had not yet risen to the expected level, but he was not fool enough to think it couldn't at any moment. He hoped the gale had blown itself out as it traveled the eastern seaboard but did not trust to it.

He had waited longer than he cared to before he saw carriage lights on the wharf; minutes later, he barely descried figures climbing down to the boat, which was invisible to him in the murk. He hung a storm lamp on the rail, its light only useful as a beacon; it barely shone upon the water below and cast its radiance hardly further than his face as he leaned beside it.

The shadow, rather than the image, of the yawl-boat drifted out of the darkness; he could almost hear it before he could see it—the wash of the oars, a voice over the water. Then came a thump against the side of the coaster, and the voice of Second Mate Forester inviting someone to "go first." In a moment a small boy came over the rail like a monkey, an oilskin some sizes too big for him roped about his middle; he looked up at the captain, wide-eyed and uncertain. Captain Amey had known about the boy, but he grunted at the sight of him anyway—a sound of disapproval.

The next thing to come over the side was a top hat, which looked heavy and wet as it rode the ears and nearly blinded the eyes that followed it. A short, blocky man ensued, and he swung a leg over the rail like a doubtful rider mounting a high-strung horse. He made two or three practice swings with the leg before committing himself to the slowly rocking deck, then stood with bent knees and arms akimbo to facilitate balance.

"Joseph Thump," he said, reaching out to be sure that the little boy was beside him. The man's eyes were wide with uncertainty, even suspicion, and he glanced about their dark surroundings as if sensing conspirators at each elbow. He raised his hat, which had done nothing to keep his head dry, and water ran from the brim of it down his wrist.

Captain Amey was not a man to stand on ceremony. "Francis Amey," he said curtly. "Your bags are aft."

There was a game look to Joseph Thump, for all his apprehension, and he pronounced his pleasure to be aboard Captain Amey's vessel with all the distinction of a newly arrived ambassador.

A second, longer man, similarly dressed and similarly suspicious, attempted to rehearse *his* arrival but was hurried by the sway of the ship and consequently stood upon the deck before he properly knew what he was about. A third fellow came somewhere between his predecessors in height and was dressed to fill out the set. Mr. Thump and the tall man helped him on board. Each man, as he gained the deck, searched first for the boy, then scanned the deck as if a horde of Huns were expected.

"Thank you, Thump. Eagleton," the third man was saying when he noticed Amey and gave the captain a doubtful look.

"Ephram, may I introduce Captain Francis Amey," said Thump. "Captain Amey, Matthew Ephram. Our baggage has arrived. It is *aft*," he added, quite liking the term. Amey looked at Ephram's extended hand before taking it. "Eagleton, Captain Francis Amey," continued Thump. "Christopher Eagleton."

"The bags are *aft*, are they, Captain?" said Eagleton with great energy. The word seemed to tickle him as much as it did Thump.

The three men had looked a little miserable as they appeared over the rail, but one would have thought the sun were shining and the breeze favorable as they introduced themselves to the captain. Amey followed the rules of decorum but looked as if he were standing over a barrel of bait.

First Mate Nelson came over the rail, startling the three passengers. The sailor peered from under his sou'wester and, speaking above the wind and rain, announced that he and Forester were ready to tow the *Loala* out of the harbor.

The captain, glad of the distraction, shouted to the third hand,

O'Brian, who was in the galley, to draw anchor. "Take us out" was all he said to Nelson before the man disappeared over the side again. Then he realized that his passengers were waiting for him with varying attitudes of expectation. "Get under cover," he muttered with a low curse, and strode past them.

The rain persevered—something above a shower and less than a downpour. The deck of the *Loala* was a black shifting plain on which the Moosepathians and Bird were left standing; surrounded by wind and water, they could see the shadows of other vessels and the wink of cabin lights, looking homely and welcoming. No light was afforded them, and despite Thump's fascination with all things nautical, it was the child who bore the practical knowledge of a ship's scheme. Bird realized that his three guardians were as apt to fall overboard as find the afterhouse, and so he pointed in the appropriate direction.

"Yes?" said Thump, leaning close.

Bird timidly said, "The aft'house."

"Ah!" said Eagleton. "The afterhouse!"

"I believe the lad wants to lead us there," said Thump very quietly.

"Bravo!" said Ephram in a confidential tone.

"Very good, lad," whispered Thump. He patted the boy's shoulder, then led the three of them as they crept after Bird to drier quarters.

It hadn't been any uncertainty in Bird's eyes that pierced Wyckford O'Hearn, it had been the absolute trust. Wyck had explained their plan to the little boy several times before it dawned upon the ballplayer that he was trying to convince himself. It was clear that Bird had not liked the idea, but he had accepted it, the way he had probably accepted many unpleasant things in his small life.

It helped (Wyckford as much as Bird) that the little boy liked the members of the Moosepath League. They were very concerned about him when they heard his tale, and if they looked at him a little curiously, it was with a degree of goodwill, rather than suspicion, toward something with which they were previously unfamiliar.

For half an hour, Wyckford waited in the rain, wondering if he were trying the patience of Horace McQuinn and Mollie Peer. The old man and the young woman seemed willing to stay, however.

After the backward splash of the rising anchor, they saw, or perhaps only sensed, the yawl-boat coming around the bow of the schooner and taking the slack from the towropes. Then the larger vessel moved upon the waters of the harbor, occluding the cabin light of another vessel as it slid past, and disappeared behind the unladen *drogher* creaking beside the wharf. A bright anchor light, further out in the harbor, caught the silhouette of the *Loala* and the yawl-boat towing her out to sea, but then the rain strengthened, and there was little hope of seeing anything but more weather and more night.

Wyckford heard a sound from Mollie, who stood beside him, and he realized that she had shivered. "We better get in," he said.

There was a flash of light as Horace struck a match; holding his pipe upside down in his teeth, he cupped the flame and put fire to the bowl. An island of radiance captured the three of them for a moment, then there was only the resultant glow of the pipe and the ghostly plume of smoke rising briefly in the rain. "I'd say they were safely off," said Horace.

"I hope safe, in this weather," said Wyck.

"They're not going far. Old Amey is a rum one, no doubt—as hard a pill as ever ran his easting down—but he's able. Brought that old bucket up from Portsmouth by himself just so's he wouldn't have to hire on a second crew."

Wyck thought the captain sounded like a man who would take chances, but said nothing. "Say a prayer," Wyck's mother would have told him. "Say a prayer, let it go. Only God is meant to know."

When I get that boy back, he thought, *I'm taking him to the farm and Ma can make him one of her butter cakes.*

Horace lost the fire in his pipe and tried another match. Wyck turned to Mollie and was startled to find her watching him. She, in turn, was *not* startled, and did not look away.

Three things surprised Ephram, Eagleton, and Thump when the door to the afterhouse was opened. The first was the size of the chamber; the *Loala*'s quarters had been built flush with the rails, adding space on three sides. The second was the cheeriness of the room; it was brightly lit, warm and dry, in a word, *cozy*, with a little potbellied stove radiating cheerily and snug berths built into the walls.

The third element of discovery was a tall, narrow fellow with sparse, straw-colored hair who was seated among a pile of baggage and sipping from a steaming cup. He had a pleasant look on his gaunt face, his eyebrows raised in expectation, his smile welcoming. "Good evening, sirs!" he said in a voice of surprisingly stentorian depth. "Come in, come in!

> *"Come in from the night*
> *Come in from the storm*
> *To the hearth that is bright*
> *And the heart that is warm!*

"Barthelmass to the wayward travelers," informed the fellow, "from *The Aged Tavern*, act the first, scene the third!" He stood, crossed one foot before the other, and performed a stately bow.

The boat rocked on the harbor surface. The man teetered with it slightly. Ephram, Eagleton, and Thump leaned together just outside the door and observed this performance, thereby forming a human canopy over Bird, who also paused before descending the bulkhead stairs. Thump made a noise of recognition.

The man was not to be daunted by hesitation, but launched into another encomium for the comforts within.

> *"What better place to meet new friends,*
> *Than that small room where Comfort tends*
> *The benches where we'll seat ourselves,*
> *And take the bottles from their shelves?*
>
> *"What golden keep or castle high*
> *Can ever hope to draw the sigh*
> *From worn and weary traveling men*
> *That's conjured by this simple den?*

"The old scholar to the wounded foot soldier, from *Many Were the Days*, act the second, scene the fifth."

"Good heavens!" said Thump. "It's the man on the street! Marvelous!" he declared. Thump allowed Bird to enter the *simple den*, then clambered down himself and extended his hand. "Joseph Thump," he said with great enthusiasm. "We met only this afternoon! We were talking about Mr. McQuinn!"

"Goodness sakes alive!" said the fellow. "How extraordinary to see you again! Amos Guernsey."

"Ephram, Eagleton," continued Thump. "You will recall that I met a gentleman today and how pleased we were to have the mutual acquaintance of Mr. McQuinn. Indeed, I was telling him about the club *and* our chairman."

Ephram and Eagleton also descended the stairs and introduced themselves. The Moosepathians were thoroughly drenched—"to the bone" is the phrase, though "to the skin" was more the case and certainly deep enough.

"Come in, come in!" continued Amos Guernsey, as if he were the genial host and they were not yet standing with him in dry quarters.

> "... whereso'er you are,
> That bide the pelting of this pitiless storm,
> How shall your houseless heads and unfed sides,
> Your looped and windowed raggedness, defend you
> From seasons such as these?"

The members of the club waited for the quote to be identified, but the tall man seemed to think it unnecessary. "Is that your own, then?" Eagleton inquired. He was reaching in his coat pocket for a notebook, with the purpose of writing it down before he forgot it.

"My own?" said Amos. He was a little perplexed at first, but soon his beaming smile had returned. "Why, yes, actually!" he declared. "So very perceptive of you to ... perceive that."

Eagleton looked abashed and waved the praise away. The tip of his tongue appeared upon his lower lip, then he said to himself, " '—whereso'er you are ...,' " and proceeded to write.

Thump couldn't get over the coincidence of seeing Amos again.

"We hadn't expected anyone else to be traveling with us," said Ephram.

"Ah, well," said Amos. "Last-minute plans. Life of the stage."

"You are an actor," said Ephram. This was something Thump had not ascertained.

"I have that pleasure," said Amos, "to tread the boards and parlay playwright's wit to theater air. In tragic *dungeon* or comic flirt, my life is signifying other lives for three hours and twenty-five cents before the cunning public."

The drenched men applauded (Eagleton nearly dropped his pencil and notebook), and Thump declared, "That is yours, surely!"

"Thank you, thank you. But where are you gentlemen bound?"

"Not very far," said Ephram. Slowly, his wet condition and a subtle change in the movement of the boat were becoming apparent to him. "To Cape Elizabeth."

"My very destination!" shouted the gaunt fellow.

"Marvelous!" said Eagleton. He was working on Amos's most recent words, scribbling furiously.

"To be very honest with you, sir," said Thump, "ours is a serious calling, and we will not be sorry to have a capable man such as yourself along the way."

"And who is this?" asked Amos. He seemed to notice Bird for the first time, though the boy, still wrapped in his oversized oilskin, had caught the actor's glance more than once.

"This is Bird," informed Ephram.

"Bird!" said Amos. Something about the man's quick grasp of his name raised the little boy's eyebrows.

"He is our charge," added Ephram, glancing to be sure the bulkheads were without ears. He leaned close to Amos. "There are forces at work—diabolical parties that would stop at very little to get their hands on this child."

"Dear me!" said the actor, a hand to his breast.

Ephram may have unsettled himself with this thought. (Certainly his fellow Moosepathians appeared a little troubled.) "Diabolical," said Ephram again.

"Indeed?" said Amos. "Well, we shall keep a watchful eye." He patted Bird's head, then gave a brave wink and brushed his damp hand upon a sleeve.

To a landsman, the task would have seemed out of all proportion for a yawl-boat and two oarsmen, but the tide and the chop were with Forester and Nelson; the towline remained taut, and the *Loala* passed from the harbor like a thief in the night, a specter among a roomful of sleepers. The hulls and rigs of larger vessels fell behind as silently as dark clouds, their anchor lights and cabin lamps like bleary eyes through the blowing rain.

28. Merry Meeting

"DID YOU KNOW JOHN POOR?" asked Sundry of John Neptune.

"Not as well as Isherwood knew him," said the old man.

"I met him once," said Mister Walton, and when Sundry looked interested, he described a powerful man with grim, dark eyebrows and a wide-set mouth that contradicted the light of humor in his eyes. "He was a little jowly by the time I met him," said Mister Walton, "but his hair was without a thread of gray, and the ladies were quite fond, I have been told, of his curls. He moved like a bear."

"I am not hearing much in the way of quibbling," said John Neptune.

There did seem to be a disappointing lack of quibbles among those gathered to dine at Brunswick's Tontine Hotel. Despite this shortage of argumentation there was much in the city to interest them. The day had grown stormy, and in the twilight, the elms across Brunswick's broad Main Street could be seen, from the dining room of the hotel, shifting and shivering. Mister Walton wished they could tour the local environs, but a hard rain had already begun to fall.

John Neptune had promised them a lively evening, however, and he suggested they put on their rain gear. When the Indian retrieved Eugene from a boy who had been paid to watch the raccoon, he led Mister Walton and Sundry out into the storm and toward the river, where the houses of mill workers and tradesmen lined the way in neat clusters and where the bright lights of an old tavern beckoned. The great man-made falls were behind them, and beneath their roar (and that of the gathering wind and rain) could be sensed the rush of water against the shore, the ripple of back currents and eddies, as the river reasserted its natural pace.

The sound of voices raised in song leaked from the old building, so that it thrummed like a beehive. Smoke from its chimney barely lifted above the roof in the sheets of rain, and figures could be seen through its streaking windows as they approached.

The state of Maine had officially prohibited the selling and consuming of spirituous liquors forty-five years before, and most of the old taverns had been forced to close down or modify their stocks as a result. Some operated counter to the law, of course, and not all of them in great secrecy, but they were expected to be in the less reputable sections of the larger cities and towns or in less accessible places along the coast or the forested interior.

Mister Walton was surprised to see an old alehouse so bright and crowded, and the closer they drew to the building, the more impressed he was with its obvious age. With its broad front and peculiar little gables, it had the look of that era when the architecture of the Old World haunted the practical necessities of the New; and when they came to its door of oak and iron, he looked up at the sign that swayed in the weather above them and was delighted.

Two men were represented there, greeting one another, articulated in a primitive, if pleasing, manner, like the flat caricatures in a child's drawing. One represented an Indian, with his buckskins and feathered head-dress, the other a colonial European in tricorner hat, old-fashioned coat, and breeches; they were shaking hands, and in ornate script above them was the single word *Merrymeeting*.

The song that shivered the rafters had reached its final stanza, and when John Neptune opened the door, the volume of male voices rose, the light from within spilled into the yard, and the smells of smoke and food and the headier scent of things stronger than cider greeted them with almost alarming friendliness. Sundry's Yankee caution drew him up before he crossed the threshold into the dry interior. Mister Walton stopped and laughed aloud. John Neptune did not hesitate, but preceded them into the brightly lit tavern, with Eugene perched on one shoulder.

> "So, all you fine fellows come join in the round;
> The tune is quite merry, the words are profound—
> With a mollie toddle hoodle and a merrie tarry hay,
> As the evening drops her cloak about another merry day!"

A cheer went up, and the men entering the tavern could not say if it was for the song so well sung or for themselves so well met.

Hands were raised, pipes puffed, and laughter greeted them. Mister Walton and Sundry marveled at the noise and commotion. The room was large and plain, held up by broad beams and posts as large as ancient trees. The chairs and tables were unadorned and worn smooth with time and use. There was a massive fireplace at either end of the room, and each of these was blazing against the autumn chill. Mister Walton would not have been surprised to see the crowd of men dressed like those on the sign without, with buckled shoes and powdered wigs or buckskins and feathers; but as it was, they were regular in their attire.

Several people, including three women, one matronly and two of more youthful appearance, were serving the guests, and a happy fellow with a crafty smile received the newcomers. "Come in, John. Come in, my friends," he called from the other side of the room. "Warm yourselves! Dry yourselves!" He hurried through the crowd to greet them.

"A song or a story! A song or a story!" came a general cry.

The tavern keeper made himself heard above the shouts and laughter. "Please, join us," he said. Mister Walton was about to suggest that there was no room to comply with this invitation when the crowd parted and three chairs and a table appeared in its midst. Some shook their hands as they passed; others nodded or shook the end of a pipe. Several called out John Neptune's name, and everyone laughed to see the beady-eyed raccoon blinking from behind the old Indian's head.

"What will be your pleasure?" asked the proprietor.

"A glass of Moxie, please," said old John Neptune, "and a bowl of milk for my friend."

"Yes, yes. And for you, gentlemen?" There was perhaps a hint of the conspirator about the man.

Mister Walton expressed an agreeable bemusement. It was not difficult to imagine that the tall mugs and pewter tankards on the tables and in the fists about him sloshed with ale and rum. He was a well-traveled man, and though of law-abiding disposition, he was not so shocked by this sort of prohibited indulgence. But if he could look with forbearance, and even good humor, upon the indiscretion of others, he was still at heart a law-abiding man.

"A mug of hot apple cider would be of great use to me," he decided.

"And for me," said Sundry. He had been observing the scene with more curiosity than complete understanding.

"How have you come to Brunswick, Mister Walton?" asked a man when the three newcomers had been identified.

"My young friend and I have come from Portland, by way of Bath. We are on our way to Hallowell so that I may fulfill a certain invitation, and having a day before my presence is required, we took the advice of Mr. Neptune and adopted his plans for the evening."

"Ah!" said a fellow some tables off. "We need a story from this one."

There was general consensus to this, and the man who questioned Mister Walton explained. "It is the custom, here at the sign of the *Merry-meeting*, to justify one's place with a tale or a song. Our friend John Neptune has long since joined our ranks with a tale, but now it is your turn."

"A tale is an amiable form of toll," said Mister Walton. He winked to Sundry, who frowned a little, thinking, perhaps, that it was impertinent to suggest that Mister Walton needed to justify himself to anyone. "I will tell you something that happened to me only last July, and it is very solemn."

Of course, it was anything but solemn, and the fact that he told it as if it were made it less solemn still. From his first sentences the crowd leaned forward, and rapt expressions focused upon him. The story is familiar to Moosepathians, and it is only unfortunate that Mister Walton's performance of it was not more carefully recorded.

It was the tale of how he had been tricked into delivering a wagonload of illegal rum to its owner, which he made hilarious by celebrating his own gullibility and reveling in the absurdity of attempting to control a runaway horse when his hat was crammed over his eyes.

More than one member of the audience seemed to recognize the identity of the trickster in this narrative, and once Mister Walton heard the name of Horace McQuinn being whispered. There was applause when he ended his tale by wetting his whistle. John Neptune nodded his approval. The raccoon was entertaining those at nearby tables by accepting little tidbits from them. The hot cider was rich and sweet, with a slight hint of charred wood. It had been heated in the old manner, by plunging a red-hot poker into the pitcher.

"More cider for the man," said someone. "He's talked himself dry."

Sundry also asked for his tankard to be replenished, and he smiled at the young woman who came to their table. Her brown hair was done up behind, and the high laced collar of her blouse accentuated the beautiful complexion of her cheek. She was of a healthy disposition and had not allowed the fashion of the time to constrict a waist that was not by nature waspish; but since everything about her was in strict relation, she was the picture of that phrase "pleasingly plump." She had a spray of light freckles across her small nose and gray-blue eyes, and she smiled back at Sundry from beneath long lashes.

But when she went to pour the steaming concoction of cider and spices into his tankard, there proved to be only a dollop left, and she let out a heartfelt sigh of apology.

"Some of us get what we deserve, I suppose," said Sundry philosophically.

"I don't imagine you're as bad as that," she said, and the smile returned to her face. "I'll get you some more," she added, and the glance she gave him might have indicated that she planned to get him something else entirely.

Now Sundry was not bad at all, in relative terms, and he reddened appropriately, though he was made bold to submit his toll next.

"What have you to offer, young man?" asked an elderly fellow whose eyes swam a bit from his own version of cider.

"I believe I might sing a song if I could have some accompaniment."

It was not a daring request in this company, and though several volunteered their friends or raised their own hands, Sundry gave the nod to the elderly fellow himself, who produced a fiddle and bow from a box that the young man had spied beneath his seat. "What is your pleasure?" asked the old fellow.

"Do you know *'The Jolly Tinker'*?" asked the young man.

"I'd throw out my fiddle if I didn't."

"It's the same tune," explained Sundry, "but a different song."

"That's fine now. Where do you sing?"

Sundry gave him a note, and the fellow plucked and tuned for a while. When the moment arrived, the crowd grew quiet, Sundry stood and, after a verse from the fiddler, sang out in a very presentable baritone:

> *"What would you have me do, my dear,*
> *What would you have me say;*
> *For what I truly want to hear*
> *Is the date of our wedding day.*
> *Don't you know I do,*
> *Oh, indeed, I do.*
> *Shake the reins to race my lassie.*
> *Yes, you know I do.*
>
> *"I'd ask of you a needle, love,*
> *That fell from out the sky;*

That would never know a stitch of cloth,
Or have a single eye.
Don't you know I would,
Oh, indeed, I would.
Shake the reins to race my lassie.
Yes, you know I would.

"So I thought about her words by night,
And my thinking must have been good,
For I caught the needle she asked of me
From a pine tree in the wood.
Don't you know I did . . .

"I slipped my arm about her waist,
So soft and wonderfully fine,
And in my youth and in my haste
I asked her next design.
Don't you know I asked . . .

"I want a single dollar, sweet,
Of stuff that cannot bend,
That's coined without a country's seal
And no man ever can spend.
Don't you know I do . . .

"So I thought about her words by night,
And my thinking must have been grand,
For I found the dollar she asked of me
At the seashore, made of sand.
Don't you know I did . . .

"I looked into her blue-gray eyes;
I swear I must have been hexed,
For I wasn't cautious, shrewd, or wise.
'What do you want of me next?'
Don't you know I asked . . .

"I want a precious seal, my heart,
Though its mark will never tarry,
But must repeatedly be pressed.
Find it and we shall marry!
Don't you know I do . . .

"I didn't wait to think by night,
For my thinking then was fine.

I hugged my dear with all my might
And sealed her lips with mine!
Don't you know I did,
Oh, indeed, I did.
Shake the reins to race my laddie.
Yes, you know I did."

A shout of approval from everyone proved that Sundry had paid his toll successfully. "You must write that down for me," said John Neptune. "A riddle concerning a needle is something I myself have encountered, though I answered it differently."

"I would be happy to," said Sundry. "Perhaps you would tell me about *your* riddle."

"You will hear it, I think," said John Neptune.

"Have you ever known a girl with blue-gray eyes?" wondered the fiddler. He was retuning his instrument. Someone had taken a tin whistle from his pocket and was tootling with it.

"I have met a very pretty woman of that description," said Sundry, speaking so that he could be heard above the music and talk. He glanced around the room and found the young woman with the blue-gray eyes laughing.

She was watching him, as was everyone else, and she did not look away when their eyes met but gave him a knowing, even admonishing, smile. She had never heard the song before (it was, in fact, of Sundry's own invention), but she was quick to guess that the reference to the color of the sweetheart's eyes had not been a coincidence. Sundry's brave display was perhaps *too* successful, and he blushed from ear to ear.

"Wonderful!" Mister Walton was saying. "Wonderful!" He patted Sundry's shoulder. In a tone expertly directed to his young friend's ear, he said, "It is all so jolly, like an ancient carol or an old painting. I feel as if we were visiting our great-grandfathers."

It is a sad truth that we often attribute great jollity to times preceding our own, but anyone who has read Henry James from the nineteenth century and Henry Fielding from the eighteenth might agree that, in this case, Mister Walton's feelings were justified. There was a very un-Victorian sense of ribaldry about the place, and even the women carried out their duties with a certain relish, brushing close to a man's leg while darting him a warning glance or shaking a fist at another with a sly smile. Sundry decided that it was the nature of their employment, working and weaving among so many men, that lent them such an air of practical ease; and he wasn't sure that he disliked it so very much.

There was a flash of something serious in his friend's eye, how-ever, and he said to Mister Walton, "You are thinking of Henry Echo."

The portly fellow nodded. "I can't help but wonder how he spends tonight."

"He should be with us," said Sundry. His throat felt dry, and he drained his second tankard of hot cider. He looked across the room again and saw that the brown-haired woman was gone; the other young woman (her sister, as it turned out) came up with a smile and offered to fill his tankard again. "I'm afraid I need to make some room first," he said with a hand on his stomach.

The second woman had darker hair and eyes than her sister, and she was slim where the other was not, but just as pretty. "Towards the back," she said. "Through the door and the long hall and out the door beyond there's a path."

Sundry nodded, indicated that he would have more cider, and rose to follow her directions. He weaved through the tables and the crowd and found an old, narrow door, beyond which was an old, narrow hall and the young woman with the blue-gray eyes walking toward him.

"Good evening," said Sundry. She smiled that knowing smile again. They passed very close to one another, and she was amused by his nervousness. He glanced back when he came to the outside door and saw her swishing saucily, head turned to smile back at him. He was afraid, for a moment, that she would collide with the inside door, but she caught it with her hand without even looking.

Sundry, however, *did* run into the outside door. There was a double clunk as it bounced from his shoulder, then struck the side of his head as he turned with a start. The other door had already swung shut with a bang.

Rain greeted him, and wind, but it was a welcome balm after the heat and press of the tavern. He rubbed the sore spot at the corner of his skull and hurried along the path to the outbuilding. Upon his return, he paused just inside the back door and shook the dampness from his sleeves. He wondered if he had made a fool of himself, but resigning himself to this possibility, he stepped inside the long, narrow hall.

He was partway back to the main room when the inside door came open and the "healthy" young woman also entered the hall, two empty tankards gripped in one hand. This time she hardly glanced Sundry's way, but bustled forward, very businesslike. But when she was passing him, the both of them turned sideways to make room for one another, she dropped the tankards, threw her arms around his neck so that she could pull herself up, and kissed him very fully and very forcefully upon the lips.

Sundry had hardly time to respond before she let go of his neck, dropped to her feet, picked the fallen tankards from the floor, and hurried businesslike through the outside door.

"Sometimes," she chimed sweetly, "you get what you deserve."

He could hear her laughter as the door shut behind her.

29. Cliff Cottage

LATE IN THE EVENING ON THE ELEVENTH OF OCTOBER, Eagleton wrote: "A *night of such wild adventure and intrigue I have never known!*" and safe to say, it was.

As the wind rose, the quarters in the aft'house of the *Loala* grew increasingly talkative, but what might have been music to the ears of an old salt was so much untranslatable din to Ephram, Eagleton, and Thump. There was the sound of the harbor water and the creak of the ship and the strum of the towline playing through the hull like the lowest string of a bass violin. They were ghostly, unexplained sounds, and even Amos exhibited signs of worry as conversation waned and they found themselves listening to the storm.

Only Bird was unperturbed; he climbed into a berth and pulled a blanket over him. The journey took one hour and seventeen minutes, according to Ephram's watches. Thump expected the tide to shift in three hours and twelve minutes; Eagleton, that the weather would clear by sunrise. The first two or three times that these data were announced, Amos had said, "I beg your pardon?" but after that the actor simply smiled.

The movements of the boat grew more alarming as they crossed open water and the announcements regarding time, tide, and weather came at shorter intervals. Bird snored softly.

Then the motion of the ship slowed; some axis of pitch or sway stiffened as they altered their relative position with a current or the tide or the wind. Once the ship was relatively still, the captain came barging into the aft'house to announce that they had reached the agreed-upon dock. Bags and passengers were hurried onto the deck. Thump stirred the little boy with a gentle shake, and soon they were all wading through the rain and squinting at a tiny pier and up a precipitous staircase that rose to the top of a dark bluff. Lights blinked through the storm from atop the cliff, and the members of the club gaped up into the dark and all about them in hopes of seeing shelter that was more easily reached.

Nelson, Forester, and O'Brian were already charging up the staircase, loaded down with bags, and the captain shouted out the necessity for the others to follow suit, and quickly. "You've paid for me to see you safely up top," he growled. "Well, head up and wave down at me when you get there."

In another moment, the sailors had returned, half-running, half-sliding down the stairs as nimbly as they would have negotiated the ratlines of a square-rigger. "Keep a tight hold, now," Nelson warned the boy, but Bird was up the steps like a squirrel.

The surface of the dock was treacherous with rain, and the wind pulled at the men as they climbed, half on their hands and knees, up the stairs. Ephram suggested that they tuck their hats beneath their coats to keep from losing them, and it is sure that they would have done so if they hadn't.

Amos was the first to reach the top, after the little boy, and he stumbled away from the edge of the bluff. Bird lay down so that he could see how the others were progressing, then looked over his shoulder and saw the shadow of the actor standing over him. Thump's face rose out of the murk, and Bird reached out as if to keep the man from falling.

"Thank you," said Thump, quite touched. For a moment he considered offering the boy a membership. Then, like the anchor man in a tug-of-war, he kneeled his stocky frame at the edge of the cliff and helped his friends.

"It's very exhilarating!" said Ephram in a tone of voice he might have employed had he been falling instead of climbing.

"Quickly, gentlemen!" said Amos. "We must get inside!"

From the top of the bluff they saw the sprawling form of Cliff Cottage for the first time and could even make out the first few letters of the establishment's name above the front porch. Lights burned in the foyer, and they thought they had never seen anything so congenial. From the southeast they heard the bell at Portland Head, and when their eyes followed their ears, they could see a ray of light dimly through the rain.

"Oh!" said Eagleton. "We are supposed to wave down at the captain!"

"Good heavens, you're right!" shouted Ephram over the wind. Amos gaped as the three friends inched themselves back to the edge of the cliff and waved down into the blackness.

"Is he there?" wondered Thump.

"I think he's gone," said Ephram.

"He didn't wait for us to wave," said Eagleton.

"Matters very friendly at Cliff Cottage," Eagleton wrote later that night. *"Thump's wallet went missing."*

"My wallet has gone missing," said Thump. They arrived at the lobby of Cliff Cottage, their clothes soaked, their bags and trunks gathering dark puddles about them. It was late in the evening to be checking in lodgers, but it was also late in the year, and Mr. Bailey was pleased to see these well-dressed, if wet, gentlemen at his desk when he answered the bell.

"What's that you say, Thump?" asked Ephram.

"My wallet," said Thump, and he ran his hands in and out of various pockets as he spoke. "My wallet is gone."

"Dear me," said Eagleton. "His wallet is gone," he said to the manager. A small sum of earnest money had been requested of them, and Mr. Bailey was glad of it now.

Thump was wandering among the bags, casting about the floor. He looked up. "Good heavens! If I lost it outside, it will have blown away."

"Or on the stairs, Thump," said Eagleton.

It was embarrassing, though of course his friends were ready to see him any amount, but Amos stepped forward and announced that he was *flush*.

"Perhaps your collar is too tight," suggested Eagleton considerately.

Amos declared, " '*If I had but a guinea, you would have ten shillings; but as my pockets reek with coin, you shall come away with no more than you can eat and no fewer beds than you can occupy.*' " The actor bowed. "The generous stranger to the unfortunate traveler, act one, scene five, of *At His Best*."

The three companions were very pleased with the sentiment and felt they had gotten something for nothing simply by hearing Amos's brief performance. Amos's expression changed quickly, though, when he reached into his coat pocket. "What's this?" he said, and tried a second pocket. "I don't understand." He shifted slightly, turning sideways to Ephram, Eagleton, and Thump, and thereby revealed Bird, who had been standing behind the actor.

Bird was holding a leather purse and several loose bills in his hands like a communal cup. Amos saw what the boy had and was about to reach for it when Thump gave a delighted shout.

"My wallet!" he pronounced. "My good boy, however did you find it?"

"In his coat," said Bird, looking at Amos. It was the longest phrase they had heard him utter.

"How in the world!" wondered Ephram.

"What a coincidence!" said Eagleton.

Amos was still foraging through his pockets, of which there were many, as if he couldn't believe what had happened. "I don't understand," he kept saying. He laughed nervously and flinched when Thump reached out.

"My good fellow!" Thump was saying as he shook the actor's hand. "How can I thank you enough!"

"Oh, well," said Amos, not sure of what was happening.

"Teasing our friend, were you?" said Ephram with a smile.

"Teasing?"

"When did you find it?" asked Eagleton.

"Find it? Outside, actually. You dropped it coming off the stairs," he said to Thump. He demonstrated his own quick action. "I snatched it up. Wasn't even sure what it was in the dark."

"You must have remarkable night vision," said Ephram, and he leaned forward to peer into Amos's eyes.

"When the lights go out, you must find your way offstage," Amos said, laughing.

"Hiding the boy behind you with the wallet," said Thump. "I was a little nervous for a moment."

Bird frowned at Thump, as if trying to understand something that required intense concentration. "It was in his coat," he said again. Thump patted the boy's head warmly.

"All's well that ends well," said Eagleton.

"Eagleton!" said Ephram. "I believe that's Shakespeare!" and for some reason this made the three friends laugh heartily. "Quoting Shakespeare with an actor in the room!" said Ephram. "Very brave!"

"I beg your pardon, gentlemen," said Amos, "but I feel I am in a very mortifying position." When he had their complete and serious attention, he said, "Having declared myself well-to-do, I am now forced to announce that *my* wallet is missing."

"Oh, dear," said Eagleton.

"Though you rescued mine," said Thump, "you miss your own." He looked distressed. "But you shall not want, my friend! Sir," he said to the manager, "anything this man needs shall be on my bill."

"Bravo, Thump," said Eagleton. He was very moved.

The manager's eyebrows were raised, and his mouth was open; he had to make a sort of mental inventory of his facial parts before he regained control of them. The eyebrows fell; the mouth closed. "You are sure," he said.

"Why, yes!" said Thump. "Most certainly!"

Ephram patted his friend on the shoulder. Amos put up some objections to this solution, but in the end Thump took care of the bill after the actor was assured that he would be allowed to pay Thump back.

Eagleton wrote:

> *Cliff Cottage is sprawling with halls and rooms. One can imagine*
> *these spaces filled with light and laughter at the height of the season,*
> *but tonight, with the storm rattling the shutters and the dining room*
> *echoing emptily as we passed through it, I had the sense of loneliness*
> *and disuse.*

In summer, certain travelers could not be blamed if they were disappointed by their first sight of Cliff Cottage, when white dresses and striped suits populated its lawns and sails filled the harbor below. Cliff Cottage was bound to disappoint the romantic in search of some crumbling Gothic lodging or stone house upon a barren promontory. It did not loom, it was not melancholy, it hardly pondered in the light of the summer sun or the gentle breath of a summer's night.

In fall, when the summer guests were gone, when the trees surrounding the cottage (and *cottage* had a much different meaning a hundred years ago) turned to red and gold or stood skeletally against the sky, when the pleasure boats left the harbor and the chairs and bureaus in empty rooms were covered in sheets—then Cliff Cottage might take on some aspect of the fanciful image its name suggested.

The manager lit an extra lantern in honor of his new guests and led them upstairs, where rooms were readied for them. Amos suggested that Bird be billeted with him, since he was the one in debt for his room and board, but the Moosepathians cited the responsibility that had been given them and, thanking Amos for his thoughtfulness, decided that Thump and the boy would share quarters. The manager ordered a cot for the boy.

Not much had been revealed to the members of the Moosepath League concerning Bird's situation. Horace approached Ephram first with vague intimations of intrigue and foul doings. Very impressed, Ephram invoked the chairman but was reminded by Horace that Mister Walton and his aide-de-camp were out of town. Together they went to Eagleton's, and with Eagleton they went to Thump's. Then they each went (or stayed) home to pack.

Horace assured them that the safety of this child was in their hands, that they alone could be entrusted with guiding the boy from the clutches of sinister forces bent on using him for their own nefarious schemes. (These were Eagleton's words; Horace's manner of styling the boy's predicament was no less colorful and not immediately comprehended by his audience.)

The affair sounded to Eagleton very much like the one in a book he had read, *Mrs. Ludley's Luck,* by Reginald Obinwald, and Thump showed so much interest when the plot of this story was sketched that Eagleton very kindly offered to lend it to him.

But it was the mention of Mollie Peer that sealed the involvement of the Moosepath League. They recognized the name immediately from Mister Walton's description three nights before. Children were to be considered, of course, but they were a little vague to Ephram, Eagleton, and Thump. (Their chairman was fond of children.) Service to a young woman of Miss Peer's merit was something they understood very well.

Some sleep fitfully through a night of wind and rain. Ephram dreamed that night of the *Loala* endlessly sailing over stormy seas. Eagleton stayed up in his room for an hour or so, writing in his dampened journal. (The ink ran in this passage, and the words are difficult to read.)

Thump, as soon as he was in dry nightclothes, curled up in his warm bed. (The manager had provided a heated soapstone for everyone.) He was a little too weary to start the book that Eagleton had lent him, but he hesitated before turning out the light on his bedstand. It seemed to him, as he lay there, that he had been remiss.

Climbing from his bed and shivering in his bare feet, Thump crossed the floor. Bird had the moose badge pinned to his pillow. He looked up at Thump with large, round eyes; the man's beard looked particularly impressive hanging over the front of his white nightshirt. Thump peered at the lad as if something about him would suggest what needed doing. He thought back on his own childhood, enumerating the events that customarily led to bedtime. He cleared his throat. "Are you comfortable?"

The question engendered a look of wonder on Bird's face. He nodded.

Sometimes Thump felt thirsty before he went to bed. "Are you thirsty?"

Bird shook his head.

"I see," said Thump. "Very good." He started to walk away but turned back. He had the indistinct memory of someone listening to his prayers when he was young. "Have you said your prayers?" he wondered softly.

Bird did not respond to this.

A thought occurred to Thump. "Do you know your prayers?" he asked.

The little boy shook his head again.

For some reason this seemed very sad to Thump. He wasn't sure what to say. He considered instructing the little fellow, but perhaps the child was not an Episcopalian; there was no knowing what sort of prayers he was supposed to say. His own childhood was returning to him in small bits, and he remembered *tucking in*. Leaning over, he made an attempt to snug the blankets around the little boy, saying, "I'll say them for you."

And once he was back in bed, Thump curled up with his hands folded beneath his pillow and whispered his own prayers twice.

from the *Eastern Argus*
October 11, 1896

A STRANGE CASE

**A Schooner Mysteriously Disappears
in the Night.**

**Where Are Capt. Amey and
the Crew of the *Loala*?**

*A Diligent Search Fails to Reveal
Any Traces of Them.*

One of the most mysterious cases that have ever occurred in this vicinity was the general subject of conversation among the local shipping men late yesterday afternoon.

Occasionally, a man drops out of sight as completely as though the earth had swallowed him, but when a captain, crew, and vessel vanish in the night and a diligent search fails to discover any trace of them, it is little wonder that people begin to look mystified and form all sorts of conjectures as to what may have happened.

One day last week the coasting schooner *Loala* came creeping into the harbor. Nothing special was thought about the matter until it was learned that Captain Amey, who was in charge of her, had sailed the vessel here from Portsmouth, N.H., without any assistance whatever.

It seems that Captain Amey's men deserted him at that port, and as the captain said to a friend who inquired about the matter, he would be d——d if he was going to ship two crews and he consequently took his chances on sailing the vessel to Portland alone and as there is a providence said to watch over two very large classes in society, he arrived in safety, as previously stated.

Captain Amey secured a crew here and also obtained a charter through J. H. Blake to carry a cargo of grain for a Portland firm to Bangor, where he resides.

The captain at once had his schooner towed over to the elevator wharf and awaited his turn for the cargo. His turn would have arrived yesterday morning, but when the time came, the *Loala* was missing, and so were Captain Amey and his men.

The whole outfit had vanished during the night, and not the slightest clue was left to indicate where it had gone. At first it was supposed that during the gale which came up late Saturday night the vessel had broken away from her moorings and had drifted onto the flats. It did not take long to prove this supposition was false, and then a general search for the missing craft commenced.

Every wharf was visited, and the harbor was swept time and again with a spyglass, but all in vain. At nightfall the searching party was compelled to admit that the case utterly baffled them and they had not the slightest idea as to where Captain Amey had gone.

It does not seem at all likely that he would start for his home in Bangor without a cargo when there was one waiting for him to take to that port and nobody can imagine where else he could have gone.

If the vessel broke away from her moorings and the captain was obliged to run her down among the islands, all hands will probably turn up safe and sound, but if Captain Amey ran outside Saturday night and was caught in the fierce gale, there is very slight prospects that either he or his crew will ever be heard from again.

Book Four

OCTOBER 11, 1896

30. Fond Farewells

IT WAS NOT THE EFFECT OF DRINKING that Mister Walton felt when he awakened late on Sunday morning; he had not indulged in anything stronger than apple cider the night before. Nor did he suffer from the hour of his retirement; he and Sundry had not stayed "until the last gun was fired." No, it was certainly the heady, noisy atmosphere of the *Merrymeeting Tavern* and its merry company that resounded in his head. He stretched and groaned elaborately, then decided that a proper breakfast would go a long way toward remedying his hazy senses.

Sundry had already broken his fast when Mister Walton stepped into the hotel's dining room. The young man was mostly hidden by a newspaper, unfolded and raised before him, but his friend and employer recognized him immediately from his long legs, stretched carelessly before him.

"Good morning," said Mister Walton melodiously.

The paper was lowered, and Sundry beamed from his reclined position. "Good morning, mister," he said brightly.

These were the first words he had uttered to Mister Walton some months ago when they first met, and the memories they spurred made them both chuckle.

"I took a stroll this morning," said the young man with a sigh when Mister Walton sat down.

"You *have* been ambitious."

"I wandered down to the river."

"To get a glimpse of the *Merrymeeting Tavern*, I would guess."

"I did, actually," Sundry said with a frown. "But I didn't find it."

"The young women there were very pretty."

"I thought so." Sundry shrugged a little sadly. The experience at the *Merrymeeting*—most particularly that brief, flirtatious kiss—had affected him greatly, and he had gone to bed last night and awakened this morning with a rich commotion of romantic melancholy occupying his heart and mind. It was a sensation that he was loath to lose, but it occurred to him that Mister Walton, thinking of the coming evening with Miss McCannon, harbored deeper feelings; and so Sundry rose out of his own comfortable reflection (not to mention the confusion of missing the tavern by day) and suggested that they leave forthwith.

Mister Walton was readily talked into continuing their journey on the first available train, and within the hour they were taking the trolley to the station. Sundry chuckled with pleasure at the beaming expression upon his friend's face; the man's natural congeniality was heightened further by the pleasure of his anticipation, and people found themselves beaming back at him before they knew what they were about.

Once a porter had taken their bags, Mister Walton and Sundry went out onto the platform and took in the sights before boarding. A dry fall breeze shook the leaves of the adolescent trees planted about the station, and the midmorning sun glinted from the train's windows. The engine let out a chuff of steam that swept past them while they waited for others to mount the steps of the nearest car.

The conductor called, "All aboard!" and Mister Walton and Sundry were ready to comply when old John Neptune appeared. He carried his drawstring sack with him and looked pleased that they were so happy to see him.

"Now you can tell me about the riddle of the needle," said Sundry while they were boarding. The train gave a low whistle.

The Indian paused at the top of the steps and said, "It was a riddle of a needle, a mirror, and a rock."

Mister Walton, who had not heard any of this the night before, was curious. "A needle, a mirror, and a rock?" he asked.

John Neptune nodded gravely. He raised one hand and demarcated the dimension of something with a thumb and forefinger. "It was a very flat rock," he said. Then, without further elucidation, he moved down the aisle, found a seat, and set his bag beside him.

Sundry prepared himself to hear about "the needle, the mirror, and the very flat rock," but John Neptune sat back in his seat and closed his eyes. Before the train was under way, the old man was asleep, and before the train was very *long* under way, Mister Walton was snoring lightly, his portly frame leaning against the side of the car, his head propped against the window.

That was when Eugene escaped from his sack.

*   *   *

"I want to know how you got that creature on board in the first place," said the stationmaster at Richmond, where they had been "kicked off" the train.

John Neptune held Eugene before him and considered what he might do with the raccoon. Mister Walton was in good humor, if a little concerned that their reaching Hallowell had been delayed. He ignored his desire to press forward, however, and considered the paramount problem to be that of safely confining Eugene so that together they could continue their travels.

"He was in a sack," said John Neptune, who had been kicked off the train without that item.

"Mr. Steuben was not amused to have a raccoon on his train, I take it."

"The conductor was indeed a little stern with us," said Mister Walton, that familiar glint of drollery like light from behind his spectacles.

"The lady across the aisle thought it was a rat," explained Sundry. Eugene had taken a liking to the woman's fur stole.

"I wished I'd seen it," said the stationmaster.

Mister Walton's shoulders shook. "I am sorry you were not there. But we are a little uncertain about our reception if we attempt to continue along the line."

"Get something a little more secure to put that animal in and *I* won't refuse you a ticket."

"We'll have to find a box of some kind," said Sundry.

"I think I will stay in Richmond for a while," said the Indian. "I have a friend who lives here, and there are some nice woods a little to the west." He considered the raccoon again, almost affectionately. "He may be a family totem, but even relatives can be troublesome."

"Do you think he is old enough to survive by himself?" asked Mister Walton.

"I have great faith in him," said John Neptune. He scratched the creature behind the ear, and the raccoon took a nip at his thumb.

They hired a horse and carriage at the livery, and Eugene was given the run of the trap as they took him and his interim master west of the town. The fall roads were hard-packed by summer traffic, so the way was easier than it might have been in another season. The village of Richmond quickly fell away to outskirt settlements, then to field. Clouds were gathering, the trees lining the way evidenced a rising wind, and Mister Walton remembered that another storm was expected on the coast.

A wood did appear over a particular hill, and Sundry pulled alongside a break of trees, where he spotted a likely-looking path. John Neptune climbed out with his *"relative"* and sat down on a stump. The animal peered with its beady eyes over the Indian's shoulder. Mister Walton and Sundry waited by the carriage and watched as the Indian stroked the raccoon. Two crows traded raucous comments from a stand of birch at the edge of the wood.

Eugene suddenly realized that he had no collar or leash, and he dashed several yards down the path. John Neptune laughed. The raccoon nosed around a circle of mushrooms grown brittle with the cool nights and the final ravages of voles and mice. The animal blinked at the man on the stump, then waddled into the bracken and was gone. It was all very unceremonious and (thought Mister Walton) a little melancholy.

"Thank you, gentlemen," said John Neptune, "for coming along, but I think I will stay here for a while."

Mister Walton had re-secured his hat and turned his collar against the strengthening breeze. He looked behind them toward the fields, above which gray clouds were gathering. "There is a storm coming," he said.

"There often is," said the Indian.

"We certainly don't mind waiting to see if Eugene comes back looking for you."

"Oh, I am very certain he is gone."

Mister Walton looked to Sundry for the next possibility. They had no way of knowing how old the man was; he might be eighty. But he looked very certain and comfortable sitting on the stump, gazing along the line of trees. "I was always more partial to the shoreline than the forest," he said aloud, though he might have been speaking to himself. "My father considered it a weakness in my character. 'All those waves, crashing, crashing,' he used to tell me. He thought it was bad for the digestion."

"I am partial to the ocean myself," said Mister Walton.

" 'The raccoon fishes in freshwater,' my father would say, but I have seen a family of them prying open mussels and clambering in tide pools for periwinkles." He looked up at Mister Walton. "It's nice here, though. I think I will stay for a while and walk back to town, where my friend lives."

The old Indian might have been eighty years old, but he didn't appear frail or foolish. He wanted to sit in the fall air and walk back to town. He may have been better suited to it than Mister Walton. "It has been a pleasure knowing you, sir," said the portly fellow. He shook John Neptune's hand, and Sundry came up to do the same.

"You were very good for Henry Echo," complimented the old man.

"I'm not sure that any of it did him very much good in the end," said Sundry. He was thinking of the man's abstraction and sadness.

"We will see" was all the Indian would say.

Mister Walton watched the man as long as he could as they drove away and only turned forward when the brow of a hill came between them.

31. Phileda

MISTER WALTON PASSED SEVERAL HOUSES on either side of Hallowell's Second Street before he came to the red maple, the guardian cherubs, and the two flights of granite steps. These last ran somewhat counter to one another; the first tacked to port, the second toward starboard, before reaching a fieldstone walk. Gazing up from the street, past these switchbacks, the portly fellow wondered wryly if the steps were meant to accommodate the gait of a captain who is newly come from sea.

Beyond the steps and the walk, which was flanked by two younger maples, was the house itself, a late Georgian home with a gambrel roof and two stories that loomed benignly over the sloping lawn and the unpaved street. The house, painted yellow, was handsomely collared with evergreen hedges and set among brilliant foliage. Mister Walton's shoes sounded amiably upon the stone walk, and he could hear his own hurrying pace as he reached the door, where a brass lion with a ring in its mouth glowered at him. He took the ring in hand and gave several moderate knocks.

He waited, feeling anxious and awkward to be discovered, hoping to make a casual impression. The wind noised through the variegated leaves, and he turned to view again the crown of the great maple. The door did not open. No footsteps approached. He glanced at the curtains on either side of the door for some sign of movement, but he was disappointed. He knocked again.

His step was less hurried as he descended the granite flights. He had wired Miss McCannon, saying that he would arrive "by evening," and there was no reason for her to know that he had come so early; he feared it was a little impolite of him to have done so. He chided himself for his eagerness to be here; it seemed so childish to him now. He stopped when he reached the street and gazed at the McCannon home.

"Toby?" came a familiar voice. It took him a moment to realize that it was not coming from his own head. "Toby?"

Phileda McCannon and another woman stood slightly above him on the slope of the street. The breeze rising up the hill was pulling at Phileda's hat, so she held it firmly on her head with one hand, a gesture that heightened her look of surprise. (Her companion looked not surprised but curious.) In the crook of her other arm, Miss McCannon held three books. Her dark brown hair was done up almost carelessly behind her, but several locks of it had gone astray, and one of them tickled the tip of her nose. Mister Walton was a little flustered to see her so suddenly, but her smile was so bright and so genuine in its pleasure that it swept away his self-consciousness.

"Miss McCannon," he said.

"*Mister* Walton," she said, her smile briefly gone. "If you are to escort me to the ball, I expect you to address me with a good deal less distance."

"Phileda," he corrected himself.

"Thank you," she said, and for a moment, just before she offered her hand, he had the giddy sensation that she was going to embrace him.

Now that the matter of address had been settled between them, Phileda presented her companion, whose curiosity was not lessened by the preceding dialogue. Mrs. Miriam Nowell was of an age with Phileda, though she dressed with more of an eye to the latest fashion and cultivated a less direct manner. Introduced as a friend and neighbor "since childhood," Mrs. Nowell did not offer her hand (a woman's prerogative) but expressed gratification in meeting Phileda's escort.

"Phileda has done much for local rumor by keeping you a secret, Mister Walton," said Mrs. Nowell wryly.

"I fear I shall prove a disappointment, since any conjecture must rise above my head," he said with a smile.

"The truth is always more interesting, sir," she disagreed.

"Or at least stranger," said Mister Walton, causing a little delight in both women.

"I have promised Miriam that I will walk home with her," said Phileda, "and as that is in the direction of your hotel, I can show you off a bit before the evening." Mrs. Nowell waited on the sidewalk, and Phileda took Mister Walton's arm. "I will just run up and put these books in the hall," she said, and led him back up the steps with such briskness that he might have wondered if the wind hadn't suddenly got behind him and pushed. She was filled with excitement to see him and was telling him about her brother, Jared, who had gone back to Harvard after his digs at the shell heaps in Damariscotta this summer, how her grandmother had planted the red maple at the foot of the bank, and what fun they would have at the ball.

She threw open the front door and breezed into the hall, where she tossed her books on a chair. He had never known her to be so talkative, and he was laughing with pleasure at her enthusiasm when she paused for a moment and looked at him with an impish smile.

"I am glad to see you," she said.

He had his hat in his hands, and his eyes were bright behind his spectacles. "The feeling is mutual," he replied with the hint of a bow.

"Yes," she said. "Let us take a walk."

At forty-one, Phileda Verona McCannon was six years younger than Tobias Walton. Her manner of dress was appropriate to her middle years and the dictates of the time; she did not draw attention to herself with bright colors or with the latest in flounces and furbelows. Her hats were practical; her shoes, high-buttoned and black. But she had an energy that any young person might envy. Her blue eyes were bright and able to communicate fond amusement or wicked irony with equal facility. Her hair was of a shade with the chestnut when it breaks from its shell in the fall. There was only a suspicion of gray above her temples.

She had been considered plain as a young woman; she had considered herself plain and had suffered predictably for it. But age had worked in her favor, as it often does not with beauty—age, intelligence, humor, and the inspiring example of a maiden aunt who had traveled the Amazon and shot a grizzly bear in the Yukon. Activity had kept Miss McCannon in the very figure of her youth, and a natural athleticism lent grace and decisiveness to her movements.

She was very attractive for a woman considered plain, and Mister Walton was not the first to take note of this contradiction. The contradiction itself was intriguing and somehow increased her appeal. Mister Walton was flattered to escort her and a little panicked to think of his own obvious middle years and of the other better-preserved fellows who must have found themselves enchanted by Miss McCannon's contradictions.

Her idea of a stroll was less leisurely than some people's, but Mister Walton was up to brisk movement and a great walker himself; had he not been, her presence on his arm would have inspired him with the energy necessary to keep up. As for Mrs. Nowell, she seemed accustomed to Phileda's pace.

"That is Old Kalf's house," said Phileda, pointing down at a building of obvious colonial origin. "I will tell you about him sometime," she promised. "Can you stay in Hallowell after tonight?"

"I would like to," Mister Walton said simply, and he could forbear a glance in the married woman's direction. Such a question might seem altogether forward coming from Phileda; but, again, her friend knew her too well to show surprise.

Phileda smiled. "Tomorrow we will go and look at the smoking pine."

"The smoking pine?"

"Phileda will do no less," suggested Mrs. Nowell, "than change you into a true enthusiast of her hometown."

"Though this is my first visit," said the portly fellow with that grand glint in his eye, "I arrived today thinking already that there was much to recommend it."

It was a surprise to see Miss McCannon blush a little, though there was an expression of pleasure and gratitude in her own eyes. "Is Mr. Moss with you?" she asked.

"He did come."

"I am sorry I couldn't invite him to the ball. The affair is so popular that they sell tickets."

"I am sure he will be fine. Sundry has an ability to discover his own amusements."

"I like him very much," said Phileda McCannon.

"He speaks highly of you."

He thought he heard Mrs. Nowell laugh quietly.

Phileda was not to be outdone, however, and very deftly turned her friend's mind back to its former curiosity. "It was nice of him to send me a message when you and your friends hurried so unexpectedly from Damariscotta this summer. I read the papers and, of course, your letters, but I want to hear all about your adventures firsthand. Buried treasure! Kidnapping!"

"My part was very small," said Mister Walton, and though indeed it may have been, his statement sounded modest.

"And this after quelling a bear at the Lincoln Hall!" Phileda laughed. She was clearly enjoying the effect of this upon her friend.

"The bear, fortunately, was quite quellable; but, yes, it *was* a remarkable few days," he admitted.

They paused so that Mister Walton could be introduced to two elderly women whom they met along the way. "They are extremely curious about you," she said when they bid good afternoon to the women and continued their way along Second Street.

"Are they?" he replied.

"Oh, yes. Extremely." She was smiling.

"And they haven't even *heard* about kidnappings and bears," said Mrs. Nowell.

32. Amos's Strange Sensation

THE ELEVENTH OF OCTOBER, true to Eagleton's word, dawned bright and clear over the islands of Casco Bay (it has been said that there is an island there for every day of the year), gentling the recently turbulent waters with a cool breeze.

The members of the Moosepath League reconnoitered that morning, taking breakfast in the vast dining room with a few other guests who shared lodgings at Cliff Cottage. Amos Guernsey joined them and was interested to hear what little they knew concerning the boy named Bird. It was all spoken of very carefully, since the lad was sitting with them. Bird was as silent as ever, though doing great justice to the meal, which made up in quality what it lacked in variety.

The day was spent recovering from the previous night's adventures. Thump began *Mrs. Ludley's Luck* late in the morning, and in the afternoon the Moosepathians took their little charge into the village of Cape Elizabeth, where there were some shops, and purchased him several suits of clothes and a tweed cap.

Ephram, Eagleton, and Thump did not let Bird out of their sight, and Thump, in particular, seemed to relish the role of guardian. Ephram and Eagleton were singularly gratified to see Thump ambling around the lawns of Cliff Cottage, with the little fellow walking along beside him. The one appeared almost bearlike, with his stocky frame and remarkable beard, his expression of deep concentration; the other might have been a cub, willing to wander with his parent and doing so with every consideration for his protector's quiet thoughts.

The sight was so pleasing that Ephram and Eagleton joined the two. As a foursome, they stood on the breezy cliffs and looked out over the city they had so recently quit, then faced the endless ocean to contemplate the breakers below and the surging whitecaps that stretched beyond sight.

They did not see Amos that day until dinnertime, but that evening he retired with them to the south parlor of the hotel. Thump was anxious to return to *Mrs. Ludley's Luck*, and very quickly he was immersed. (Mrs. Ludley had just discovered that the carriage driver she had hired after discovering the note on the pigeon's leg was the same man that had intervened in the embarrassing incident on the trip back from England.)

Ephram and Eagleton took turns reading to one another from the old newspapers and magazines they found in the parlor, and Amos occasionally graced these vocal renditions with bits of appropriate dialogue. Bird quietly listened to it all. The evening had progressed in this manner for an hour or so when Amos sat straight in his chair and said, "Oh, dear! I have the strangest sensation!"

"Is your collar too tight again?" asked Eagleton. They were all concerned.

"I have had an odd sensation myself," said Thump.

"You, too?" said Amos, as if amazed.

"Possibly it's the clams," suggested Ephram, and Thump nodded.

But Amos's perception was nothing so prosaic (or dire, perhaps). He stood and reached out a hand, like a man groping in the dark.

"Good heavens!" said Eagleton.

"I feel," said Amos, "a presence!" He moved toward the door with stilted steps. "Yes, there is a strong presence even now among us!"

Thump feared that the actor had detected his complications with the clams. "High tide at nine twenty-one," he announced.

"Someone is here," said Amos, attempting (despite the misunderstanding) to hold on to the drama of the moment. The manager came into the parlor just then and (upon request) announced the Baroness Blinsky and Major Alcott.

"Oh, my!" said Amos Guernsey.

The names rang small bells in the minds of Ephram, Eagleton, and Thump. They stood as the new guests stepped into the room.

The baroness and the major did not disappoint. She was wide and imperious, with a blunt, upturned nose that was seen mostly from the underside; he was long and ascetic, with long, ascetic mustaches and a narrow chin and nose. She did not respond to the bows and greetings from the room, and he barely did; the tassel of the red fez that he affected shook slightly.

"The spirits are very taxing," she said, waving a hand in front of her face. "There is trouble and confusion in this room. Oh, please! Come to me with questions so that I might relieve the air of this ethereal congestion!"

Ephram, Eagleton, and Thump were so far from coming to the woman with questions that they were each privately thinking of bolting from the room. It was difficult to say when any of them had ever been in the presence of such an imposing matron.

"Eight forty-three," said Ephram.

"Cool and clear expected through tomorrow," announced Eagleton. "Chance of showers next evening, wind in the southwest."

"High tide at nine twenty-one," said Thump again, possibly for the benefit of those who weren't in the room before.

"Baroness Blinsky!" Amos was saying. "Major Alcott!" Suddenly, every expression in the room was appended with an exclamation. The new guests looked vaguely amused with Amos's astonishment. "How I have heard of you! *'What news arrives before your famous countenance that offers terror to the common man!'* The landlord to George Washington, act three, scene four, of *The Rescue of Ann Beam.*"

"Come, come," said the baroness, exhibiting both indulgence and impatience, like a mother with a naughty but beloved child. Her voice had a shrill quality to it that did not seem in keeping with either her title or her reputation. "Find me a seat," she said.

Ephram, Eagleton, and Thump made haste to offer theirs, and Amos pulled a wing-backed chair from behind the door, but the baroness chose the sofa and settled herself noisily into it. The major stood at the arm of the sofa, looking bored.

There was silence then. The baroness peered about the room, ducking and weaving her head as she looked past the many phantoms in the room. She stopped her search when she locked eyes on Bird, who looked bemused rather than awe-stricken.

"There are some very interesting sprites about," she said.

33. Several Figures in the Night

"AND HOW IS MISS MCCANNON?" asked Sundry when Mister Walton returned to their rooms at the hotel. The young man was putting away his employer's clothes against an extended stay.

"Oh, fine," said Mister Walton, "very fine!" and there was nothing in his voice to indicate if this was the state in which she was found or the manner in which he saw her.

"Did she harshly reprimand you for running off to another woman's rescue last summer?" asked Sundry when they were at dinner. The last blush of twilight was lost in the brilliance of the dining room's chandelier, and they could see themselves in the windows opposite.

"She did reference that moment," answered Mister Walton, "and quite praised your merit in sending her an explanatory note."

Sundry thought this was as it should be and again expressed his admiration for the woman. "She is a woman with plans, I think," he called when Mister Walton was shaving.

Mister Walton came to the doorway of his room and regarded his young friend uncertainly. "Plans?" he said. It was not like Sundry to conjecture lightly upon such a subject.

Sundry sat in the little parlor that connected their rooms, his long form draped unceremoniously in a corner chair. A newspaper occupied his lap, but he was not paying attention to it. "She probably has an itinerary planned for you," he said. "For tomorrow," he added when this did not clear things up for the portly fellow.

"Oh, yes," said Mister Walton. He had been a little confounded to think that Sundry might think what Mister Walton thought he was thinking; and now he was more confounded to think that Sundry would realize *what* he had been thinking. "I believe she has some plans, yes," he said. "She is going to show me a smoking pine." He stood in the doorway and raised his shoulders at Sundry's expression of inquiry. There was silence while Mister Walton returned to his chore. "It seems a shame that one doesn't keep one's hair and grow bald about the face," came the older man's voice from the other room.

This was the first bit of information that Mister Walton had offered, without prompting, since seeing Phileda McCannon that afternoon. Sundry thought there was hope for him, after all. When Mister Walton was all but dressed for the gala, Sundry attended him with a black tie, which he expertly fixed about the man's shirt collar.

"I've been thinking about our fellow Moosepathians," said Mister Walton.

"Honestly?" said Sundry. "You surprise me."

Mister Walton held still for Sundry's knot, chin up, eyes to the ceiling. He laughed deeply. "Am I as easily read as all that?" he wondered.

"Your situation is," said Sundry.

The older man touched the tie when it was finished, then turned to a mirror. "And Henry Echo," he said quietly. He looked as dapper as Sundry had ever seen him. But Mister Walton thought he looked like just another portly bald man, and he adjusted his spectacles, either to alter what he saw or how he saw it. "She is very grand," he said with a sigh.

Somewhere downstairs, a clock struck half past seven. "Good heavens!" said Mister Walton. "Is that all it is?" He had half an hour's wait before Phileda came by with a carriage to pick him up. "I have only known her a very few days, when you add them up," he said after five minutes of pacing, which followed five minutes of trying not to pace.

"You've exchanged letters several times," said Sundry. "My mother always says a letter is as good as a week together for knowing a person."

"Ah!" said Mister Walton, and he went to the bureau in his room, on top of which was Phileda's invitation to him. He stood there and read the opening lines of the letter.

Dear Toby,
*   I was wonderfully pleased to find your letter when I arrived this morning . . .*

He sat beside his bed and read the letter over again.

Sundry returned to the parlor and his newspaper.

Not long after Mister Walton left that evening, Sundry began to feel himself at ends. There was little in the newspaper, which was two or three days old, to pique his interest, and the books in the sitting room, downstairs in the Worster House, proved to be romances of the most obvious sort. The hotel itself was quiet as midnight, and he realized that most of the guests must, like Mister Walton, be at the ball.

He thought about the young woman with the blue-gray eyes.

The clock in the foyer struck nine when Sundry decided to take a walk. It was chilly out, and the wind was blowing from the east; Sundry found his coat but eschewed a hat. There are times when it is good to get the wind in your hair and let it brace you about the ears. He had a general idea of the direction of the ball but could see or hear nothing when he reached the street and looked over the buildings above him on the slope.

He was alone, it seemed, on Main Street. A few lights burned above the storefronts. A sign swung in the wind. Across the way, behind the waterfront buildings, the Kennebec River was a dark presence. Somewhere a dog barked, and there was the smallest hint of music in the air, so soft and tiny with distance that he had to wait for a lull in the wind to catch it again. After a moment he heard the suggestion of voices, and a pipe perhaps, so remote that he couldn't identify a single note. It was as if the cheer of the Merrymeeting Tavern had followed him upriver.

He attempted to place the sound, turning into the wind and cupping an ear. It seemed to come from downriver, and he, with nothing to do, followed it. He had not gotten very far when he was startled by, and seemed to startle in turn, a man standing in the doorway of a shop.

"Good evening," said Sundry.

The man on the steps waved a hand and said something inarticulate. Sundry had an odd feeling about the fellow, as if the man had been watching for him. *I wonder what he's up to,* Sundry thought, and decided that he must have interrupted a lovers' tryst. He picked up his pace accordingly and made his way quickly to the southern end of Hallowell's business district.

Fog had come off the river, and the further away from the center of town he walked, the more the mists rolled in over the land. The sound of voices and music—there was a fiddle playing, he was sure—rose as he went, and finally he came onto a treeless bank that led steeply to the shore.

There was a large building below, some distance away, its lights glowing like will-o'-the-wisp through the fog, the color of fireflies. He had a curious notion, standing there at the top of the bank, and when the fog was briefly lifted by the breeze, the notion settled into the pit of his stomach with the certainty of hard fact.

Sundry peered through the regathering mist but could not mistake the sign above the door—a colonial European and an Indian shaking hands. It was not just the *same* sort of sign but seemed the *very* same sign and the very same building, and from the voices rising out from it, he could believe that they emanated from the very same throats.

It was impossible, of course, that the Merrymeeting Tavern had somehow moved up the Kennebec like a phantom ship, but he hesitated, nonetheless, to descend the bank. Perhaps, he thought, if he peeked in the windows first. He could almost hope that the young woman with the blue-gray eyes would be there, and with this rising, illogically, in his chest, he took one step in the direction of the building by the river and stopped.

A figure was working its way up the steep hill—a man who was singing, under his breath, a song that Sundry had heard two nights before in Brunswick. The man was breathing laboredly by the time he neared the brow of the slope, and he straightened his posture to regain his bearings and saw Sundry.

"Give me a hand here, will you, lad?" he asked in a deep voice.

Sundry went two or three steps down the slope and took the man's arm. He was a compact old fellow with white hair, beard, and mustache. Sundry could see little of his face in the dark, but a clear eye regarded him with interest as they reached the top of the hill.

"I am obliged," the old fellow said. "I don't know why they put a building down in a place like that without a proper path to reach it."

"What is the name of it?" asked Sundry.

"The Merrymeeting, son," said the man.

Sundry was no less confounded than he had been moments before. "The Merrymeeting? I was at an establishment of that name."

"Where was that?"

"In Brunswick."

"Oh, yes, that's the place."

"I beg your pardon?"

"The Merrymeeting."

"But that was in Brunswick."

"Yes, I know." The old man shook his head as if it were a wonder to him. He chuckled. "Did you lose a day or two?"

"Not that I noticed."

The fellow laughed again. "Once, upriver from here, I found them roaring it one night in June. I came out a few hours later, and summer was gone."

"Gone?"

"It was September eighth, I think, 1883." The white-bearded man produced a pipe from his pocket and struck a match. "I was a little put off at first." The match lit a handsome, wrinkled face and bright eyes.

Sundry was sure his leg was being pulled, but he wasn't so sure that he wanted to go down the bank to see for himself.

"They are fine people, but they know nothing about moderation," the man said. "I am surprised that you didn't at least miss a day or two. Who brought you there?"

"My friend and I went with John Neptune."

"John Neptune! Good heavens! No wonder! John Neptune!" The old fellow shook Sundry's hand. "Isherwood Tolly," he said.

"Mr. Tolly!" replied Sundry. "John Neptune spoke of you more than once!"

"Did he still have that rascal Shotgun?"

"He named him Eugene, though, after his grandfather."

They were walking now, toward town, and Sundry cast a regretful glance back at the Merrymeeting. How bad would it be to lose a day or two, or even a season, among such company? Then he laughed at himself.

"Where are you going?" Mr. Tolly was asking, and when Sundry told him he was only taking a walk, the fellow insisted that they have tea together at his cousin's place on the other side of town. "You will have to tell me about old John. We have the devil's own time catching up with one another these days."

On the other side of town, dark though it was, Mr. Tolly showed no hesitation at the precipitous stairs that led from the street to a small building half-perched on pilings upon the shore. Sundry took the stairs with less alacrity, feeling his way carefully where the small light from the end of town was obscured by the overgrown bank. A plank walk brought them to a door. (Sundry only saw that it was a door once Mr. Tolly had opened it; the house was nothing but a boxy shadow against the river and the opposite shore.)

"Darker than a wolf's mouth in here," said Mr. Tolly, and he disappeared into the gloom.

Following him, Sundry thought he could see the dim blush of embers in a grate. Then a swarm of sparks, brilliant in the dark (though they shed little light), rose up as the old man shook the coals with a poker. Sundry was able to see the edges of furniture or the suggestion of a rug upon the floor from the resultant glow of the hearth. By this light Mr. Tolly located a lamp, and soon a soft radiance filled the room.

The word *snug* could not have been better defined than by the chamber thus revealed. There were heavy curtains on the windows and a thick rug upon the floor. Two chairs (one armchair looked big enough for two people to curl up in) and a rocking chair stood close to the hearth so that anyone seated might warm their feet.

"Let me get a pot going," said Mr. Tolly, and he shuffled through a narrow doorway. Sundry heard the draft and flue of a stove being worked and a sloshing pot as it was laid upon a hot surface. "Sit down, sit down," said Mr. Tolly when he returned to the little parlor.

The young man had been peering at several framed pictures on the wall—one of an Indian and a leaping buck particularly intrigued him—and before sitting, he took in the presence of books on shelves and an old gun on the shadowy wall opposite the fireplace.

"John Neptune!" said Mr. Tolly again.

"Your cousin lives here?" asked Sundry, wondering if they were disturbing someone.

"He'll be asleep," assured the old man. "Dead to the world. I'm surprised we can't hear him snore."

Sundry was still curious about the Merrymeeting and considered how he might ask about it again without appearing foolish or impertinent.

"So where did you see him last?" Mr. Tolly inquired before the young man could speak.

"Just this morning, in Richmond," said Sundry.

"Richmond? This morning? Good heavens!"

"He said he hoped to catch up with you." Mr. Tolly chuckled. Sundry remembered something then, and he leaned forward in his seat. "I've heard speak of you from other folk as well," he said.

"That can't be good," said Mr. Tolly with a glint of humor in his eye.

"On the contrary," said Sundry. "I was told that you and John Neptune deserve a statue at Monument Square."

"That is generous of someone."

"It was said that Portland owes you a debt that few remember."

"John Neptune a good deal more than I." Mr. Tolly relit his pipe, chuckling around the stem. "The race for the Atlantic and St. Lawrence," he said between puffs. He thought about this for a moment, then took the pipe from his mouth and whistled. "Fifty years ago come next March! Fifty years! John Neptune looked like Pontiac himself the day I met him. Of course, he comes from a long line of chiefs and shamans. It is sometimes difficult to separate the deeds of one John Neptune from the deeds of another."

"But this particular event belongs to the John Neptune of my acquaintance," prodded Sundry.

"It does indeed," replied the old man.

"And to yourself."

But Mr. Tolly was only half-listening. Smoke rose from his pipe in threads and puffs and hovered like a blue mist in the room. Sundry had read of Indian shamans painting pictures with the smoke from their pipes, and he could almost believe that Mr. Tolly was doing this for his own edification—forming shadows of other days so that he might properly remember them.

34. Needle, Stone, Mirror

"THERE WAS A THIRD FELLOW, ACTUALLY," said Isherwood Tolly. "Another John by the name of Poor. You may have heard of him."

"I have, just recently, yes," said Sundry, and he told Mr. Tolly what he had learned from Henry Echo about John Poor; about the meeting between the Montreal Board of Trade and the Boston agents and how imperative it was to Portland's cause that a speedy driver be found; and also how Mr. Tolly himself had fit this description.

"I was thirty-six years old," said Mr. Tolly, "and you will find, young man, when you reach that era in your life, that you are at the height of your powers. I was sufficiently grown to have a bit of wisdom by then, but yet there was enough youth left in me that I still looked for diversity in my experience and even excitement.

"I had been a farmer once, but also sailed before the mast, trapped furs on the Canadian border, and worked a feldspar mine down by the coast. I had labored at half a dozen other things as well and had done just enough to know that I wanted to do more still. So somewheres in the mid-'40s—'44 or '45—I found myself in Portland and hired on as a stage driver.

"I had a knack with the horses, you see, and a feel for the terrain and drove a sleigh as well as I did a coach. I had several inland runs, delivering mail and small goods and people to places like Buxton and Hollis and Limerick and Fryeburg and Denmark. I liked a speedy pair of animals and a light rig, was known for shaving time from a run whenever I made it, and I don't know that I as much as broke an egg. I like to think I wasn't reckless.

"Portland was different then; more boom than bustle, if you take my meaning. There's a lot of moving about these days in the city, but fifty years ago, Portland was *growing* like a well-fed boy, in great bursts and swells. That was before the fire, of course, and much has come and gone."

Sundry, who had only recently migrated to Portland in the service of Mister Walton, was trying to imagine the city in an earlier era, before the railroad depots and the telegraph poles.

"Things were more muddy back then," said Mr. Tolly simply, and he let out another puff of smoke. "Well, as I say, I was pretty vital myself, and it didn't take much convincing for me to warm to a challenge. We picked out the fastest horses, borrowed a little sleigh that the company was liverying, and Skully Peaslee came charging out, just as John Poor and I were bundling under several furs, and put a crock of hot stew between us. The doors were thrown open.

" 'Do you know where Montreal is?' asked John Poor.

" 'A little north and west, isn't it?' I said, and he asked no more.

"The storm had already begun as we trotted onto Fore Street, small flakes of snow spitting out of a darkening sky. The wind was on the rise, and soon we were driving into the teeth of it, and to this day I couldn't tell you how I saw my way through such a blizzard, along paths I had never seen. But the clouds cleared with the next day, and beneath a brilliant sky we mingled with the commerce of Montreal, and John Poor was before the Montreal Board of Trade before it had made a commitment to the city of Boston. He convinced them to postpone their decision, and the Boston delegation was in an absolute rage.

"I paid a little more attention to the newspapers after that, and the language between the two cities grew more shrill than anyone from either of them would care to remember. Then some brilliant editor stewed up the notion to have a race that would determine which city could deliver a letter the fastest from England to Montreal—and the winner take the contract.

"I wasn't surprised when John Poor showed up at the livery, asking for me. I was ready for the two of us to do it again, but he informed me that he wouldn't be going this time. It seems there were certain politic reasons for his staying behind, though he didn't explain them out. I took him at his word and considered who to take with me, since it was important that another come along in case of unforeseen incident.

"On the first of March, two letters aboard two steamers left Liverpool, the one for Boston, the other for Portland—and we waited. Two weeks later, I still hadn't decided who to take with me, though I knew the steamer could arrive any day. The horses were groomed and kept; the sleigh was festooned with ribbons and an American flag. I kept close to the livery, which was close to the waterfront, and we waited." Mr. Tolly lifted himself from his reverie and considered the high-pitched whistle from the kitchen. "Tea water is ready," he said.

Sundry hadn't noticed but was anxious to hear the rest of Mr. Tolly's tale and offered his help in readying the brew. The pot whined when it was taken from the stove, and Mr. Tolly fidgeted around for the tea and the tea ball. The young man was interested in how John Neptune would fit into Mr. Tolly's tale but decided not to interrupt a good storyteller with questions.

Soon they were back in the parlor, a steaming pot brewing on the table before them. Mr. Tolly tapped out his pipe, gazed into it with one eye scrunched up, and decided the pipe was in need of a cleaning. He unwound the stem and gazed through it to the lamp, then took out a jackknife and began to scrape at the bowl.

"I had a troublesome dream one night," he said, recommencing his tale without ceremony. "A strange and uncomfortable sort of vision where trees fell in upon me and a great river flooded past and wild creatures dogged my heels, and I saw another man—an Indian, he was—dreaming with a vexatious smile. I had never seen him before, but there was something otherworldly—aside from the fact that it was a dream—about him. I thought, in my dream, that he was putting a spell on me, and I woke in the small hours of the morning in a terrific sweat."

"Was it John Neptune, then?" asked Sundry, unable to put the image of this threatening shaman together with his knowledge of John Neptune.

"No, it wasn't John Neptune, but I met that worthy that very day—that morning, in fact—on my way to the livery. He was standing on a snowy sidewalk, peering into a store window—not the man in my dream, but he was an Indian, and I was nervous of him as I passed. I have had enough strange experiences in my time so that I don't thoroughly discount an odd dream—not just a nightmare, mind you, but an *odd* dream—and so I was making a fairly wide circuit around him when he spoke up.

"His voice was as low as it is now, and it startled me, I admit, when he asked, 'Which hat do you think is the best?'

"After repeating himself two or three times, I was coaxed into joining him before the window and philosophizing on the worthiness of several head coverings displayed there. I grew more comfortable with the man as I stood there with him, and finally I told him that one of his race had occupied a dream of mine the night before.

" 'What was he doing?' wondered the fellow. There was a snow flurry that morning, and his black hair was dotted with flakes. He had the clearest eye and the straightest gaze of any man I had ever met.

" 'Why, he was sleeping,' I said, and explained the remainder of my dream. He listened with great interest, and upon questioning, I told him about my impending mission to Montreal. He was greatly concerned, and though I did my best to impress upon him that I needed to stay near the livery, he insisted that I follow him to his rooms on Summer Street. 'I'm not sure it's a good time for a visit,' I told him.

" 'Buying a hat can wait,' he said to me, and it wasn't till many days later that I looked back and realized he was joking with me.

"On Summer Street we came to a house where John Neptune and his great-uncle John Neptune kept a room on the third floor. He was a very old man then and known, I would soon learn, as a great shaman."

Isherwood Tolly put his pipe together again and fished about for his tobacco before realizing that it was on the table before him. "John Neptune explained to his great-uncle John Neptune the nature of our visit," he said. He paused with the bowl of his pipe in the tobacco sack. "I described my dream again. The snow had turned briefly to sleet and scratched at the windows. I had my back to them, telling my story and feeling a little foolish that so much had been made of it; the power of the dream was fading from me." Mr. Tolly crammed some tobacco into the bowl of his pipe, returned the pipe to his mouth, and pulled the drawstrings of the little sack.

"Then," he continued, "Great-uncle John Neptune pointed to the window directly behind me. 'Look,' he said. 'Is that the man?'

"I turned and was staggered with sudden fright, for there on the window, formed by the sleet that stuck there, was the very image of the man in my dream!" Mr. Tolly took a deep breath; just the memory of that moment gave him great pause, and Sundry waited in respectful, if avid, silence while the old man picked up the thread of his tale.

"The face of the man from my dream was quickly gone from the window, swept away by a whip of a breeze, but my hair was still standing on end. The two John Neptunes talked for several minutes, and the upshot was that John Neptune turned to me and said, 'I will go to Montreal with you.' And you know, I was very glad to have him; though not half so glad as I would be once we were under way. Here, let me pour you some tea," said the old man.

"Oh, let me," said Sundry. He all but leaped to the table and doled out two cups, which were immediately forgotten.

"Now, let's see," said Mr. Tolly, and he leaned back in his chair. Even his pipe was forgotten now. "Great-uncle John Neptune went to a little box at the foot of his bed before we left him, and he took from it a drawstring sack, which he opened and the contents of which he spilled onto the floor. 'Take three things,' he said to his great-nephew, and John Neptune considered the items strewn before him.

"There was nothing that looked of the slightest value to me—trinkets mostly—household things, a kitchen knife, a wooden spoon. I remember a feather and a framed picture of a bear and a red ribbon. John Neptune pondered this collection, and soon he very deliberately picked from it a needle, a stone, and a small looking glass."

"The needle, the stone, and the mirror!" said Sundry delightedly.

"You know about this?" asked Mr. Tolly.

"Only that John Neptune solved a riddle concerning them. I didn't realize that he was hinting at the same tale."

Mr. Tolly chuckled softly.

"But who was the man in your dream and on the window?" wondered Sundry. The thought of this apparition gave him a shiver.

"On the way to the livery, John Neptune explained that somewhere another shaman was making magic against our enterprise; someone in Boston was leaving nothing to chance and had recruited a man of magic, possibly to lay a spell upon me but more likely to cast one on the journey itself.

"The very next morning, I was roused at dawn by a furious knocking at my door. A man from the livery rushed in with the news that the steamer had been sighted. I asked him to go to Summer Street and alert John Neptune, but it seemed the Indian was waiting for us at the wharf.

"It was still March, and it had been a powerful winter for snow. Drifts and banks blocked the light of the sun before the storefronts, and from the sidewalks these piles of snow looked like canyon walls stretching the length of a block. Children were already up that morning, sliding on the tallest of the snowbanks, pulling each other on makeshift sleds through the streets. The city was waking to the news, and many a man arrived, hastily dressed, at the waterfront, to be there when the steamer nudged the wharf and the letter was given over to the next leg of the race.

"John Neptune was indeed waiting for me, and I was surprised to see him talking to the horses. Indians of the eastern tribes are not known for any particular love of horses; the forests that were here when our people arrived and the craggy shape of the land were not as congenial to riding as were the plains of the West. The Iroquois, the Micmac, the Abenaki, and all the tribes here were extraordinary footmen, able to cover many miles in a day with little rest or nourishment. But they had no great love of horses.

"So it surprised me to see John Neptune stroking our horses' ears and whispering to them, and half in jest I asked what they were talking about.

" 'I was just telling them,' he said, 'that whatever they are, on this journey they are one thing.'

"This was cryptic to me, but the steamer was nearing its berth, and already the gathering crowds were cheering. Sailors were waving from the decks, and we could see the captain in his pilothouse.

"I will not belabor the point. It was a grand send-off, and John Poor delivered the letter himself from the boatswain of the steamer to my hand, which he shook heartily as he wished me luck. The day was brilliant with the winter sun. I whipped up the horses, the crowds parted, and I found myself driving amid fur-clad walls of cheering Portlanders. None of us had any idea that the steamer to Boston had arrived two hours earlier.

"As we charged through the morning streets, the crowds thinned till there was only the occasional pedestrian waving to us. One fellow, who didn't know who we were, shouted angrily at us for our imprudent speed.

"The first fifty miles of our journey were uneventful, and I must say that I was beginning to have fewer misgivings. We sped through hamlet and field, and the fields rose into forests, and the hamlets grew further apart. We would stop at each prearranged stage for fresh horses, and each time John Neptune would take a moment—a precious moment, I was beginning to think—to talk to them and tell them, 'Whatever you are, you are one thing.'

"It was late in the afternoon when I noticed the forest growing tangled and close. I was not unused to the woods in that part of the state, but I had never seen such close-knit trees or so many trunks rubbing one another as they moved with the wind. The trail narrowed, and the reflected light of an overcast sky dwindled as the trees leaned over us like wary giants.

"A branch nearly took my hat from my head; another snapped at my outside hand. John Neptune turned his face away from a reaching limb. The horses ducked their heads as they moved beneath the thick branches of a great pine; they slowed their pace and finally came to a halt. We were looking into a solid wall of trees and bushes, branch and limb.

"I was angry with myself for having gotten off the trail, but John Neptune assured me that this was not the case. 'Look behind,' he said. The dread I had felt in my nightmare and that shock I knew when I saw the shaman's face upon the window rushed back to me as I looked over my shoulder to find an identical wall of trees closed in behind us. The horses shifted nervously, blowing steam into the air with anxious snorts.

" 'John,' I said, almost in a whisper, 'what do we do?'

"But he had already gotten down from the sleigh and was moving through the snow to the horses. He held in his hand the needle that he had taken from his great-uncle John Neptune's collection of trinkets. He talked to the horses quietly, and he seemed to be showing them the needle.

"When he returned to the sleigh, I said, 'What did you say to them?'

" 'I told them, whatever they are, they are one thing,' he said, 'and I told them that they are the needle and the woods are the weave.'

"The horses appeared calm now, even eager to go forward despite the fortress of wood before us and not the smallest hole—that I could see— through which to drive.

" 'Get them moving,' said John Neptune.

" 'Where?' I asked.

" 'To Montreal,' he said, and he reached over and shook the reins for me.

"I protested, but he took the reins and drove us with some speed toward the wall of wood. The horses, against all prior experience and common sense, answered his chucks as if they were blind. I would have jumped from the sleigh if John Neptune had not gripped me with one powerful hand."

Isherwood Tolly leaned forward in his chair and expressed his next thought with the utmost seriousness. "And then we were through the wall of trees," he said. "They did not part, we did not find a path amongst them; we were simply through them. I can explain it no other way. But the forest continued to loom around us, and wall after wall of snowbound trees appeared before us like the gates of a city pulled shut. 'John,' I said, but he only handed the reins back to me.

" 'They are the needle,' he said then; 'the woods are the weave. Keep your hands and feet in.'

"And we continued, John exhorting me to greater speed until we seemed to be going faster than ever. 'I can't see the trail,' I protested.

" 'I don't think it matters,' he said, 'as long as we head in the right direction.' He smiled and said, 'We may even save some time this way.'

"We had two more stages with fresh horses ahead of us. I can't tell you how many miles we made through those forests, but after two or three hours, they fell away again, as if they had given up trying to stop us. And then we came to a village and trotted into a yard where a man waited with a lantern. John Neptune jumped out of the sleigh and whispered something to the horses.

" 'What did you say to them?' I asked.

" 'I told them that they aren't a needle anymore,' he told me. But the next team of horses he whispered to before we left, and I thought better of the practice.

"We were off again like a shot, sledding through an open country of fields and settlements and meadows. It was long past dark, and we traveled by the light of half a moon that had already passed its zenith. The hoofbeats of the horses were muffled and dull in the snow, the shush of runners like a constant wind beneath us; the shadows of houses and trees were blue upon the white overlay. Smoke rose from chimneys, gray against the black sky and starlight, dogs barked as we passed, and figures stood in lamp-lit doorways.

"We could hear the river long before we could see it. The night was so quiet, the expanses so wide and empty, that the roar of that water might have drifted fifty miles. I drew rein when we came over the last rise and saw the water, a dark surge overflowing its banks and pounding against the small bridge we were supposed to cross.

"I have seen rivers at flood, glutted by torrential rains or the snowmelt of spring, but there had been no thaw yet, and I had never seen anything quite like this stream. There seemed almost a consciousness to the water, as if it had risen up in defiance of the land and its banks and the feeble span above it. Great waves crashed over and against the bridge, and no one in their right mind would have attempted to cross it.

"But John Neptune had no intention of crossing the bridge; much to my amazement and horror, he pulled from his bag the stone that he had taken from his great-uncle John Neptune and went to the horses.

" 'What did you say to them now?' I asked when he returned.

"Very matter-of-fact, he said to me, 'I told them that whatever they are, they are one thing. And I told them that they are this stone.'

" 'Stone?' I said. 'How can we get across that torrent as a stone? Why, a stone will sink!'

"Then John Neptune raised the stone for me to see. It was small, about three inches in diameter, and very flat. 'It is a skipping stone,' he said.

"My horror and amazement did not abate, and I let out a shout when my companion grabbed up the reins and snapped them over the horses' backs. '*Hay-yuh!*' he shouted, and those two horses bolted over the snow as if they had never stopped.

"I buried my head in my hands and let out another shout just as those creatures flew past the edge of the bank. A great cold spray spattered us. I felt as if we were riding over giant cobblestones and clung tenaciously to the side of the sleigh.

"Then we were on the other bank, and those horses continued to skip over the snow, hardly leaving a trace of their passing, and I felt like St. Nicholas, ready to take to the air behind his enchanted deer.

" 'John!' I shouted. 'Should we stop them?'

"He handed me the reins, saying, 'We are making good time, I think. And there may be another river to cross.'

"There were *two* more swollen rivers to cross, as it happened, and each time, I gave the horses their head, and I do mean *head*, since whatever they were, they were one thing! Fifty miles from Montreal we came to the last stage at the edge of another forest. John Neptune disabused the horses of the notion that they were a skipping stone and let them be two things again.

"The man at the stage spoke French, and I couldn't understand him, but John Neptune and he talked for some time. 'He thinks we should not go further tonight,' said my companion. 'He says there are things crashing through the woods that have encouraged him to put another bar on his door.' Indeed, the man was still speaking and gesticulating his warning. 'Creatures that only walk at night,' said John Neptune, translating, but he only shrugged and seemed unmoved. He thanked the man for his concern, but then he whispered to the new horses while I hung two lanterns on the sleigh, and we were off for the final leg of the race.

" 'That shaman is doing a good job,' said John Neptune.

"The way was well traveled and wide through the forest. The lanterns threw extraordinary silhouettes among the trees, tall shafts of darkness that fluttered and fell past on either side against the depth of the forest. I was a little mesmerized by the flickering light and shadow and found, after all those hours, that I was driving the sleigh on pure instinct.

"Very gradually, I became aware of something running alongside us in the woods, some dark form that paralleled our movements, just beyond the first screen of trees that bordered the trail. I turned to say something to John Neptune and saw another form on the side opposite. Then something flew past, among the trees, and still another loping shape came into view.

"I thought they were wolves, at first, till the first figure appeared upon the path before us. It scrambled into sight from behind a stand of boulders, shuffling in the snow like a hunting dog; but then it straightened up like a man—a very tall man—and waited for us.

"Well, I drew the horses in, as you can well imagine, and they seemed content to stop, blowing and snorting with fear, their eyes wild and reckless. I had to stand in the sleigh and exert all my force to keep them from charging back and tipping us over.

"John Neptune leaped from the sleigh and caught hold of their bridles. An unwolflike howl rose from beside us, and we could hear the sound of strange feet crunching in the snow. I could see dozens of figures—only shadows, really—watching us from the forest or drawing closer to the trail.

"John Neptune whispered again to the horses and showed them the little looking glass that he had taken from his great-uncle John Neptune, and the animals became very calm.

" 'Are they a mirror now?' I asked him when he returned to the sleigh. I had taken a rifle from under the seat and laid it across my lap.

" 'They think they are,' said John Neptune quietly.

" 'I'm not sure what help a looking glass is going to be here,' I said.

" 'Go ahead and we will find out,' he said.

"I nickered at the horses and urged them forward. They seemed to be without fear as they approached the figure on the trail. It was something like a bear, I thought, but then again, something like a man, and yet nothing like bear or man. I had never seen anything like it, and I can tell you that I have met with some peculiar things in the woods. It was larger than I had first thought, which was large enough, and it let out a deep noise that seemed to resonate in the trees and the reins in my hand.

"But as we approached, the figure grew less sure of itself; it returned to all fours for a moment, then straightened again and stared with wide, dark eyes as we passed.

" 'It has seen itself,' said John Neptune, and this time I did not need to be told to put on speed. I was only too glad to make distance between ourselves and that creature. Other things came out of the forest, however, stranger things still. Some watched us pass in bafflement; others—those I did not look at too closely—screamed with fright at the sight of us and fled. Shapes followed us on either side—we could hear as well as see them—and more than once something flew from the darkness, only to veer away at the last moment.

"After an hour or so we saw less of these things. They seemed to have lost interest in us somehow, as if the influence upon them had waned and they were returning to the functions that would normally draw them from the sphere of human knowledge.

"It was a two-hundred-and-fifty-mile journey, and we traveled it in eighteen hours and sixteen minutes. The outskirts of Montreal slid past us before the dawn, and we were glad to see the lights of the city draw close and envelop us.

"A man charged out of the city hall as we approached, leaping and shouting that we had arrived. I knew from his excitement that we had won, and in truth we were ahead of our Boston rivals by four hours. Others came out of the building, and the man at the fore hurried up to us, only to take one close look and faint dead away." Mr. Tolly took note of his pipe all of a sudden and searched about himself for a match.

"So Portland won the railroad line because of your driving and John Neptune's enchantments," said Sundry.

"Well," said the old man, light glittering in his eyes, "that's what they say."

"But why did the man faint? Was he that excited?"

"John Neptune had forgotten to stop and tell the horses that they weren't a mirror anymore."

Sundry chuckled.

"That fellow," explained Mr. Tolly, "charged out, took one look at those horses, and saw himself pulling that sleigh! I don't know that he ever got over it. He'd been drinking, however, and we hoped that his condition would moderate the memory of what he had seen."

"Really? And did it?"

"Actually, he became a priest, I think."

It was near midnight when Sundry left Mr. Tolly. They could hear snoring, sure enough, coming from another room. "I'm sorry not to meet your cousin," said Sundry.

"Come back again," said the old fellow. They shook hands, and Mr. Tolly stood on the walk and took in the air as Sundry disappeared up the steep stairs and returned to the road.

Walking back to the hotel, Sundry wondered how Mister Walton's night at the ball was turning out, and then he fell to thinking how Portland had prospered by the Atlantic and St. Lawrence Railroad. He didn't even know that Commercial Street was built to accommodate the new line or how the wharf district was improved upon and increased. He thought of John Neptune, whom they had left in Richmond. And he thought of the Merrymeeting and the girl with the blue-gray eyes.

Watching from behind a tree on the other side of the street, Adam Tweed's henchman, Sketchy Rowse, was careful not to be seen a second time.

35. Diversion and Duty

THE HOME OF MRS. CAPT. LEDLAND BLYTHE, on the corner of Lincoln and Middle Streets, was imposing in its extent and in the view it commanded atop a broad knoll overlooking the Kennebec and many a more humble rooftop. When Miss McCannon and Mister Walton arrived, the fall gala, already in progress, could be heard. Music and chat and laughter blended through the walls to form a congenial welcome to the ears; every light in the house burned brightly, and the smoke of wood fires spiced the air.

A young man took the bridle of the horse when they pulled up before the front door and took over the reins when they stepped out.

It was a consummate fall night, with a bracing wind off the river and brilliant stars in a moonless sky, and they paused to quietly revel in it. There was perhaps nothing really wrong with Mister Walton's collar, but standing at the very bow of the cul-de-sac, between two hedges, Phileda reached up and tweaked it slightly—an intimate gesture that was seasoned with a happy smile.

"Did Sundry miss something?" he wondered.

"No," she said enigmatically, and took his arm.

The wide double doors opened before them as they mounted the steps, and two liveried men took their coats and hats. A third man, similarly accoutred, led them through the front hall to a ballroom, from which the largest share of noise arose.

"If you will wait, ma'am, sir," said the fellow, "I will announce you." And with full appreciation of the comic affectation, he declared, "Miss Phileda McCannon! Mister Tobias Walton!" which delighted Mister Walton, since the man had not asked their names.

There was a good deal of laughter then; it was the joke of the evening that everyone should be introduced in this fashion, and the unmarried women, with their leap-year escorts, drew the loudest reactions.

There was not just laughter but admiration, for Miss McCannon's dress was bold in its simplicity, which she carried off very well. Her gown was blue, with long sleeves and accordion shoulders; hers was not a figure of great extremes, so a cascade of frills at the bust distracted the eye and a lack of frill or pleat at the skirt drew attention to the purity of line there.

Mister Walton carried his portly frame with unconscious dignity and ease and demonstrated, by his attire, the ability to buy and to dress.

The periphery of the room was lined with men in their ties and tails, women in their fall gowns; small islands of conversation dotted the parqueted floor, and from a raised platform in a far corner a band (sort of a string quartet with the addition of a banjo and a flute) played something softly. Phileda's friend Miriam and her husband came from the crowd to greet them, and Mister Walton was introduced to Mr. Nowell.

"Very glad to meet you," said the husband. "My wife asserts you have stories to tell."

"I fear," said Mister Walton, "that Phileda has overstated my involvement in some interesting affairs."

"She has not *overstated* anything, Mister Walton," said Mrs. Nowell. "It pleases her to tease us with hints and references. 'Kidnappings! An escaped bear!' she says, and answers our queries with 'You must meet him.' "

Mister Walton laughed heartily.

A very handsome woman of later years appeared at Miss McCannon's side, and they embraced affectionately. Mrs. Blythe was eighty years and a month and proof of the bard's contention that "*age cannot wither . . .*" She had an exceptionally clear eye, and every lineament of her youth was somehow manifest in her aged features. It did not surprise Mister Walton, after some minutes in this woman's vigorous presence, to discover that her husband, himself eighty-four years of age, was at that moment captaining ship somewhere between Hallowell and Barbados.

In the course of their conversation (during which they found themselves a little apart from the others), Mister Walton *was* surprised to hear Mrs. Blythe refer to Phileda as "my cousin."

"You are related, then," he said to the hostess.

"Not that my parents ever knew," said the woman, "but I call her my cousin because I like her so much."

Mister Walton stood with his hands clasped behind his back, his round middle thoughtfully preceding him. "It is an amiable way to collect a family," he said.

"It is the only sure way to gain relatives you can endure."

Mister Walton thought of Sundry Moss and the members of the Moosepath League. He said, almost to himself, "I was fortunate in the people to whom I was born as well as in my friends."

"My own relations are tolerable, on the whole," replied Mrs. Blythe, "though I warn you, one approaches who does not always equal that description."

Mister Walton caught the flash of something guarded in Phileda's eye, and he turned to greet this newcomer. The woman who approached was a good twelve or fifteen years younger than he, and attractive in a sly sort of way. Her pretty auburn hair was in ringlets that would have suited a woman half her age, and yet she wore them with a full measure of self-assurance. She had large blue eyes spaced narrowly over a perfectly straight nose and a full lower lip that was both expressive and evocative. This lower extremity did not seem to join the rest of her face in an otherwise inclusive smile. She seemed the human equivalent of a very beautiful fox.

The man on this woman's arm was the physical antipode of Mister Walton. Tall and slender, his features were large; his eyebrows, black angles. He had a fine head of silver hair.

"Minerva," said Mrs. Blythe. The older woman let the younger come to her, and then she embraced her—not falsely but as she might a child she would care to scold. Implicit in the hostess's voice and movement was the admonition to behave. "Mister Walton," she said, "may I introduce to you my cousin, Mrs. Bateson Wallace."

"Mrs. Wallace," said Mister Walton.

The woman extended a languid hand and rested it briefly in his. "Mister Walton," she said carefully, "this is my friend, Charleston Thistlecoat."

"I am very pleased to meet you, sir." Mister Walton offered his hand, and Thistlecoat took it with the air of a man who reserves judgment.

"Charleston has just gained the controlling stock in the *Portland and Rochester*," said Minerva Wallace offhandedly.

"I have ridden your railroad, sir," said Mister Walton pleasantly.

"I myself never travel by rail," Thistlecoat said quietly.

"It reaches some very excellent places," said Mister Walton with a twinkle in his eye.

Others in the group were introduced even as new people joined them. Thistlecoat took a conspicuous interest in Phileda, who greeted him and Mrs. Wallace with barely the hint of distance. Mrs. Wallace glanced from Phileda to Mister Walton with curiosity or amusement arching her brows.

Minerva Wallace affected to find nothing humorous unless it was spoken by her escort, and Charleston Thistlecoat gave to every utterance the same bit of weight, so that it was very difficult to say when he *thought* he was supplying Mrs. Wallace with reason to laugh. He did bestow urbane smiles upon Phileda McCannon, however, and when Mrs. Wallace insisted they move on, he said to Mister Walton's escort, "Miss McCannon, you will do me the service of putting my name in your dance card for a waltz."

"I will do that, Mr. Thistlecoat," said Phileda gracefully.

"I, too, must have a place there, Phileda," declared Mr. Nowell.

"I already have Mister Walton's name on *my* card," said Mrs. Blythe.

Phileda gave her friend Miriam Nowell a reproving glance, since that woman must have preceded their arrival with a report (however favorable) of Mister Walton's character.

Mister Walton, meanwhile, deemed it wise to take occupation of as much of Miss McCannon's dance card as social dictates allowed—and quickly.

It has been said that the *grand march* was first instituted by French society, perhaps by the Sun King himself, as a means of placating private indiscretion with public virtue. It was deemed proper to reserve the first dance of an evening for a legal spouse, if one was had, and yet some fickle hearts might care to adorn another with that honor. The grand march, therefore, was enough like a dance to signify, in a public manner, that duty had been done, yet enough *un*like a dance to appease the jealousy of a mistress or the hurt sensibilities of a gigolo.

The very idea of a grand march in Maine in the fall of 1896 was filled with humor rather than intrigue. Mrs. Blythe, in the absence of her husband, was escorted by an elderly cousin as she led the procession, and there were only the servants to fill the office of audience, except the performers themselves, who were audience to each other.

Mrs. Blythe considered duty done, however, and had no compunctions in claiming Mister Walton for the first true dance of the evening—a *scottische*, which is a type of polka. The hostess was as nimble as a schoolgirl, and Mister Walton was famous, wherever he had danced, for his agility, and they were the favorites to watch while they capered. Applause followed them from the floor, and Mister Walton, though his inclination would lead him to other pastures, was polite enough to offer Mrs. Blythe some refreshment.

A *Portland Fancy* was next on the card, and Miss McCannon, who had danced with Mr. Nowell in the last, now danced with another fellow. She waved gaily to Mister Walton and Mrs. Blythe as she and her partner skipped past.

"She looks twenty years old," said Mrs. Blythe with obvious pleasure, and when Mister Walton only smiled after Phileda, the hostess said, "She has told me a good deal about you."

"I thought I was a great secret," he replied, still smiling.

"Phileda and I have always been close, especially since her mother died."

"I am grateful, then, for her sake."

Mrs. Blythe dismissed this with a wave. "I've known her since she was a child."

"I am envious, then, for mine."

"Captain Blythe might be envious of *you*," said the elderly woman. "He has always counted Phileda as his pet, and she has leave to abuse him even more than I. He depends on her teasing, I promise you."

The portly fellow knew well (and well appreciated) Miss McCannon's teasing. He laughed softly. "*I* have no claim that would make him envious," he said with a blush.

Mrs. Blythe made a vague sort of sound. "*There* is another interesting woman," she said, and indicated by a subtle gesture a beautiful woman, perhaps ten years Mister Walton's senior. "She always graces us with her company," continued the hostess, "but never a man with her favor."

"There is something melancholy about her," ventured Mister Walton.

"Do you see it? Phileda said you were perceptive." Mrs. Blythe spoke not as a gossip, for gossip takes pleasure in others' misfortune, but only as an interested and compassionate spectator of life. "Elizabeth Verrill. The war brought complications to her life that none of us will ever know, Mister Walton. She has been away for some months, visiting family in Massachusetts."

The woman wore her hair, where silver vied with coal black, in an old-fashioned manner that was not the less attractive for being out of style. Her eyes were pale blue and did have the look of sadness, almost weariness, to them, yet showed interest with whomever she was speaking.

A quadrille came next; Mister Walton was accosted by Mrs. Nowell (on the strength of its being a leap-year ball), and they were paired off with a couple to whom he had not been introduced. Mr. Nowell, in the meantime, escorted Miss McCannon to the punch bowl, where presided the hostess. "And what have you two been talking about?" asked Phileda.

"Oh, nothing of consequence," said Mrs. Blythe with a smile that purposely belied her words.

Circumstance continued to keep Mister Walton and Miss McCannon on opposite sides of the ballroom, the center of which moved with dark coats and colorful gowns. He was looking for Phileda, in fact, just before the first waltz, and when he caught sight of her, she was already speaking with Charleston Thistlecoat. Mister Walton was unsettled watching her step onto the dance floor with the tall fellow and considered himself small for it; he was *stopped short*, as it were, and wished for a quiet minute and an unoccupied corner in which he might regroup his thoughts.

Phileda smiled mildly, then gave Thistlecoat one hand and rested the other lightly on his shoulder. She appeared to enjoy herself as, with the rest of the dancers, they wheeled gracefully past Mister Walton; he wasn't sure if she saw him. Thistlecoat was talking, eyebrows raised, eyes peering down his straight nose at her; she listened with polite attention.

For the briefest moment, a very odd thing happened inside Mister Walton, for a stroke of anger flashed against his heart; a vague, unnatural *touche* that was not reserved for any one person but was broad enough in scope to do for all—himself included. He flinched, as if he had been stuck with a pin.

"Good heavens!" he said in a whisper. "Good heavens!"

He realized, when he considered what disturbed him, that his only claim upon Phileda was to escort her to the ball. And even if Charles Thistlecoat seemed a little "lofty," he did prove to be a graceful dancer. Phileda was not a girl, of course, and if she accepted a man's invitation to dance, she would accept it gracefully. Mister Walton would not have been so taken with her if she had been anything else.

"It was very kind of you to bring Phileda tonight," came a voice at his side. Mrs. Wallace stood there, watching the dancers, seemingly uninterested in Mister Walton's reaction.

"It was not kind at all," he said. "It is my very great pleasure. And, of course, she brought *me*, which perhaps says more for *her* kindness."

"Really?" said the woman, as if this amused her but scarcely. She turned an exquisitely languorous gaze upon him. "Well," she said, "it is very kind of you to say so."

"Since returning to Maine," he answered, "I have met a good many people, and Miss McCannon is one of the finest."

"Charleston does seem rather taken with her," said the woman with half a smile. She scanned the dance floor till she had picked them out.

Mister Walton's uncharacteristic stab of vexation had dissipated, and he was left to study Mrs. Wallace (which he did rather than look for Phileda and Mr. Thistlecoat and therefore appear too curious). Minerva Wallace affected great poise and reserve, which he suspected did not run very deep. She was, he was sure, a whorl of complex reactions centered around simple motives. His mother would have said that Mrs. Wallace, despite being beautiful, was "not very happy," and he was ready to believe this—a conclusion that did not make him like the woman more or even pity her but to look upon her as if she were of a separate race whose behavior was fascinating to catalog.

She was ready to say something else when, much to Mister Walton's gratitude, Mrs. Blythe joined them. "What have you been telling this man, Minerva?" she said, humor mitigating the note of counsel in her voice.

"We've been talking about Phileda, if you must know," said Mrs. Wallace. "I was remarking that Charleston seems rather taken with her."

"As well he should be," said Mrs. Blythe. She cast a glance, almost a wink, in Mister Walton's direction. "I will think more highly of him for his good judgment."

"Yes," said Miss Wallace. She turned her gaze, uninterested and dismissive, upon her elderly cousin. "I know you have always liked her. There's Audrey," she said, and followed her own wave in the direction of a woman who stood several yards away.

Mrs. Blythe looked as if she were doing her best not to make a face.

"Those are deep waters, I fear, Mrs. Blythe," said Mister Walton with more amusement than severity.

"I do not know how very deep they are, Mister Walton," she replied, "but they are certainly very dark."

The music came to an end, and the waltzers left the dance floor. Charleston Thistlecoat led Phileda McCannon to the opposite side of the room, where one of the punch bowls stood.

"He does have a sense of humor," said Phileda about Thistlecoat later in the evening.

Mister Walton had not suggested otherwise and did not argue with her when she said this. "It is perhaps a little dry" was all he said.

"More ironic than dry, I think," she returned. She had apologized for abandoning him, and they were waiting out a dance while she explained that she had dispensed with most of her social duties for the night. "You were in serious conversation with Minerva," she said, perhaps revealing something by admitting that she had noticed.

"She thought Mr. Thistlecoat rather taken with you," he replied puckishly.

"Did she?" Phileda laughed, and the sound was so clear of anything but heartfelt humor that Mister Walton found himself gazing at her, his own face beaming. Her hand slipped into the crook of his arm.

When they did waltz that night, they said very little.

Book Five

OCTOBER 12, 1896

❖

from the *Eastern Argus*
October 12, 1896

MARINE ITEMS

*Various Happenings of the Harbor
and Wharves.*

The Schooner *Loala* Was Heard
From Yesterday.

*Large Shipments of Grain Have
Been Made From Portland.*

The wind came around to the "nor'ard," as the old salts say, about noontime yesterday, and the large fleet that has been in for shelter immediately made preparations for departure. One by one they hoisted sails, and at sunset but very few of them remained.

Captain Amey and likewise the schooner *Loala* were heard from yesterday, and all fears concerning the vessel's safety were dispelled.

It seems that the captain discovered that the schooner needed some repairs, and late Sunday he had her towed over to a secluded portion of the Cape shore in order to make them.

Nobody seems to have noticed the departure of the *Loala* from the elevator, and as the captain neglected to inform anybody as to where he was going, it was only quite natural that many shipping men were completely mystified.

Before any news of Captain Amey had been received yesterday, another vessel had been given his charter, and now he will have to wait for cargo.

The run of herring during the . . .

36. The Level of Private Thought

IN A GIVEN SEASON, any city will have many tales to interest its people, and Portland was no exception in the days after the gale of October 11, 1896. The impending visit of William Jennings Bryan and Arthur Sewell was spending ink in the local papers, as was a murder investigation in Parsonfield. The gale itself continued to engender news; the foremast and foretop gallant mast of the barkentine *Golden Sheaf* were lost in the teeth of the storm, and the next day, the ship was towed into Portland; many came down to the waterfront to survey the damage.

For a day or so there was also concern over two disappearances—that of a small boy, unnamed in the newspapers, and of the coaster vessel *Loala*. Two days after the storm, when the telegraph line to Cape Elizabeth was repaired, news came that the *Loala* had safely come there for repairs, though it sounded a near thing to some to sail, or even tow, a vessel in need of fixing through gale winds. Most of the mariners on the wharf conjectured that she had put out before the storm reached its peak but thought it, anyway, a chancy thing.

The tale of the missing boy, for lack of detail to report, was quickly forgotten by the general public.

There are many levels of *buzz* in a community, and Angus McAngus, reporter for the *Portland Daily Advertiser*, once numbered them to a colleague thusly (and in this order): general knowledge, news, gossip, rumor, communal suspicion, public intuition, neighborhood secrets, and private thoughts. The further down this ladder, the more mysterious the level of buzz and the more it interested him. Angus understood that any story might exist on more than one level, and his job, of course, was to find the level that most closely approximated the truth, then to decide which level looked best in print.

The tale of the *Loala* was a case in point; one day, the ship and her crew were gone, with no one to witness when or where (and particularly *why*) she had left the harbor in such a storm; the next day, it was reported that the *Loala* had been taken into Cape Elizabeth, ostensibly for repairs.

The general knowledge in this instance was that the *Loala* and all hands were safe; the news was that Captain Amey lacked sound judgment; the gossip was that he was mad; the rumor was that he was running contraband; communal suspicion (as far as Angus could tell) was that the illegal cargo was not your run-of-the-mill spirituous liquors.

The neighborhood secret was what Angus was truly curious about.

His own private thoughts were stoked by deeper private intuitions.

He had nothing to do with either story in the *Daily Advertiser*, but he had read the account carefully in all the papers. The first had raised a puzzle; the second, which professed to solve the puzzle, raised in its stead a suspicion. Then rumor breezed Horace McQuinn's name in Angus's ear, and Angus was reminded of the strange conclave he witnessed at *the Crooked Cat* on the night before the *Loala*'s disappearance.

Angus greeted Officer Skillings on his way into the *Eastern Argus* on the afternoon of October 13, and though the newspaperman was braving rival territory, he did not fail to take note of the policeman's demeanor. Angus was known among the constabulary partly as a reporter for the *Daily Advertiser*, partly as a man about sports, and partly as a man about town. He trod a fine social line in his relationship with Dotty Brass; with his frequent attendance at her establishment, some might have said he trod the further side of the line. For all that, he was well liked among the *cops*.

With his long silver hair and fashionable togs, a perpetual expression that somehow balanced doubt and amusement, and a large cigar invariably crammed in the corner of his mouth, he was instantly recognizable to the greater part of the city's population—well-to-do or poor, honest or otherwise. Officer Skillings greeted Angus with a reverse nod when they met just outside the *Eastern Argus*, but there was something tentative and preoccupied about the policeman that Angus thought curious.

Skillings had the look of a man who was doing his best to appear engaged in some activity not readily apparent to the common observer. He met Angus's eyes with his own for the briefest moment, then looked away and took several steps down the sidewalk, looking tentatively purposeful. Angus, who had other things on his mind, took the outside stairway that led to the second-floor offices of the *Eastern Argus* and disappeared inside.

The rumble of the presses was conspicuously absent from the building, as if the pulse of the Printers' Exchange had momentarily ceased. Life itself, however, continued to be evident to Angus as he stood in the narrow hall.

"—said you had nothing to do with the boy," came the voice of the *Argus*'s editor, Frederick "Fritz" Corbel.

Angus considered whether anyone had heard him enter before easing the door to with a quiet click. From an open doorway, halfway to the other end of the hall, he could hear the voice of a woman raised in barely concealed annoyance. "Well, I didn't, to be sure; but having been implicated in the situation, however mistakenly, I feel obliged to look into it further."

"But you just happen to think he's at the cape."

There was no answer.

"*I* would think, since the police have decided to believe your story, you would do well to attend the next charity ball or coming out or soiree and call it good." There was a hint in Corbel's voice that the police may (or may not) have believed the woman's story, but as an editor, *he* was reserving judgment.

"I could wish for more than charity balls and social events," said Mollie Peer, whose voice Angus recognized.

"Are you hard up for expenses?" asked Corbel.

Mollie was insulted by the question. "I am not." But the conversation had been derailed by an expert. Angus winced, as at a paper cut.

"Miss Peer," said Corbel, "Bryant and Sewell are coming to Portland next week, the most political hay we'll pitch for a year."

"Yes?"

"And if I send you down to city hall to report the goings-on in the back room, do you think the big boys are going to let you in?"

There was no reply.

"Do you think that Chief Hiram is going to let you talk to his latest prisoner down at the cells? Do you think any editor in his right mind is going to send a young woman, such as yourself, down to the tilty end of the waterfront to question the drunks and no-accounts about some kid's disappearance?"

There was no reply.

"If you *did* know something about this business, there might be something for you to write about, but as things are, this is the sort of thing Peter Mall can handle standing on his head, and for all I know he's writing about it even as we speak."

"Your first mistake, Miss Peer," said Angus, appearing in the open doorway to Corbel's office, "was asking. Better to go forth and make excuses afterwards than to ask and be told no." The dormant length of a cigar protruded from the corner of his mouth.

Mollie Peer held a dark velvet purse in her lap and was wearing gloves and an understated hat that was punctuated with a single purple plume. Angus, who was something of a connoisseur of women's fashions, thought she looked as stylish in her nearly *out* of fashion Persian lamb jacket and oversized collars as those ladies more closely accoutred to the times.

She did not seem very pleased with his interruption.

Fritz Corbel never *seemed* anything at all; whatever he felt at any given moment was all too plain. "Doesn't anybody knock? When did you come in? What are you skulking around for? You make as much noise as Uncas, padding about the forest in his moccasins! Is that how you fill that scandal sheet of yours?" He turned to Mollie. "Didn't I tell you to shut the door?"

"I don't believe so, no," said the young woman, one exquisite eyebrow raised as if she were warning a noisy child. In the face of Corbel's rant, Mollie's response was filled with a remarkable lack of trepidation.

"What are you looking for, work?" asked Corbel of Angus. His own cigar smoldered furiously, and he looked appropriately like an engine letting off steam.

"Just a good story, now that the baseball is done."

"Well, there is nothing happening here."

"On the contrary," said Angus. "I would say that your reporters are stirring up stories where there were none before." Angus had been haunting the police station the last day or so, and twice he had seen Mollie come in to be questioned regarding the disappearance of the little boy.

"She's not a reporter," said Corbel, which caused the barest flinch from the young woman. "She writes a social column. And," he said, glancing at Mollie over the stacks on his desk, "she had nothing to do with it. The cops had her confused with someone else."

"There seems to be a fair measure of disappearance lately," said Angus, prodding with the subject that was really on his mind.

"Have you lost something now?" asked the editor wryly.

"I was thinking of the *Loala*."

"The coaster? She's in Cape Elizabeth. Don't you read your own paper?"

Angus shrugged; he brushed at something on his cheek. Corbel's stare dipped, in a space of a blink, from Angus's eyes to the young woman and back. There was significance in the quick glance, though the editor's face showed no more expression than before.

Angus took the man's meaning in the space of a second blink; it was no secret that Eustace Pembleton, a wild man at best, had been making the police station noisy with his complaints (just short of threats) against Miss Peer, Wyckford O'Hearn, and Horace McQuinn. Angus recalled the odd assembly he had caught sight of at the Crooked Cat that Sunday night. "Whatever Pembleton's reason for accusing you, Miss Peer," said Angus, "he's a dangerous man."

"He's mad," said Corbel.

"And he's twisted up, somehow, with Adam Tweed, who's more dangerous still—and perhaps as mad."

"Tweed?" said Fritz Corbel, his own instincts for a story showing plain with the sudden interest on his face. "It's the first I've heard of Tweed having anything to do with this."

"I saw Pembleton and Tweed together the night of the kid's disappearance," said Angus. It was not natural for him to spill this sort of news to his archrival (and, to be truthful, his oldest friend), but he knew, from years of experience with Fritz Corbel, that the man was genuinely concerned for the young woman's safety.

"You didn't see McQuinn in your travels that night?" asked the editor.

"Horace?" Angus glanced at Mollie to see how this was setting with her. It didn't seem very likely that she was as unconnected with the affair as she protested. Even a madman like Pembleton needed some reason to fix blame, though it could turn out that she was simply *there* when the boy disappeared. Ladling out a little news, Angus might learn more than he enlightened yet. "Horace was there, I guess," he said, "but he wasn't with them."

"What do you mean, he wasn't with them?"

"Let's just say they weren't taking him into their confidence. There was another one with Tweed, though." Angus searched his memory and came up with the image of a tall stick of a man with straw-colored hair. "A long, spindly fellow, an actor—yes, an actor; though I'm not sure when he plied his trade last." Corbel's attention was on Angus now, and only Angus saw Mollie's dark eyes widen. "I can't think of his name," finished the silver-haired reporter.

"An actor," said Corbel to Mollie, as if this made matters worse. "God bless us all!"

"I would stay close to the society gatherings for now, Miss Peer," said Angus. "O'Hearn won't have much to do with baseball over; he could watch after you."

Mollie shot Angus a glance that spoke volumes, none of which were meant to amuse.

"Stay away from O'Hearn," said Corbel. "He admitted to taking the boy in the first place, though he claims not to know where the kid got to."

Mollie, who had said almost nothing since Angus arrived, stood from her chair and bid them good day. Angus straightened himself away from the doorjamb to give her room to pass. When her back was turned, Corbel shot another glance at Angus, then said to Mollie, "Do we get some news tomorrow?"

"News?" she said. "Do you mean, my *column?* I'll send it with someone."

"If Mr. O'Hearn is barred from your company, Miss Peer," said Angus as she passed him, "may *I* escort you somewhere."

"You are welcome to your share of the sidewalk, Mr. McAngus," she answered without stopping. "If we are going in the same direction."

Angus gave only a cursory glance in Corbel's direction before following the woman. Fritz Corbel didn't know which of them was the keener to know what the other knew or which of them would get it.

It may seem contradictory to those of us in the latter days of the twentieth century that in an era of "carefully" considered social standards, such as the end of the nineteenth century, a woman could take a man's arm without considering it an intimate gesture. It was, perhaps, the descendant of some ideal—the putting oneself under protection—that lived still and allowed a young woman like Mollie to take the arm of a bare acquaintance such as Angus McAngus. Indeed, social mores almost dictated that she should, the supposition being that if she ought not to give the man her arm, she ought not to be walking with him. And so the reader must not make too much of the situation to know that Angus McAngus took the street side of the walk (another prerequisite, to protect the lady from being splashed by passing traffic), offered his arm, and that she very naturally took it.

Angus was a little surprised to see Officer Skillings outside the Printers' Exchange again, then amused to catch a look of disappointment on the policeman's face when it was clear that Mollie had an escort. "One of your readers?" he asked her.

"Yes, I believe Officer Skillings *is* very astute in his choice of journals," she said easily.

He laughed both at the riposte and at the pleasure of having this attractive young woman on his arm. His dandyish charm was not without its effects on some women, and he wondered if he could work it on Mollie. He walked her around a puddle on the sidewalk. A small gang of boys shouted to him from across the street.

He waved to the boys, saying, "Who is this actor I saw with Tweed and Pembleton the other night?"

"If *you* saw him, you would know better than I," she replied, but she took her arm from his—an almost involuntary movement—and looked ready to part company with him.

He was quite taken with her, as impressed by the controlled manner in which she responded to the unexpected question as he was by her physical endowments. He liked smart women as well as physical endowments—something to which Dotty Brass could attest. "A tall stick of a fellow," he said, "thin blond hair, not much to look at."

Mollie stopped, and Angus pulled up. "Amos—" she said.

"—Guernsey!" he finished. "That's him! Amos Guernsey."

"Amos Guernsey was with Eustace Pembleton and Adam Tweed?"

"You know him?" Angus asked.

"Yes," she said quietly, registering a sudden misgiving.

"Where *is* the boy?" he asked. He was sure that she was about to tell him when he brilliantly connected two seemingly disparate events. "This doesn't have anything to do with the *Loala*, does it?"

Angus had overplayed his hand. "The *Loala*?" she said. "Do you mean the boat that disappeared? They found that, didn't they?"

"Yes, but it was an odd business, leaving in the middle of a storm. For repairs, they said." He watched her carefully, feeling like the fisherman who sees the line shiver and reels it in to find the bait gone.

A mask had risen in Mollie's face to hide the confusion. "I thought we were talking about the little boy?" she said.

"Never mind," he said hastily. Maybe he liked endowments in a woman better than intelligence, after all.

"Thank you for your kind escort, Mr. McAngus," she said, backing away from him and giving him her winningest smile.

"Which way are you going?" he asked.

"This way," she said, and hurried in a direction perpendicular to the one they had been walking.

She knew who Amos Guernsey was, Angus thought to himself, *if that means anything*. She was very tall and very fetching as she hurried through the traffic and up a side street. He made no disguise of his admiration, and a little sigh from him went after her.

It took three or four blocks of vigorous walking for Mollie to pick through a welter of apprehension and raise up the most disturbing element in Angus's news. It seemed improbable that Amos Guernsey would be seen in the company of Adam Tweed and Eustace Pembleton, though not impossible. Putting Horace in the picture raised a series of separate doubts, but it had been well established that Horace McQuinn knew everyone in Portland's darker environs. What most troubled Mollie was the memory of Amos on the day of Bird's rescue (or kidnapping) and particularly of the actor's claim of penury and of his barely concealed threat of disclosure.

Mollie was convinced that she had put paid to Amos's initial threat;

but what else might the man do to see his palm crossed with a few coins? He *had* followed her that day on the waterfront. Had he been following her since?

She was on Congress Street now, vaguely aware that she should be looking for an idle cab. Several long wagons, filled with lumber and bricks, thundered past; the men sitting on the building materials shouted in loud voices to one another. She realized that she was repeating her mistake—that *Angus* might be following her even now. She wasn't sure whether to turn around and let the reporter know that she knew (if he were there) or quietly mislead him somehow. If Angus was following her, she was not disturbed by his interest; she understood it too well. Angus wanted the *story* not only for his paper but for his own finely honed curiosity.

There were several businesses across Congress Street, and during the fleeting breaks in traffic she tried to glimpse in the store windows a suspicious reflection. Standing on the curb with such indecision plain in her face, and even in her posture, she garnered attention from other passersby.

To be truthful, she had been in a state of uncertainty since Saturday night, when they sent the child off with the members of the Moosepath League. She did wonder where they were. The lion's share of her disquiet, which she barely understood, arose from her sense of Wyckford O'Hearn's sadness as they watched the yawl-boat disappear into the rain and the night.

Conflicted feelings of another sort had met her that night with Mrs. Makepeace at the door to the boardinghouse. It was well past ten o'clock when Mollie arrived, alone and dripping in the hall, and she had been subjected to a fierce interrogation. Mrs. Makepeace had given Mollie a good deal of license in the past, all out of keeping with a young woman in a respectable establishment, but this time Mollie was not able to fully exonerate herself. Hilda, of course, had been nearly out of her mind with worry and had not helped matters by bursting into tears in the parlor. Mollie almost wished that she had let Wyckford come in with her—he had offered—so that he could have shouldered some of the emotion.

It had taken the kind offices of the redheaded giant's own landlady to quiet Mrs. Makepeace's objections and save Mollie from eviction. Mrs. Barter came down that Sunday afternoon—*Yesterday was it?* Mollie wondered—and explained it all, or a safely truncated version, to Mrs. Makepeace. The two ladies sat to tea and commiserated over the youthful indiscretions of their tenants, but before they were finished, they were in something of a contest regarding the excellent qualities of their respective charges.

Then the police had arrived, and Mollie was twice questioned by them.

Now she was moved by a wave of fresh doubts as she imagined what Amos Guernsey might have been doing in the company of Adam Tweed and Pembleton. *Perhaps,* she thought, *I should find Wyckford O'Hearn and tell him.* But she hadn't really learned anything, and she worried that she would only cause the man further worry. It was also true that Amos was as likely to know the seedier denizens of the waterfront as Horace McQuinn.

What if Amos is watching me now! she thought. This brought her head around, and she scanned the busy street, scowling as if she had already caught sight of the man. Neither Amos nor Angus was in sight, however, and she chided herself for letting her imagination seize her so. It was still the middle of the day, and she was amid busy streets, and yet the phantom eyes of Eustace Pembleton and Tom Bull, as well as Amos Guernsey and Angus McAngus, seemed to brush her shoulder as her steps hurried in the direction of home.

37. Sun in the Afternoon

ON THE TWELFTH OF OCTOBER 1896, the *Portland Courier* read:

> The recent sunlit hours are in keeping with October's tradition in our fair city. The strength of sun and the resolve of wind conspire to produce one of the most amiable climates and affords that proportion of cool, though not cold, degrees as to facilitate a man at labor or a woman on a brisk walk. Contrarily, the darker hours, or those properly lit by moonlight, have smacked of November and remind us of what is to come. The day might be dry and sunny, but the evenings of late seem to bring with them clouds and wind and rain—more of which, we are told, is to be expected tonight.

It is well the days proved so amiable, since Cliff Cottage in its off-season was filled neither with people nor with diversion. It was indeed the activity, suggested by a pleasant day, that proved of great merit to the Moosepath League and the endeavor of a rainy night that so nearly brought disaster.

On the morning of the twelfth, Eagleton rose with a likable thought, and that was to hire an open carriage and treat his friends to a tour of the local sights. This scheme was forwarded, ratified, and put into action.

They spent the morning anticipating an outing which would prove doubly beneficial, providing them with amusement *and* taking them briefly from the environs of Baroness Blinsky, who, to tell the truth, made them a little anxious, with her spirits and sudden communications from the astral plane.

(Before she had gone to bed, the baroness had let out a sudden and startling cry, put the back of her hand to her forehead, and said, "Good heavens, Alcott, Wildfeather is terribly put out tonight!" Wildfeather, as it happened, was the baroness's spiritual familiar—the ghost of an American Aboriginal who had been contrarily described in the esoteric journals as both wild and somber. Strangely, the Moosepathians were not eager to meet Wildfeather that evening, and each quickly made his excuse for bed.)

It was during lunch that a second scheme was suggested by none other than Amos Guernsey; the fate of the day was sealed. "I would like to propose," said the actor, "a séance." He raised a glass of cider as if he had proposed nothing more than a toast.

Sunlight streamed through the south-facing windows of the dining room at Cliff Cottage, casting crosshatched shadows on the table linens and the polished floor. The air was warm, the day was bright, and yet something just below a shiver made itself felt through the Moosepathians.

There were eleven people at the long table. Mr. and Mrs. Sherman Stroad, an elderly couple from New York, as well as a drummer by the name of Ezra Staples sat with Ephram, Eagleton, and Amos on the one side; and opposite them were Bird, Thump, Baroness Blinsky, Major Alcott, and Miss Astoria Hempel, who was not yet middle-aged but taking in the country air like a dowager for her health.

"A séance?" said Ephram. He glanced warily in the direction of Baroness Blinsky, who looked as if such a thing had never occurred to her. She had been explaining to Thump how the "Masters of Tibet" communicated to her through esoteric means (such as mental imaging or telepathy—or sometimes by post), and Thump had politely allowed his plate to grow cold so that he could give her his utmost attention.

"The elements will be very favorable tonight," said Baroness Blinsky.

"A séance?" said Eagleton. His fork hovered above his plate, and he looked like a man who is listening intently for a small sound.

"It is not usual for the baroness to exercise her great powers at such short notice," intoned Major Alcott. He had not taken off his red fez, even for breakfast.

"A séance?" said Thump. He considered his plate as if he hadn't noticed it before.

"I'm sure I am very excited!" said Miss Hempel. Before Amos's proposal, she was almost giddy; now she was positively light-headed. She had large (and, to be honest, very pretty) blue eyes that flashed with alarming impact upon the bachelors at the table, but she had reserved her most heartfelt looks for Mr. Thump. "Oh, Mr. Thump!" she said. "I am *sure* I am very excited!"

Thump could not decide how to reply to this communication; Miss Hempel's face was rosy, and her breast swelled with a great sigh, none of which facilitated a solution.

"We must be circumspect regarding our energy," warned the baroness.

"Oh, yes, of course!" said Miss Hempel, a little reined in.

"Bobby, what are they saying?" asked Mrs. Stroad.

"It's a séance, Mumsy," said her husband.

"When? When is this going to happen?"

Amos asked the baroness, "Shall it be tonight?"

The woman put a thumb and forefinger to the place between her eyebrows, which nearly met above the bridge of her nose, and said, "Yes, it will be tonight. Wildfeather has important communications to . . . communicate."

"I believe I will be to bed," said Mrs. Stroad, and there was the hint in her voice that it could not be a very significant sort of event if she were not in attendance, and if it were not to be a significant event, then she had no intention of being there.

"You, of course," said the baroness, scanning the members of the club, "will be there."

Ephram looked to Eagleton; and Eagleton, to Thump; Thump looked to Ephram, then turned to Eagleton, who looked back at Ephram. "I believe—" began Ephram. He looked to Thump, who looked to Eagleton.

"—there is a difficulty in that," continued Eagleton. He turned to Ephram, who had started the sentence, but Ephram turned to Thump.

"—we must keep the boy with us at all times," finished Thump. His friends were both admiring of, and grateful for, this coda.

"You must bring him with you," insisted the baroness. "Children are very favorable to the masters, and the presence of a child at the table will facilitate communication with the other side."

On their way to dress for their afternoon outing, with Bird in tow, Ephram said, "I say, Thump, have you ever attended one of these . . . séances?"

"I myself was going to ask you much the same question," returned Thump. They saw that he was thinking and, knowing that great things often came of this process in him, waited for him to be done with it. Finally, he brightened and said, "It *was* the same thing, actually."

This continued affinity of mind encouraged them. It bode well for the human race if they, despite their separate political affiliations and religious backgrounds, could think so alike. "Eagleton?" said Ephram.

"I must say," said Eagleton, "that the words in which my own curiosity were about to be formed had much the identical ring to them."

"Extraordinary!" said Ephram.

"I was just about to say!"

Conversation in the hall continued along these lines for several minutes before they more or less simultaneously suggested that they prepare for their excursion.

Bird watched them with continued interest.

"Marvelous!" said Ephram.

The sights proved splendid that day, which continued sunny and warm. A degree of tension, however, manifested itself among the three friends, or, rather, within them (a direct result of the activity that had been proposed for that evening), and they were grateful for Eagleton's inspiration.

"Cape Elizabeth was *not* named after Queen Elizabeth, as is commonly imagined," read that gentleman from a chapbook he had purchased at Cliff Cottage. They had stopped to gaze at the lighthouse and the battery at Portland Head from their carriage.

"I never knew," said Ephram.

"It says here that it was named by Captain John Smith after the daughter of James the first and Queen Anne of Denmark."

"It was very nice of him," said Thump.

Their driver took them back along the Shore Road, past the Birch Knolls and Pillsbury Bluff. There were other folk taking the air, walking along the streets and roads that commanded the water, and the club members were quick to touch their hats as they drove past the ladies. (A serious nod was deemed sufficient for the men they met.) Bird, who wore a tweed cap, observed his guardians at this nicety, and soon was touching his brim to the ladies with a degree of goodwill that the Moosepathians quite admired; it reawakened within them an appreciation for the excellence of this custom.

They drew near two women as they entered the cul-de-sac of Sea View Avenue, and with great energy these four raised their hats. The ladies—one of middle age, the other perhaps a daughter in her latter twenties—smiled and nodded in return. Then the younger woman's eyes grew wide, and her mouth formed a perfect O to complete the picture of absolute surprise.

While driving by the two women, Ephram never returned his hat to his head but sat straight-backed, staring forward, with his black topper some inches above him, as if he were attempting to balance it upon thin air.

Eagleton turned as they went with nearly as much astonishment on his face as there was exhibited on the young woman's. "Goodness sakes!" he said. Thump, who was facing toward the rear with Bird, straightened his already exemplary posture, perhaps in an attempt to overcome a lack of height so that he could look over the back of the carriage. "Goodness sakes!" said Eagleton again. "Wasn't that Miss Riverille?" Ephram did not respond.

"I think you are right, Eagleton," said Thump, for it did appear to be Miss Sallie Riverille, whose pleasant presence had so agitated their friend Ephram at a public event the previous July.

Ephram said nothing. He had not turned around or lowered his hat. There was a look of consummate uncertainty upon his face.

"My goodness, it is!" concluded Eagleton. "Here they come! Driver, pull us up, if you please!"

Sallie Riverille was indeed waving as she hurried the older woman in the direction of the carriage, and there was a very wonderful smile inhabiting her face. The carriage was drawn to a halt, and Eagleton vaulted out with an almost cavalier aplomb. "Ephram," he said with great joy for his friend. "I do believe she is very anxious to greet you."

Courtesy outranked all else in Ephram's disposition, even fear, and because of this, he was able to climb from the carriage with a good deal less élan than his friend. He had not yet returned his hat to its perch.

In Mister Walton's absence, Ephram was considered the deputy chairman, and it was to his example that the eyes of his friends often referred. Eagleton had never seen a person tip his hat for such a long interval, but it occurred to him that the civility of the gesture might increase with the amount of time it was maintained. In deference to his friend's wisdom he lifted his own hat again and held it above his head as he and Ephram advanced upon Miss Riverille and her escort.

The effect of this eccentric approach upon the young woman was hilarious. "Oh, Mother!" she declared. "Didn't I tell you how amusing they were? *Mr.* Ephram! *Mr.* Eagleton! How wonderful to see you when the season had promised so little distraction. Oh, Ophelia will be mad with envy!"

"Miss Riverille," said Eagleton when Ephram did not speak up. He was a little shaken himself at the mention of Miss Simpson (with whom *he* had spoken at the Freeport Ball). He watched his friend from the corner of his eye so that he might not make the mistake of lowering his hat too soon, and they were only saved from this awkward posture by Mrs. Riverille, who kindly offered her hand. Ephram's courtesy demanded that he lower his hat so that he could take the lady's hand gently.

"I am Mrs. John Riverille," said the woman. "Sallie has told me so much about you."

"Matthew Ephram," said that worthy. "At your service, ma'am." He looked at Sallie with the light of terror in his eyes.

"Mr. Ephram," said the young woman again; she offered her slim hand. It was cool in Ephram's palm, and he held it briefly, with as much care as he would have handled a small bird.

Sallie Riverille had a small, oval face and a lovely complexion (*like a cameo*, Ephram had often thought); none of her features were remarkable by themselves—all brief and unassuming—but together they formed a pleasant aspect, so that her eyes, which squinted somewhat from behind a pair of round spectacles, were like twin gems hidden in tiny settings, and her modest mouth surprised a person with its ability to shine when she smiled, which was often. Her dark brown hair was piled high to reveal a graceful neck, and her large, feathered hat framed her face to the most advantageous effect.

She smiled now as she gave her hand to Ephram, and the force of her expression upon him was electric. A church clock happened to be in his line of sight, and he consulted it, saying, "Forty-two minutes past two o'clock."

"Brief showers expected tonight," said Eagleton, who had been pleased to find the morning's *Portland Daily Advertiser* at Cliff Cottage. "Winds in the east, tapering off near morning."

"High tide at four-eighteen," said Thump.

Mrs. Riverille, who had heard a great deal about these men (including what had been perceived as their eccentric humor), let go with a laugh that was as delighted as her daughter's. "Oh, you gentlemen!" she cried. "Sallie, I thought you had exaggerated!"

Eagleton accepted the hands of both mother and daughter and quickly took the reins. "We had no idea you would be in Cape Elizabeth today, Miss Riverille. Did we, Ephram?"

"I don't know why that should be," the young woman said with good humor. "I live here, after all."

"We had no idea! Did we, Ephram?"

Ephram managed a silent shake of the head, then articulated something like a hiccup.

"You wouldn't have, would you," said the young woman with a look of false peevishness, "since Mr. Ephram never inquired."

It occurred to Eagleton that the young woman with whom *he* had spent the evening of the fourth—one Ophelia Simpson—might also reside here in the Cape, and his own powers of speech summarily vanished.

Sallie and her mother seemed not to notice; they were introducing themselves to Thump and Bird. Bird made them laugh by tipping his hat, and Sallie ruffled his hair; she remarked on his moose totem. "I do like your little friend, Mr. Ephram," she said. "I think I shall ask him to escort me at the next gala I attend." She looked very pert when she said this, and her mother wagged a finger at her, though she smiled behind it.

Eagleton and Thump, who knew their friend so well, feared for Ephram's heart when Miss Riverille flashed a crafty look in his direction.

If Ephram was at all interested in this young woman's company, there were two mighty factors in his favor. The first was Sallie herself, for she thought him handsome and charming and gentle, which were three virtues she quite liked in a man. The second determinant, and perhaps the most powerful, was Mrs. Riverille's desire to see her daughter *well matched*—by which phrase she meant *wealthily* matched—and it had not been difficult for her to ascertain, through the customary channels of social gossip, Ephram's financial station, once she had discovered his name from her daughter on the day after the Freeport Fourth of July Ball.

With Eagleton and Ephram both mute, it was up to Thump to come to the fore, which he did with remarkable acuity. "Séance tonight" was the first thing that popped into his head.

"Oh, my!" said Mrs. Riverille.

"Baroness Blinsky and Major Alcott presiding," informed Thump. "Lodging at Cliff Cottage."

"My goodness!" said Mrs. Riverille.

"Our good friend Miss Hempel is staying there!" said the daughter.

"Yes," said Thump, agreeing with this view of matters. "Miss Hempel is very excited, to be sure. She mentioned it herself."

"Oh, Mum!" said Sallie. "Perhaps Astoria would act as chaperone, and I could attend!"

Ephram's expression grew a little wild.

"I don't know, dear," said the mother. "A séance! My goodness!" The Methodist church, of which they were members, did not take a very tolerant view of such goings-on. Then again, Sallie's father had always maintained that these mediums and spiritualists were a lot of charlatans practicing, in his inelegant phraseology, "a lot of humbuggery." So, if there was nothing to it, what could be the harm? "Well," she said, "let's give Astoria a call."

"May we offer you a ride?" asked Thump gallantly.

The mother, who thought they had put forward quite enough forwardness for the time being, declined on the grounds that she needed the exercise. The company parted with mutual well-wishing and handshakes, and Miss Riverille allowed her hand and her smile to linger with Ephram as she bid him adieu.

"Forty-seven minutes past two," said Ephram, and the young woman scolded him happily for a rascal.

"Don't forget showers tonight," said Eagleton. "Wind in the east."

"Oh, you gentlemen!" declared Mrs. Riverille.

The men and Bird were returning to their carriage now.

"High tide at four-eighteen," said Thump.

The driver snapped the reins. The women waved. The men lifted their hats and never put them back till they were out of sight. Bird held his cap above his head like his guardians, but there was an impish look in his eye as he turned to keep the ladies in sight as long as he could.

38. Misspoke or Misled

A GANG OF CHILDREN HAD TAKEN the playing field on the Western Promenade, now that the local team would not return till spring. The turf was damp from the storm, and Wyckford knew that they would probably scar up the outfield, though he hadn't the heart to discourage anybody from playing the game he loved, especially these boisterous kids with their homemade bat and ball.

It was always a melancholy time for Wyck, and he never stopped to think how it might appear for a big hulk of a fellow to be mooning about the ball yard like a dejected schoolboy. Some seasons he looked back upon with the sort of regret one feels for grand moments that are beyond recapture; the more he tried to relive them, the more they slipped away. This year he would have been looking back with the sort of regret one feels for moments never captured to begin with; he would have been looking back if his mind hadn't been occupied with the little boy he had sent off with strangers two days before. He wondered where they were.

Wyck had been questioned twice by the police, once at Mrs. Barter's house, where the landlady corroborated his story (he was rather shocked that she would prevaricate, even for a good cause), the second time at the station, where he was grilled by the chief himself. It had not been pleasant, but Wyck managed to stick by his version of events.

There was a good deal of loud banter between the teams (allegiance changed with swinging fortunes as the game progressed), and one muddy runt in the batter's box was staring down the pitcher, who stared back from about half the distance to the mound. Wyck was not mindful of the grin that touched the corners of his face as he watched the little batter swing the crudely fashioned bat. A notion struck Wyck with a sudden pang that Bird had probably never even seen a ball game, much less played in one—and might never.

"Are you Wyckford O'Hearn, mister?" came a voice from first base. With no bag at the corner, a hat had been commandeered as the object to tag.

"Yes," said Wyck. He was always a little surprised to be recognized.

The kid at first base grinned over his shoulder, his face dirty and gap-toothed, bare hands resting on knickers. "They say you hit a ball out to Congress Street once."

"Who told you that?" asked Wyck.

"My brother."

"I never believed anything *my* brother told me," said Wyck, smiling.

"He said you knocked it to Congress Street and it hit a horse."

Wyck nodded in the direction of the batter, who was a left-hander. "You better stay in the game or he's going to hit you."

"Alice can't hit anything," said the boy.

"Alice?"

"Her brother is supposed to be watching her. It's his bat and ball, so we let her play."

"Alice?" Wyck stared down the line at the kid in the batter's box and realized he was watching a little girl in boy's clothes scowl after a high pitch. He was reminded of his own childhood in Veazie, where there might not be enough boys to make two teams and a plucky girl or two would be recruited to fill out the rosters.

Now that he was older, he wasn't sure if he approved of females playing ball, but he couldn't help but like little Alice, with her smudged grimace and her hair tucked up under her hat. The ball came in low and inside, and the girl was able to get a piece of it. Sure enough, the first baseman was throwing another comment over his shoulder at Wyck when the out-of-round ball bobbled between his position and the unoccupied mound. Alice made first base standing and stuck her tongue out at the pitcher, who had evidently been blistering her with rough baseball chatter.

Before long, other members of the outfield took note of Wyck, and he was asked to "knock some out to them." He was a little amazed by the bat and the ball, the former a fairly heavy oaken stick that had been whittled into a shape resembling its office and the latter a piece of stolen leather that had been cleverly stitched by a shoemaker's son and filled to near bursting with feathers from his grandmother's bed. Wyck didn't dare knock it hard, but he popped it high so that they could scramble about in the field for it.

A carriage pulled up on the road just above the left-field foul line, and a tall, dark-haired woman stepped from it. The late-afternoon sun was behind Mollie Peer, outlining her figure to agreeable effect as she looked down at them. One of the older boys let out a low whistle.

"Mind your manners," said Wyck, casting the boy a sharp glance.

"Is that your sweetheart, Mr. O'Hearn?" asked another.

"No, kid," he said with an odd note in his voice. "That's not my sweetheart." Something in his upbringing (and in his nature) considered it ungallant to wait for the woman to come to him, so he signaled to her that he was on his way and handed the bat and ball to a pair of small hands.

There was enough of the athlete in Wyck that he didn't quite lumber up the bank, despite his size, and watching from the field, the kids were half-convinced that here were two emblems from some American legend: the giant ballplayer and the tall, beautiful woman standing almost in silhouette above.

Wyck had his bowler hat in hand as he approached her. "Miss Peer," he said. He was still a little put off by her frank appraisal.

"Mr. O'Hearn, I'm glad I found you. Mrs. Barter thought you might be down this way."

Wyck wasn't sure why he felt embarrassed, but his ears reddened. "I was showing some of the kids—" he began, then said, "What's wrong?"

The carriage behind Mollie moved slightly as the horse shifted; the animal let a snort out into the cooling air. A wind stirred from off the water, and a single curl of hair at Mollie's temple shivered a little. Wyck was struck by that single stray lock and forced himself to look away from it. He realized, then, that Miss Peer had said something that he hadn't heard.

"Pardon me?" he said.

"I'm a little concerned about Bird," she said again. Wyck thought this an odd thing to say; he had been concerned about the boy since he first laid eyes on him. "There's a man I know," she began, "with whom I have an understanding. No, not that sort of understanding—a business arrangement. He's an actor."

There was a palpable tension between them, though they were scarcely near enough for him to shake her hand if they had both reached out. Watching from the field, the children half-expected some dramatic moment—an embrace, some indication that Wyckford either misled or misspoke in denying that he and Mollie Peer were lovers.

39. What You Don't Hold

"WHY WOULD THIS FELLOW care anything about Bird?" wondered Wyckford. Mollie had been telling him about Amos while they rode, though Wyck sensed he was not hearing the entire tale.

"For the same reason that Adam Tweed cares about him, or Eustace Pembleton, for that matter. They think he represents some knowledge that will profit them. Pembleton, of course, fears that someone *else* will profit."

Wyck grunted. He didn't even like hearing Pembleton's name. "So where is he, this actor?"

"I don't know. But I saw him just before I came down to the waterfront that day. Then I caught sight of him on the wharf, so I am sure he followed me. If he knew Tweed was looking for the boy, it would explain what he was doing when McAngus saw him. Your friend Horace was there, too."

"Where?"

"Angus didn't say."

Wyck liked McAngus, but it bothered him to think of the dapper reporter conversing with Mollie. "How were you talking with McAngus?" he asked.

"I told you, I was at the *Argus* when he came in to see Mr. Corbel."

Wyck grunted.

"That's going to be difficult to quote," she said.

Wyck tried to look interested in what was passing by the window. They were seated in opposite corners to make room for two pairs of long legs— his sprawled awkwardly before him, hers hidden beneath skirts and petticoats. She occupied the shadowy side of the carriage, her eyes bright beneath her hat, her gloved hands resting on the pommel of an umbrella. He thought she was looking at him, but when he glanced her way, she, too, was gazing out the window.

"Have you got any family?" he asked, and when she regarded him, trying to decide if he were being derisive, he added, "I know about your mother and your brother, but—"

"My father's a blacksmith."

"Really?" he said. "I've done some smithing."

"Yes, I can believe it," she said, and he wasn't sure what she meant.

"Is he here in Portland?"

"On Munjoy."

There were several moments of silence. "I wouldn't have guessed your father was a smith," he said quietly.

Something complicated crossed her face. "You wouldn't have guessed I was from the hill," she said.

"What *I* am is written all over me." Wyck smiled wryly. "You're a little better hidden, is all."

"If this were truly a classless society, there would be no surprise in seeing a smith's daughter at a charity ball or reporting the social news."

"A *what* society?"

"Classless."

He thought about this for a moment. "You're a suffragette," he noted.

Mollie felt the need to take the bait. "And do you think that women *shouldn't* vote?" she asked, a little fire showing in her eyes.

"My mother would knock me over the head if I did." He smiled again.

"So your mother is a suffragette," she said, and there was just the hint of condescension in her voice.

"No," he said, never losing his smile, "she just thinks women should vote."

" 'If you don't join the cause, you can't fight the war,' " said Mollie.

"Who said that?"

"Susan B. Anthony."

" 'There are some,' " quoted Wyck, " 'with a barrel of public grievance and a pint of private compassion.' "

"And who said that?" she asked.

"My mother." And still he smiled. Then he grinned. Then he laughed. It was a low chuckle that she mistook, at first, for the rumble of carriage wheels over new cobblestones. "I guess you wouldn't have guessed *my* mother would have said such a thing."

That same set of complications passed over her face; then she found herself chuckling with him, though it was a moment before anything like a smile broke through her expression. "I would like to meet your mother," she said.

"Saints preserve me," he said, putting on a passable Irish brogue. "I wouldn't survive ten minutes between the two of you." He continued to chuckle till his old misgivings caught up with him. He pulled a sigh and looked out the window again. "I am awful worried about that kid," he said.

"I'm sorry," she said after a moment. The truth was that she herself was beginning to worry. She kept thinking about the little boy's shoes, so obviously big for him.

"If this were a classless society," said Wyck, "there wouldn't be any charity balls."

She was startled by the remark. "No, I don't suppose there would."

"Nor social columns, either."

In the shadows she rolled her eyes. *I guess I don't have to meet his mother, after all.*

Mrs. Barter was waiting for them when the carriage pulled up to her gate. She had her apron in her hand, watching with interest as Mollie stepped from the carriage without waiting for Wyck's assistance.

The landlady had never actually seen these two together, though she had gone to Mrs. Makepeace's and pleaded the young woman's case upon Wyck's request, and she almost smiled at the discernible tension between them. *Goodness sakes!* she was thinking. *They might harm each other more than it's worth!*

Wyck had his bowler in his hand as he came up the walk, casting his eyes from side to side, as if he were searching for a hat stand before he even came through the door. He looked worried, which was a reflection of Mrs. Barter's own state of mind. "Come in," said the older woman, "I have the tea on."

As it happened, there was little to be said after Mollie's news, which they each had heard by now. Wyck could not bring himself to sit, but stood against the kitchen cupboard with a teacup, like a child's toy in his great hand. Mollie had taken off her hat, and standing to one side of her, he could see the light from the window in her hair, which glowed with an almost blue-black luster.

Any information they had was woefully inadequate. They had the word of a reporter from a rival paper that an acquaintance of Mollie's was seen with Tweed and Pembleton. They had had no idea until the papers printed a second item regarding the *Loala* where Bird and his guardians had gone and still no idea where the Moosepath League and their charge were staying. "What you don't know you can't tell" had been Horace's philosophy. "What you don't hold you can't spill." Horace himself might not know.

Horace had made himself scarce these past two days, but Wyck thought he might be able to find him. The redheaded fellow did not waste time; he laid his unfinished tea on the table, took up an extra cookie, and said good-bye.

There was a fidgety minute after he was gone; he was such a big man, it felt as if half the air in the room had rushed out in his wake. The room seemed lighter to Mollie, now that he wasn't standing in it; she supposed he had been blocking the window above the sink. She glanced after him, sipped at her tea, then said, "I want to thank you again for coming to my defense with Mrs. Makepeace." She laid down her cup and took the sort of deep breath that indicates someone is preparing to leave. "I should be going, I suppose. I'm sorry if all this adds up to nothing in the end."

"I won't be able to defend you a second time if you follow him," said Mrs. Barter, who was not to be fooled.

Mollie's startled expression might have passed for a lack of understanding.

"There is no telling where he will have to go to find Mr. McQuinn," said Mrs. Barter, pronouncing Horace's name with a certain emphasis.

"I don't understand," said Mollie testily, "how we can pride ourselves on being so civilized if it is too dangerous for a woman to walk the city alone!"

Mrs. Barter was calm in the face of Mollie's anger simply because she understood exactly what the young woman was feeling. "Civilization is one thing, Mollie," she said. "Nature, I fear, is quite another."

The young woman rose from her chair and retrieved her hat. "I suppose if he finds where they took the boy, I'm not to go there as well."

"With Wyckford? You had better be careful how you travel, for your own sake. You're safe, of course, with Wyckford; he's a very gentle man for someone who knocks down a wall now and then. He is a *gentleman* as well, or I wouldn't have sent you after him this afternoon. If you're careful how things look, you should be able to follow your story. Young women can do more on their own these days than when I was young."

"Well, you don't make it sound like an accusation, at any rate."

"Things will get better," said Mrs. Barter.

Mollie thanked the woman for tea, and Mrs. Barter saw her out, then watched her disappear down the hill. Mrs. Barter didn't know but what she was more worried for Wyckford than Mollie, if the two of them spent much time together. There was such an odd mix of mistrust and regard between the two of them, but Mollie had an edge that might be as dangerous to herself as to others. She considered the state of young hearts and hoped Miss Peer was wise enough to handle Mr. O'Hearn's with care.

What you don't hold you can't spill.

40. The Persistence of Melody

"DID YOU DANCE TO THAT TUNE last night?" Sundry asked from the parlor connecting their rooms.

Mister Walton appeared in the doorway, looking uncertain. "Is it very tedious?"

Sundry chuckled. "Not at all."

"I'm sorry," said the portly fellow. "It's been in my head ever since I got up."

It had been in Sundry's head as well, but he didn't say as much. "It's very nice," he said instead. "I wonder what it is."

Mister Walton considered the melody (and the dance and Phileda) again but could not come up with a name. "It's German, I think." He returned to his room and inspected his tie in the mirror. "Phileda is taking me on a tour of the sights," he said. "You are welcome to come with us."

"Thank you, but I think I will look up a fellow I met last night," said Sundry.

"Really? I never did hear what you did while I was out."

"I got the tale on John Neptune."

"Good heavens! Did you find out why Portland owes him such a debt?"

"I did. And about the race for the Atlantic and St. Lawrence."

"I can't wait to hear!"

"*And* the riddle of the needle, the stone, and the mirror."

"All of that!"

"It's all the same tale."

"I hadn't realized."

Sundry came into Mister Walton's room and stood at the window. A carriage had pulled up to the Worster House. "It's more than *I* could have guessed. I'd tell you, but you probably don't want to keep Miss McCannon waiting."

Sundry went down to the street with Mister Walton to say hello to Miss McCannon, who very graciously asked him along. What pleased Sundry was the knowledge that had he accepted her invitation, neither she nor Mister Walton would have felt the day was wasted. One characteristic they shared was the ability to take the situation at hand and make it as happy as possible. Sundry graciously declined.

Hallowell's Water Street was not so busy at midday, and Sundry took notice when a second carriage pulled from the opposite curb (he hadn't seen anyone enter it) and drove in the same direction as his friends. His thoughts turned quickly to the Merrymeeting, however, and he wondered how far downriver he had gone last night before he reached the building on the shore. It had been rather dreamlike, the entire business, and he laughed at himself for being so romantic. But then, in Brunswick, by the light of day, he hadn't been able to find the tavern.

Sundry looked up the other end of Water Street, and something puzzling caught his eye. He did not linger upon it, however, but turned back and went up the steps of the Worster House. From the window of the hotel's front parlor he watched as a large man walked cautiously to the corner of the building, where he loitered, as if waiting for something (or someone).

Phileda McCannon was very proud of her town, and Mister Walton thought she had reason to be as they paused to look down from one of the loftier avenues. Hallowell had been incorporated as a city years before, but its population and its principal settlement belied this status. Phileda knew Mister Walton's fascination with history and legend, and she was well able to provide him with the local lore. One ancient home in particular she pointed out from the top of the hill.

"That is Old Kalf's home," she said. Overlooking the rooftops and chimneys, Mister Walton could see a tiny house, which was so obviously of the colonial period that he half-expected a man with a tricornered hat and musket to step from its front door. "Old Kalf was a Finn," explained Miss McCannon. "*And* a wizard. There have been two very famous storms, peculiar to our city, and he is responsible for at least one of them."

"Could he control the weather, then?" asked Mister Walton. "Our friend Mr. Eagleton would be breathless at the thought."

"He could summon weather, it has been said. But his *control* of it, once it answered his call, remains in question."

The aged house, its clapboards gray with years and neglect, sat on a ridge partway up the slope that overlooked the Kennebec. It was shaded by two yellow oaks whose age was evident in the posture of their limbs, if not their height. Shadows surrounded the property, and this one place upon the sun-soaked ridge gave the appearance of a dim and secretive dell.

They left the horse and carriage and walked toward the top of the slope. The sun shone warmly on Miss McCannon as she sat against a stone wall. She had taken off her hat, and the dry autumn wind was working to undo her hair; several strands flew before her face. Mister Walton felt self-conscious, suddenly, watching her, and he looked past her to the other side of the hill.

"There must be a house among those trees," he said, "though I can't see one. I see smoke rising among them."

"Do you?" She followed his gaze. "How wonderful! Of course, *you* would see it!" And she almost laughed.

Mister Walton was mystified. "Am I imagining it, then?"

"Not at all." She reached out and briefly touched his hand. "But not everybody *does* see it. There is no house there; only the pines."

They could not see the ground upon which the tall, straight pines grew, only the top half of the trees themselves running down the further slope.

"It is the season for burning leaves," he said. "But generally not among evergreens."

"No burning leaves," she assured him.

"Now I'm not sure if it's smoke at all," he said. He took off his glasses and squinted at the pines.

"No one is," she said mysteriously.

"No one is sure that it is smoke?"

She laughed with delight, enjoying his mystified expression.

"Ah!" he said, remembering. "You promised to show me a smoking pine!"

"I did, but we must walk there, by a path in the woods. It is a mile or so." Her tone indicated that he might be unwilling to go so far.

Contrarily, a walk through the woods with Phileda McCannon was more than Mister Walton could have hoped for. "The forest in fall and good company," he said to indicate that he could think of nothing better.

She took his arm, and they strolled to the crest of the hill. In one hand she held her hat, and she seemed absolutely unconcerned that the wind was making free with her hair. He thought it beautiful, tousled like that, as he thought it beautiful the way her glasses perched on her nose and the confident way in which she walked and her smile and . . .

"What are you laughing about?" she asked happily.

"I feel very young," he said.

She considered his round face. "You are, Toby."

He laughed again. "Am I?"

"And very wise, I think, for one so young."

Without looking at her, he said, "Well, I *am* with you, aren't I?"

A street or two below the crest of the ridge, a man stepped out of a carriage, paid the driver, and trudged up the slope.

41. Some Words with Wildfeather

THE SÉANCE HELD AT CLIFF COTTAGE on the evening of October 12, 1896, is mentioned in at least two diaries and obliquely referred to in the police columns of the local papers. Most of the participants were gone from the cape by the morning of the thirteenth, including Baroness Blinsky and her purported husband, Major Alcott, as well as Amos Guernsey, Bird, and all but one of his three guardians. We are highly obligated to the Moosepath League's scrupulous historians, and of course to Christopher Eagleton's account, for our understanding of what transpired. In his journal, on the night of the twelfth, Eagleton wrote:

> It was with great interest last night that we met Baroness Blinsky and her estimable husband, Maj. Halberd Alcott. We were understandably fascinated to meet a people of such high rank and peculiar talent, though we found the baroness's manner unusual. It was Mr. Guernsey who, at lunchtime, proposed the evening's divertissement, and it must be admitted that we three were somewhat trepidatious to take part. But with the example of our courageous chairman (wherever he may be), we were emboldened to join in the proceedings that followed. Thump is quite enjoying his book.

The handwriting, uncharacteristic of Eagleton, is shaky and difficult to read and thought by some to be proof that it was written in the dark confines of a swiftly moving carriage.

A disturbance, oscillating between the mild and the volcanic, went everywhere with the baroness. She and the major were expatriates—the baroness from some mysterious burg in the Ural Mountains, he from Harvard; no one has ever been able to ascertain the origin (or, for that matter, the authenticity) of their titles, but they expected to be addressed thusly, and people were usually polite about doing so. Strange ripples of discontent emanated from them ("Spirits everywhere sap my strength with their insistent noise," she explained), and the baroness looked out from her inner thoughts, which were rumored to be deep and filled with turmoil, with all the gracious expression of one who is passing a pigsty.

They were a well-contrasted couple, not unlike Jack Sprat and his wife, and were thus characterized by cartoonists of the day.

Theosophy was the ideology they espoused, a creed defined by the dictionary as "*dealing with the mystical understanding of God, of which historical religions are considered by its adherents to be only the* exoteric *expression.*" This seemed, to some critics, an opportunity to slough off the inconvenient strictures of ancient creeds and to skeptics an excuse to construct whatever suits a person most. There had been attempts to initiate a theosophical chapter in the state of Maine, without success; but what people will not eat in public, they might taste in private, and Baroness Blinsky toured the southern counties of the state, demonstrating her psychic abilities (mind reading, levitating, materializing letters from the deceased) and holding séances in people's homes.

Mr. Bailey, manager of Cliff Cottage, was of two minds regarding Baroness Blinsky and her professed talents: The one worried that a séance or any such occult practices in his hotel might bring public censure upon his head; the other imagined that even a little dubious notoriety couldn't hurt him in the off-season and might draw a curious lodger or two. That afternoon, he was balancing these two minds in his one head when he met the baroness in the front lobby, and it occurred to him, upon sight of her, that he had no desire to refuse the woman—so fear of public opinion proved less daunting than fear of the baroness—and he accepted her list of items needed for the night's séance with a cordial smile.

Ephram, Eagleton, and Thump returned to Cliff Cottage with Bird late that afternoon and found the hotel filled with an agitated murmur. The baroness was readying herself for her ordeal, they were told. It was unfortunate that she chose the dining room for her preparations, but she had decided that this was the psychic center of the building, and it also meant that she was easily served several courses of food several times during the day in anticipation of the vast energy she would be spending that night.

The members of the club hardly got within ten yards of the dining room when her great moans convinced them to take the evening meal in their rooms. Even there they sensed her noisy rumblings, which traveled along the water pipes and through the registers with a great "*Ohmmmm!*" and a powerful "*Oeegahhhh!*"

"This séance," Thump wondered, "do you suppose it will be a lengthy affair?"

Neither of his friends could answer this. "I do wonder where Mr. Guernsey is," said Eagleton; they had not seen him since lunch. Since it had been the actor's suggestion to have a séance in the first place, it followed that he must know what to expect from such an event. They had read of the Theosophical Society in their respective papers and even seen reference to séances held in the homes of well-to-do folk, but none of them had a very clear idea of what happened beyond the inexplicit picture of several people holding hands around a table.

Thump had vague notions of floating heads and disembodied voices. He was a little shaken by this thought, and he patted Bird's shoulder as if the boy could read the image in his brain and was in need of reassurance.

Eagleton envisioned table tipping and crystal balls.

Ephram had been stopped by the idea of holding hands, for it occurred to him that he might be seated, that night, next to Miss Riverille. A cold sweat formed upon his brow.

Evening drew apace. Outside, the wind followed the example of previous nights and rose as the sun set, as if Aeolus had paused the entire day to catch his breath. The anxious concerns of the club members did not decrease as the hour of the séance drew near, and with the prospect of Miss Riverille's arrival looming, Ephram in particular was not of a frame of mind amiable to the confines of a small room; he might have found the limited vistas tedious, as he paced the floorboards, if he had been at all conscious of them.

However, Eagleton and Thump put their nervous energies to good use, and a variety of valets could not have rendered Ephram more attention than did his friends. No female accoutrement was ever given more thought than was Ephram's tie; he was required, in fact, to stand for several minutes while Eagleton and Thump peered at the cravat beneath his chin as if it were a recent gallery acquisition. Thump leaned close to the article, hands behind his back, and made several sounds, the meaning of which was not altogether clear.

Bird watched these proceedings with mystification. Beads of rain pattered at the window, and a gust of wind hugged the casing.

"I say, Ephram!" said Eagleton, and then he proceeded *not* to say, though his expression gave the impression of one who *has* said very much.

Ephram, who was prepared for a compliment and even had the vague idea that he had received one, blushed modestly.

"Don't you, Thump?" insisted Eagleton.

Thump felt safe in acquiescing. "I do!" he declared. "I really do!"

Ephram looked from one to the other of them, communicating perplexity with the knit of his brow, and his friends took this to mean that he was unsatisfied with the state of his cravat. Consequently, they reapplied themselves to the task, the end result of which was that the tie looked to Bird's untrained eye exactly as it had before.

"What a remarkable thing, meeting Miss Riverille and her mother!" Eagleton said, not for the first time.

Ephram stood straight and looked courageously indeterminate.

* * *

If possible, Ephram became less articulate as Miss Riverille's arrival drew close, but he was ever mindful of the time, and he did manage to announce the hour when it was upon them. The three men hurried with their young charge to the lobby of the hotel, where they were pleased to hear silence emanating from the dining room.

Sallie Riverille's friend Miss Astoria Hempel met them in the lobby. The men were dressed in their evening toggery and had even managed to apparel Bird in something like formal wear, though he had asked for, and not been denied, permission to wear his moose badge on his lapel. (Eagleton's extra cummerbund was wrapped around the boy three times.) Miss Hempel, herself handsomely costumed for the occasion, was suitably impressed.

Bird sat on the lower step of the front-hall stairs and watched as the three men passed one another, back and forth, pacing. Miss Hempel waited demurely in a wicker love seat and admired them. Thump's pacing was brought temporarily to a halt when she winked at him.

The hour came and went. Ephram looked concerned. He consulted one of his three watches. "One past," he announced.

The front door of Cliff Cottage opened then, and a carriage driver held it so that Sallie Riverille could enter with a cool breeze and a little rain. She was dressed and coifed to such effect that one might suspect she had spent every hour since their meeting that afternoon in producing it. Not so formally dressed as at the Freeport Ball, she yet had found occasion for silk flowers in her hair, inserts of contrasting fabric in her dark blue gown, and a neckline considerably lower than had been evidenced earlier in the day.

If there is a level of speechlessness deeper than absolute silence, then Ephram demonstrated it vividly. Indeed, his speechlessness was so profound that it seemed to draw the words from Eagleton and Thump as well.

"Am I too early?" asked Miss Riverille.

Eagleton and Thump shot alarmed glances at one another. Ephram opened his mouth but said nothing. Miss Hempel hurried to Miss Riverille's side with an exclamation regarding her friend's dazzling effect. Even Bird was not unmoved; he stood at the foot of the stairs and looked as if he had missed the young woman all his life.

"Not early at all!" blurted Eagleton.

"No, no!" insisted Thump.

"Not to say you were late!" assured Eagleton.

"Not at all!" said Thump.

"Certainly, not. Indeed, Miss Riverille, one couldn't be more on time."

Eagleton was warming to his thesis when Ephram surprised everyone, including himself, by saying the most extraordinary thing. "Miss River-ille," he said, "to see you tonight and to imply that you could ever arrive too soon would be to suggest the most absurd of all contradictions." Until the events of the evening came to their dizzying climax, these were the only words to pass through Ephram's lips, but from the expression on Sal-lie Riverille's face, they sufficed.

"Intermittent showers expected," said Eagleton. "Gusty winds, giving way to fair weather by midmorning."

"High tide at three minutes past five," said Thump.

The room chosen for the night's event was in the northeast corner of Cliff Cottage, and it was here that the weather was most evident—rain sifting at the windows, the shutters groaning in the wind. The room itself was dim; there were heavy curtains at the windows, and the few lit candles about the room wavered with mysterious drafts. A table was positioned in the center of the room with several chairs, spaced equally about it; the largest of these sat opposite the door. There was a cloth-covered object on the table.

The walls of the room were crowded with paintings and trophies of the hunt, so that eyes and fangs glared down from their perches; antlers and snouts cast peculiar shadows in the dim light.

The company hovered in the hall and took turns peering inside. A sin-gle light from behind cast their shadows through the door, so that a host of heads and shoulders occupied the carpet. One of the heads and the accompanying shoulders did not, to Eagleton's mind, fit anyone in the group. The shadow was crowned with a conical outline and seemed to belong to someone tall and thin. Being the tallest and thinnest among them, Eagleton raised a hand experimentally but saw no corresponding movement from the silhouette in question. The shadow appeared to be wearing an impressive pair of mustaches, which Ephram could answer for, but Eagleton was sure that Ephram's shadow was the one furthest to the right.

It occurred to Eagleton to number the heads on the carpet against those in the party, and very quickly he accounted for everyone but Bird, who was not tall enough to cast a shadow with everyone standing around him, and yet there was still one shadow more than seemed necessary for the people attending.

Then it occurred to Eagleton that if there was one more shadow than there were people, then there must be one more person among them to cast it. He turned and was gradually aware of a tall, heavily mustached man standing just behind Thump, and before Eagleton realized that it was Major Alcott, he let out a startled "A*h!*"

Miss Hempel let out a sympathetic cry, and then Ephram gave an anxious "*harumph*," and Sallie followed suit with a squeak. Everyone, in fact, took their turn in quick succession, as if each had been asked to give the sharpest and most eccentric sound in their repertoire. Only Bird did not participate, which was ironic, since the general effect was that of a startled aviary, and Thump himself (whose voice was normally the deepest) managed a fair imitation of an alarmed seagull.

Major Alcott, the tassel of his fez hardly stirring, did not respond to this peculiar greeting (perhaps he was accustomed to such responses), but only droned a message from Amos Guernsey, who apologized for missing the séance.

"Good heavens!" said Eagleton, the first to recover. "Is he ill?"

"I fear the anticipation of tonight's ceremony has played poorly upon his nerves," said Major Alcott.

This did seem too bad, and since the séance had been Amos's idea, Thump forwarded the proposition that they "do it another night."

"The baroness has prepared," said Major Alcott dryly.

While this was discussed, Mr. and Mrs. Stroad appeared in the hall, having decided to join the séance. Mr. Bailey, who escorted them, inquired if all was well, for he had heard the commotion and was feeling uncertain about the proposed event. The major did not calm Mr. Bailey's fear; rather, he drove him off with a look of mild disdain; whereas the arrival of the Stroads impelled the unnerved party forward. They were directed to speak only in whispers once they entered the room.

Incense permeated the room, and as their eyes grew accustomed to the darkness, they could see tendrils of smoke rising from the table.

The Stroads seated themselves, and after some indecision, the remainder of the party found their places. The largest chair was reserved for the medium herself, and clockwise from it they were arranged in this manner: Major Alcott, Bird, Thump, Miss Hempel, Ephram, Miss Riverille, Eagleton, Mrs. and Mr. Stroad.

Thump found that the incense floating above the table was tickling his nose in a not altogether agreeable manner. The smoke filled the air like a haze and further obscured what the lack of lighting had already made indistinct. On the wall opposite, there hung the head of a bobcat, and its eyes seemed to be blinking with the light of the candles.

There was a sturgeon mounted over the major's head, and Eagleton was rather taken with the notion that it was smiling at him.

The door from the hall shut as if of its own volition; the room darkened further, and the quiet click of the latch was like the period at the end of a subtle sentence.

Bird, whose shoulders barely reached the surface of the table, peered around himself with more curiosity than apprehension. The other members of the circle sat quietly as they awaited the next occurrence. Wind rattled at the side of the hotel, and a short downpour could be heard against the curtained windows. The air above the table appeared to swim, and those directly opposite one another grew less distinct.

The baroness was in her seat at the head of the table, and no one had seen her arrive. Miss Hempel let out a small cry, and the others showed signs of amazement. Thump could no longer deny the effect of the incense on his nose, and he made a little noise, like a cat sneezing. He considered apologizing, but Baroness Blinsky stopped him with a wild look.

"How many are we?" she groaned.

Eagleton began to count.

"We are ten," intoned the major.

That's right, thought Eagleton, nearly speaking aloud.

"Ten spheres of the mystic realm," moaned the baroness after a moment of silence. "Ten levels on the masters' path. Ten masters in the final sphere." She took a long, vocal breath before expounding, "Here is an auspicious number."

She startled them again by jerking her hands over the table and waving them above the cloth-covered object. She whipped the cloth aside and revealed, to Eagleton's satisfaction, what appeared to be a ball of blue glass seated upon a metal stand. With her hands, she made some passes over the crystal ball as she peered into it. Ephram saw the image of her chin bobbing upon its blue surface.

She took another long, loud breath and spoke again. "The spirits are favorable to our enterprise. Those waiting on the other side are eager to communicate with those of us upon the earthly plane. Secrets they have to reveal, boons they crave of us. Do not tremble to hear the voices of those long departed!"

Several of them did tremble.

"Join hands," commanded Baroness Blinsky.

Slowly those in the circle did as they were told. There was hesitation among them; it was not natural for any of them to take the hands of strangers, and most of them were strangers or near strangers to those near to them. Most of them, in their trembling, could feel the hand in theirs tremble as well.

"*Perfect love casteth out all fear*," it is said, and it is not to be known how perfect Ephram's feelings were for Sallie Riverille at that moment, but his own hand was remarkably steady. He would always remember that evening not for what was occurring across the table, before the crystal ball, but for the presence of the young woman beside him. Since he found himself sitting in such close proximity to Miss Riverille and now feeling her slim hand in his, all anxiety regarding the night's diversions had left him. The loveliest sunset, the most mellifluous birdsong, the most exquisite sweets, were nothing to the sensation he experienced just then; and yet he knew that he was unable to fully perceive the extraordinary beauty of that hand—the softness of it, the elegant structure of its tiny bones, the very creator who had been its architect and invested it with life.

Ephram had not the slightest notion that Miss Riverille was looking at him. She was herself calmed by, and grateful for, the steadiness of his hand without ever suspecting that it was she who had made it so.

Others at the table were not so distracted, though Thump had to remind himself not to squeeze the hands of Miss Hempel, who would perhaps not mind, or Bird, whose own little hand barely covered the center of Thump's large palm. Eagleton, who had been right in his prediction of the crystal ball, was waiting for the table to rise. The elderly Stroads, who had started the séance with great aloofness, were both frozen in attitudes of nervous expectation.

"Ohhhhhhh!" articulated the baroness. "Ohhhhhhh!" She shivered, and these vibrations rippled around the table, arm by arm, till they returned to her. "Oh, spirits!" she groaned, her voice charged with emotion, though her tone was barely above a whisper. "Oh, spirits! Come to our table, come to our side! Join with us, enter our circle, let yourselves be known!"

There was a collective gasp as a radiance grew from the very center of the crystal ball. Its blue light struck the baroness, so that her face was cast in strange shadows; it rose from a dull glow to a light that rivaled the candles in the room.

A breath of cold air passed over the table. The candles went out.

The shadow of the baroness towered above them, limned in that blue radiance. Eagleton felt an unpleasant pricking at the nape of his neck as the medium encompassed the ball with her hands and the stick images of her fingers writhed upon the ceiling.

"Come!" she chanted. "Come!"

There was silence while they waited for the subject of her request to make itself known. Eagleton hardly dared turn his head, but he glanced from side to side, wondering from what dark corner this communicative spirit would appear. Thump was startled by a low growl emanating from beneath the table. He felt his skin tighten at the temples and his arms thrill with goose bumps till he realized that the sound came from his stomach.

Ephram thought the growl sounded like an unhappy cat and considered peering beneath the tablecloth.

"He is recalcitrant," said the baroness abruptly, and her voice startled everybody. "He was greatly offended during our last session by an untoward remark regarding porcupines."

It was not Thump's habit to discuss the quilly animal, but he was struck, at the mention of it, by an apprehension that he might say the word "porcupine" if asked to speak aloud. He was not really keen on seeing a spirit in the first place, and the notion of an offended one certainly did not appeal to him. It occurred to him that a member of the spirit realm might be capable of reading his mind, and he did his best to banish anything like a porcupine from his thoughts; the end result of which was that great ranks of the creatures proceeded to march through his brain.

The baroness gave a low moan, and this time the shivers communicating from arm to arm did not originate with her. "I sense the shadows of unanswered questions," she hissed. "Nothing is more apt to draw him hither. Wildfeather, we call you to us! Come! Come!"

And then he came. They could hardly tell if he had dropped from above or risen from below, but the luminescent face of a man suddenly hovered over the table. Long and thin, its face shone with a ghastly green light; his hair was black and fashioned into lengthy braids. The baroness seemed the only one at the table who could not see the apparition, for she said, "Wildfeather, are you with us?"

"I come from the happy hunting grounds!" said the spectral face.

It was extraordinary that no one in the circle broke his or her grip, but there was a sense of electricity that seemed to hold them together like magnets of opposing poles. The Stroads wore identical expressions, too extreme to properly describe. Miss Riverille and Miss Hempel were only slightly less astonished. Eagleton and Thump were amazed, there is no doubt. Ephram looked more curious than afraid. Bird's wonder was that of a child who has not learned to fear anything but the living.

"Ah, Wildfeather!" said the baroness. "What have you to tell?"

"There are those who walked among you," said the eerie figure. Ephram was sitting directly behind the glowing form, and Sallie and Astoria, who were to either side of Ephram, had only marginally better views of the old Indian.

"Who walked among us?" asked the baroness.

"Among you there are those who walked," came the reply.

"He speaks a riddle," said the medium. Her eyelids fluttered, her face raised to the light generated by the specter. " 'Those who walked.' Those who walk, pace, ambulate, stride—strode! Of course. What have you to say about the Stroads?" she moaned, now that she had solved the mystery.

The glowing figure then communicated a message to Mrs. Stroad from some late relative, and it neither helped that the message was a little vague or that Mrs. Stroad was a good deal deaf.

"What is he saying?" she repeated. "Stuff and nonsense! Tell Aunt Cremona to mind her business!"

It was very odd how accustomed they grew to the shining visage and how very natural it seemed that it should have appeared to speak to them.

"Someone has lost a pearl button," said Wildfeather, and no sooner had Miss Hempel let out a small gasp than the very article fell from the ceiling onto the table before her.

This caused a stir, and the baroness had to instruct everyone to remain seated and holding hands. "There is something deeper that Wildfeather waits to tell us. I can sense it. Now, my friend from beyond, tell me what powerful thing you have to impart."

"I sense the presence of the moose," said Wildfeather in deep tones. "I sense the presence of my totemic familiar."

"Ah!" sang the medium, her hands raised above her. "The moose! The moose! What can be meant by 'the moose'!"

The members of the club were naturally struck by this turn in the conversation, and Thump felt himself rise above his own apprehensions regarding porcupines, so that he considered shouting, "Here we are!"

The face, glowing above them, stared into the gloom beyond. "The moose has brought that which belongs to the other side," he said, his voice taking on the rhythm of a chant. "Great peace is meant for the young soul who is meant to fly among those who were lost before him."

A qualmish feeling crept over Thump.

"Great fortune is bestowed upon those who have brought this winged gift to the place beyond the masters," the apparition was saying. "Great is the peace awaiting them when, in their time, they step into the next world."

Eagleton felt a sense of undefined horror as he listened to this, and when the meaning of the riddlelike chant became clear to him, he looked across the table to Bird, who was not there. The stunned expression on Eagleton's face drew Thump's gaze; then the direction of Eagleton's stare turned Thump's head to the little boy at his side.

There was a tiny hand, made of wax, in Thump's hand, and he

dropped it with a sudden cry. Eagleton jumped to his feet, Ephram fell backward in his chair, and the entire table rose in the air before them.

The face of the Indian vanished, the light of the crystal ball went out, and the room was in complete darkness.

42. Shadows and Sleeping Furniture

It does not take deep philosophy to understand that the more people you put in a given space, the less room you have; and it is only marginally less evident that panic might make one person seem like ten, and therefore nine like ninety, but it is perhaps helpful to point up these principles in order to explain what happened and why.

It seemed long minutes of shouting and struggle before Miss Hempel found the door and let enough illumination into the room so that someone could turn up a light, during which interval there sounded several collisions among the bodies and the furniture. Interestingly enough, the gaslights had been turned off at some other source, so candles had to suffice, once someone was able to locate a box of lucifers. When the room was once more under the command of some form of light, the Stroads proved to be the only members of the fractured séance who were still seated.

"Good heavens!" cried Thump. "What has happened?"

"Thump!" said Eagleton. "Where is the boy?"

Sallie was helping Ephram untangle himself from his chair. "Dear me!" he kept saying. When he got to his feet, he commenced to brush himself off till he realized what his fellow Moosepathians were intimating. "Dear me!" he said somewhat more emphatically.

"Ah! The boy!" said the baroness, her tone melancholy, yet peaceful. "Wildfeather has taken the boy to his bosom—to the other side, to the land beyond the masters."

"Well, you tell him to bring him back immediately!" declared an outraged Thump.

"Sir!" said the major in his most commanding voice. "You will speak to the baroness in a proper tone!" He had lost his fez in the confusion, and his hair was in disarray.

Thump had never felt such conflict; his natural reticence, not to say his courteous disposition, were at war with his astonishment and vexation. "That boy was given over to our safekeeping!" he insisted.

The baroness put on a look of heavenly peace and joy. "And you have delivered him nobly into such safekeeping that does not exist among our earthly trials."

"No!" said Thump indignantly.

"I've heard enough!" pronounced the major.

"What's happened, Bobby?" Mrs. Stroad was asking.

"I don't know, Mumsy," returned Mr. Stroad. "The boy seems to have chased after the ghost."

"Is this some sort of terrible joke?" demanded Miss Riverille.

"Come, Major," said Baroness Blinsky. "I am leaving. I will not stay in this hotel another night, not with such belligerent energy about. Honestly, do some people a courtesy—!"

"It seemed a strange sort of ghost," Mrs. Stroad was saying. "What was he on about?"

"I didn't understand a bit of it," admitted the husband.

"A strange ghost indeed," said Miss Riverille, pointing behind the baroness. "One who doesn't cover his tracks very well." The curtain before one of the windows wavered, and once the room was momentarily quiet, the rain could be heard clearly from behind it. "What would you want with that child?" demanded the young woman. The baroness and the major looked vaguely startled by the accusation. "Mr. Ephram, quick. They've taken him that way!"

"Good heavens!" he shouted. "Sinister forces bent on using him for their own nefarious schemes!" He charged the curtain, but Thump was there before him, tearing it aside to reveal not a window but a door leading to a porch. Their feet sounded loud as they hurried into the night, and Sallie and Eagleton were quickly behind them, the young woman with a candle, which was sheltered by a glass chimney that she had taken from one of the gas lamps.

The cliffs that gave the cottage its name stood within a stone's throw of the porch, and it seemed unimaginable that anyone would elect to take that path on such a murky night. The wind blew, and rain dampened their faces. Miss Riverille passed a hand over her spectacles. Another wing of the building paralleled the cliffs, and Eagleton spotted a door to this section on the other end of the porch.

By the time they reached the further door, which was unlocked, a frightened Astoria Hempel had joined them, the storm following as they entered a dark hallway. They entered in a cluster, and the wind slammed the door shut behind them, which raised a concerted yelp. Sallie almost dropped the candle as they clutched one another. The memory, or perhaps, more accurately, the effect, of the glowing apparition had not left them, and it did not matter how unconvinced some of them were of its authenticity.

Once the fright of the slamming door had passed, there was another silence, and they listened intently, peering into the absolute darkness of the long corridor. A howl of pain—not a child's—rose from the other side of the gloom, and after another collective yelp, Thump led the party with a charge into the shadows beyond. He had not gone far when he took a complete somersault in the middle of the hall.

When the candlelight caught up with him, a small regiment of porch chairs and lounges, hibernating for the winter beneath white sheets, could be seen filling half the hall, and it was over one of these that he had fallen. Ephram and Eagleton helped Thump to his feet.

There came another bellow, and they hurried among the ghostly shapes till they reached a wall which significantly hindered further progress. They had passed several doors on either side, and one of them stood immediately to their left. Sallie raised a hand to indicate the need for quiet, and except for a chorus of nervous breathing (and a similar chorus from without as the wind pulled at the corners of Cliff Cottage), they could hear nothing. The candlelight wavered, and the shadows in the hall bowed and quivered. Even their breaths were silenced at the sound of a creak, and Sallie reached for the door and pulled it open.

A narrow stairway reached up into shapeless gloom; the compass of candlelight touched the top step and ventured no further. A shuffling sound came from above, and it was plain that their quarry had taken the stairs.

Matthew Ephram was remarkably composed; the wonderful calm he had attained while holding Sallie Riverille's hand had not left him and had only been strengthened when she called to *him* to investigate the moving curtain. (Perhaps, in retrospect, he was more stunned than composed.)

Whatever he was feeling, he acted quickly. Taking the chimneyed candle from Miss Riverille with an "I beg your pardon," he disappeared, with somewhat stilted steps, up the stairwell. The sphere of light dwindled, and his shadow traveled at cross-purposes with the lengthening shadows of the stair treads.

"It is not unlike the seventh chapter in *Mrs. Ludley's Luck*," said Thump. " 'The Steps in the Old West Wing.' "

"It is very like," agreed Eagleton, "and does put one in mind."

Ephram, meanwhile, had come to the top of the stairs and another hall, where he paused long enough to take stock of something at his feet. It was Bird's moose badge, its pin bared and red with someone's blood. He heard the sound of a door groaning in the darkness of the hall, and as he went forward, he winced at the creak evoked by his own steps.

The wind and rain were louder here on the second floor, in the dark, alone. There was a terrific slam of something falling behind him, and the unexpected clamor propelled him impetuously down the hall.

He came to a large room with draped shapes and shadows reaching from every corner and device; one tall object appeared distressingly human beneath its sheet—a hat rack, perhaps. Rain beat upon the windows, and the wind banged a shutter in a nervous rhythm. Ephram heard voices behind him. He crept ahead, feeling vulnerable, the candle shining in his hands; it dazzled his eyes.

Then he saw him, a tall, broad-shouldered man pressed against one wall; his eyes caught the light like a cat's, and he held the back of one arm to his mouth like an animal nursing a wound. There was anger in the man's face, and in the moment of discovery, he let out a low growl just as the little boy in his grasp wrenched himself free.

Bird ran toward Ephram with a little cry. Ephram watched with something between horror and uncertainty as the man strode toward him. Ephram wasn't sure what to do with the candle; if he dropped it, they would be plunged into darkness. Bird grasped his leg. The man was within two strides of Ephram, who looked to either side for a place to set the candle. There was a shout and two large bangs at the door behind him.

From the moment that Ephram had first laid eyes on him to that in which he saw the man's fist rushing toward his nose was a matter of only a few seconds. For the second time in a matter of minutes Ephram was plunged in darkness, and he didn't know which went out first—the candle or himself.

43. Flying with Bird

JOSEPH THUMP WAS OF SUCH A STALWART NATURE physically that as he paced before the hearth in the parlor, he more surely obstructed its light than would the average human soul. Even his shadow seemed more substantial than that of most people (indeed, more substantial than Amos Guernsey himself, who fidgeted in the corner), and it was Thump's coming and going before the firelight, like a series of clouds before the sun, that first caught the attention of the stricken man's rising perception.

"Please let me know when Astoria returns with my mother," came a sweet voice, and Ephram felt an intuition of well-being; like a traveler who, long in the dark, senses as much as sees the coming dawn.

"I cannot imagine how such a thing could happen!" This was the product of a man's vocal cords.

"I am shocked! Deeply shocked!" said another man. " *'What devils feast upon the innocent presumptions of faultless folk!'* The philosopher to Katherine in *Heart's Content,* act two, scene six."

"Is he waking?" said the first man's voice.

"Oh, the poor, dear man!" was expressed in soft, feminine music. "Such a terrible bruise on his handsome face!"

"And to take advantage of the baroness's good intentions!" said the second man. "To spirit away this child from beside the major himself! *'Fear and forsooth! What foul calamity hath befallen these fast friends of mine!'* Ambrosius to Barthelmass, from *The Aged Tavern,* act three, scene one."

"I am not at all sure about the baroness's good intentions," said the woman.

"I do hope that you understand," said the first man, "I had doubts concerning the whole affair, though I have never heard anything untoward regarding Baroness Blinsky and the major."

"I believe he *is* waking."

"Thank heavens!" came a heartfelt sigh upon a warm, sweet breath. Ephram could feel it on his aching cheek, and it was like a balm.

Rising from his senseless state, he had been listening to these voices, and it was not unlike hearing a conversation across a large room or drifting down a hall to the parlor where people are conversing. The speakers' voices rose in volume and clarity, and he began to place them—Mr. Bailey and Thump, Mr. Guernsey and Miss Riverille.

Ephram was hearing many footsteps, as if people were rushing about the room. He opened his eyes and looked into the sympathetic eyes of Sallie Riverille. The room in which he found himself was brightly lit, and Thump was pacing between Ephram and a blazing hearth. Ephram was on a sofa, covered in a quilt up to his shoulders. The manager was apologizing to him. With a dovelike sound, Sallie Riverille let go his hand to touch his brow.

The others hurried over to see him, and the manager pressed close behind, staring over Thump's shoulder. They weaved their heads slightly, as if endeavoring to peer through a foggy window. "Good heavens, Ephram!" said Thump. "Are you awake?"

"I do believe he is!" declared Amos.

Their voices sounded unnaturally loud. "I had no idea!" said the manager, as if protesting a specific charge. "Upon my word, I didn't!"

"Perhaps we shouldn't crowd too close," suggested Miss Riverille, meaning that *the men* should not crowd too close, since she had taken Ephram's hand once more and had no intention of giving it up. Thump, Amos, and Mr. Bailey distanced themselves accordingly.

"The boy," said Ephram quietly.

"He's quite safe, thanks to you," said Sallie Riverille.

Bird appeared at Ephram's side, expressing his concern with large eyes. On his chest was the moose badge, which Ephram had recovered.

"My word, sir," said Amos. "What quickness of mind! What forthrightness of thought!"

"Ever in the fore!" rumbled Thump with great feeling.

"Eagleton?" asked Ephram.

"Readying the carriage!" announced Amos, one finger waving in the air. "Rousting the ostlers! To wit, to make clear the way!"

Ephram was alarmed by this proclamation, and he turned to Thump for explanation. He looked unusual, lying there with the covers up to his chin and his eyes wide with astonishment.

"I am very sorry if you gentlemen think it necessary to leave," the manager was saying.

"We did not catch the fellow, Ephram," said Thump apologetically.

"There is no reason to think he worked alone," said Amos.

Thump did his best to explain. "Mr. Guernsey was quite sure he saw figures lurking outside the hotel."

"Sinister forces. Nefarious schemes," continued the actor. "Why, the entire hotel might be surrounded." The manager thought this construction unnecessary. Ephram was not hearing all that was said; he had realized that Miss Riverille was stroking his hair.

Eagleton arrived, out of breath and on the run; with great pleasure he discovered Ephram among the conscious inhabitants of the room, and without thinking, he took the stricken man's other hand and shook it heartily. Thump, who perhaps thought himself remiss, followed with his own heartfelt grasp.

"Marvelous!" Eagleton was saying. "Marvelous!" It was then that Ephram noticed that Eagleton was dressed to go outdoors. "We are off, beyond the reach of these scoundrels!"

"Off?" said Ephram.

Amos, who had somehow become a part of their company, was extremely agitated. "Before the noose tightens!" he declared.

"The noose?" said Ephram.

"We must take the boy away from here," said Amos, "since clearly we have been discovered." This was not said with much caution, and Mr. Bailey threw up his hands as he raced from the room.

"Oh," said Ephram; he honestly intended to release his hand from Miss Riverille's lovely clasp and lift himself from the sofa. Miss Riverille had other ideas and held tight to him, even as she leaned forward and said, "You can't move yet, Mr. Ephram! You need time to recover from your ordeal!"

Eagleton and Thump looked to one another. The idea of charging off into the night had not originated with either of them, and they were, in fact, trying to recall who had first offered the notion. Ephram was perplexed. To be absolutely truthful, he had very little desire to quit his present station.

There are certain womanly attributes that have ofttimes been numbered with three figures; and Ephram was in a position, relative to Miss Riverille, to appreciate each of them, and at close quarters. She was not a large woman in any of these merits, but as she embodied them, they were sympathetic to one another. In the words of one great thinker (regarding another woman entirely), "She was as complete as an acorn." It was well that Miss Riverille took Ephram's part in the ensuing discussion, since he himself continued to lose track of it.

It fell out, however, that he must make a decision, and the entire business had to be explained again.

"We must be off!" said Eagleton, caught up in the moment.

"Not keen to leave you behind," said Thump.

"Ever in the fray!" said Eagleton.

"We know how disappointed you would be to miss out," agreed Thump.

It would not be fair to suggest that Eagleton and Thump were thinking merely that there was "safety in numbers," for they honestly believed Ephram would be eager to fly into the face of danger, notwithstanding that they hoped they were flying *away* from it. "My friends," he said quietly. "I am deeply touched, and I would like nothing better than to continue this adventure—"

Eagleton and Thump looked abashed.

"—but I *am* feeling . . . less than myself."

Thump had tears in his eyes. Miss Riverille brushed Ephram's hair from his brow. "We shall carry you!" declared Eagleton.

"No, no!" said Ephram rather loudly.

"We shall stay!" proclaimed Thump.

"You must think of our charge," insisted Ephram, never letting go of Miss Riverille's hand or wavering from his conviction.

"Unselfish beyond words," said Eagleton, shaking the invalid's free hand. The sofa vibrated with the gesture.

"I'll catch up with you," Ephram promised.

Thump pumped Ephram's hand. "We are heading east," he said.

"East?" said Miss Riverille. A bright notion occurred to her. "Gentlemen, you must go to Brunswick, where you will find hospitality at the home of the Simpsons."

"The Simpsons?" said Eagleton, his voice having developed a small squeak.

"You *do* remember my dear friend Ophelia, whom you quite charmed last Fourth of July?"

"I did?" said Eagleton. "I mean, I do? I mean, yes . . . certainly . . . remember . . . of course . . . Miss Simpson . . ." And it was all true, if difficult to follow, for he had remembered very little else these past few months.

"You must go to her address, which I will give you," said Miss Riverille. "I will send a telegram ahead. They are fine people, the Simpsons, and your situation will not be met by a lack of sympathy."

Thump thought this suggestion very strong to their purpose. "Yes" was all that Eagleton said. Amos did not appear so convinced, and he voiced a lack of confidence in the plan, but Miss Riverille was already dictating the Simpsons' address to Thump.

"Miss Simpson," said Eagleton dreamily. "Are you sure we shouldn't wait with you?" he asked Ephram.

Holding Miss Riverille's hand, Ephram was a great deal *more* sure than he was of most things. "Oh, yes," he said. He reached into his pocket to retrieve one of his watches. "Twenty-three minutes past ten o'clock."

"Skies expected to clear before a southwest wind," said Eagleton. "Fair and cool tomorrow."

"High tide at three past five," said Thump.

Their bags were taken to a waiting carriage. Thump left the room three times before Eagleton was pulled in his wake. Amos was voicing some weak objections to the proposed itinerary. Bird waved as he hurried off with the two club members, and Amos quickly brought up the rear.

Ephram relaxed. There was a scent of perfume near Miss Riverille. The fire in the hearth snapped; the light from it danced with shadows across the room. "Everyone is well?" he asked the young woman. They were alone, and yet the calmness he had exacted from holding her hand held such sway over him that he was able to articulate this thought.

"Yes," she said. "You were very brave."

"Your friend?" he said quietly.

"Astoria?" She leaned close to him, the better to hear him, and it was an act of great intimacy.

"Yes," he said.

"She should be back any moment now," said Miss Riverille. "She has gone to get my parents," and she only just straightened her head out of the way as his head came up and he sat bolt upright on the sofa.

The rain was gone, and a quarter moon was high in its path, silvering the swift fair-weather clouds. Top hats bobbed in the light from the foyer of Cliff Cottage, and coattails and capes fluttered with the wind. Leaves spun at the feet of the horses. Instructions were given to the driver, Bird was lifted inside, Thump climbed in, and Eagleton held the door for Amos Guernsey.

"Miss Simpson," Eagleton was saying; but then a curious expression came over him that stopped Amos; for a moment, something like disquiet occupied the actor's countenance. Eagleton held the door, and Amos paused with one boot on the carriage step. "Do you have some Indian in you, Mr. Guernsey?" said Eagleton finally.

"I beg your pardon?" said Amos.

Eagleton marveled at what he had not noticed before. "In this half-light, you bear the most striking resemblance to Wildfeather!"

"I beg your pardon?" said Amos again.

"The baroness's spiritual familiar," explained Eagleton. "Of course! You weren't there, so you couldn't know, but it really is most remarkable!"

Thump looked out the door, and the resemblance was clear to him as well.

"My grandmother was full-blooded Indian, actually," said Amos. "Mohawk, I think."

"How marvelous!" said Eagleton, the look of wonderment leaving his face to make room for a bright smile. "You must tell us about her!" He patted Amos's shoulder as the actor climbed into the carriage.

But the thought of Ophelia Simpson returned to Eagleton once he was seated, and uncertainty crept over him once more. Thump had inquired after Amos's lineage, and the actor was already telling great tales about his grandmother (though there seemed to be some confusion whether she was his mother's mother or his father's) as the reins were snapped and the carriage trundled from the yard.

"Actually, both my grandmothers were Indian," Amos was saying.

Book Six

OCTOBER 13, 1896

❧

44. The Opposite Direction

EAGLETON AND THUMP THOUGHT THE ATMOSPHERE in the Tontine Hotel's dining room at lunchtime Wednesday was strangely contentious. All about them, men at other tables forgot their meals in the heat of arguments that led to many raised fingers and strong declarations. Stranger still was that the subject of altercation seemed to be the same from table to table. "I believe they are discussing grass," said Eagleton, and considering the volume of these conversations, he could not be faulted for curiosity.

"Hmmm?" said Thump. Interested as he was in the quarrelsome environment, he found it difficult to concentrate on more than his lunch. They had slept late, having arrived in Brunswick in the wee hours, and missed breakfast. They were all hungry, in fact, and even Bird did not eat in accordance with his name. Amos was the last of their small party to arrive at the table, and while closely seconding Thump in his attention to the board, he was the first to raise the subject of their hurrying away.

This was an issue of some moment to Christopher Eagleton, since he understood that their plan was to seek the hospitality of the Simpson family, the daughter of which had, on the previous Independence Day, greatly mesmerized him at the ball in Freeport. Amos's suggestion that they leave Brunswick seemed to affect a muscle in the lower-right hemisphere of Eagleton's face, so that a portion of his jawline twitched like a cat's ear. Bird was quite taken with this manifestation.

"I am rather concerned," said Amos, patting Bird's head, "that those villains who took advantage of ourselves and the baroness last night will have found some means to follow us."

"Do you think?" asked Eagleton.

Bird's head turned back and forth with the conversation.

"I think very much," said Amos, which was as true as anything he had ever said to them. "They are desperate men, I am sure, to attempt such a kidnapping beneath our noses! '*What fuller proof needs be obtained of their base employ?'* Louis the XIV to the captain of the guard; act one, scene seven, of *How Power Was Preserved.*"

"Good heavens!" said Thump between mouthfuls. He was thinking of Ephram and Miss Riverille, left behind.

"We must not light long upon any single perch," said Amos.

"Miss Riverille did say she would wire the Simpsons this morning," said Eagleton.

"We should stay as far away from the Simpsons as possible."

"We should?" Eagleton was shocked.

"One failed plan on the part of desperate men can only lead to more desperate measures," said Amos. "And whatever *we* have planned to do, we must do the opposite."

"How extraordinary!" said Eagleton.

"Ephram and Miss Riverille will think we have gone to the Simpsons'," interjected Thump.

"And who else will think it?"

"Certainly Ephram and Miss Riverille will say nothing!" said Eagleton. He was astonished and not sure he shouldn't be a little offended.

"Of course they won't," placated Amos. "But how were we discovered at Cliff Cottage in the first place? How did they spirit this little fellow away before our very eyes? These are deep waters, gentlemen, and forces of untold abilities, to find us so quickly and effect such a plan."

Eagleton and Thump turned to Bird to be sure that, even as they spoke, the same was not being done again. "Are you saying that we should not bring ourselves to the Simpsons'?" asked Eagleton.

"I have the impression that *Miss* Simpson is a young lady who holds some charm for you," said Amos.

Eagleton's posture straightened.

Thump cleared his throat.

"Certainly, if this is the case," said Amos, "you do not want to lead danger into her house."

"I hadn't thought of that," said Eagleton honestly.

"Good heavens!" said Thump again, his eyes wide.

"With such miscreants upon our trail," said Eagleton almost in a whisper as he formulated the thought, "we might be a hazard to anyone near!" Ephram and Eagleton hadn't considered how they came to be discovered at Cliff Cottage (any more than they questioned why Amos Guernsey had attached himself to their cause). "What should we do?" wondered Eagleton. To make a plan and yet to plan to do the opposite seemed very unusual.

"In my travels upon the stage, I have come to know many places and more people, my friends, some of which are—in parlance—'out of the way.' By train we can reach Bath and there hire a carriage to a lodging of which I know and in which you might *never* be discovered."

Eagleton's eyes were wide. "And where is this place?"

"If we knew," said Thump with great caution, "we would have to go someplace else."

"Of course," said Eagleton. "Do the opposite of what has been planned!"

It was a perfectly rational idea. They had been charged with protecting the young boy, but circumstances begged that they *not*, in the meantime, endanger others. Eagleton felt a vast disappointment that he was not to see Miss Simpson—it was a shame that they hadn't planned *not* to see her—but his sense of what was honorable rose above this melancholy, so that if he was not happy about their decision, he was at least sure of its being right.

"We will get our things together as soon as we eat," said Eagleton, then, "Oh, dear!" He was trying to think of how to do the opposite of what he had just suggested. "This is going to be very difficult."

Bird had stopped eating. His hands were rested at either side of his plate—a knife in one, a fork in the other—though they did not look relaxed, only halted. His large eyes followed the conversation and perhaps the emotions underlying it, and whenever they lit upon Amos, they seemed to be working at a puzzle or an optical illusion, as if he were not sure of what he was seeing.

Within the hour they were gone from the Tontine Hotel.

45. The News That Day Was the Accident on Commercial Street

MOLLIE DIDN'T KNOW when she had ever seen Mr. Corbel when he *wasn't* sitting at his desk, his face surrounded by piles of journalistic debris and punctuated with the inevitable cigar, like a living, grimacing firetrap. She was almost embarrassed to find him standing alone in the middle of the room, as if she had caught a turtle out of its shell.

"I guess I spoke too soon," he rasped.

Mollie waited for some further elucidation.

"I said you were always on time," he explained.

"Am I late?"

"For you, you are." He walked up and took the copy from her hands. It was all very odd, as if she had walked into the wrong newspaper.

"You were probably right about that kid," he said offhandedly.

"What do you mean?" she asked.

"You haven't read the paper," he said. She cast an eye over his desk and saw what looked to be the day's edition of the *Eastern Argus*. "Page six," said the editor without looking around. He was searching for something on one of his shelves. "Second column, I think; about halfway down. Looks like they *did* take him to the cape."

The item was just where he had placed it:

News from Cape Elizabeth

The word from Cliff Cottage last night was breathless, it seems, as members of the recently inaugurated club the Moosepath League indulged in a little hocus-pocus with the celebrated Baroness Blinsky and her mate, Major Alcott. It was a séance, in fact, and several other guests and at least one member of the local community joined in the ceremony, during which a great deal of excitement ensued.

The baroness's famous guide to the spiritual realm, who sometimes appears in feathers and loin cloth to startle the women, was the first act in the evening's entertainments, and for a brief moment it was believed that he had made off with a child, who was also a guest at the hotel and who remains unidentified.

Not in attendance, surprisingly enough, was an actor named Guernsey, whom some will remember in the role of George Washington three years ago, though he looked less like that great man in his presidential prime than he did a scarecrow at Valley Forge.

Constable Pear, who answered a late call from the proprietor of the hotel, George Bailey, did not arrive in time to meet most of the personages involved. . . .

"That must be *Amos* Guernsey," Corbel was saying. "Angus was saying yesterday there was an actor mixed up with Tweed. I remember that fellow, though I didn't see him perform Washington, more's the pity." Fritz Corbel thought he had found what he was looking for, and he walked over to his desk and sat down before he realized that Mollie was gone and the paper as well. His door was open, and he could hear the door down the hall slam shut.

* * *

The streets were choked with traffic; the day was so fine that anyone with a reason to be out was answering it. Pedestrians filled the sidewalks and slowed the movement in the streets as they crossed; horsemen and carriages and wagons created a steady clamor that echoed from the buildings. When the cab unexpectedly came to a halt, Mollie put her head out the window and asked the driver what he saw from his perch.

"There's been an accident up ahead," he replied. He was standing on his seat, and he let out a sorrowful "*Ach!* There's a horse down, I think." He looked as if he wanted to climb down and comfort his own animal.

They were hemmed in without even a side alley to escape by, the crowd gathering ahead of them. "Meet me on Pine Street," she shouted, and when she reached the curb, she shouldered her way through the mob. Before she reached the scene of the accident, which was hidden from her by several halted vehicles and a growing cordon of police, she came to an alley that took her to the next street over and began the vigorous climb to Pine Street.

Mrs. Barter was at home, but she did not know where Wyckford was. He had not been able to find Horace McQuinn the day before and was perhaps out looking for the man again. The carriage was there for her when she hurried from Mrs. Barter's, and she asked the driver to take her home.

She was hurrying up Mrs. Makepeace's front walk and wondering what to tell the landlady when she was startled by Officer Skillings, who materialized on the lawn, calling her name. Mollie nearly let out an oath but slipped into a habit of her father's instead, saying, "Gar! Officer Skillings, you near frightened the life from me!"

"I beg your pardon, Miss Peer," he said. Cap in hand, he looked like an admonished schoolboy. "I only wanted a word with you, if I may."

She could hear something her mother had said a hundred times. "You are not careful with people, Mollie." Mollie knew she should feel sorry for the man, but she had no time to fend him off or generously salve wounded pride and broken hopes. "I'm very much in a hurry, Officer."

"Call me Sam, please, Miss Peer," he said, looking down at his hat as if he didn't know what it was. "It was just that I was—"

"Truly . . . Sam, I cannot stop to talk," she said with as much kindness as she could muster on short notice.

He put a hand up as if to get a word in, but she was already up the steps, saying, "I'm sorry. My life right now just doesn't allow for anything so congenial as a simple conversation."

Sam Skillings stood below the porch steps for a moment and scratched his head before replacing his hat. He glanced quickly to a moving curtain and thought he caught a glimpse of the landlady. He raised a hand to wave, though she was already gone; then, with hunched shoulders and shaking head, he plodded back down the walk.

Mollie left her door open and hoped she was making enough noise to interest Mrs. Makepeace. "I'm going to Cape Elizabeth this morning, Mrs. Makepeace," she said when the woman poked her head in. Mollie had nearly finished packing her bag. "I may be staying a night or two."

"Is this to do with the little boy again?" asked the landlady frankly.

"I will be honest with you, Mrs. Makepeace. I had every intention of *not* being honest with you."

"That was a very rough bunch with him," said the older woman, not without a hint of sympathy for the child. "I'm not your mother," said Mrs. Makepeace, the meaning of which was difficult for Mollie to interpret.

"At any rate," said Mollie, "I am less apt to do the opposite of what you ask of me than I was my mother."

"Then I won't tempt fate and ask you not to go. But I will enjoin you to take care of appearances and to take greater care of yourself."

Mollie picked up her bag, retrieved her purse, and stopped in the door, where she kissed Mrs. Makepeace. She was more than a little relieved to find that Skillings was gone when she hurried out to the carriage.

"Mrs. Barter said I might find you leaving for Cape Elizabeth," said Wyckford O'Hearn. Mollie found him outside the station, a brown satchel held in the crook of one arm, the way one might carry a small animal. His derby was not the rakish accoutrement of a few days past, tilted so carefully upon his red hair, but simply a hat planted on the top of his head like an old and nearly forgotten habit.

They said very little till they were on the train; the journey to Cape Elizabeth would hardly take ten minutes, and they balanced themselves on their respective seats, opposite one another, as if prepared to bolt and run.

"The man I told you about yesterday," she said, "has been with Bird and his guardians." She hadn't thought to bring the issue of the *Eastern Argus* she had appropriated from editor Corbel.

"What does it mean?" asked Wyck.

"It is not a coincidence, is all I know." Mollie thought of Amos's threat of blackmail, which showed more grit, if less sense, than she would have credited him; and she tried to imagine that the man would actually threaten anyone, much less a defenseless little boy. And when she thought of Bird, her memory always took her back to his shoes; first his bare feet and then his oversized shoes.

Wyck was watching her, and there was the look of approval in his eyes, as if she had exonerated herself (against her behavior of a few days ago) just by arriving at the station and sitting there with him. There was something, almost a smile, at one corner of his mouth, and he looked at her with more ease than he had since challenging the lie about her mother.

She would have liked to kick him.

46. Playing Catch

"A séance?" said Wyckford. The word did not come naturally to his lips, and he frowned when he said it.

"That is what the paper said." Mollie had not mentioned the item's suggestion of an attempt to abduct the boy.

The ballplayer's frown only deepened. He shook his head. "The poor kid won't know whether he's on foot or horseback." They could feel the carriage lurch away from the Cape Elizabeth station.

"Most children don't," said Mollie.

Wyckford thought about this for a while. Mollie leaned forward so that she could see the grand houses they were passing. "No, I don't suppose I understood very much," he admitted. He could hardly remember when he was Bird's age. "I didn't understand how to stay out of trouble, mostly. *You* must have been a Tartar."

"I was an exemplary child," she said, arms folded, eyebrow raised.

"Were you?" he replied, as if he couldn't imagine it.

Perhaps a little too exemplary, she thought.

Before she had reached her ninth birthday, Mollie had earned the reputation of a snitch among the neighborhood children on Munjoy Hill, and for a time she wore the distinction with a fierce and unrelenting pride. It didn't matter that she was left out of many of the games and much of the play that went on beyond the eyes and ears of adults; she had her catechism, which was only a little more strict than the one taught at school.

But tattling never proved very satisfying; people seldom punished a wrongdoer as harshly as they would if they had simply caught the culprit red-handed. Her own mother often let her brothers off with a cuff to the head or a swat of the broom whenever Mollie laid their offenses at the seat of judgment. Giovanna Peer would level a superficial blow to Bobby's ear for swearing or rap Ian's knuckles for stealing apples, then turn to Mollie and as likely give *her* a rap or a blow and shout, "Don't tattle!"

Mollie's tattling came to an end one day when she announced her intention to reveal her brother Malcolm's latest sin and Malcolm came back with the absurd notion that he would tell on her tattling. The taunts flew between them, gathering steam and volume, and it happened that the entire scene took place within earshot of their father's forge.

Edgar Right Peer stepped out from the shed and watched this conflict for a minute or so before letting his presence be known. "Mollie," he said, "what's this about snitching on your brother?"

She had never run to her father with her *tales*; he always seemed so innocent of wrongdoing himself that she felt he wouldn't understand another's transgression. Or perhaps she secretly feared that his innocence would be scarred by the knowledge of sin in the world.

What Mollie, in her youth, did not realize was that her father had come from a line of Orangemen, that he had taken on the mantle, if not the absolute heart, of Catholicism in order to marry her mother, and that he knew very well what men of both persuasions would stoop to in the name of righteousness.

But the nine-year-old girl was at a loss for words (which was not typical), and what filled the ensuing quiet was Malcolm's low chuckle.

"Malcolm," said their father, "go tell your mother what you did." This was not what either of the children had in mind; Mollie in particular felt that her thunder had been stolen. "Come here, Mollie," said Edgar Peer, and he turned back to the forge.

Just inside the shed, Mollie leaned against a doorjamb and waited while her father fed the fire. He did not seem to be in a hurry, and after a while, she wondered if he had forgotten about her. When he did speak, he startled her. "Mollie, dear, you're not a tattletale, are you?" When he received no answer, he said, "People don't like a snitch, you know."

"But if someone's doing something wrong—" she began.

"Mollie, why do you go to your mother with a tale about Malcolm?" She had thought this self-evident and only blinked at her father.

He changed the question. "Do you do it for his sake or your own?"

"Perhaps a little too exemplary," said Mollie in the carriage, hardly realizing that she spoke aloud.

There is a story behind that, thought Wyck. He wished she would talk more so he would have an excuse to look at her directly. When she leaned forward to peer out the window, light fell upon her face, and everything about her countenance—her dark eyes and expressive brows, her black hair, the paleness of her cheek—awoke in contrast.

"It seemed a distance from Munjoy Hill to Plum Street," she said, "but it's a good deal further from Plum Street to Cape Elizabeth."

Wyck knew what she meant; well-to-do was the principal form of social strata here at the cape, and this was evident from any road or byway. The homes were handsome and well spaced, the grounds manicured and neat. *Captain's Quarters* was how the cape was sometimes referred to on the Portland wharfs. ("Is that the *Laurie B.* coming round Captain's Quarters?")

"I've never been here before," said Wyck, who thought the journey from his family farm in Veazie to Mrs. Barter's house on Pine Street was no distance at all. It was not long before the carriage pulled into the yard of Cliff Cottage. Wyck insisted on paying the driver, and though Mollie suspected that he could ill afford it, she did not argue with him.

Cliff Cottage stood like an afterthought upon its bald knoll, a large, ungainly structure, looking inert and lonely in the autumn light. They approached the hotel, carrying their small bags and presenting a puzzling aspect to Mr. Bailey as they approached the glass doors. Mollie was dressed as any lady who had come to spend a night or a month at his establishment.

Wyckford was dressed neatly enough, but the cut of his jacket and the material of his vest would have shouted his laboring origins even if his burly walk and uncertain expression had not. He might have been a drummer, though they tended to dress with too much flash and rarely looked uncertain. The redheaded man deferred to the young woman (Mr. Bailey thought that most men might), though there was nothing of the servant about him.

"Can I help you?" asked Mr. Bailey when they had entered the foyer.

"Yes, thank you," she said. "We are looking for members of the Moosepath League."

"Oh, my," said Mr. Bailey.

47. Intruder from Another's Tale

THE OLD CAPE AND ITS OUTBUILDINGS AND BOATHOUSE were gray with years and elements and disuse. The stairs and walkways, the landings that reached down the overgrown slope to the shore, were weathered and worn to the look of driftwood, as if they had been raised from litter left behind by the tide. Brambles and tall grass ranked the path from the road, and narrow, unhealthy trees screened the view of the cove till one came within sight of the house.

By rail, Amos Guernsey had led Eagleton and Thump and their

charge to Bath's noisy waterfront of shipyards and shipping firms. After disappearing for an hour or so, Amos returned to the train station, driving a carriage, which took them south, along the Kennebec, past the old sawmills and over a narrow bridge to a head of land known as Winnegance.

As he drove, the actor assured them that his "friends" would help them along the next stage of their secretive wandering. In truth, Eagleton and Thump were a little turned around and had, by the minute, less idea where they were; and yet they were encouraged, since they had no idea where they were going, that they could not be going on a more opposite course than they had planned, if they had had a plan.

They were not so encouraged by their first sight of the gray buildings standing above the shore and the rickety wharf, nor very convinced that someone could be living among them. But there was a face at a window, and the front door cracked ajar as they approached the porch.

Amos halted his little entourage just short of the porch steps. "Brownlow!" he called out. "Brownlow, is that you?"

"Who wants to know?" came the reply from behind the door.

Eagleton and Thump shared a sense of danger, and Thump pulled the little boy behind him.

"It's Amos," the actor was saying. "Amos Guernsey. Tom Scale said we would find you here."

"Did he," came the voice, implying more statement than question.

"I have a proposition for you," said Amos.

There was a noise from behind the door that did not sound altogether optimistic about this possibility, then a deliberative silence. "You come up," came the voice.

It was understood that "you" was to be interpreted in the singular, and Amos went up the steps with a good deal more bounce than would have either Eagleton or Thump. The actor stopped at the door, which opened enough so that he could step inside. Conversation could be heard, and presently Amos stood in the doorway and called the others. "Come in, come in!" he said, as if there had never been any question of their being welcome.

Eagleton went first, stepping softly, as if he might wake someone. The inside of the house was plainly furnished, but it gave more signs of life than did the outer walls. There were rooms to either side of a narrow hall, and past a flight of stairs they could see a kitchen, brightly lit from the south. Amos stood in a curtained parlor to their immediate right.

"Come in, come in," he continued to say.

There was a low fire in the parlor hearth, hardly smoking, and past this, in the further corner, was another man. He was seated, and a primitive crutch, made of sticks and line, leaned against the end of the mantel close by. A tall jug stood on the floor by his feet. He looked to be as tall as Eagleton, if more ruggedly built, and simply sitting there, he gave the appearance of agility and athleticism. He had a close-cropped beard and trimmed mustaches; he was a handsome man with dark eyes and dark eyebrows. He had plaster on one ear, and they were a little shocked to realize that a portion of that extremity was missing.

"Brownlow," Amos was saying, "may I introduce to you two members of the amiable Moosepath League." And he proceeded to do this, adding Bird to the list. "Gentlemen, Mr. Brownlow Davies, fellow thespian and accomplished treader of the board."

"You will pardon me if I don't get up," said the man with no sound of apology in his tone or expression upon his face. It was plain from his voice that he *had* gotten up, for they had heard him at the door. His head was slightly lowered, so that he looked up at them from beneath his expressive eyebrows. A shotgun leaned against the wall, behind his chair.

So far from noticing any of this, besides the shotgun, Eagleton and Thump were unswayed from their natural amicability; they greeted the man with genuine openness and pleasure and came forward to shake his hand.

"Very good of you," said Eagleton, without specifying (or really knowing) what the man had done to occasion this praise.

"Any friend of our friend, you know," said Thump.

Davies hardly stirred himself to return the gesture and considered the two men with suspicion. There was something older or more worn about Brownlow Davies as one looked at him, and Eagleton and Thump could see the gray in his hair as their eyes grew accustomed to the dimmer precincts of the house. Others might have detected in him a feral quality, like an animal that is doubly wary for being injured—the wolf just escaped from the trap.

"Brownlow has recently lost his position as a result of injury," explained Amos. "I thought we might benefit from one another—we by his attachment to certain river people and he by some stipend for his services."

"Most certainly," said Eagleton. Thump was of like mind; the loss of a "position" perhaps explained Mr. Davies's gray lodgings, and the members of the Moosepath League were known for nothing if not for their ready sympathy.

"And this is your charge," said Davies. He looked at Bird the way a person might consider an object if he had been told (though not convinced) that that object was of some value. Eagleton and Thump were a little put off by the man's demeanor, but he turned his attention back to them and recovered himself; he even smiled. "I have associates arriving presently," he said, "and a boat will be here in the evening that they plan to load, so you will find a passage from this point that others will be at great pains to follow."

"You will be swallowed up, my friends!" declared Amos Guernsey.

"We can never repay you," said Eagleton. "I myself could never have thought in a manner so opposite."

"Quite admirable in its conversity," agreed Thump.

Amos waved this praise away, and they thought from his expression that he might blush. Neither Eagleton nor Thump seemed to think it strange that any boat would rendezvous at the decrepit wharf below. "High tide at eighteen past five," said Thump cheerily.

"Continued fair," announced Eagleton. "Light breeze from the southwest expected by evening."

Amos was delighted with these forecasts and predicted that they had put the villains behind them. " *There still be days, like old, when untried innocence is watched by fate and trouble turned by gentle destiny!*' George Washington to Tom, act three, scene the last, in *The Rescue of Ann Beam*."

Mr. Davies felt strongly about bringing the horse and carriage down from the road, and Amos went out to accomplish this. The day was shining and the sun was at its height when Eagleton and Thump clumped out to retrieve their bags, and till their eyes were reacquainted with the light, the trees and the leaves looked pale and bleached. Bird tagged along, and their feet shushed in the long grass. Thump caught his coattail in a raspberry bush, and it took some minutes to extricate him.

They stood on the porch and looked out over the slope and the cove. "Winnegance," said Eagleton, as if to affix the place as well as the word in his memory. Winnegance, to be sure, was a village that they had passed through, but the name would always conjure in their memories the image of that gray house and the surrounding thickets.

It seemed strange to them (city dwellers) how very overgrown it was; so fragile and tenuous was the human grasp upon the natural landscape that the house, which might have been built only seventy years ago, had weathered to the color of an ancient tree and become the home of insects and small creatures. Vines and even small trees encroached upon the walls and pushed leafy tendrils between the floorboards of the porch; the yard itself was a chaos of competing raspberry plants and alder shoots. A single path wound through this like a maze till it reached the steeper portion of the hill and plummeted in a direct line to the bony wharf.

Many songbirds had already left for southern climes, but a chickadee called from a nearby tree, and some lazy insect's buzz inhabited the sunny air. The dry scent of fall rose up and intermingled with the salty tang of the cove and the Kennebec beyond.

The boathouse loomed below, tilting on a relatively horizontal bit of shore; it put Eagleton in mind of a barn, which made him think of livestock, which conjured up the image of Sundry Moss's uncle's cow. He was still fascinated by the animal's ability to predict the weather, and he said aloud, "I wished I could have seen that cow."

"Yes," said Thump, nodding.

The Moosepathians were reluctant to return to the little parlor, though the day had cooled and the fire in the hearth was pleasant. They had a vague sense, now that they were away from Mr. Davies, that they had been in the lion's den; that the lion had not growled at them or offered to eat them was perhaps only a consequence of his having just fed, and they weren't sure (or, rather, they wouldn't have been sure if they had articulated their feelings so pointedly) that they wanted to be near him when he grew hungry again.

But a lifetime of courteous habit is in itself a powerful thing, and it seemed, after a time, ungracious to avoid their host any longer. Brownlow Davies was drinking from his jug when they came inside. Amos, who was seated on the other side of the fire from the dark man, looked relieved to see the other guests. "Come in, come in," he said, laughing nervously. He seemed to have run out of theatrical dialogue suddenly.

Cold meat, bread, and cheese were to be had in the kitchen, served in somewhat primitive conditions. Nicety did not win over hunger in their approach to the meal, however, for they had not eaten since leaving Brunswick. Mr. Davies did not join them, but had his meal in his chair by the fire, washing it down with whatever sloshed in his jug.

"Medicinal necessity," he told Eagleton and Thump when they watched his imbibing with curiosity. He laughed in a low tone, and if he meant to imply any irony, it was lost on them. "Doctor's orders for the ankle," he added.

Amos watched the liquid gurgle from the jug with solicitous concern. It took continued doses to fulfill the physician's behest, and it was not long before the look in Davies's eye grew indirect and his ability with the jug less agile. He cursed when he spilled some of the drink, and the Moose-pathians were a little astonished, not to say horrified. Amos laughed nervously again.

Thump was so brave as to retrieve *Mrs. Ludley's Luck* and found enough light in the parlor by which to read. He was quite anxious for the titular heroine (Mrs. Ludley had just returned to the grove in the woods with the carriage driver, and they were searching for the cigar box lost by the brother of the woman who called to them from the tower), and Eagleton was pleased that his friend had become so engrossed with the volume.

Amos and Eagleton spoke quietly; Mr. Davies seemed disinclined toward conversation as the afternoon wore on. Bird sat in a chair beside Thump and looked at the pictures in a *Century* magazine that they found in the kitchen.

Soon Mr. Davies was snoring, and there seemed a degree of contradiction between the wary manner in which he had greeted them and this sudden lack of vigilance. He did not immediately awaken when the front door opened, startling everyone else, and his "associates" stepped into the hall.

48. The Bottom Line

WYCK WENT WHITE when he heard about the attempt to abduct Bird. The story was a little eccentrically told, and in the course of Ephram's description, the fact that the boy had been temporarily lost was presented as something of an afterthought. "Then we went searching for the boy," said Ephram.

"The boy?" piped Wyck. "Bird, you mean?"

"Yes, indeed."

"You *searched* for him?"

"He was missing, yes," said Ephram, as if still puzzled himself.

"Missing?"

"They had taken him —"

"*They?*"

"Yes, they had," agreed Ephram.

"Who are *they?*"

"Hmmm? Well, I'm not really sure who they are, actually, but they had taken him. Sinister forces, I fear."

"Is he all right?"

"Yes, first rate. *I* took a blow to the head, but I'm feeling much better." His words were confirmed by a purplish lump above his right temple.

"And where are your friends and the little boy now?" Mollie wondered.

"In Brunswick," replied Ephram. "Mr. Guernsey was so kind as to take them there."

"Mr. Guernsey," said Mollie. "And how did you meet with Mr. Guernsey?"

"Do you know him? I'm thinking we should offer him a membership. He was on the boat, you see—a friend of the captain's." The story was more or less got out of Ephram, eventually, despite the occasional turn in the narrative. At one juncture he described the strangeness of a fish on the wall. ("Eagleton was a little startled.") At another he philosophized on the wisdom of storing unused furniture in dark corridors. ("Thump was not expecting it, I am sure.") His tale was entirely derailed when Miss Riverille hurried into the dining room. Sallie was a little wary to find Ephram conversing with such a striking woman; but after introductions she facilitated the telling of last night's tale.

Mollie and Wyck did not add to Ephram's worries by revealing their own concerns regarding Amos Guernsey, but Sallie was suspicious of the man. "But they haven't gone to the Simpsons'," she announced when Ephram invoked Amos's kind leadership and the name of Brunswick again. "I nearly forgot; that is why I hurried so to get here! I wired Ophelia this morning, telling her to expect them, but she has just wired back to say they have not turned up." She took a telegram from her purse.

EASTERN TELEGRAPH COMPANY
BRUNSWICK

OCTOBER 13 P.M. 12:15

HILL STREET — CAPE ELIZABETH

MISS SALLIE RIVERILLE

MR EAGLETON AND FRIENDS HAVE NOT ARRIVED. SENT BOBBIE TO THE STATION BUT NO WORD OF THEM. ??? WHAT SITUATION? ANXIOUS TO HEAR.

OPHELIA

"But what does it mean?" asked Ephram.

"It means that Amos is up to more tricks," said Mollie.

Ephram was relieved to hear it.

Waving from the drive at Cliff Cottage, Sallie wished more than anything that she could go with them and felt as if all hope of interest and romance in her life was trundling away from her. It did not matter that Mr. Ephram had shaken her hand several times before he finally climbed into the waiting carriage or that he seemed himself so hesitant to leave.

"You must let me know what happens," she said to him. "You must come visit me."

"Yes . . . er, well, I would . . . very much, of course . . ." He was still gripping her hand, shaking it vigorously. "Certainly . . ." Then he straightened to his full height, like a soldier on parade, and pronounced, "Miss Riverille!" and stepped stiltedly to the carriage.

She watched the horse and trap disappear down the road. Astoria was in town visiting friends (regaling them with last night's adventures, no doubt), and Sallie's parents would not be pleased that Sallie had come here alone.

But it didn't matter. Life had returned to normal. Mr. Ephram and the lovely Moosepath League were once more figures of daydreams and imagination. Her shoulders slumped; she felt that even her hair drooped unbecomingly. Was it only last night that she had been so famously decked out and registered such wonderful compliments from those gentlemen? Her spectacles fogged.

"Oh, pooh!" she said.

The horse seemed to share their impatience, speeding through traffic with nervous energy; and when they arrived at Cape Elizabeth station, the train was waiting to be boarded, as if the very engine and cars Mollie and Wyck left there had kindly, if anxiously, changed ends and tarried for them. Ephram paid the driver and dashed after his bags and companions just as the conductor was giving the last call of "All aboard!"

"What if they went in another direction?" Wyckford said once they had settled themselves.

It was true that since their quarries had not shown themselves to Miss Simpson, there was reason to guess that they had not gone to Brunswick. "There might be word of them by the time we arrive," suggested Mollie. Now that she was *on the case*, she had no desire to let indirection stall their movement, and as no other direction was proposed, she deemed it wise to go to Brunswick rather than go nowhere at all. "We can be pretty sure they are not here, at any rate," she said. "Perhaps they *have* gone to Brunswick but after second thoughts scrupled to involve Miss Simpson and her family."

"Good heavens!" said Ephram; the thought was so rife with gallantry and drama. "What a fine thing!" he declared, quite in awe of his missing friends.

"I should have stayed with him," said Wyck. His mind was a loud clutter of uneasy thoughts and images of Bird in desperate circumstances.

Mollie gazed out the window, past gouts of steam, at the shifting crowd on the platform. She turned away from the view and glanced from Wyck to Ephram. "We all thought it best at the time," she said.

Ephram was inspecting his three watches and did not appear hurt or offended by the possible connotation of Wyck's words. As for Wyck, he was a little too worried, at the moment, and a little too straightforward in his speech (as a general thing) to perceive how his words might have been taken till that glance from Mollie. He apologized to Ephram, abashed at his own thoughtlessness. "It was a grand thing for you gentlemen to help the little fellow," he added.

Ephram, who hadn't understood the need for an apology, balked at the praise that followed. "It is nothing to what our chairman might have done," he said, unaccountably shaking the ballplayer's hand. "It is in times such as these that I look to his example." He straightened in his seat, filled with the thought. Mollie and Wyck were sure some words of wisdom were pending, but if Mister Walton was a man worth emulating, they were not to be blessed at this moment with a sample of his example.

Mollie watched the two men from beneath the rim of her hat. Wyck was still waiting on some erudition from Mr. Ephram, and Ephram, vaguely conscious of her dark eyes, peered through the window opposite. These men had nothing in common—in their appearance, in their social status, in their demeanor—save one trait. Mollie was reminded of something she had read long ago in the pithy end of a newspaper column: "*What greater wisdom is there than kindness?*" Her opinion of the world might seem a little brittle to some, but these words had stayed with her (haunted her, perhaps), and she was vaguely convinced, just then, of their accuracy.

49. The Hallowell Following

SUNDRY WONDERED WHY THE MEN WATCHING HIM and Mister Walton were so imprudent, almost as much as he wondered why he and his employer were *being* watched. Standing to one side of the window in Mister Walton's room, he could see one of them standing by a telegraph pole up the street.

"I wish John Neptune were here," said Mister Walton, who knew nothing of Sundry's discovery. "It is an Indian business, and he might know about it."

"Did the pine smoke, then?" Sundry wondered.

"I certainly thought so from a distance." Mister Walton took his spectacles from his nose and rubbed them with a handkerchief. "There is a grove on the other side of this steep hill, behind the hotel, and hovering over the tallest tree—said to be the reincarnated chief of an outcast tribe—there is a misty sort of disturbance. The tale, as Phileda conveyed it, was a strange mixture of tragedy and charm, as I suppose are many legends."

Mister Walton returned his spectacles to his nose with a sigh. There was a surprisingly wistful air about him, thought Sundry, considering that he had been keeping company with Miss McCannon. Indeed, Mister Walton's time with Phileda had been nothing but pleasure if one discounts the self-doubt that is a requirement among men of any age who go courting.

When, on the previous afternoon, he and Miss McCannon reached the curious grove of trees and the smoking pine, circumstances could not have been more favorable to a soul of romantic inclination. The grove itself stood upon a slope overlooking a valley of farms and fields. The trees were ancient, which, along with their loneliness upon the hillside, gave Mister Walton the impression that he was standing among monoliths that long ago marked a sacred place or the poles that once held the roof beams of an Aboriginal lodge. The day was warm enough to encourage a cricket or two, and their *chirr* added a helpful touch of melancholy.

The conversation had been pleasant, even sweet. (Miss McCannon's voice and therefore her words were by nature both these things to him.) And while strolling among the pines, there came a moment when he felt something serious might be spoken—not a pledge or a promise or a proposal but a word to acknowledge that there was more than simple fondness between them.

An unpleasant ripple of doubt coursed through him then, and he wondered, not for the first time, though not so profoundly, if he were taking the meaning of her companionship for granted. Was he, in fact, signifying her natural kindness and affectionate temperament with his own hopes? And was he, then, placing an unfair burden upon her friendship? Must she assume the encumbrance of his expectation as the price for her gentle familiarity?

In truth, it was Mister Walton who must assume the encumbrance of his own misgivings as the price for the gentlemanly nature of his soul. He did not think poorly of himself (else he could not have thought so well of others), yet the most successful in balancing self-knowledge and self-esteem have moments of self-doubt.

Phileda McCannon had been aware of a brief cloud in his expression and had inquired as to the state of his thoughts. He responded with a very small (and rare) prevarication, wondering aloud about Henry Echo. She, in turn, was wise enough to neither take him at his word nor hold the lie against him. And though the remainder of the afternoon was bright with her company, Mister Walton had been haunted ever since by an apprehension that his single instance of opportunity might have come and gone.

Talking with Sundry about the legend of the smoking pine, it was this uncertainty that plagued him, and a cloud, similar to that which Miss McCannon had spied, fell in and out of his typically sunny aspect.

"So what is it today?" Sundry asked his friend.

"Tea at the Nowells'," said Mister Walton, who was putting the finishing touches on his afternoon garb, "and you are invited. Phileda's friends are beginning to consider you mysterious."

"I promised Mr. Tolly I would come by this afternoon," said Sundry.

"Are you sure, then? I hope to meet this Mr. Tolly myself someday."

"He has a good many tales to tell, I can promise you. You should hear the one about the bear that saved his farm in Shirley Mills."

This caused Mister Walton to chuckle. "If you're sure."

Sundry was trying out his own small lie and did not like it. From the foyer of the Worster House, he watched the second carriage pull onto Winthrop Street and follow Mister Walton's trap up the hill. Then he took note of the large man standing at the corner of the hotel and left through a back door.

Stuart and Miriam Nowell's home on Middle Street was a reflection of its occupants—rather grand and friendly, a large brick house, half a century old, constructed on the fortune and promise of the ice trade, which was practiced with unparalleled success upon the Kennebec.

Though a servant stood at the periphery of the hall, Mr. Nowell met Mister Walton at the door and heartily shook his guest's hand. "Come in, come in!" he declared. "Phileda has been baiting us with bits of your adventures, and we are eager to hear it all from Aeneas himself."

"Don Quixote, more like," said Mister Walton with a laugh. He patted his middle. "Or Sancho Panza."

The host let the joke go with a smile and escorted Mister Walton to the parlor. Phileda smiled from a sofa by the further window, and beside her sat the long and ironic form of Charleston Thistlecoat. Mister Walton was delighted to see the one and surprised to see the other. Their physical proximity did not gladden him, to be sure, and he was doubly troubled by the dark sensation that flitted through him as he stood in the doorway.

"Our cabal is complete," said Mr. Nowell. "I believe you have met everyone." There were also in the room Mrs. Blythe, who had so graciously hosted the Harvest Ball, Minerva Wallace—next to whom Mister Walton was seated and who looked like the cat with the canary—and two or three other folk whom Mister Walton had met at the gala.

"Phileda tells us, Mister Walton," said Mrs. Wallace, "that you are the chairman of something called the *Moosepath League*," and she pronounced these last two words with a very deft mingling of incredulity and condescension.

Thistlecoat looked as if something from the moose path had reached his nose (and not pleasantly) even as he was doing his polite best not to show it. "I think Mister Walton has been having us on," said the man. "It is an unlikely name."

"Nonetheless," said Mister Walton, "it is a very real one. As a name, it is *uncommon*, I would say, as are its members, whom I have the honor of calling my friends." He said this with the happiest of smiles, and it was as pleasant a warning as Charles Thistlecoat could rightfully expect.

"I suppose with such a name," said Thistlecoat, with a negligent wave of his hand, "you must *gallivant* about the woods and perform all sorts of *grand* deeds on mountains and things."

"We haven't yet," said Mister Walton, looking mischievous, "but it is in our charter, I think."

The laugh seemed to be on Charleston Thistlecoat, somehow, and Phileda threw a hand before her face to keep from shouting. She had never seen Toby fencing before, and the manner in which he met Thistlecoat's irony filled her with delight.

Thistlecoat himself flashed his teeth in a smile.

Despite his abilities in the field of badinage, it was not entirely a pleasant outing for Mister Walton, and looking back upon it, it would seem less pleasant still, since unexpectedly it would be the last opportunity he had of Phileda McCannon's company for some time.

The carriage waited on a street perpendicular to, and a house or two above, Middle Street. Sundry didn't see the driver immediately, since the man was down with his horse, braiding its mane. He had an unlit pipe in his mouth and was humming to himself, and Sundry approached him with a confident smile.

"Afternoon."

"How are you."

"Fine, fine," said Sundry. "The fellow told me to pay you and tell you he won't be needing you to stay."

"Oh? Did she let him in, then?"

"Let him in?" Sundry was stumped for the briefest instant. The driver clearly thought his fare was involved in romantic subterfuge. "Yes," said Sundry, "she's been having fun with him, I think. But enough is enough."

"Some girls will send a fellow over hot coals," said the driver sagely. "My wife, Mary, made me ask her seven times!" Sundry settled up with the man, and they exchanged more homilies regarding the eccentric nature of women. The driver sent on his best wishes to the couple and shook the reins.

Sundry hurried back to Middle Street. The idea had not occurred to him before, but perhaps these men were interested in Miss McCannon, not Mister Walton or himself. Could they be in the employ of a jealous admirer?

He had no idea which home belonged to the Nowells, but he was able to spot his quarry standing in the break between two hedges on one property while watching the front of a brick house on the next. He was a thin fellow, with a thin beard and mustache and thin features. He was dressed well enough, and he wore a derby cocked back on his head. Sundry approached the man with the same *bonhomie* with which he had greeted the driver.

"Can you see anything?" he asked happily.

The man between the hedges started violently. He had been in the act of lighting a small cigar (another act of ineptitude for a spy), and match and smoke fell from his hand and lip. "What?" he asked, standing straight and fearful to take his eyes from Sundry to retrieve his cigar.

"I don't think they'd mind, really, if you dropped in," continued Sundry. "I've been invited myself, so why not think of yourself as my guest."

"I don't know what you're talking about!" said the man, looking past Sundry, then up and down the street.

"No need to be bashful," said Sundry. "We're all friends."

"I'm just trying to get my smoke lit out of the wind," said the man, and he made a grab for his cigar.

Sundry had it first, however, and as he held it out to the man, his smile never altered. The man wavered between fear and anger—presumably between flight and fight—but he snatched the cigar from the young man's hand and hurried off down the street, then up the side street, where he had left carriage and driver. Sundry called out, "I told him you wouldn't be needing him anymore."

The man cast a glance back and hurried down Middle Street. Sundry stayed some yards behind, and the thin fellow's walk grew stiffer and swifter with each look back. There is very little to say about this odd little chase except that Sundry seemed to drive the man and his confederate out of town altogether. The thin man stopped only a moment in front of the Worster House to berate his large companion, and Sundry thought they might be forming some strategy with which to address this new situation.

But Sundry hailed a policeman who happened by Main Street, and while he garnered unneeded direction, the two men hurried off in the direction of the railway station. A train was chafing there, and the conductor had only made the final call when the two men scurried from the station house, tickets in hand, and boarded the nearest car.

Sundry sat on a bench at the platform and watched the train depart, next stop Augusta. He had driven them away, but he still had no idea what they had been about, and he wasn't sure, after all, that he had handled it very well. Someone had left a newspaper on the bench, and he perused the back of it before picking it up. He was surprised to find a copy of the day's *Portland Courier* and had spent enough time in that city to think of this found object as something of a gift.

After a few minutes, he rose from the platform, tucked the paper beneath his arm, and (not wanting to be a complete liar) strolled off in the direction of Mr. Tolly's cousin's.

It was awkward, and even painful, to see Phileda driven home with Charleston Thistlecoat and Minerva Wallace, but they had arranged their departure very artfully. Mister Walton, who had confirmed his amiability despite Thistlecoat's manner and Minerva's catlike commentary—that is, graceful *and* pointed—found it difficult to insist on escorting Phileda home without appearing jealous. "Perhaps you will allow me to see you home, Mrs. Blythe," he said, which he would have done at any rate, and she, who knew it, accepted.

The elderly woman's society was to be cherished, but Mister Walton found himself a little hard-pressed to be jolly, knowing that others had the company, however temporarily, of Miss McCannon. It had been, on the whole (and through no fault of their hosts), a trying, if quiet, afternoon.

"Well, *that* was a trying afternoon," said Mrs. Blythe when they had settled themselves in Mister Walton's rented trap and he had started them on their way.

"I feel somehow," he admitted, "that my presence was not conducive to a peaceful gathering."

"Nonsense!" said Mrs. Blythe. "Minerva hasn't known a peaceful gathering since her christening, and even there, if I remember rightly, she poked her father in the eye."

The woman's blunt manner was something of a remedy to Mister Walton, and the relief he felt made room for a small chuckle.

"And Mr. Thistlecoat seems to have a high opinion of some things," she added, "mostly to do with himself."

It was the portly fellow's nature to be charitable, and he made some excuse for Thistlecoat's manner.

"There is no use beating around it," she insisted. "Some people are bound to be trouble to everyone else. How is Phileda?"

Mister Walton was a little startled. "I don't know—"

"*You* don't know? If *you* don't know, who should? You've spent the last two or three days with her, haven't you?"

"I suppose I have."

Mrs. Blythe didn't pursue this line of inquiry.

"I am fortunate for her friendship," said Mister Walton almost sadly.

"Friendship!" said the old woman. She thought on this. "Yes," she conceded, "I suppose Ledland and I wouldn't have gotten very far if we didn't like each other pretty well."

He smiled. From what he knew of Mrs. Blythe and what he had heard about her husband, he thought they probably liked each other a good deal. He had turned onto Winthrop Street and was taking them up the eastern side of town, toward the Blythe estate.

Phileda had not said much to him that afternoon, and of course Mister Walton wondered if his had been a poor showing with Charleston Thistlecoat. The Nowells had been charming, and tea had been very nice, but the entire business left Mister Walton with a terrible feeling of loose ends. *Perhaps*, he thought wryly, *I have stayed too long after the ball.*

Charleston Thistlecoat's attentions to Phileda had been obvious. He had a way of looking at people as if he were sizing them up for his own purposes, and it had not worn well with Mister Walton to see this look leveled upon Phileda.

It *had* been a trying afternoon. He felt a little weary, as if he had been treading water for hours. When the Blythe estate came into view, he was a little glad, since it meant that he would have time to think by himself, and a little sorry, since Mrs. Blythe's company had buoyed him up.

"I *am* sorry," he said when he helped her down from the trap. "I haven't been very good company."

"Not at all," she replied. "A little quiet with another person can be curative." There was something else on her mind, though, and she hesitated before letting him see her to the door. "She really couldn't say no to their offer of a ride, you know."

"Oh," he said with a dismissive wave. "My goodness, I have no claim on her!"

"Don't be so sure," said Mrs. Blythe, and she greeted the servant at the door cheerily.

But it was amazing how a few kind words (four, in fact) could affect him, and he drove off for the Worster House with a lighter heart and brighter view of his prospects. Instead of himself, he was thinking of Phileda once again.

50. Matching Colors

THERE WAS A VERY BLOND YOUNG MAN outside the Brunswick station who was very plainly waiting for someone to get off the train and just as plainly distracted by something he could observe from his vantage point at the further end of the platform. Mollie took note of him immediately, and she asked him if he were in the employ of the Simpsons.

The young man (Bobbie, as he had been named in Ophelia's telegram) was surprised to be so identified and struck by the handsome woman who had categorized him. "I am, ma'am, yes," he said, and gave himself a quick inventory to see what had declared him. He wondered if Wyckford and Ephram were the men for whom he was waiting.

"I take it, from your presence here," said Mollie, "that Mr. Eagleton and Mr. Thump have not arrived."

The question corrected his misapprehension. "No, ma'am, they haven't."

There was the sound of something—far distant, it seemed, like a hammer against a plank—an almost hollow crack, followed by the roar of many voices; and it was a measure of Wyck's deep worry that he looked with only half interest over Bobbie's head, across Brunswick's wide Main Street to a tree-lined common where a runner was taking the turn at second.

The young man looked over his shoulder longingly. "It's the Penobscots and the Quibblers," he said, and when he realized that this did not entirely clarify matters, he added, "We have an event every year, here in Brunswick, called the Great Quibble, and there's always a ball game. Once a year they take the best of the town players and the Bowdoin players and form a team they call the Quibblers, and they invite some other team to meet them."

"They picked a good team to play," said Wyckford. The Portland Bantams had gone up against the Indian team twice; and though they had split the wins between them, the games had both been close and hard fought. They had been as exhilarating as any games Wyckford had ever played, and he thought that the teams had brought out the best in each other. "What should we do now?" he asked of Mollie.

"Perhaps Bobbie will be good enough to take Mr. Ephram to the Simpsons' to see if they have heard anything. Miss Riverille may have wired since we left. I will go across to the game and find the reporters, who will know where a person might stay if he wants to remain inconspicuous. It's possible that someone may have noticed three men and a little boy. Mr. Thump's beard is quite admirable."

"I'll stay here," said Wyck, "in case they show up on another train."

Mollie glanced over to the game, surprised that Wyckford seemed to care so little about it. "Yes, that's probably the best." Bobbie was already ushering Mr. Ephram toward a carriage in the station yard, and she spared no time in hurrying across the street.

"Be careful who you talk to," called Wyck. He hoped, after he had said it, that she hadn't heard him. The ballplayer found a bench that he could drag to the corner of the platform, and he sat down on it and halfheartedly watched the game. *If I just get him back!* he kept saying to himself. *If I just get him back!* And then he wasn't saying it to himself, but repeating it under his breath like a prayer.

Tom Corsline would have been annoyed by any distraction if it had come in any other form, and *form* for Tom was perhaps the conductive word in this instance. "Mollie Peer," said the young woman as she held out her hand. "The *Eastern Argus*." She had easily recognized him as a newspaperman, if not by his demeanor, then by the notebook into which he was scribbling.

"Tom Corsline," said the reporter. He glanced toward home plate and watched a strike come in. The game was tied at two runs apiece, and the Penobscots had opened the fourth inning with a double that had been stretched to three bases on an error. The second man up had popped a shallow fly into the left fielder's glove. "Are the ladies reporting the games in Portland now?" asked Tom.

Mollie gave him her sweetest smile. "I'm looking for someone—three men and a little boy, actually. They have been traveling, and I have reason to believe they may be staying in Brunswick."

She described the members of the Moosepath League, Amos, and Bird and even hinted that they were an odd quartet to be traveling together. She did not explain why she was looking for these people, although she did let slip that she was with friends. This disappointed Tom, but it was a pleasure to be in her company, and they talked for some minutes before it was plain that he could be of no help.

The Penobscot at bat popped a high foul ball, and the catcher was able to get under it for the second out. The pitcher covered home plate, and the man at third came back from his lead.

"Did you say that one of these fellows had a prodigious beard?" asked another older man, who stood only two or three feet away.

"That would describe it, yes," said Mollie.

"And there was a little boy with them?"

"Yes! Have you seen them, then?"

"Just this afternoon, at the Tontine, having lunch. They must have gotten in late last night because *I* hadn't seen them before."

"Yes, they would have!"

"Very friendly fellows. Asked me if I would like to join their club. The Moose something." The man shook his head. "The Moose—"

"The Moosepath League," said Mollie.

"Ah, yes!" The man laughed quietly.

"Where is the Tontine?" she asked.

The man pointed down the street. "But I think they left soon after lunch. I'm sure I saw them with a carriage and a pile of bags."

Mollie was thanking the man for his help when the next man at bat connected with the ball in a splintery snap. The roar of the crowd went up and redoubled as the pitcher made an extraordinary dive to his right and terminated a hard-hit grounder. The runner was charging for home, and the pitcher rolled sideways onto his feet and fired the ball to the catcher. Home plate became a tangle of limbs as the runner slid and the catcher pivoted himself and the ball into the base path.

The sound of the crowd was deafening, players on both teams froze, the umpire threw his arm up and called, "Out!" It had all happened in a matter of seconds—the smash hit, the head-spinning play at the mound, the catcher's deft snag at the ball, and the collision at the plate.

Then the crowd grew quiet as the runner sat up to inspect his leg; he rubbed his knee and exhibited a wry smile. The catcher kneeled beside him, and several players from both teams hurried over and surrounded them in a huddle. After a short conference, the Penobscot was lifted from the field and carried to a place among his teammates.

"Maybe we should give them the run," said the catcher, one of the town players who was fearful that he had contributed to the injury. The Indian players were appreciative of this gallant notion but waved the incident off as part of the game.

Mollie let herself be distracted by this brief drama. Tom Corsline had hurried over to the Penobscot bench, and she could see he was scribbling furiously in his notebook. "They only brought nine men," said someone at her shoulder.

"Too bad," said another. "It was a tight game."

Wyck stood at the end of the station platform. Behind him, in the distance to the east, he could hear the whistle of a train. He had been watching the commotion on the ball field as well as he could with the crowd standing between him and the action at the plate. He had seen these sorts of delays before, had felt the weight of waiting and the silence of the crowd, and heard the applause for an injured man carried from the field.

Out of that crowd strode Mollie Peer, and Wyck, despite his fretting, was so taken by the figure she cut—comely and confident—that he did not at first notice the man walking with her. When he turned his gaze so as not to appear to be staring at her (which he was), he marked and recognized the lithe fellow in the athletic suit. Wyck stepped down from the platform and held his hand out to the man. The ballplayer shook Wyck's hand firmly.

"Mr. Sockalexis," said Mollie. "Mr. Wyckford O'Hearn. Mr. O'Hearn, Mr. Louis Sockalexis."

Wyckford already knew the man; Sockalexis was only the most remarkable player he had ever faced. "You won't remember me," said Wyckford.

"I do," said Sockalexis. "You drove in the game-winning run the first time we played in Portland."

"Yes, well, you threw me out at home and stopped the tying run the second game. I thought you were at Holy Cross."

"Late start," said the Indian.

"The Penobscots have an injured man and only eight players," said Mollie. "I told them I had a ballplayer for them across the street."

Her proprietary tone touched Wyckford in a way he could not have predicted; there was something not entirely wry behind her humor. He was surprised, however, that she would suggest such a thing under the circumstances, and he respectfully declined. "I'm afraid it's important that we reach our friends," he explained apologetically. "Otherwise, I would dearly like to oblige you, sir."

"I've had word of them," said Mollie before a reply could be made, "but they've been to Brunswick and gone, it seems."

"Where?"

"As soon as Mr. Ephram returns from the Simpsons', I'll have him escort me to the Tontine Hotel, where they stayed last night, and we will make inquiries."

"But what if they come back and no one is here?"

"The Simpsons' boy will bring Mr. Ephram, and we'll ask him to wait. Come, *Mr.* O'Hearn," she said, "we have all the bases covered. You need something to occupy you, and it won't do Bird any good if you're worn out from worry."

Mr. Sockalexis appeared vaguely amused by this exchange. Wyck shrugged. "I haven't a touch of Indian in me," he said.

The Penobscot smiled broadly. "You're redder than I am," he said.

Wyck ran a hand through his bright hair and laughed for the first time since Mollie met him at the Portland station that morning.

"The Irish and the Indians have much in common," said Mr. Sockalexis with continued humor, "for both have been considered descendants of the lost tribe of Israel."

51. An Argument to the Inch

BOBBIE PULLED THE CARRIAGE into the yard of a grand house overlooking the Androscoggin River, and they had hardly come to a stop when a young woman rushed out the front door and down the steps. Ephram sensed that he was a disappointment to her, though she was too kind to show it. "Miss Simpson," he said, doffing his hat and climbing down from the carriage.

"Mr. Ephram," she said, a bit out of breath. "I do hope everything is well with Mr. Eagleton and your friends. Sallie's wire was rather ominous."

Ephram had no desire to cause the young woman further concern, and yet it was beyond his power to deceive. "It has been an adventure, Miss Simpson," he said, "but you will know whereof I speak when I say that the situation could not be in abler hands than those of Eagleton and Thump!"

Ophelia Simpson had no idea what the situation *was* and, to be sure, had only known the handsome Christopher Eagleton for the space of two or three hours and had not devised an opinion of him outside the accomplishments of his good looks and the sweetness of his nature. She did, in fact, harbor certain fears for the man in any endeavor where innocence and cheerfulness were not required. She questioned Ephram politely and was able to ascertain the general nature of their recent exploits.

Bobbie stood by and listened with interest. No proper explanation for his duties that day had been offered to him, and he hoped, while remaining quiet, to learn what was up.

"Is this Mr. Eagleton, then?" came a voice from the front door.

"Daddy," said Miss Simpson, "this is his friend Mr. Ephram."

"Frederick Simpson," said the father as he shook Ephram's hand.

Ephram was impressed with how little the daughter resembled the father. He was stocky of build, and she was long and narrow; he was florid of face, and she possessed a perfectly white complexion; his hair and mustaches were dark, and she was blond; his features were large and gregarious, and hers were quietly handsome. She had an engaging space between her two front teeth, which added to an already youthful appearance.

"Are you ready to take me into town?" the father was asking Bobbie. "I must go to town," he said to Ephram, by way of apology for his abrupt exit. "I must quibble."

Ephram's eye widened. He hadn't meant to indicate any disagreement.

"Oh, Daddy!" said Ophelia. "Mr. Ephram, you must excuse my father, he is going to take part in the event there. They call it the Great Quibble."

"I call it the Grand Quibblation," announced the father. "Though there are those who insist on naming it the Great Quibblation or the Grand Quibble. These distinctions are of the utmost importance."

Ophelia rolled her eyes. Ephram was fascinated. He wished Eagleton were here to record this extraordinary phraseology, and the thought of his friend reminded him to inquire if any message had been sent from Sallie since he had left with Mollie Peer and Wyckford O'Hearn. Ophelia was quite moved by the delicate manner in which the man invoked her best friend: "Miss Riverille," he called her with the sort of tremolo another might inflect when speaking of a masterwork of art or an inspiring piece of music.

But nothing had been heard since Sallie had wired that Mr. Ephram was on his way with friends.

"Your friends are well, I hope," said Mr. Simpson. "Ophelia says you were having some complications."

"We are waiting to hear from them, sir," said Ephram.

"Yes, well, I hope you do. Ophie will be very disappointed if she doesn't catch sight of your Mr. Eagleton again."

"Daddy!"

"What?" said the father. "Yes, well."

There was a peculiar impasse. Bobbie stood at the bridle of his horse, the ears of the animal and those of the young man about equally pricked.

Mr. Simpson hesitated between the duty signified by the Quibblatory speech in his hand and the responsibility he had as a host. Ophelia, denied the company of Eagleton, was loath to give up the presence of his friend, and Ephram himself was, as always, a model of uncertainty.

"It's thirty-two minutes past two o'clock," said Ephram, which did nothing for anyone's decisive abilities. But Mr. Simpson, as it turned out, had some genius, and he managed to strike two birds with one throw by inquiring if he could drop Ephram off anywhere.

It was an odd visit, Ephram never venturing further than the driveway. He expressed, quite handsomely, his hope that he would see Miss Simpson soon, bowed to the young lady, to her father, to the driver, and (as he was in a fixed frame of mind) to the horse.

"Wish me luck, my dear," said Mr. Simpson.

"Happy quibbling," said Ophelia. She looked very pretty, in a melancholy way, waving to the carriage as it left the yard.

Ephram felt a bit guilty, having had the company of Miss Riverille *and* Miss Simpson in one day while his friends were somewhere dealing with sinister forces and nefarious schemes. "I am sorry," he said to Mr. Simpson, "that I will not be able to attend your event."

"Yes, well, it does promise to be a corker!"

"Does it?" said Ephram, who was not familiar with the term. "A corker!"

"The length of the lawn!" declared Mr. Simpson.

Ephram felt as if he knew less about the coming event the more he heard about it. "The lawn," he said.

"I am arguing for three and three-eighths inches."

"You are?"

"Indeed. I was going to argue for three and a quarter, but we've had a mild fall, and the lawn managed to gain another eighth of an inch. It meant changing slightly the tenor of my philosophy, but the instant I realized that the lawn had increased, I knew I could argue as vociferously for three and three-eighths as I could three and a quarter!"

"How remarkable!"

Mr. Simpson shook a finger in the air, and he was very impressive as he commenced to orate. "What! Think you that we shall elevate the opinion of our neighbors by cropping at three. Or worse, perhaps two and a half will be imagined the measure by which our fame is made. I say that the neighbor observing, as we trim at anything under three and three-eighths, will correctly speculate that we have less to occupy our time than the good Lord intended. Appearances indeed, and between the appearance of our yard and the appearance of ourselves, where do we choose?"

"It would never have occurred to me!" said Ephram.

"And can there be," continued Mr. Simpson, "that slothful man who passes over the rising grass at three and a half with no qualms!" He noticed that they were nearing the center of town and returned to his less disputatious manner. "And the like," he said. "I have some estimated figures regarding insects in tall grass and the lack of plushness in short—"

"Plushness!" marveled Ephram.

"I'm not sure it's a word," admitted Mr. Simpson. "There may be some debate over it."

"It's quite a good word," said Ephram, "even if it isn't one."

"Thank you. I rather like *plushness*; in a lawn and ladies' laps it is an imperative!" He was sorting through his papers. "I just hope I'm prepared for the rebuttals."

"I think you are admirably ready!" said Ephram.

"Do you think?"

"I am quite convinced by your argument."

"I haven't even gotten to the good part. Freedom, liberty, women, and children. It's quite rousing, really. Yes, well, here is the town hall. It's been a pleasure meeting you, sir."

"And you, sir. I wish the best for your debate."

They shook hands once again, and Mr. Simpson climbed from the carriage, looking ready to take on the opposition.

Bobbie shook his head as he looked after his employer.

Ephram was wondering how long the lawn was at his parents' home.

52. The White Bullet

WYCK WAS GLAD ENOUGH that he wasn't replacing the shortstop, for it was sufficiently challenging to play alongside men he had hitherto only played against without assaying a position with which his large size and rolling gait were not compatible. First base seemed a good omen, though he played left field for the Bantams, and the glove provided him actually fit his broad hand.

He was hastened to the field as soon as he and Sockalexis arrived amid cheers from both teams as well as the crowd. The game scorer was given his name, and play resumed.

He felt exhilarated and unprepared when the first batter hit a drag bunt up the left-field line and the third baseman neatly scooped it up. The throw to first was accurate and abrupt, though it did not arrive in time. Feeling the ball in his hand, Wyck was suddenly in the game. He glanced over the crowd along the right-field line and could see Mollie across the street, watching. *That wasn't a good idea*, he thought, and did his best to banish her, however temporarily, from his mind.

The delay in the game had had its effect, which seemed to favor the batters for the time being. Sockalexis, known for his fast pitch, was off speed throughout the inning; and the rest of the Penobscot team, who made a habit of turning marginal plays into *stoppers* and tight situations into game-winning breaks, seemed equally out of pace.

The fourth inning proceeded with very little involvement from Wyck and three runs for the Brunswick Quibblers. Wyck, who was as superstitious as any player, worried that his presence was jinxing the team. His larger worries, concerning Bird, were not forgotten but tucked behind his concentration on the game. The worry had become second nature to him, an involuntary process; and in this he had taken on the mantle of a parent, which was remarkable, since it seemed so unremarkable to him.

It was during the fifth inning that Wyck thought he recognized the pitcher for the other team, and before he could put a name or an identity to the face, he had an odd sense of foreboding. "That fellow on the mound looks familiar," he said to Sockalexis when they regrouped at the Penobscot bench.

The Indian peered at the pitcher. "His brother pitches for Lewiston."

Wyckford nearly gasped. His final at bat of the season, culminating in a strikeout in three pitches, had lingered in his system like a low-lying disease, slowing him down without absolutely debilitating him. "His brother struck me out," he said.

"I know," said the Indian. "I read the papers. I wouldn't mention it to the pitcher."

"He probably reads the papers, too."

Sockalexis could see the near horror in Wyck's eyes. "He's not a professional, like his brother."

"No, but he looks like him," said Wyck.

"The ball he throws isn't any smaller than anybody else's," said the Penobscot.

If I can only look at the ball and not that last pitch his brother threw me, thought Wyck.

The pitcher was grooming the mound, scratching at it with his feet like a rooster. The first of the Penobscot batters took some swings at the plate.

Very quietly, Sockalexis said, "My grandfather said to me once, 'You should imagine the deer calling the arrow, like a lodestone.'" The Indian smacked his fist into his hand. "You must think of the ball calling the bat."

"Does that work for *you?*" asked Wyck, amazed by the thought.

Sockalexis shook his head. "No."

It took a moment, but when Wyck did laugh, it was wholeheartedly.

"But my grandfather didn't play baseball," said the Penobscot.

In the sixth inning, Wyck glanced in the direction of the station and saw that Mollie was gone, replaced now by Bobbie. Ephram must have returned. It was just as well, he thought; the rest of the game promised to be unremarkable; and it was a measure of his state of mind that he thought this. The great ballplayers, of which certain contemporaries numbered Wyckford O'Hearn, always believe that something remarkable is going to happen and that they have as good a chance to make it happen as anyone else. The great ballplayer (the great anything, perhaps) craves the moment of decision, the narrow alley of possibility, the juncture where action is both necessary and precarious.

Wyck was ready to perform, to catch a ball, perhaps even hit one; his playing instincts, his reflexes, had been taught enough over the years to generally behave in a manner that would not shame him. But he was not thinking, certainly not believing, that he would do anything remarkable.

The game, as it progressed, bore this out. He was called upon to catch accurately thrown shots to first base, he tagged a man out in a fairly close situation and got on base on an error in the top of the seventh. Sockalexis became that man of iron that people would recall years later, delivering fastball after fastball, and though the rest of the team managed to claim bases, they were unable to drive one another home.

The game continued at 5–2.

It was in that proverbial inning (that is, the ninth) to which all hopes fly that the Penobscots came to life. The leadoff man poked an opposite-field double up the right-field line, and he was given leave to take third when the next batter reached first on a line drive. To the team, there was more in the air than simply getting on base; there was the sense that they had coalesced to a single purpose, and watching them, Wyck felt himself part of it and almost wished that the next batter would not *clean up* with a home run so that he himself might have the opportunity to play that narrow alley.

At an even count of one, the Quibblers' pitcher hurled the ball, and the sphere curved to the inside, where the batter was ready for it; the result of which was a leveraged ground shot that bounced in front of the pitcher and over his head, allowing the batter to reach first and the man on first to advance as the second baseman leaped forward to take the hop. It was, however, not long enough to encourage the man on third; the catcher took the snapped throw from the second baseman and gave the game a breather as he eyed the loaded bases.

Wyck advanced to the plate, feeling the welcome weight of the bat hanging from his right hand. There were shouts and catcalls from the spectators, all good-natured; the wind blew from the southwest; the Quibbler outfield played at a medium distance. Beyond them, the great oaks and maples were filled out in red and gold, the dry rush of their leaves communicating in a steady hush beneath the noise of the crowd.

The westered sun fell out from behind a cloud, and the peopled common was etched in the orange light of fall; long shadows stretched across the grass. Wyck swung the bat lightly with one arm, sweeping the tip of it below his knees; then he hefted the length of ash with both hands, set his shoulder against the field, and made a slow pass over the plate, watching the pitcher as if he were aiming for the man. *Imagine the ball calling the bat*, he thought, and it made him smile.

The Quibblers' pitcher (who had read the newspapers, by all accounts) was a little surprised by that smile, it was so uncalculated. He paused on the mound and somehow missed the signal from the catcher. Wyck was, in turn, surprised to see a flash of uncertainty in the thrower's posture, and he stepped from the batter's box to settle himself again.

The pitcher took a couple of hen scratches at the mound when he returned. He took a stance. Some fifty nonregulation feet of clarified air separated them, and the buttery light captured the glint in Wyck's eye and the set of the pitcher's chin like a magnifying glass. Wyck thought the crowd had quieted; he thought he could hear the movement of the pitcher on the mound.

The ball came in fat and heavy and wide.

Wyck stood straight before it reached half the distance between them and watched it slide past, barely making the catcher's glove.

"Ball one!" declared the umpire.

Wyck stepped out of the box again, tapped his shoes, and caught sight of Louis Sockalexis on deck.

"Imagine it calling the bat," said the Penobscot.

Wyck laughed, stepped into the box again, and leveled that same strange smile at the pitcher. The man took his windup and hurled a fastball at belt level, but inside.

"Strike!"

Wyck looked amused when he shot a glance at the umpire. He shifted slightly, leaned into his stance, and took one slow swing before raising the bat above his shoulder.

The catcher took his time getting the ball back to the pitcher, then settled down behind Wyck. The pitcher was looking in the direction of the Quibblers' bench. He glanced toward home plate, back to the bench, to home plate, to second base. He dug in, kicked, and threw.

The ball came in as fast as any pitch Wyckford had ever seen—an express, the Flying Cloud, the fastest horse, the electrical charge racing along the telegraph wire, a round white bullet at a level to the ground and a distance from Wyckford that could only have been managed by a month of his mother's prayers.

The shout of the crowd was as much from surprise and startled nerves as from any real sense of what had happened. The bat and the ball met like angered bulls, heads butted and horns locked for something less than an instant. The crack was deafening. The white sphere surged like a rocket, racing so that the eye was fooled into thinking it gained speed as it climbed. The pitcher lifted his head and watched. The infielders turned as they craned their necks. The outfielders shielded their eyes.

The gorgeous cloudlike billows of gold and red on the other end of the common shook with the breeze, and the bounding sphere sailed over them and disappeared. *"It was the longest shot this reporter has ever witnessed,"* Tom Corsline would write.

That might have hit the horse on Congress Street, thought Wyck.

There was silence.

Wyck looked back at Louis Sockalexis, who gave out a great roar of laughter. Mollie Peer was just stepping through the crowd, her eyes gazing out over the trees. Ephram, behind her, was peering at an untied shoelace. The players on the Penobscot bench leaped to their feet and let out a howl, and Ephram jumped with surprise. The Quibblers on the bench leaped to their feet and roared their approval, and Ephram jumped again.

The base runners began their carousel of movement as if in slow motion.

Mollie smiled at Wyck and raised her eyebrows, almost reprovingly. *What did you do?* she seemed to be asking, like a mother who has caught her child at a minor misdeed.

For the rest of his life Wyckford would look back on that moment, and it would lend him the strength to live with what afterward occurred.

53. News from the Moosepath

"ONE OF THOSE FELLOWS IN WINTHROP has confessed," said Sundry. He had the *Portland Courier* unfolded before him.

"Ah," said Mister Walton, who had just entered the parlor with a package in hand. "It was a terrible thing." He gave the package a close look. "This seems to be from our friends in the club."

"Sunny again tomorrow," said Sundry.

Mister Walton chuckled at Sundry's affectionate mimicry. "A book," said the portly fellow when he had opened the package. "*Where Would She Turn?*" He read the accompanying note. "They are sorry not to have sent us off but hope I will enjoy the book, which is a favorite of Mr. Thump's. How nice of them!" Mister Walton adjusted his spectacles and peered at the note. "There is something about a Hubbard squash and piano stools."

Sundry let out a low whistle and straightened in his chair. "Speaking of whom . . . ," he said. He folded the *Courier* so that a single item, headed by the name Cape Elizabeth, appeared for Mister Walton's perusal.

"This here?" asked the bespectacled fellow.

"Yes, indeed." Sundry wondered if it was time to mention the men who had been watching them.

Mister Walton held the paper beneath a table lamp and began to read. Sundry stood and looked over his shoulder. "A séance!" said Mister Walton, and added, "Madame Blinsky—I've heard of her. Good heavens!"

54. Crosscurrents

THE BOAT CAME with the very hind of twilight, when the trees and leaves before the porch were a single whispering silhouette in the evening breeze and two bright stars in the east showed over the roof of the gray house. It was a small two-masted fishing vessel that came into the cove with the eddying currents of a shifting tide, lighting like a dragonfly against the end of the tumbledown wharf.

There were two men aboard her, and they did not hail up to those waiting on the porch; one of Brownlow Davies's four "associates" went to speak with them. Davies himself stood uncertainly with the crutch under one arm and announced that when the time came, he would need help down the steep bank. His colleagues had been amused to find him snoring in the parlor with the half-empty jug beside his chair, but he had awakened in a dark mood and countered their gibes with a growl.

"I think his ankle is bothering him," deemed a charitable Eagleton to one of the men.

"I think his skull is bothering him," said the man.

"His ear has been injured, certainly," agreed Eagleton.

Inexplicably, to Eagleton, the man laughed.

These fellows, who had arrived earlier in the day, were curious about Eagleton, Thump, and Bird, but Amos, who was known to them, was cautious in his explanation, saying only that they were in need of transport. Davies would say less, which made the men more curious still.

But there was business to occupy their minds. In the room opposite the parlor there was a worn carpet, brought from some eastern land to grace a seafarer's home. Now this was lifted, and a trap door was revealed and raised in turn. One of the men nodded in the direction of Eagleton and Thump and frowned at Davies.

"*We're* not coming back here," said Davies.

The entire affair was mysterious, and the Moosepathians observed what they could with the utmost fascination. The four men dropped themselves into the space below, and soon there were various grunts and bangings as (it was explained) another entrance to the cellar was opened.

It was more than two hours later that the boat arrived (without Ephram to apprise them, Eagleton and Thump did not trust to the exact time), and soon the four men were rolling large barrels out from under the porch and easing them down the steps to the wharf and the waiting vessel.

Eagleton and Thump offered to lend a hand, but the men declined in a very jolly, if perplexing, manner.

"Wouldn't forgive ourselves if one of these took hold and blew up," said the tallest of them, and they all laughed heartily.

Thump smiled. It was all very spirited and robust, and he was put in mind of Theodore Roosevelt's ideology of the "strenuous life," with which Thump was very sympathetic and of which he had read a great deal.

Eagleton reflected on the phrase "took hold and blew up" and raised the concern that they were moving explosives. "Should we take the boy from the vicinity?" he wondered.

"They are having you on," said Amos with a wink.

"Having me on?" Eagleton was not familiar with the phrase.

"They're rubbing your elbow," said the actor, and when Eagleton inspected this portion of his anatomy, Amos said carefully, "They were joking with you."

"Oh!" said Eagleton. He waved a hand to indicate how clear it was to him now. "Good heavens!" He laughed. "If only Ephram was here."

"*And* Mister Walton," said Thump.

"Ah, yes," sighed Eagleton. "Mister Walton would have liked it."

"Are they moving explosives?" asked Thump.

Once the two Moosepathians were assured that the barrels contained simple molasses ("In one form or another," muttered one of the men), Mr. Davies led the idle contingent back inside; his medicine, it seemed, had given him the shivers, and Eagleton and Thump wondered if it were as curative as the dark fellow thought it to be.

It was not long before the sounds below them rose again to grunts and bangs; then the men came up the trap door, closed it, and covered it. Amos asked that one of them (the previously mentioned Tom Scale, as it turned out) take the hired carriage back to Bath, and after some laughter and jesting, much of which seemed eccentric to the club members, the men filed from the hall and were gone. It had already been ascertained that the captain, who had not made himself present beyond the deck of his vessel, was waiting for some moonshine by which to sail, and Amos thought it wise if everyone took to their bunks for an hour or two, till the time of departure had arrived.

There were small rooms, hardly more than narrow garrets, beneath the eaves of the old gray house, and with no more than a single, untidy cot in each of them, so that Bird was billeted on his own for the first time since coming under the guardianship of the Moosepath League. Eyes wide, the little boy took in everything (what little there was) in the room he was given and showed no emotion regarding his situation. He had a habit, Thump had noticed, of pulling at a tuft of hair behind his right ear, and he was doing this, standing in the midst of the tiny room alone.

A quarter moon peered through the very tops of the trees on the opposite shore of the cove, and the light of it reached Eagleton's cot. Rising into a state that was vaguely conscious, he became aware of the need to make a nighttime call. The room felt chilly outside his covers, but nature will have its way, and his condition eventually wore upon him till he was awake enough to rise and reach for his jacket and shoes. (Amos had invoked nothing more than a simple nap, and Eagleton and Thump had decided to "rough it" by sleeping in their clothes.)

Eagleton shivered in the night air and threw on his jacket. He took a step back to his bed to put on his shoes and stubbed his toe with a great deal of force. For a minute or so he sat and gripped the injured digit, then gingerly pulled on the shoe. The toe sang out when he put weight upon it, and he limped as he moved down the hall. The floorboards creaked, and passing Thump's room, he could hear his friend snoring. He paused before Bird's door, which was open, and watched with satisfaction as the little boy slept.

At Amos's door, he was startled by a low hiss. Eagleton stopped, wondering what could have made such a noise. The sound came again, and he realized then that it was coming from Amos's room. "Hssst!" it came again.

The sound gave him gooseflesh even when he realized that it was Amos himself making it. "Yes?" said Eagleton softly, his voice low and grumbly from sleep; he hardly dared clear his throat.

"Is that you?"

Eagleton thought about this for a moment. There seemed to be only one answer, and he gave it. "Yes," he whispered again. He did have a very definite catch in his throat and did not sound like himself.

"Let us get started, then," Amos said through the door.

"Yes," Eagleton whispered hoarsely. The thought gave him a great deal of excitement, and he hurriedly limped on his sore toe back to Thump's door. "Thump!" he stage-whispered. "Thump, old friend! We are off!"

"Hmmm?" said Thump.

"Thump!" said Eagleton, hurrying over to the man's bedside.

The man made a sound; then his eyes opened suddenly, and he almost knocked heads with Eagleton when he sat up. "Eagleton?" he spoke aloud.

Eagleton expressed, by the sudden gyrations of his hands and the startled look upon his face, the need to proceed quietly. Thump accepted this without question, as had Eagleton, and searched out his jacket and shoes.

A low murmur came from the next room, which was Bird's, and Eagleton peered out Thump's door in time to see a tall figure struggling with a smaller figure in the shadows at the end of the hall. "Good heavens!" whispered Eagleton, and then he shouted, "Good heavens!"

The figures had disappeared down the stairs, and Eagleton charged after them. "They have him, Thump!" he shouted, though the end of this declaration was somewhat attenuated by the need to concentrate on his footing as he tripped down the steps. The noise Eagleton made resounded throughout the house, and he did not stop in the hall; he tumbled out the front door like a cannonball and floundered down the porch steps into the brush beyond.

What occurred in the next few moments is easily confused. Eagleton was vaguely aware of following a pair of struggling figures as he pushed through the bushy path. There was a shout from the slope above and movement from the direction of the road.

"Stop!" came a voice not far from Eagleton.

"I've got him!" shouted the tall figure of Amos as he descended the path toward the wharf and the boat, and it was at that moment that Eagleton realized who was charging off with the boy. "Quickly, Amos!" he shouted. "Get him to the boat!" But his voice was lost in a great babble of shouts and commands. Hands gripped him, and he was dragged by several men up the slope.

Thump, meanwhile, hadn't the time to tie his shoes, but came down the front stairs of the house and the steps of the porch with similar speed, if a bit more grace, than had his friend. He did not see Amos disappearing down the bank with Bird but caught sight of Eagleton being dragged by three or four dark-clad men toward the road. With a shout, he charged in this direction, but then his unlaced shoes proved the undoing of his gallant intentions.

It has been noted, in photographs of the Moosepath League's charter members, that Thump described a certain *blocky* aspect; he was, it has been said, nearly as broad of shoulder as he was tall, which is something of an exaggeration. Nevertheless, once he had taken a complete somersault and tucked himself into a self-protective ball, he was of a shape conducive to rolling down the slope; and this is what he did, with extraordinary speed.

Amos had only just leaped into the awaiting vessel when Thump, who had gotten up terrific momentum, rumbled down the short, sloping wharf and dropped into the boat, the gunnels of which had lowered with the ebbing tide, like a ball in a cup. This was all the more remarkable, since the boat had actually been cast off and had drifted a foot or so away from the dock; Thump's spinning form carried in a neat arc through the air before landing with a loud noise very much in keeping with his name.

This precipitate arrival was of great surprise to the captain and crew, not to mention Amos, but they were too busy getting away to pay it much heed. Thump, understandably, was stunned.

Meanwhile, Eagleton was struggling with his captors.

"This isn't him," growled someone.

"Who was that running down the hill?" asked another.

"The one running or the one rolling?" wondered a third.

"We've stumbled onto something else entirely, gentlemen," came an official-sounding voice. "It's no wonder we were taken by surprise."

"There's more than tea and biscuits on that vessel, I'd bet my head!" said the second man.

The boat had already caught a breeze coming off Winnegance Creek and was making the turn around the next head of land.

Several forms swarmed in the direction of the house, and Eagleton, who ceased his struggles for the time being, watched with a little horror as they mounted the porch and charged through the front door. A window exploded from the near gable end of the house, and a chair landed on the ground below. There came a crash from inside, the sound of a door being knocked down. A dark figure climbed from the window, hesitated, then lowered itself down the side of the house while hanging to the sill.

Behind Eagleton there was a man who let out a satisfied *"Ah!"*

Just as arms reached out the window for the man hanging there, he dropped to the ground. There was a grunt of pain, and he rose uncertainly, took two limping strides, and came to a halt. He was surrounded. After some struggling, he was half-carried, half-dragged, to the place where Eagleton was being held. Several lanterns were unshuttered, and the man from the window came into the circle of light. With a growl, Brownlow Davies lifted his head.

"What did you do to your ear, Brownlow?" wondered one of the crowd that gathered round. A light was shone directly into the actor's face.

"Take it away from his face," came a quiet voice, and the lantern was turned aside.

Gaping about, Eagleton could see now that several of the men were in police uniforms. A short man came into the light and approached Davies. "Let him see me, please," requested this man. The light was turned upon him.

Davies narrowed his eyes.

"I am not sure we have been properly introduced, Mr. Davies." The fellow did not extend his hand. "I believe you visited me the other night without stopping to say hello. My name is Henry Echo."

55. And Then There Was Thump

"Shall we throw him overboard?" came a growly voice from the cabin.

"Good heavens!" said Amos. "I'm not going to murder him!"

"He'd come to. The water's cold enough."

"Yes, well, I am not," said Amos. He stood at the companionway with his back to the captain. The two crew members awaited orders a few feet away.

"Was that Tweed and his gang, then?" wondered the captain.

"I don't know, really," said Amos, "though I think not. I thought I saw uniforms among them when I came out." He was still out of breath.

"Gory!" cursed the captain. "They'll be stirred all up and down the river." He needed the light of the quarter moon to sail by but knew his sails would stand out in that same light, particularly through a pair of field glasses. "This is why my crew and I don't get off the boat." He had changed his original course, and they were sailing up the wide stretch of the Kennebec. The wind was behind them, and the ship was plowing against the current. There was the occasional light along either shore and ahead of them a more general glow to indicate the denser environs of Bath. A sleeping shipyard slipped by. The wind in the sails sounded loud in the night air.

Amos had made his way to the stern of the vessel when he realized that Thump was rousing. The man sat with his back to the stern board and blinked. Bird had gone to Thump immediately and was scooched down so that he could peer with concern into the man's bearded face. Thump had lost his hat, and his hair was in wild disarray.

" 'What vast tally shall we leave after us,' " said Amos grandly, " 'tripping up the hounds of destiny, fast upon our heels.' "

Thump looked up at the actor.

"Bridget to James, act two, scene five, *The Romance of Philadelphia*."

"I believe I have seen that one," said Thump quietly. Then he considered the meaning of Amos's citation and said, "Eagleton!"

"We are numbered one less once more," admitted Amos, "and indeed the whole affair reminds me of those ten little Indians."

Thump stood uncertainly just as the schooner was heeling, and in catching hold of the man, Amos surely kept him from pitching overboard.

"Ephram," said Thump. "And now Eagleton." He said no more, conscious of the little boy standing beside him. He reached out and patted Bird's head, as if to encourage the little fellow despite their diminishing ranks. "Where are we going?" he wondered.

"Quite the opposite from what the captain had planned," said Amos.

Thump was not sure that this tactic was working for them but said nothing. He stood at the gunnel and watched with Bird as Bath came up on the port side. The wind ruffled his unruly hair. The little boy glanced back at Amos with a frown.

Amos caught the look. "They almost got us that time," he said quietly.

Bird looked away.

*   *   *

For half an hour they watched for pursuit; then the captain took the vessel toward a break in the land to the east, and they sailed past the twin points of Preble and Sasanoa, into Hanson Bay and the upper reaches of the Sasanoa River. The current, as much as the breeze, began to pull them, and in the second hour following their departure, they came to the swirl of water known as Upper Hell's Gate; the captain and his hands were grimly occupied with assaying these turbulent narrows for long minutes.

Thump, who had less idea where he was than he had earlier that day (which was none at all), understood, despite his lack of nautical knowledge, that they were taking a precarious route by moonlight, and he stood with Bird (who perhaps understood better) under his arm. The lower reaches of the Sasanoa boiled around them, and the ship was pitched about in the conflicting currents and eddies.

They were deposited a little roughly from Hell's Gate and found themselves once more beholden to the breeze as they came into the relatively calm waters of Back River. The names of these places would have meant nothing to Thump if he had heard them—Hockomock Bay, Flying Point, Castle Island. ("Not on an island," he heard Amos say to the captain.) Thump was only aware of treeless hills and long stretches of rocky shore gleaming in the moonlight, great houses on the ends of land and clusters of buildings where fishing communities, some of them ancient, clung like barnacles to the riverside. He shivered with the night wind, and it occurred to him that Bird would be cold. He took off his jacket and put it over the boy's shoulders.

It was such an adventure! Thump was a little at sea just thinking about it. And yet there were his friends to consider. Ephram's head must be repaired by now, but had Eagleton been captured by "sinister forces"? Was it less than a week since his friends were happily dining at the Shipswood Restaurant? Then he wondered where Mister Walton and Sundry Moss were, and what they would say when they heard of the club's great adventure.

"Underground," Thump thought aloud. "We have gone underground." He had read this phrase in a book once—*The Rose Beneath the Street*, by Mrs. Rudolpha Limington Harold. ("*Rose shivered in the darkness of the doorway*," read the book, "*and watched in terror as her fiancé stalked down the rain-washed street, whip in hand. 'He'll have the police after you,' said the kindly old washerwoman who had pulled her out of sight and into a momentary safety. 'You'll have to go underground.'* ")

They themselves (that is, the Moosepathians) had been warned off the law by Horace McQuinn, but if Eagleton was in the grip of "sinister forces," what was Thump to do? He was beginning to think it was time to call in the police.

The moon rode near the top of its path as they flew among the darkened shores and ledges, watching the mysterious shapes of land grow out of the distances, pass by, and fall behind—a pine-clad island, a single eye of light in a fisherman's dockside home. They flew with the fall wind—the current by which or against which the geese hurried south, the leaf chaser, the comely herald of sparse winter.

It was past midnight when a large sloping shore rose up before them, and Amos and the captain conferred quietly. "There's a ferry to the mainland," Thump heard the captain say. The sails luffed, and the ship was driven in a graceful arc to a point of land. A dock materialized from the darkness, its shadow like the form of some creature lurking beneath the water. "Hop on and tie us up," said the captain, speaking to Thump for the first time. He nodded in the direction of a coil of line in the stern.

Thump did not hesitate, all too willing to be of some assistance when he imagined himself to be in the captain's debt. Bird moved after him, and Amos quietly slipped behind. Thump took an end of rope, stepped onto the gunnel and up to the wharf (there was a moment in which he had to adjust his bearings), then looked for a post or a ring on which to fasten the line.

He wasn't very handy with a knot, and this bothered him. He frowned down at the line in his hand and made a practice loop in the moonlight. Perhaps he should just wrap it around a few times and hold it while someone else came ashore.

There was the sound of something banging, as if someone were kicking the side of the boat. Thump wandered a few feet down the wharf, then turned and realized that the ship was drifting away. He pulled at the rope, reeling it in, then realized with a sick feeling that the other end was not attached to anything; it fell with a splash into the river.

"No, no, no," Amos was saying. He looked to be struggling with the little boy, who was trying to leap overboard. "Good heavens, Mr. Thump!" Amos called. "We've forgotten to fasten it, and the tide is taking us! Dear me, can't let the little fellow fall overboard, can we?"

The boat was growing less distinct. The moon had slipped beneath a cloud. Thump ran to the end of the dock, waving the end of the rope like a kerchief. "What shall I do?" he called, almost whispering.

"We'll meet you down that way," said Amos, waving inland. "On the other side of the island."

"The other side of the island?" said Thump, horrified. How was he to find them? How was he to find the other side of the island? "Island?" he said. "Good heavens!"

Something was troubling Thump, and he decided that it was a matter of Moosepathian pride. They had been given charge of the little fellow, and one by one they had fallen by the wayside. However noble was Mr. Guernsey, Thump deemed it a mark upon the character of their club that this duty had fallen to one outside their charter. Mister Walton would never have allowed it.

If only I had been injured, and not Ephram! thought Thump. *If only I had been taken instead of Eagleton! Either of them would have handled this much better than I!*

Looking over his shoulder as he puffed up the slopes, he could still see the sails of the schooner gleaming in the moonlight or the vessel itself obscuring the moon's watery scatter of silver dollars. He stood atop one of these banks and considered the view before him in light of his unease. He had only one recourse, and that was to go forward, which he did, charging with great energy into a tree.

He was in a grove of birches, beyond which there was a stone wall and a road. The moon had barely lowered, and it occurred to him, while he rubbed the bump on his forehead, that if he kept his shadow in front of him, he would eventually come to the eastern shore of the island. This meant crossing the road instead of following it, and soon he was chasing his own silhouette as it hurried before him, silent over the October grass.

When Amos was sure that Bird would not jump overboard, he let the little boy stand by himself at the aft end of the ship. The child pulled at a tuft of hair behind his ear, and his expression was difficult to read; it was, in fact, no expression at all, which troubled the actor. "We shall find him," Amos assured the boy, his manner jocular. They might have been out on a pleasure trip. "We shall pick him up on the other side of the island. In the meantime, I will watch out for you, my little friend."

The captain glanced between Amos and the boy, and there was no knowing, from that look, what he himself knew. They were rounding the southern tip of Westport Island, down Knobble Bay to Robinhood. Time became the shoreline that passed by, and distance began to eat the light of the moon.

It was in the midst of Goose Rock Passage that Amos caught sight of the first boat, sails filled, moving toward them from a tiny cove on Westport. Then, to the starboard, a second boat appeared out of the dark hump of MacMahan Island. Amos hurried from one side of the schooner to the other, peering past the flecks of moonlight to ascertain the nature of this unexpected accompaniment. The two vessels were slightly ahead of them and drawing in like the closing gates of a city.

"Do you know them?" asked Amos. He stood in the companionway and the captain did not look back.

"I do," said the man, and his flat tone spoke volumes. He was conning them in to meet these shadowy vessels.

Amos felt as if a cold hand had gripped his stomach, and he moved to the port side to consider the distance to Westport—a span too great, for he could not swim. He looked toward MacMahan, but that island was further still. Then he turned to the back of the boat and saw Bird watching him, as quiet and expressionless as ever. This was the greatest distance of all.

The boats came alongside, a little less expertly than the captain's arrival at the dock in Winnegance, and the thumps of the hulls were like hammer strokes. Amos wanted to retreat to the back of the ship but couldn't bring himself to stand beside the child.

A dark figure came over the side and, with help from the captain himself, handed a second figure onto the deck of the fishing vessel. This form paused, almost comically, to take in its surroundings. The round hat was tipped back; the eyes gleamed in the midst of a half-scrubbed, unshaven face; teeth flashed in a wolflike smile.

"There he is!" came a wild voice from one of the other boats. "There he is! He's mine! I tell you, he's mine!" Several other voices growled and threatened but could not shout the first man down. Amos shivered.

"Are you cold, Amos?" asked Adam Tweed. He was searching in a pocket for something, and what he pulled out looked to Amos like a page torn from a newspaper. "You should stay out of the paper, Amos."

Thump heard the trot of horses rising and falling out of the darkness with the inclination of the land. They were coming from the north, and there were several of them. He had passed a grove of trees and was skirting the end of a pond when he caught sight of another road—a pale stripe through the fields—and though it was wider than the one he had crossed earlier, it discouraged him with its emptiness until he heard the sound of hoofbeats.

He had reached the top of a small bank when the horsemen surprised him by drawing up some yards away, discernible as shadows in the moonlight. He counted seven men on horseback and could hear two of them talking—debating, it seemed, without any real disagreement in their voices. He heard the trace of an accent—a Scottish burr perhaps—and had the unaccountable feeling that his luck, and that of the club, had altered.

"Halloo!" he called from the top of the bank, then used an expression he had picked up while learning to use the telephone. "Hello!" He could see and hear the effect of his greeting; heads came up, horses shifted nervously, a voice called back. He hopped and slid down the bank to the road, and the two men who had been conferring trotted up to meet him. "Good night to you, gentlemen," said Thump, but this sounded as if he were bidding them good-bye. "Good day," he amended, then said, "Good evening."

"It's good morning soon enough, sir," said one of the horsemen, the r's in his speech rolling pleasantly.

"I fear I have been stranded, gentlemen," said Thump.

"Have you, now," said the first fellow. He leaned forward, and Thump was aware of a pleasant middle-aged face and long white hair.

The second man was tall and authoritative in a quiet way. "What brings you to the middle of Westport, sir?" he asked as he dismounted.

"A boat, sir," answered Thump. "Well, a boat brought me to the shore, and I brought myself to the middle, actually." He thought it important to be accurate.

"A boat? Not a boat from Winnegance, certainly?" said the first man. The other horsemen sauntered their mounts closer to the conversation.

"Yes!" declared Thump, astounded by the man's understanding of the matter. "That is it exactly!"

The tall man looked bemused, perhaps even *amused*, but there was no mistaking the first man's good humor. "Left you high and dry, then," he said with a laugh. "Been drinking up the profits, have you?"

"I beg your pardon?" said Thump.

"Can you smell it on him, Charles?"

"But how did you know about the boat?" wondered Thump. His scalp tightened as he realized that these men might be the very *sinister force* that had taken Eagleton. He stepped backward.

"Whoa, there," said the tall man. "Why don't you come with us."

"But how did you know?" Thump asked again.

"It's all over the wire, sir," said the man with the burr. "The police that took your friends were not expecting to nose out contraband, but they were quick to rouse the telegrapher at Winnegance and send the message up and down the coast. Since then your vessel has been spotted twice, you see, so there's no sense in avoiding the inevitable."

None of this was said unkindly, but Thump was mystified. After a moment's silence, he could only think to introduce himself. "Joseph Thump," he said, and extended his hand.

"Charles Piper," said the tall man, "sheriff of Lincoln County. This is my associate, Colonel Taverner, of the customs agency."

"Sheriff Piper!" said Thump, astonished. "Colonel Taverner!" He spoke as if he were greeting old and unexpected friends, and indeed he felt very warmly toward them since hearing such admirable stories concerning them from Mister Walton and Sundry Moss. This reaction was not what any of them had expected, and the sheriff's bemusement spread throughout the troop. "Wait till I tell our chairman!" declared Thump.

56. Telegrams and Trains

"MISTER WALTON," said Sundry softly. He could see his employer's bald head above the covers, his portly middle rising and falling with the measured breath of sleep. The man's spectacles lay folded on the nightstand beside a volume of Fielding. Sundry stepped into the room. "Mister Walton."

The man made a questioning noise.

"There's a telegram come for you."

"Is it my aunt?" asked the man.

"Your aunt? I don't—"

Mister Walton came awake and realized what he had said. "Of course it isn't," he said to himself.

"I am sorry to wake you, but there's a telegram."

"Not at all." Mister Walton sat up and asked for his glasses. "A telegram," he said, and paused, the spectacles on his nose, his hand still on the bow. "Good heavens!" He blinked and read the message again. "Good heavens!" he repeated. He passed the paper to Sundry, who read:

EASTERN TELEGRAPH COMPANY
BATH

OCTOBER 14 P.M. 6:45

WORSTER HOUSE — HALLOWELL

MR. TOBIAS WALTON

CAUGHT INTRUDER AT WINNEGANCE. ALSO MR. EAGLETON WHO CLAIMS YOUR FRIENDSHIP. CONCERNED REGARDING CHILD IN POSSIBLE DANGER. LOOKS FOR YOUR GUIDANCE. I CONCUR.

HENRY ECHO

"*This* is very unusual," said Sundry. "Does he mean he caught Mr. Eagleton with the prowler?"

"It does sound—"

"First séances, then this," said Sundry. "What has the Moosepath wrought? And what child?"

"I don't know! But it sounds as if Mr. Eagleton is in some difficulty."

"He caught that rascal," said Sundry, almost to himself, "at Winnegance. But Mr. Echo said he was leaving the state."

"Yes, I wonder if he wasn't sending us away for our safety," said Mister Walton. "Or perhaps to put the guilty parties at their ease." He was still sitting up in bed, attempting to understand what the telegram meant.

"'*Also Mr. Eagleton* . . .'" read Sundry. "Does he mean that he caught Mr. Eagleton as well? Do you suppose it's really him?"

"Oh, dear," sighed Mister Walton.

"Do you want me to go down to Bath and see what is happening?"

Sundry could see Mister Walton vacillate on this, and he knew before his employer what the outcome would be. "No, Sundry," said the bespectacled fellow. "I wouldn't feel right after they have asked me to come. And a child in danger! They would be better off with you rather than me, but they shall have the both of us."

"They could do worse," said Sundry. "It is strange, though, that the telegraph apprises us of someone else in hazard." He wondered if this could have anything to do with the men he had chased off yesterday.

It was true—news of Cordelia Underwood's kidnapping had reached them (the previous July) by wire as well; but there was another aspect of the situation that troubled Mister Walton. "Oh, dear," he said, "and things were left in the air with Phileda." He was also thinking that Charles Thistlecoat was still in town. "This time *I* shall write a quick note of apology. Perhaps this will amount to nothing and we can be back before nightfall."

Mister Walton rose, then, and Sundry began to pack. The portly fellow was splashing his face with water from the pitcher on the washstand when a dream he had regarding Miss McCannon and Charles Thistlecoat returned to him. His heart sank a little, and he had to pause to catch his breath.

They were nearly ready to go when a knock came at the door. Mister Walton came out of his room just as Sundry was thanking someone with a coin and saying good day. He passed Mister Walton another telegram.

"What's this?" said the portly fellow. "Maybe it will explain everything. Good heavens! It's from Sheriff Piper!" He perused the message and said only, "Oh, dear! Now Mr. Thump!"

Mollie dreamed that night as well—of her brother Sean, who was jump-ing ice cakes in the cove with the other boys. She was ten and hadn't tat-tled on anyone since her father had reproached her on the subject. It *was* a dream, of course, and never like the real event; only the dread was genuine.

She was remembering this dream, which had vanished into some-thing vastly different (an old ash tree and a robin's nest), while taking her turn at the Brunswick station. It was midmorning, and though she had in-sisted that they stay in Brunswick ("We'll find them more quickly if we aren't all running around in circles"), she was herself impatient with the self-imposed duty.

Wyckford had paced the platform for half an hour before Mollie drove him off, and he went to find Mr. Sockalexis, who had spent the night at the Tontine. Mr. Ephram had gone to find the papers in case there was some clue regarding the whereabouts of Mr. Eagleton, Mr. Thump, and Bird. *And Amos*, Mollie reminded herself. *Just wait till I get my hands on Amos.*

A train approached from the north, the column of steam rising above the rooftops and the engine and the weight of the cars upon the tracks rumbling closer. She had the intuition that Messrs. Eagleton and Thump would arrive with their charge (and Amos, perhaps) on one of the trains from the east and hardly paid attention to this line of cars as it halted be-fore the platform. It was, in fact, the eye of a young man—sensitive to the presence of an attractive woman—that may have been responsible for what happened next.

Sundry and Mister Walton were changing trains, ready to head east themselves, the motivating telegrams in the older man's coat pocket. Mol-lie glanced at the passengers coming off the one car and, seeing neither the tall Eagleton nor the broad-shouldered Thump, took no lingering no-tice of anyone. Sundry, however, took lingering stock of Mollie, admiring the abundance of her, when slowly a vague sense of recognition came over him.

Mollie glanced back, as if feeling Sundry's gaze, and raised a critical eyebrow as he lifted his arm in an irresolute wave. Both of them felt they should know one another, but it had been dark when they met, and a good deal had happened to the both of them betweentimes.

"Miss Peer?" said Mister Walton, at Sundry's shoulder.

"Of course," said Sundry.

"Mister Walton?" said Mollie. She stepped across the platform.

"Miss Peer, how good to see you again."

"Mister Walton," she said, "I am sure *I* have the greater benefit in seeing *you*. And Mr. Moss." There was something in her demeanor that suggested more than simple politeness.

"We are at your service, Miss Peer," said the older man.

"It is the opinion of the local paper, Miss Peer," came a voice, "that the *'two and a half inchers'* won the day." Matthew Ephram was navigating the platform with the merest corner of an eye, the rest of his sight fixed upon the newspaper before him; he did not see Mister Walton and Sundry till he came to a full halt, lowered the paper, and said, "I am very sorry for Mr. Simpson, for I thought his points regarding the phases of the moon were admirably—"

Ephram ceased all movement of his feet, his mouth, and his hands in the process of turning the newspaper page; one might have believed that even his internal functions (his brain included) had suffered a momentary lapse, he looked so comprehensively halted. Only his eyes belied this illusion, for they glanced from Mister Walton to Mollie to Sundry and back to Mollie and Mister Walton. They performed this pattern again, and he felt very odd, as if he had stepped into the wrong story. "Mister Walton," he said without any real emotion carrying the name. "Mr. Moss."

"Mr. Ephram," said Mister Walton, whose concern for two of his fellow Moosepathians was slightly mitigated by his pleasure in seeing the third.

Ephram's cessation of movement lasted a bare moment. "Mister Walton?" he said again, question coloring his voice. "Mr. Moss?"

"Sir, how are you?" said Sundry.

"Mister Walton!" declared Ephram. He thrust his paper beneath his arm, then shook Mister Walton's hand with such vigor that the great fellow would have been excused if he thought a newly arrived train was vibrating the platform. "Ever in the fray!" pronounced Ephram. "Come forward in the hour of greatest need to pilot the ship of adventure! Sinister forces, I assure you, Mister Walton! Nefarious schemes, Mr. Moss!" he continued as he gripped the young man's hand. "Why, if Eagleton and Thump only knew!"

"It is to those gentlemen that we hurry!" said Mister Walton.

"Good heavens!" said Ephram.

"Then you know what has happened!" said Mollie, a little astonished.

"We know next to nothing," admitted Mister Walton. He fished through his pockets for the telegrams, which he put in order before passing them to her. "Sundry and I were in Hallowell when these arrived. But what could Mr. Thump have been doing to warrant the law?"

"The law?" said Ephram.

"This is more than we know," said Mollie when she had read the telegrams. "Who is Henry Echo?"

"We only met him ourselves a few days ago," said Mister Walton. "But am I mistaken in thinking that you are looking for Mr. Eagleton and Mr. Thump?" Ephram nodded energetically. "Perhaps, then," suggested Mister Walton, "we should postpone explanations for the trip to Bath."

"We must get Wyckford first," said Mollie.

"I beg your pardon?"

"Mr. O'Hearn," she corrected herself.

"He's a baseball player," explained Ephram.

"He is?" said Mister Walton, not enlightened by this knowledge.

"He knocked down a brick wall, I've been told," continued Ephram.

"Well," said Mister Walton, a little amazed by this communication, "by all means, let us have him."

57. In a Single Place

IT WAS DURING THE ADVENTURES of the previous July that Mister Walton and Sundry Moss attended Charles Piper and Colonel Taverner on a night watch for smugglers at Fort Edgecomb. There in the dark they first caught sight of Bird and Eustace Pembleton as they escaped. In Boothbay Harbor, on the very next day, Sundry, who had not gotten a definite look at the child, came to the aid of a little boy; and these two children—the one at Edgecomb and the one at Boothbay—he discovered to be one and the same.

Now, three months later, Sundry was powerfully affected by the story told on the trip to Bath; Wyckford O'Hearn, looking large and awkward, staring into his hat, had earned Sundry's admiration. Mister Walton, whose sympathies were easily roused by any innocent creature, was affected in a more general manner; his age, perhaps, allowed him to be as touched by the fear and sadness in the redheaded man.

Sundry and Mister Walton agreed that Amos Guernsey's part in all this sounded shifty; and they were impressed, not to say astonished, by Horace McQuinn's place in the tale. The trip to Bath was hardly long enough for it all, and Mister Walton was just able to explain his and Sundry's presence in the most truncated way when the carriage they hired set out in the direction of Henry Echo's lodgings. "There is one thing that doesn't seem to fit," said Mister Walton, directing his words to Mollie Peer as they climbed High Street, "but perhaps you can make it clearer to me."

"There *is* something I have been wondering about," she said.

"Why expend such exertion chasing the little boy," he said, "when they could go to Pembleton's cache and preempt anyone else from obtaining it?"

"It's the boy," said Wyck.

"How so, Mr. O'Hearn?" asked Mister Walton.

Wyckford shifted his bulk uneasily and glanced from one to the other of his fellow travelers. "There is something about the boy. Something Tweed may only suspect. But that would be enough."

"Then there is more, you think," said Mister Walton, "than some pit of ill-gotten gains."

"There is something deeper, I am pretty sure. If you had seen Pembleton when I confronted him in the cellar; and the next day at the police station."

"How can such a baby lead anyone anywhere?" wondered Mollie. "He knows the way from Pembleton's lair to the nearest rum room, it's true, but unless these stolen goods are somewhere beneath the streets of Portland, how could a child four years old lead someone to them?"

"I just want him back," said Wyck. "My curiosity can wait for that."

Mister Walton leaned forward and gave the big man a reassuring pat on the knee. "That is the direction of *our* exertions, sir."

"Oh, my!" said Ephram, who was hidden behind his paper. "They intend to debate the merits of the four seasons next year at Brunswick."

Henry Echo must have been watching for them from his window, for he hurried out even as the carriage pulled into the narrow alley. "Mister Walton! Mr. Moss!" Henry Echo called as he met the carriage. He was surprised when Wyckford stepped out first, pleasantly surprised when Mollie followed, and gratified when his two friends finally appeared.

Ephram was forced to look away from his paper as he stepped down. "Eagleton!" he shouted, for that worthy member had issued from the house in Echo's hasty wake.

"Ephram! How wonderful to see you!" They rattled one another with vigorous shakes of the hands.

"Mister Walton and Mr. Moss are with me!"

"It's too good to be true!" cried Eagleton.

"I promise you!"

"How ever did you manage it?"

"I take no credit!"

"Ever modest!"

"No, no! I was as astounded as you are now!"

"Good heavens!" declared Eagleton. "Mister Walton! Mr. Moss! We have been in exigent straits! And Miss Peer! And Mr. O'Hearn! Thump and Mr. Guernsey barely escaped! But it wasn't the sinister forces we had expected! It was the police! Mr. Echo caught his intruder! Good heavens, Mr. Moss, Mr. Echo has told me the wonderful thing you have done! I have written it all down! Good heavens!" Eagleton seemed a little over-taken by it all.

"We thought you had left the state," said Mister Walton.

"I must apologize," replied Henry Echo. "It seemed wrong to involve you further and necessary to be sure of success."

Eagleton was shaking hands with Wyckford O'Hearn and explaining, somewhat obtusely, how he and Henry Echo met.

"I have been enjoying Mr. Eagleton very much," said Henry.

"He's very enthusiastic," agreed Mister Walton.

Between Bath and Wiscasset, everyone's story was retold. Eagleton and Ephram occasionally digressed; at one point, Eagleton recalled the time that Mister Walton took the Moosepath League to the theater and Ephram mistook one of the other patrons (and a wealthy one, at that) for an usher.

"He was wearing a red vest," said Ephram. It still caused him confu-sion when he thought of it.

But as for the story at hand, the entire chain of events was remarkable, and Mister Walton shook his head in amazement. "It's a marvel that you encountered Mr. Echo!" he said to Eagleton.

"It isn't so surprising," thought Mollie aloud, "when you consider Amos Guernsey. The man who broke into Mr. Echo's home was of a cer-tain society, of which Amos seems to have considerable knowledge."

"He was a very . . . quiet man," said Eagleton.

"Mr. Guernsey?" said Ephram. He hadn't thought the actor quiet.

"Not at all!" amended Eagleton. "Mr. Davies. But I don't know if Bird and Thump would have gotten away if Amos had not carried the little boy off."

Sheriff Piper closed his eyes in the fall sunlight and leaned back on a bench at the station platform. Mr. Thump was taking instruction on the mysteries of cribbage from Colonel Taverner. The colonel's voice reached the sheriff's ears, though Piper paid no attention to the content of the cus-tom agent's words. "I hear the train," said the sheriff without opening his eyes. In his shirt pocket was a telegram from Mister Walton.

The presence of the sheriff and the custom agent at the station (along with the impressively bearded Thump) had drawn interest from many of the local people, and several exchanged niceties with them in hopes of hearing the story they suspected. Thump easily and quite innocently confused the curious with digressions on the ability of cows to predict the weather, vegetables resembling political candidates, and the effect that fog has on human perception. "I did not put much thought into the subject at the time," he insisted to one idler, "but in looking back upon it, I have considered it a topic of some fascination."

Thump stood now, his interest taken up by the approaching train.

Piper watched the man from beneath the lid of one eye.

"*I have seldom*," Thump would write in his journal, "*viewed the arrival of any conveyance with such singularity of attention, nor such warm feelings of anticipation. And yet those feelings would have been the greater had I known how completely our little band would soon be reunited!*"

Those whom Mister Walton and Sundry had met in Brunswick and Bath were not expected at Wiscasset or even *known* to Sheriff Piper and Colonel Taverner, and after introductions, Mister Walton did his best to explain that more lengthy explanations were required than might quickly be forwarded there on the platform.

"What has become of the boy?" demanded Wyck.

Ephram, Eagleton, and Thump were acquainting one another with their separate experiences—a process that seemed to be driven like a piston engine by the excited pumping of one another's hands—but Thump's joy in seeing his friends was cut short by the ballplayer's question.

"I fear, Mr. O'Hearn," said Thump with a bow, "that I have done a disservice to that cause with which I have been entrusted *and* to that honored league under which name I have taken it."

"Good heavens, Thump!" declared Eagleton.

"Certainly not!" exclaimed Ephram.

"Ephram was struck down in the execution of his duty," insisted Thump, "and Eagleton bought precious time when we were set upon last night, but I have only the tale of an unfastened rope to tell you." Indeed, the sad implication of this loose end was an apt metaphor for Thump's regret.

Again there was dissent. "How so, old friend," said Eagleton.

"What? Surely you managed further than any of us!" insisted Ephram.

"Then Mr. Guernsey is in possession of the child," said Mister Walton.

"The last I saw of them, yes," said Thump, and it was clear that he was choking back his emotion. It was a measure of Wyckford O'Hearn's sympathetic nature that he was more sorry for Thump than angry with him. Mollie was simply angry at Amos Guernsey.

"The boat that was sighted at Winnegance came into Westport early this morning," said the sheriff, "but only long enough to strand Mr. Thump there."

"And no notion where they went after?" asked Mollie.

"No, ma'am." The sheriff had not gotten the entire tale yet, and it was clear that he was trying to place all these people. "Is the boy your son, ma'am?" he asked carefully.

"No, Sheriff," she returned, startled by the thought. Then, less carefully, she said, "I am a reporter." She fenced brief glances from both Wyck and Sundry. But Mister Walton, who was trusting enough to believe what most people said, was wise enough not to take them completely at their word; the expression with which he met her eyes suspended her speech and gesture for an unnatural moment.

"Does the name Eustace Pembleton mean anything to you, Colonel Taverner?" asked Mister Walton.

"It means a bird flushed and unbagged, Mister Walton," said the wry Scotsman.

Wyck flinched.

"Your choice of words is apt," said Mister Walton.

Taverner thought on what he had said. "Mr. Thump told us that the little boy was *called* Bird. Is *he* the child in the boat that night at Fort Edgecomb, when Pembleton got away from us?"

"As I recall," said Mister Walton, "we discussed the boy's merits that night, Colonel."

"On very little evidence," admitted Taverner, who had predicted the little boy would come to a bad and somehow deserved end.

"And now we might guess where he is being taken," ventured the bespectacled fellow.

"We saw no contraband in their boat that night," said Taverner, adding the facts in his head. "And we never discovered anything on the shore."

"And yet their behavior was a little furtive," continued Mister Walton.

"If it wasn't *guilty*, Mister Walton, I'm a saint," said the colonel.

The word "furtive" brought to Sundry's mind the two strange men in Hallowell, and though he couldn't see how they could be connected to all this, he thought he should mention them to the sheriff and Colonel Taverner.

Wyck spoke up, however, saying to Mister Walton, "Do you know where they are taking him, then?"

"From what I understand about the situation," said Mister Walton, "*they* might not know where they are taking him."

"Until Pembleton and Adam Tweed catch up with them," said Mollie.

The name of Adam Tweed caught the colonel's sudden attention, and he announced then that it was time they got someplace where the entire business could be properly explained.

58. The Last of Amos

AMOS GUERNSEY HAD ONCE SEEN A CAT still a mouse with a stare, and he was uncomfortably aware of an analogous situation as he sat on a piece of driftwood in the little bay of an island while Adam Tweed watched him with animal patience. The others among them wandered the rocky beach or slept in the sun; they told stories to one another or bickered or scrounged periwinkles to cook in the fire. They were a hard-looking crew, unwashed and untutored; nearly twenty of them in all, between the three boats, and Amos wondered, not for the first time, how Tweed, who was himself an unimpressive specimen, commanded such loyalty among these brutes.

But Tweed sat on a box, leaning against a rock wall, and watched Amos without word or expression. He had a knife, and he whittled aimlessly at a stick of wood. Further up the beach, Eustace Pembleton stared at Amos with a good deal more emotion.

The actor had given them a good run, and if Tweed had been truthful, he would have admitted to surprise that Amos had taken the situation and the boy into his own hands. There was a moment when the pursuers had lost all trace of them, and if Amos had not gone in the direction expected, they might never have found him, or found him too late.

Adam Tweed still did not know, entirely, what awaited them in Pembleton's hidden cache; he did know (or, at least, suspected) that this hidey-hole was not the last or the most fruitful place to which the brat could lead him; Pembleton, who was strange enough, was strangest about this further mystery, to which the boy was key. Tweed had discerned the general location of the hidden cache during one of Pembleton's hysterical rants, so Pembleton was wise to say nothing more; it was the only reason not to drown him like a rat in a bag.

Bird sat on a rock in the very midst of Tweed's and Pembleton's scrutiny, quiet, one hand pulling at the tuft of hair behind his ear. He did not appear to be looking at the bay before him but at something within his own mind that comforted him.

Amos could not look at the child; he avoided seeing Bird, even as a shadow in the corner of his eye. The actor passed the time by enumerating, in his mind, the many roles he had played over the years—heroes and villains. *What had it amounted to?* he wondered. He had been tutored as a child, and very well. He had read the classics; he had read Shakespeare before he was twelve and understood it better than most. But one day he had asked his instructor, "Why do we read this?"

The tutor had frowned meaningfully. Perhaps all his lessons had been for naught if, in the end, he had to answer this one question. "Why?" he said. "Why, so that we might learn to live!"

But there are some lessons you can learn only if you already know them. Amos had played heroes who were loved and revered and villains who might grow rich by earthly standards and yet come to nothing—or to grief. He had learned nothing. Liars are discovered, criminals rooted out, evil dissipated by its own schemes.

The innocent friendship of the Moosepath League had amused him at first, and for a while he felt a condescension toward the exuberant Ephram, Eagleton, and Thump. Now he realized what he might have gained if he had not plotted against them. He had learned nothing, or at least too late. It troubled him that the admiration they felt for him must eventually come to grips with his actions.

Adam Tweed had watched Amos as a cat watches a mouse ever since they came ashore. In the afternoon, Tweed spoke. "Jimmy," he said to one of the other men, "when you take one of the boats back to Portland, why don't you take Amos with you and wait for me there till I come back."

Pembleton was yelling something, and Tweed threw a rock at him. Tweed got himself something to eat from the communal pot, moved his box up from the approaching tide, then sat with his back to the rock wall again and leveled that catlike scrutiny upon the boy. In a few minutes, once he was finished with his meal, Tweed came over to the child and considered him more closely. He was looking at the moose badge that Quentin McQuinn had given the boy, and he reached down suddenly and tore it loose from Bird's shirt.

Bird seemed stunned. His chin quivered.

Tweed made a noise, like a laugh, and went back to his seat, where he inspected the totem. He made his associates laugh when he pinned it to his own shirt and showed it off like a military honor.

Bird had the look of someone who has suddenly awakened to his situation. The expression on the little boy's face was sadly mature for his years, and the sight of it made something within Amos sink. Bird looked down at his shoes now instead of over the water.

59. Laying Wait

THE BLOCKHOUSE AT FORT EDGECOMB, on Davis Island, had presided over another summer, and now fall seeped beneath the great door of oak and iron and slipped like the first breaths of long-deserved sleep through shuttered windows and gun slots. The voices of picnickers, of squealing children, the lingering presence of lovers in the cool shade of the fort, in the brief shelter of the rolling embankments, were replaced with the voice of the crow and the singular attendance of the elements—the wind from the river, the patter of rain, the season's long amber light.

As the days grew short, the fort was seldom visited. When people did walk its grounds or even cross its threshold, they might sense that the wooden structure had not awakened for them, or, as in the case of Sundry Moss, they might have the strange apprehension that, to the old blockhouse, they were but figures in a dream.

There were six of them, the honorable gentlemen of the Moosepath League—Messrs. Ephram, Eagleton, and Thump—as well as Sundry Moss, Sheriff Piper, and Seth Patterson, the jail keeper of Lincoln County.

They approached from the east, and twilight's last streaks glowed behind the blockhouse from the Wiscasset side of the Sheepscott River. Some lonely bird called out as they stood outside the carriage, and there was but a small wind in the trees. Lights burned already in the houses across the river and on the opposite shore of the inlet known as the Eddy.

"Ah," said Eagleton, "the many-storied fort of Edgecomb!"

"Well," said Sundry, "there are two stories, actually, and the lookout."

The members of the club did not have the appearance of men when "the game is afoot" but looked, with their top hats and finely appointed coats, as if they expected nothing more strenuous than a sidewalk constitutional. They had insisted, however, upon attending this lookout, and since Colonel Taverner had every hope of intercepting the quarry before it reached the fort, Sheriff Piper was not averse to their presence.

"And this is where you first encountered these nightrunners?" said Ephram.

"Sundry was the only one who *encountered* anyone that night," said the sheriff. "What are you looking for, Seth?" he asked the jailer.

Seth Patterson scanned the grounds and a grove of trees some distance off. "I'm looking for Ducky Planke," he said.

"Well, Ducky caught sight of you the moment we came on the island, I promise," said the sheriff. "He won't hurt you." Piper was amused by Seth's uneasiness.

"He won't hurt me, I know," said the jailer, "but he might startle me if he comes ghosting out of the dark with those hoots and hollers of his."

"He was a little eerie," admitted Sundry, who had been witness to just such an apparition the last time he was here. "I bet he knows where Pembleton's hiding place is."

Ducky Planke was the hermit of Davis Island and the definition of that profession, if not its popular image. Though withdrawn from his own kind, he was timid rather than piqued with the human race, less human himself somehow and more a physical manifestation of some natural phenomenon, like the clouding of midges in the spring or the *chee* of cicadas in the long-shadowed meadows of early fall. The Davis family, whose island he haunted, sensed his presence always, although there were great stretches of time, particularly during the winter, when they did not see him sitting on one of the great shore boulders or moving like a wary fox along the edge of their fields.

Some thought he left the island now and then to raid the dumps of nearby homes for his ragged clothes and for odd bits of other people's refuse (a piece of broken china, a frayed shoelace)—secreted possessions which a surprised child might find in the crook of a tree limb or gleaming among a tiny cairn of stones. But crows are capable of such larceny, and as for Ducky's garments, they were often more whole than ragged. Among the Davises it was quietly suspected that the stern patriarch of their clan left things for his wild tenant in the small wood on the southwestern side of the island.

Sometimes Ducky danced at the edge of the trees, and if you were near him, you might hear the noises that replaced his Christian name. He sounded so like the eiders and teals that frequented the river that there was an unspoken, though generally recognized, ban on duck hunting on Davis Island.

Ducky's muttering quack was like the voice of the island itself, his eyes the very sight and keenness of the shore. Little that happened within view of Davis Island escaped his notice, even by dark of night, including the frequent traffic up and down the river. He had observed the previous foray against smugglers when Sundry nearly had his head knocked in by Tom Bull (Ducky had, in fact, frightened the brute away), and he was watching even now, hidden by the foliage in the very grove Seth was watching with such interest.

"He gives me the whim-whams," said Seth.

Ephram, Eagleton, and Thump were sensitive to the jailer's concerns, and they aided his cause by staring about and peering over their shoulders.

But the sound of a steam engine on the water took their attention, and from the grounds before the blockhouse they could see the *Nellie G.* puttering past, in the direction of Westport. The people on the boat waved. Sundry Moss picked out Mister Walton among them, and he led the wave in return.

"Is that Miss Peer on there?" said Sheriff Piper.

The *Nellie G.* was hardly forty feet from stem to stern, but in the tiny cove near the northeastern tip of Westport (Hairpin Cove, it was called by Mr. Parsons, who lived above it), the steamer looked like a whale in a bathtub. Capt. Amasa Williams and his single crew member, Elihu Huff, tied lines to either shore, once they had backed her in among the rocky perimeters of the inlet, and laid a gangplank to the near bank so that Colonel Taverner could report to Mr. Parsons what they were doing below his home. Mr. Parsons waved from his back door while the colonel negotiated the steep path back to the ledge and the wet and weedy rocks.

Mollie and Mister Walton returned the wave; they stood at the rail with Wyck, on the afterdeck, behind the cabin that made three-fourths of the boat's surface. The cabin was nearly the full width of the beam, so that one had to walk through to the pilothouse to reach the foredeck; and there were rails atop the cabin as well, where, on the *Nellie G.*'s more usual cruises, sightseers could better see their surroundings.

They were a party of six, altogether, counting the captain and Elihu, with more than sightseeing on their itinerary, and it was not a very official gathering, considering their purpose—Colonel Taverner being the only real representative of the law.

Sheriff Piper had been the major dissenter regarding Mollie's presence that night, and his opinion would normally have carried the day. Colonel Taverner, surprisingly, was not averse to her coming. "They are a thin lot we're laying for, Charles," said the colonel, "and will turn tail till we catch them, I warrant, or put up their hands at the first sight of us."

Mollie did not quote chapter and verse of the "suffrage manifesto," but she did invoke her position as a journalist. Sundry made certain sounds, but Mister Walton told his friend that he would be hard put to deny Miss McCannon, should *she* have wanted to go.

Wyck thought that Bird might find her a comfort, but Mollie secretly disbelieved this. In the end, the sheriff led the party on land, and Colonel Taverner said nothing when Mollie came with them. They saw the sheriff's party as they passed the fort, and she made a point of being seen.

"My wife, Elizabeth, sailed with me for three years," said Captain Williams when the subject came up, "and I was often glad to have her."

"I never knew you were married, Amasa," said Taverner.

"You didn't know Elizabeth, Colonel?"

"No, I'm sorry, I didn't. What happened to her?"

"Ah, well," said Captain Williams, "she fell overboard one day and drowned."

They arrived as afternoon fell to twilight, and Venus brightened like a beacon through thin clouds in the wake of the sun. The rocks of the cove were shadowed first, their irregular shapes and crevices disappearing in the dusk. As from the bottom of a well, from which stars can be seen by day, the passengers of the *Nellie G.* could descry certain constellations when they looked up from between the sharp banks. The tide wracked against the ledges and ran in speculative waves up the runnels of rock. The steamer rolled gently with the current.

The granite-founded, pine-clad nature of the Maine coast is never so well demonstrated as on the myriad islands that guard its pleated length and populate its bays and rivers. Wind and weather, tide and wave, have washed clean their dark shores where little but rockweed and periwinkles know to take hold. Here the earth has thrust up from the ocean and waterways to reveal its eroded bone and mineral veins; and nature demonstrates its single-minded view toward life, which is to live. Gales will not deter the scrub pines and clingy grasses; birds will nest and creatures will inhabit the raily soil; men will raise their houses and know at least that they are built on solid rock.

Wyckford, whose boyhood home was an inland farm, knew granite and stone as a continual presence, rising to the surface of tilled fields like weighty salvage; and the stone walls that line every New England farm still attest to the craggy harvest of former years.

Mollie, who came from Portland, where city streets paved cobbles over stony field and wharf and walkway thwart the hardened shore, was not so familiar with the unclad severity of the land.

Of course, she had known the shore, the beaches, and the granitic ledge, though in the circumstance of an outing or a picnic. When daylight fills the eye, the weight of rock seems less beneath a blue sky and airy clouds, and trees lift their wafery foliage in a summer breeze. By day our attention is lifted up; by night we search the ground so that we might not stumble. The sun reveals the tree; the star is beholden to the movement of the earth itself so that it might rise above the branches and be seen.

The water in the cove grew dark first, then the land, and finally the sky, fading behind the silhouettes of rocks and trees.

An owl sounded. The evening was chilly; currents of air struck the water and rose with the slope of the banks, cooling Mollie's cheeks and slipping beneath the collar of her coat. She had worn a lady's "sporting costume," which meant knee-high boots, snugly buttoned along the sides, and pantaloons, not petticoats, beneath a knee-length skirt. Her coat was of a dark twill, belted at the waist, and her hat was practical and warm rather than decorative, like a man's homburg but with a wider brim. (There had been a white feather in the band, which she had taken out.)

Wyckford paced the afterdeck, or a corner of that small space, which was described by about two and a half of his large strides. The roll of the boat seemed influenced by his movement. Mollie stood with her hands on the rail and wondered, rather than worried, about what awaited them. Mister Walton was seated on a deck chair and thought of traveling by boat the previous summer with Phileda McCannon.

"A very nice fellow, Mr. Parsons," said Colonel Taverner as he walked the plank back to the boat and dropped among them. "I expect he will be sitting by a window tonight with his binoculars."

Wyck evinced a little irritation with the colonel; the older man was, in his estimation, a little too cavalier about the situation. Mister Walton caught the look Wyck shot across the deck and exchanged a glance with Mollie, who had seen it, too.

The portly gentleman had been attempting to understand the association between Mollie and Wyck—quietly and to himself, of course. They were both strong figures, and handsome in his opinion; the romantic in him would have liked to imagine something intimate between them. They appeared to view one another with a grudging regard and walked around one another with care.

Standing on the deck in the night air, Mollie felt cold but was unwilling to be the first to retreat to the cabin where the stack from the steam engine doubled as a source of heat. She was gratified when Mister Walton suggested the warmer confines of the cabin but did her best to look indifferent to the motion. Only Wyck stayed out.

There was a single lamp lit inside, tilting to and fro with the rocking of the boat, and its glow touched everyone's face. Mister Walton remarked that the entire business was of a circuitous nature for him: "And must be more so for Sundry, since he is back at Fort Edgecomb." The remark gave Mollie leave to satisfy her own curiosity by asking for the story of that earlier night watch; Mister Walton and the colonel told her of the wait at the fort the previous July and how they had surprised Pembleton and his two odd associates and how the nightrunners had escaped.

"Sundry met the little boy the very next day, on the docks at Boothbay Harbor," said Mister Walton. "There were some older boys—young men, really—who were taunting the poor little fellow, and Sundry came to his defense."

"It is a good thing Wyckford wasn't there," said Mollie. "He would have thrown them overboard."

"Sundry did throw one of them over, actually," said Mister Walton.

Mollie suspected that there was more to this part of the story than pure violence or the kind fellow would not have followed the revelation with a soft chuckle.

"But you have come to the child's defense yourself, Miss Peer," said Mister Walton.

The respect in Mister Walton's words, in the timbre of his voice, disturbed Mollie. "I will not be false with you, sir," she said. "It was not the child's well-being that I pursued but a subject for the newspaper."

He knew this already, but it had not made him dislike her. "There was a reason, perhaps, that you chose this story rather than another," he said.

"I can't expect to get to the truth in my writing, Mister Walton," she said, "if I let myself become emotional."

He replied with that same mild countenance. "How can you expect to touch me with your story, Miss Peer, if you don't?"

"Mr. O'Hearn is greatly attached to the lad," said Colonel Taverner.

Mollie looked to the back of the boat and saw Wyck's dark bulk at the rail. "I did not do him a favor, involving him in this," she said, and there was a sympathy in her voice that put the lie to her previous words. She was almost hurt to see the big man out there alone, and though it caused her some embarrassment to do so, she excused herself and went out again.

Almost immediately, Mollie was sorry that she had gone back to the after-deck with Wyck. Not only was it cold, but the big man had little to say. He was absolutely wrought with concern for Bird, and the longer she watched him, the guiltier she felt. He reminded her of her father, and certainly Edgar Peer would have known what to say to the man.

Mister Walton appeared, briefly, with a woolen throw from inside, his expression as mild as ever. He simply smiled when she thanked him, and somehow she felt a little stronger for his kindness. She stood against the outer bulkhead with the blanket wrapped around her. Wyck stood at the rail, listening. Elihu Huff was watching the mouth of the inlet from the bow of the boat.

"I'm sorry," she said, hating the sound of her voice and the tiny words in the cold air.

Wyck hardly stirred, *had* hardly stirred for more than an hour. "Miss

Peer," he said, "if not for you, I would never have met the little fellow. Certainly his situation was not to be envied before last Friday." He turned then, just enough so that he could look over his shoulder at her, his deep blue eyes shining in whatever starlight or lamplight could gather in them. "I know you're sorry."

"Call me Mollie, please," she said.

He looked at her for a moment, as if thinking how he might use her name now, just to try it out. Instead, he simply nodded.

She was a little shocked to feel her eyes clouding, and she blinked to keep the image of him clear before her. He was too much like her father, except perhaps when he had driven that ball into the air at Brunswick; at that moment of collision—when the ball soared and the roar of the crowd rose up in a vocal backstop and Wyck stood poised, one foot ahead of the other, the bat an extension of his twisting arm and his head lifting with the loft of the white sphere—he was something else entirely. The irony was that he would never look so humble, so grateful, as at that moment.

Until he holds that boy again, she thought. He was really a very fine person, Wyckford O'Hearn. In one startling moment she thought she might reach out and take his hand. Instead, she turned her head to look up the darkened bank of the cove, hoping that the light reflected in his eyes would not glisten in hers.

"Do you think these people will give themselves up?" asked Mister Walton of the colonel.

"The young people out there?" returned the colonel.

Mister Walton chuckled.

Taverner corrected himself. "Our quarry tonight? The last time, Pembleton used the boy for a shield and made his escape. We won't be surprised so easily a second time. This Amos Guernsey does not sound a very dangerous man. In the meanwhile, I have brought my cribbage board, sir."

"I must tell you, Colonel," said Mister Walton, "I have been warned that you are very dexterous at this game."

"*Ach!*" said Taverner. "People tell awful tales!"

60. The Members Were in the Dark

"SIX MINUTES PAST TEN," said Ephram.

It seemed unnecessary to Seth to be informed of the time every half hour or so—it made the watch seem longer—and he looked a little put out to Sundry, who could see enough of the man's expression in the dark.

But others were delighted to have Ephram back on the time; "Expected clear and seasonably cool," said Eagleton. "Light winds, north to west."

"Low tide at twelve twenty-four," said Thump.

Sundry peered over the embankment; the level of the river had receded several feet since they arrived. Sheriff Piper had said they could wait inside the fort if they were cold, but the members of the Moosepath League were standing up very well in the brisk air of the October night.

"It is very invigorating," said Ephram, almost with surprise.

"I find it so," said Eagleton. "How about you, Thump?"

"Hmmm?" said Thump.

The ramparts along the southern extremity of Davis Island rendered a suitable spot for their lookout, seated in a little pocket between the earthy banks and protected somewhat from the breeze. Thump, whose sleepless night had caught up with him, yawned several times; he begged their pardon with great feeling.

"Take a walk around the grounds if you like," said the sheriff. "Only stay near the shore so that your silhouette doesn't show against the sky and walk quietly, please."

"Perhaps I will," said Thump, and choosing a direction, he proceeded along the ramparts.

Thump was normally an energetic walker, but caution had entered him since his several inadvertent revolutions down the hill at Winnegance; he craned his head forward as he went and took high steps so that he might avoid tripping over unseen roots or stones. The dark hulk of the blockhouse loomed above him like a great head on the hill, and a cluster of rosebushes below it gave the illusion of a beard in the darkness.

The grounds sloped steeply once he was past the fort, and several trees screened the shoreline. He came to a stand of rocks overlooking an inlet and a gravelly beach; he wondered if this was the place where the nightrunners were surprised by Colonel Taverner and his companions the previous July.

"Quack, quack."

Thump held his breath, listening for the sound again. A gust in the trees masked something indistinct coming from the other side of the tiny cove. As the wind died and the leaves slowed their chatter, he tensed into a hunched posture, peering into a stand of birches, their long white trunks almost glowing in the darkness.

"Quack, quack."

"Whoops!" A hand had touched Thump's shoulder, and he leaped in the air as if kicked.

"Thump!" came a voice. "Is that you?"

"Eagleton?"

"Good heavens! You gave me a start," said Eagleton.

Thump said nothing. With a hand to his chest, he could feel his heart racing through his coat. He should have expected Ephram next, but the sight—hardly more than an intimation—of that worthy stealing behind Eagleton gave him another turn. A whispered, if ardent, dialogue ensued.

"Eagleton?" said Ephram.

"Ephram?" returned a startled Eagleton.

"Thump?" said Ephram.

"Yes, yes!" said Thump, feeling pale in the dark.

"Quack, quack."

"What?" said Ephram.

"Quack, quack."

"Is that Thump, Eagleton?"

"Thump, is that you?"

"Not at all!"

"Good heavens!" declared Eagleton.

"I should say!" agreed Ephram.

A new sound, like the hoot of an owl, carried from the cove.

"Ephram!"

"Yes, Thump?"

"Eagleton!"

"What is it, my good friend?"

"I am thinking—"

"Yes, exactly!"

"Could it be this Ducky Planke of which we have heard so much?"

"I'm sure it must be!" said Eagleton.

The hoot came across the cove again. More fervent whispers followed.

"Thump!"

"Yes, Eagleton?"

"Ephram!"

"Eagleton, my friend, what is it?"

"Look! Just above that stand of trees!"

"Birches, I think," said Ephram.

"Yes, but just above them. Is something moving there?"

"I'm not sure. My eyes are not as keen as yours, you know."

"Oh, my!" said Eagleton.

"No, certainly your eyes are much better than mine."

"No, I mean, 'Oh, my, there *is* something moving there!' "

"Oh, my!" said Ephram.

"Eagleton!"

"Yes, Thump?"

"I see it!"

"Something moving?"

"Certainly!"

"Do you remember what Mr. Moss said?" asked Eagleton.

"I do indeed!" said Thump.

"This Mr. Planke is of an eccentric nature, but it was the opinion of Mr. Moss he might know the whereabouts of Eustace Pembleton's secret cache."

"My very thought!" said Thump.

"Good heavens!" said Ephram.

"Yes, Ephram?" said Eagleton.

"My very thought as well!"

"Good heavens!" came the combined voices of Thump and Eagleton.

"Perhaps—"

"Yes, Thump?" said Eagleton and Ephram.

"—we could approach this Mr. Planke and request his assistance in finding this hidey-hole!"

"Hidey-hole?" wondered Ephram.

"It was a term of Mr. Patterson's."

"I quite like it!"

It was after several more stanzas of similar conversation that the three stole around the perimeter of the cove. Occasionally, Eagleton would slow their progress so that he could strain his eyes in the direction of the nebulous form that moved above the glow of the birch trees.

Back at the ramparts, Sundry was sensing something as nebulous. "I hear something," he said.

The sheriff cocked an ear and looked down at the dark ground. Seth made a questioning noise, then held his breath to listen.

"An engine?" said Sundry.

"I don't hear it," said Piper.

"I hear something," said Seth. "Did they have a steamer?" he wondered.

"Pembleton did," said the sheriff.

"We never heard it the last time, though."

"It *is* an engine," said Sundry.

There was a long wait again, and finally the sheriff nodded in the darkness. "It's a steamer, all right. Not a large one, either."

"It's coming a good clip," said Sundry.

"Where are the others?" asked Seth.

"I'm not sure. They'll come when they hear it." But Sundry gazed into the darkness to the east, a little concerned about the three men.

"Do you hear something?" asked Matthew Ephram. "Eagleton, do you hear something?" He was crouched in a grassy declivity where a stream must run in the spring, and watched for movement among the stand of birches. "Thump?" he said. He looked to his left and descried the two other figures that had crouched there with him the last several minutes. Perhaps they thought he was speaking too loudly.

Ephram sidled up to the nearest of the shadowy forms and was a little disconcerted to find that it was not Thump but a thriving juniper bush. "Eagleton?" he whispered, but this second figure was a rustling little maple tree; and here he had thought Eagleton had been shushing him.

Movement above him caught the corner of his eye, and he peered hard at the spray of stars till he was sure that they were, one after the other, briefly occluded, right to left, by a slowly moving figure. Pretty well convinced that this could not be a tree, he tiptoed up the further slope.

On the other side of this further slope, Joseph Thump realized that Ephram was no longer with him and Eagleton. "Eagleton!" he whispered, and the figure ahead of him paused. He thought he could see the obscure paleness of a face turn toward him. "Where is Ephram?" asked Thump.

The figure skulked low and proceeded to move in an idiosyncratic manner, back and forth, along the next stretch of field. *Perhaps this is a way to remain undetected,* thought Thump, and he tried to match the peculiar movements of the shadowy form, his trouser cuffs rustling in the lengthy grass. Together they described a uniquely serpentine movement that must have puzzled anyone, were they seen. When they came to the shore, the figure clambered with remarkably little noise down the bank to the rocks below.

How can he see so well? wondered Thump as he picked his way past the brush at the top of the slope. The branches of several bushes were fascinated with his hat, his beard, and even the collar of his coat. At the bottom of the bank, he saw the figure some feet away. The form stood up from its haunches and said, *"Hoo! Hoo!"* to which Thump responded with a series of inhaled phrases that sounded for all the world like the drawn-out preludes to a magnificent sneeze.

Far off in another direction, Christopher Eagleton was hieing across the fields after the figure he had first seen, wondering how a man could run so low to the ground; in those shadows he looked rather like a dog casting for scent! The figure moved swiftly, and following it, Eagleton could see the lights of a nearby farm appear over a low knoll.

Then they were traveling through some sort of grove—apple trees, perhaps—and Eagleton was concerned that his friends might not see these obstacles. He glanced over his shoulder as he ran, then halted, looking for Ephram and Thump. He took a step or two back, but fearing to lose his quarry, he hurried on just as something called with an owllike hoot from the direction of the shore. This time he turned without slowing his speed and promptly tripped over the figure he had been following.

"Do not fear!" he declared. "We are friends!" he insisted just as the figure straddled him and a long, rough tongue began to wash his face.

"That boat is getting closer," said Seth. "I hope your friends are not too far off."

Sundry peered in the direction the Moosepathians had disappeared.

"They are very nice fellows, Messrs. Ephram, Eagleton, and Thump," Sheriff Piper was saying, a qualifying note lengthening the sentence. "They just seem a bit—"

"Uncomplicated?" suggested Sundry.

Piper chuckled in the dark. The sound of the boat engine grew in the night air. "Mister Walton is so . . . worldly, in the best sense of the word, that it is hard, sometimes, to put them together with him."

"Yes, well," said Sundry, "I've benefited as well as they from the fact that Mister Walton never had any kids of his own."

The sheriff chuckled again.

"Listen!" said Seth. They could see his eyes in the dark, wide with excitement. A new sound rose out of the southwest—another engine.

"The *Nellie G.*!"

61. The Hare at Bay

ELIHU WAS THE FIRST to hear the *Proclamation*'s engine, and he called Captain Williams out from the pilothouse to listen. Neither Wyck nor

Mollie had heard the approaching boat. The *Nellie G.* had been puffing languid rags of steam and smoke as she sat at anchor, her fires banked low; now Elihu raced down the hatch to shovel fuel into the firebox.

The captain weighed anchor himself, and the *Nellie G.* took on the shifting movement of a large animal when the gate is left open. A puff of steam, no lazy tendril, billowed from the stack. Inside the cabin, Colonel Taverner stood from his cribbage game with Mister Walton.

"We're moving," said Wyck. He hurried past Mollie and lumbered his way through the cabin to the door of the pilothouse. Colonel Taverner was there before him.

"I don't want to head them off just yet," the colonel was saying.

"We shall come out behind them, I reckon," replied the captain. "They're coming a good clip."

Mollie and Mister Walton were behind Wyck now. "So it's the little steamer they have," said the portly fellow.

"I've seen her before *and* heard her," said the captain. "She has her own sound."

Like the receding curtains in a darkened theater, the walls of the cove fell back as they crept toward the mouth of the inlet amid the echoing rumble of the *Nellie G.*'s engine; ahead of them, low-lying stars and lights upon the further shores seemed to flash into being as they were revealed.

Wyck pointed, his hand thrusting past the colonel's shoulder. Those new lights were briefly occluded, one after another, by a black shape upon the water. The salty froth of the *Proclamation*'s wake glowed in the water like guidelines.

The bow of the *Nellie G.* broke from the confines of the cove, and immediately they felt the surge of the outgoing tide against them, though the looming bulk of Westport still protected them from the inevitable head wind. The boat rolled against the current and even met with the first dwindling whitecaps from the *Proclamation*'s wake.

Colonel Taverner returned to the cabin, where he had his gear rolled in a canvas wrap on a bench. From this he produced a small megaphone, a pistol (which he strapped to his side), and a rifle.

"What are you going to do with that?" asked a horrified Wyck when the colonel, rifle in hand, made his way back to the pilot room and the door to the foredeck.

They were gaining speed now as Elihu worked belowdecks. Taverner took the handle of the door for balance as they pitched again. "I am going to encourage them to stop with it, Mr. O'Hearn," he said. "Perhaps you should see if Elihu needs help putting on steam."

Taverner was out the door and Wyck halfway down the hatch before the big man thought to shout, "There's a little boy aboard that ship!"

"He knows, Mr. O'Hearn," said Mister Walton, "but I'll go out and remind him." He was himself a little taken aback by the look in Taverner's eye. "Perhaps you should stay here, Miss Peer," said the bespectacled fellow.

"Certainly," said Mollie, then hurried after him onto the foredeck.

The bow of the boat rose over a wave as it crossed the trail of the *Proclamation*. Mollie clutched the rail and glimpsed through the window of the pilothouse at a look of wild pleasure on Captain Williams's face. She was astonished at the speed they had achieved and conscious of the little engine beneath them working harder still.

Taverner was riding the deck like an old salt, legs apart, head up. Mister Walton, only a little less sure of his footing, stood close to the rail. There was no sign yet that they had been detected by anyone on the other boat, and they said nothing while the *Nellie G.* straightened her bow between the lines of wake before them. They could almost sense the added effort of Wyckford O'Hearn in a sudden surge of speed.

Travel at night always seems faster than daylight travel, and the three on the bow experienced a sense of charging over the waves. Lights on either shore fell by rapidly; the silhouettes of trees and high banks pivoted past the accompanying field of stars.

The moon had not yet risen, and the *Proclamation* sported only a single light, but the combined glimmer of the stars and the natural phosphorescence in the churning water was enough for an old hand like Captain Williams to follow. The murky pocket of the Eddy grew before them, still half a mile away, and soon the rocky spine of Clough Point would draw back to reveal the fort at Davis Island.

" *'Some hound that doesn't bay the hare,'* " quoted Colonel Taverner, hardly loud enough for Mister Walton to hear, and no sooner did he say it than a figure stepped onto the port-side deck of the boat ahead of them and cautiously looked back. *"Ach!"* said the colonel. "Never state the obvious!"

Another, smaller figure appeared around the aft corner of the starboard deck, grabbed the rail, and looked ready to bail over the side when a third form caught up with him and clutched him by the back of his coat. Adam Tweed struggled with Bird while trying to maintain his own equilibrium; he lifted the boy from his feet and pressed him against the rail, then looked up slowly as he comprehended the presence of the *Nellie G.*

Tweed straightened and pulled the boy, kicking, from the rail.

"Light the lamp here, would you, Mister Walton?" asked Colonel Taverner. The custom agent raised the megaphone to his mouth and gave out a loud "Halloo!"

Tweed seemed more puzzled than afraid, and he frowned back at the colonel. The figure on the port side ducked into the cabin, and in another moment the *Proclamation* put on more speed. But the *Nellie G.* was already gaining upon the smaller craft, and Captain Williams took his boat around to port. The pursuers braced themselves as they dipped over the trough left by the leading vessel.

Colonel Taverner put the horn to his mouth again. "I am an agent of the United States Customs Service, and I respectfully request you precede me into the cove ahead of us, known as the Eddy."

Mister Walton lit the mirrored lantern, and shifting the door, he directed a bright light upon the aft end of the *Proclamation*. Tweed squinted against the light. "Should you show him your rifle?" wondered Mister Walton. He was unnerved to see the child so close to leaping from the boat and outraged to see him handled so violently.

"Unnecessary, I'm sure, sir," said the colonel. "I have found the common American smuggler, when caught, to be very rational, and even polite, in comparison to his brother across the water."

Tweed pulled a pistol from his coat, pointed and fired it, and a corner of the pilothouse splintered, just above Mollie's head. The percussion of the pistol reached them like the dull thump of a wave. The pilot door flung open, and the captain snatched Mollie inside.

"Of course, these are not your common smugglers," said the colonel, his head next to Mister Walton's as they clung to the deck.

Another shot rang out, and the captain steered the *Nellie G.* slightly to starboard. He glanced up at the hole in the corner of his pilothouse, cursed, then apologized to Mollie. The door swung shut with the roll of the boat, then was thrown open as the two men from the foredeck scrambled in.

The hatch was raised, and Wyck came charging up the ladder. "What is it?" he was shouting. "We thought we heard shots!"

As an answer, a third explosion shattered the glass before the captain, and they threw themselves into the cabin behind or dropped to the deck.

Peering over the sill, the captain righted the wheel, having given it a reflexive jerk. Taverner raised his head next and saw that Tweed had lowered his gun and was standing with the boy between himself and the *Nellie G.* "Well," said the colonel. "Cowards think alike. What do you say, Captain?"

"Put the coal to her, Elihu!" shouted the captain into the speaking tube beside the wheel. "Can you get a shot at him?" asked Williams.

"Not with the boy standing there!" exclaimed Wyck.

"Easy, son," said Taverner, who was still seated on the deck of the pilothouse. "You've got a good eye, I'd warrant, Mister Walton."

Mister Walton was perched in the doorway to the back cabin. "I was thought to have in my day," he said, "but I haven't *shot* a rifle in years."

"*Ach!*" dismissed the colonel. "It's like riding a horse."

"I am sure you are much the better man to—"

"There's a piece of glass in my eye," said the colonel. He pointed with his left hand at the corresponding orb.

Mister Walton leaned forward to peer at the man, but it was too dark. He took a long breath. "Should we persist, Colonel, with the young people aboard?"

Taverner's one eye was closed shut, but he leveled the other on Wyck. "What do you say, Mr. O'Hearn? Shall we leave off?"

Wyck glanced back at Mollie, who shook her head fiercely. "I don't think we have any choice, Colonel," said the redheaded man.

"I'd sign you all up to service," said the colonel, and he made an attempt to wink with his one eye, the effect of which was not pleasant.

Mister Walton had a great regard for Colonel Taverner, but he thought the man might be enjoying this too much. Still, the sight of the little boy being roughly handled had affected the portly fellow deeply, and he didn't like to think of the child disappearing now that Tweed and his gang knew they were pursued. "Give it to me," he said. He checked the chamber to see that it was loaded, fingered the safety, then crawled past the colonel and placed himself halfway in the doorway to the foredeck.

"Round starboard, Captain Williams," said the colonel. He dabbed at his eye with a handkerchief.

"What are you going to do?" demanded Wyck.

"He can shield himself with the boy," answered the colonel, "but he can't keep us from emptying their wheelhouse with a few stray shots."

"Once the pilot has left his station, we can give them a bump and bear 'em down," said the captain.

"But the boy—" Wyck was out of the hatch now, standing in full view and oblivious of the danger.

"Get down, man!" shouted the colonel.

Mollie, hunkered in the door to the cabin, reached for Wyck and tugged at his coat. "Get down, Wyckford!" she shouted.

He only partially obeyed, scooching his height nearer the floor.

The *Nellie G.* more than matched the speed of the *Proclamation*, and Captain Williams was taking her round the starboard. Tweed still stood in the aft of the fleeing vessel, defiant and undaunted, but he could see what was happening. The light of the bow lantern had passed him by, but the two vessels were very close now, and his eyes gleamed like a wolf's in the ensuing gloom. He looked down at the boy, and a sudden decision registered in his face.

There was only one sure way to slow pursuit. Tweed lifted the boy by the back of his coat and flung him into the black waters of the Sheepscott.

Captain Williams veered hard to the starboard and threw the levers that would cut the engine; Mollie shouldered Wyck aside, charged through the door to the deck, and threw herself over the side. Tweed raised his pistol again and shot into the water; when he saw Mollie go over, he leveled the pistol in her direction.

Mister Walton stood and pulled the butt of the rifle to his shoulder. Something glimmered on Adam Tweed's chest. Wyck leaped to his feet. Mister Walton caught that silver gleam in the crosshairs and fired. Adam Tweed jerked back as if he had been struck by a club, his pistol twisting in his hand and firing as he fell back against the rail. The shot whined past Mister Walton's cheek and crashed into something behind him.

Tweed fell back to the deck of the boat.

"Pray God I didn't kill him!" said Mister Walton. Shaking, he lowered the rifle. Tears had sprung to his eyes.

"We have a fallen soldier here!" said Taverner.

Mister Walton looked back to see Wyck lying in a heap upon the deck.

62. What the River Would Give Up

THE FRIGID BLACK WATER OF THE SHEEPSCOTT RIVER came over her, and for a brief instant she was ten years old again, looking for her brother, almost paralyzed with mute shock and wishing she had broken her promise to her father and had tattled on Sean for jumping ice cakes in Back Cove.

There was no perception of up or down. The engines of the *Proclamation* and the *Nellie G.* roared in her ears. She was waiting for her older brother to pull her out of the icy water; then her head broke the surface, and she cried out for Bird.

If she had been dressed more typically, she would have had to contend with the weight of petticoats and skirts, but her boots were snug to her knees and took in little water, and she had only the single short skirt and pantaloons; and she had steeled herself into a strong swimmer since that horrifying day when Sean was drowned.

Mollie brought herself half out of the water with a single stroke, looking in the dark for the little boy. She could hear splashing some distance away. Behind her the *Nellie G.* was coming around. Colonel Taverner had tripped out behind Mister Walton, who was standing at the stern with a lantern. "Come about! Come about!" the colonel was shouting.

She gasped. The cold river had momentarily stopped her breathing, and she fought off a wave of panic. The canopy of stars seemed close overhead, as if there were only a few feet between the river and the top of the sky.

"Over there!" she could hear. "Miss Peer! Over there!"

She did not know it, but Mister Walton had thrown off his coat and shoes, and only the colonel's gravest command had kept him from jumping in after her.

"Before you!" came the shout again. Mister Walton was shining the light, but her senses were so misconstrued that she had to look at the lantern itself twice before she was able to follow the shaft of light and catch sight of something dark bobbing several yards away.

"Oh, God!" she pleaded, swallowing water as the wake of the boat tossed her in the cold darkness, but she caught sight of little arms thrashing, and she knew that Bird was still alive.

She reached him with four strong strokes and feared that his struggles would be the end of them both. "Bird!" she called out, and when she scooped him from behind, he went limp in her grasp. It was the release of his self-will, a complete faith; he gave himself up to the force of her intent and the strength of her athletic body as she propelled them both through the water.

Mollie was swimming blindly, hardly aware of boat or shore; but she swam crosswise to the current, instinctively taking them in the right direction. The boat had drifted back, pivoting in the current and wind. She was feeling the weight of her clothes now. She had to remember to breathe with each dash against the water, her gasps coming in near sobs. She searched the surface of the water, fearing that she had taken them further from the boat or that the tide was tugging them away.

A life ring and rope splashed beside her, and she shifted Bird to it, fearing it would not hold them both. She treaded water, her breath rasping with the cold, her clothes feeling heavier with every movement. She pushed at the ring, but the little boy had a grip on her collar.

"Let go," she said, and she wasted energy trying to disengage his little fingers. The look on his own face, however, was determined, and he only gripped harder.

The slack in the rope took up, and the life ring was pulled across the water. For a moment it was Bird's resolute grip that kept her on the surface. Stretched between Mollie and the ring, he was the link that was pulling her in. Then he began to fail. He was not strong enough, after all, and still clutching her collar, he began to lose his hold upon the life ring. He was going to drown rather than let her go. Mollie gave a final lunge.

She was gripping him when they were drawn to the ladder. He held her neck as she let herself be pulled onto the deck of the boat and carried into the cabin. They laid them together on a bench, and she thought she caught a glimpse of Wyck on the bench opposite, looking pale and bloodless. She pulled the child's face close to her breast, away from the sight.

Mister Walton kneeled beside them while the colonel covered them with several wool throws. Mollie and Bird shivered violently together under the covers. The bespectacled fellow was white as a sheet, and he gripped Mollie's hand. "You're all right, Miss Peer," he said. "You're safe." She hadn't felt in such capable hands since her older brother had pulled her from the icy clutches of Back Cove.

"Wyck!" she said.

"He took a bullet in the chest, ma'am," said Taverner, "but I'm positive it missed his lungs. It caught in the gristle and came out high. He's passed out, though. He's lost a lot of blood, and we're hurrying him in to Wiscasset."

Indeed, she could feel the *Nellie G.* gaining steam and speed.

Mister Walton's hand was shaking in hers. "My goodness, Miss Peer, you can swim!" he was saying.

"Like a fish, Mister Walton," she whispered.

"*Ach!*" said the colonel. He stood, one eye closed shut. "Like a mermaid, Miss Peer! Like a mermaid!"

63. Foundering

SHERIFF PIPER CURSED when he heard two shots carry over the water. They could hear both of the steamers clearly but couldn't see them yet, for the boats had not come far enough up Clough Point. The first shot had sounded indistinct, and he could not be sure that it wasn't the cough of an engine or one of the boats striking a rock.

The second shot came soon after, and there was no mistaking it.

Sundry jumped up from his place against the rampart and ran east along the shoreline without a word.

"What is it?" asked Seth, though he knew only too well.

"It's the colonel," said Piper. "He's misread his quarry."

"Is it the colonel shooting, do you think?"

There came another percussion, echoing along the shoreline and between the hills. "I'm almost sure it's not," said the sheriff. *They're not smugglers, after all,* he was thinking, and he had yet no notion of Adam Tweed. "Let's follow Sundry," he said.

"I wonder where the others got to," said Seth. He had begun to think that he had dreamed the members of the Moosepath League.

They could see Sundry as a shadow further down the shore, and they almost caught up with him before he began to hurry off again. The sheriff called to the young man, and Sundry stopped only long enough to shout back that he couldn't see anything yet.

Several shots in succession stilled them all. The sheriff recognized the report of two different guns. "That was Taverner, I'd guess. The next to last."

Sundry drifted back; he was in an agony of apprehension and indecision. The sound of one engine was drawing closer. "Mister Walton is with them" was all he could say.

"I know, son," said Piper. "It doesn't seem to fit what we know about Pembleton."

"He's crazy, I think," said Sundry. "He's vicious, but he didn't appear to have the nerve—"

"Who was this fellow he was seen with, Adam Tweed?" wondered Piper.

"I don't know him," admitted Sundry.

"Maybe the colonel has just made his acquaintance."

Seth pointed down the river. "There's something!"

"It's Pembleton's boat!" said Piper. "Come along," he told Seth. "Keep down and we'll see where he puts in. Sundry—"

"Mister Walton is back there. I'm coming, too."

Piper didn't want anything tragic to happen, if it hadn't happened already. "See if you can scare up your friends," he said. "We don't want them running into someone who's panicking with a gun."

In his concern for Mister Walton, Sundry had forgotten Ephram, Eagleton, and Thump; he suspected this was a way for Piper to keep him out of harm's reach, but he couldn't abandon the three fellows to such dangerous possibilities. "I think they went this way," he said, and hurried off.

Sheriff Piper and Seth Patterson hurried back to the bulwarks of Fort Edgecomb and recovered their weapons, by which time the *Proclamation* was plainly visible against the gray gleam of the river. The little steamer seemed itself agitated, as if unsure where it wanted to go or how it was to do it. For a moment they thought the boat was going to put in by the fort, but it veered away from the shallows at the last minute and headed north again.

"We'll need the carriage," said Piper, and while he kept an eye on the boat, Seth ran off to the place where they had left the horse and carriage. Ten minutes later they were pulling up at the Wiscasset bridge, leaping from the driver's seat and scrambling down the northern shore of Davis Island, rifles in hand.

As if nobody were at the wheel, the *Proclamation* was veering for the tidal flats. The moon showed the faintest influence over Edgecomb, a bluish glow paling through the trees, but even this weak light revealed details in the shoreline, caught the ripples of current in the river, and limned the figure of Eustace Pembleton, who was kicking an inert figure on the deck of his boat.

"He'll kill him!" said Seth.

"If he's not already dead." Piper stopped at the edge of the water and shouted: "Pembleton!"

The wild man froze and stared up at the shore, searching for the source of the commanding voice. Then the boat ran aground, listed to one side, and dumped Pembleton into the shallows. Someone was driving the engine hard; of a sudden, the boat made a pitch against thin air, her propeller sawing the surface of the water. Pembleton was standing in the shallows screaming, but the boat spun dangerously close to him.

Then it stopped. The stack puffed smoke and steam, which cast shadows across the shallows in the light of the rising moon. Several figures, including that of Tom Bull, abandoned ship, and together with Pembleton, they charged across the flats, climbed the shore some distance away, and disappeared among the dark meadows and slopes beyond.

A light by the shore went up. Someone had awakened to the sound of the engine and the shouting.

"Good Lord, the water is cold!" said Seth as he followed the sheriff out to the boat. They climbed onto the deck, fearing the worst, but it was no one they knew. The man was breathing, and except for the obvious damage done by Eustace Pembleton's boots, they could find no wounds on him.

Then Seth marked the tin badge. "Look," he said, and unpinned the totem. The crease in it was unmistakable. "He was hit by a bullet."

"How could a piece of tin turn a bullet?" wondered Piper. The question was academic.

"I've seen bullets make strange tricks," said Seth. "It was a moose," he added, pointing to the animal engraved there.

"Yes, well, a moose is the proper creature to get between you and a fair shot," said the sheriff.

He looked back from the tilted deck at the shore and the river and the bridge rising out of the shadows with the increasing moon.

Standing near the bridge, just a few yards away from where the horse and carriage had been left, were the silhouettes of three men, two of whom had top hats, which they raised and waved to Seth and the sheriff.

"Is that a dog with them?" wondered Seth.

Book Eight

OCTOBER 16–30, 1896

❀

64. The Telling Portrait
(October 16, 1896)

"It's a moose," said Mister Walton. He touched the tin badge pinned to Bird's shirt, his finger following the crease left by the bullet, and he felt himself pale somewhat to see this object—a target of his dangerous intent—fastened over the child's heart. "It is very fitting," he added, however, "since it was great good luck to me."

Sundry, who stood in the doorway, was not so convinced. "It gave you a mark to aim for, but it protected the wrong person."

"Ah, Sundry," said Mister Walton, "you misunderstand. This little emblem has saved me from taking another man's life." His smile was very soft, and its affect was all out of proportion to its degree of intensity.

Sundry felt his own expression soften under its influence. Mister Walton's reasoning didn't answer for him when it came to a man who would throw a child into the river at night, then shoot at him and his rescuer, but if it delivered his friend from any anguish, Sundry was satisfied.

They were in the parlor of the Wiscasset House (an old haunt for Mister Walton and Sundry), and they waited for Dr. Cushman to come down. They heard someone arrive at the front door, and a moment later, Colonel Taverner looked in at them. The doctor had removed the piece of glass from his eye the night before, and now the colonel wore a black patch that lent him a piratical appearance. "How is the lad?" he asked.

"Not very comfortable, I'm afraid," said Mister Walton.

"A little medicinal spirits would not be out of place, I think," said the old soldier.

"The doctor has taken care of that, I think."

"He is a good man, then."

The doctor appeared while they talked. He thought it worth a little of

Wyckford's energy for him to see Bird safe and sound. "I haven't told him the worst of it," said the doctor softly.

"And what is that?" wondered the colonel.

"The bullet came out clean, and I see no signs of infection yet, but his shoulder is split in pieces. I don't see how he'll ever swing a bat again."

"*Ach!*" was all the colonel said. Mister Walton and Sundry had heard this news already.

"It's a shame," said Dr. Cushman. "I saw him play three years ago; the only man on his team to hit off New Bedford's pitcher, three for four, two home runs and won the game."

Mister Walton took Bird upstairs, with the colonel in tow. The room they entered was dark and close. On the other side of the room, by a curtained window, sat Mollie Peer. Occupying the four-poster bed and looking strangely small was Wyck, his eyes shut, his brow creased and damp with sweat. His breathing was shallow; his face was pale and waxy, his hair a wet mop upon the pillow. He did not open his eyes when the door opened, and Mister Walton wished he had thought to warn the child about Wyck's appearance.

But Bird walked to the bed without hesitation. He touched Wyck's uninjured arm. The man's eyes opened groggily, but the first sight of the little boy seemed to lighten the pain from his face. "Good boy" was what he said in a small voice. The child's hand fit in the man's like the bud of a flower. "You have to learn to swim, like Miss Peer, here," said Wyck.

"Mollie," came the woman's voice from the shadows.

He corrected himself. "Like Mollie. You stick with these gentlemen, now, do you hear me?" Wyck had been told that Tweed was convalescing from broken ribs on a cot at the Lincoln County Jail, and Tom Bull had been cornered and captured somewhere along the shore just that morning, but Pembleton had not been found. "Thank you for bringing him in," said Wyck to Mister Walton, which might have meant several things.

Mister Walton escorted Bird out again, but Colonel Taverner lingered at the door. He glanced to the other side of the room, at Mollie, and did not know what to make of her. "The boy thinks he can take us to Pembleton's hideaway," he said. "The sheriff thought you might like to come, Miss Peer."

There was a silence before she spoke. "Thank you, Colonel, but I'll stay here."

The colonel nodded. "You get better, lad," he said.

"You did well, Colonel," said Mollie, "trusting to Mister Walton's eye." The colonel glanced behind him. He could see the back of the man as he went, hand in hand, with Bird down the stairs. "It wasn't his eye, lass, that I was trusting," said the custom agent.

He saw her head rise up and sensed the questioning expression.

Colonel Taverner slowly closed the door. "It was his judgment."

After their strenuous, if unsuccessful, pursuit of Ducky Planke, Ephram, Eagleton, and Thump had met the news of the events aboard the *Nellie G.* with great alarm, then waited with the others in the parlor of the Wiscasset House till the small hours of the morning, when the doctor pronounced Wyckford O'Hearn out of immediate danger. But having been involved with anxious situations themselves in recent days, these latest circumstances only served to amplify an already profound exhaustion, and they did not stir from their rooms before the height of the sun or the heat of the following afternoon.

Sundry jumped down from the driver's seat when he had pulled the trap onto the grounds of Fort Edgecomb. He opened the door and waited for Mister Walton and Bird, then Sheriff Piper and Colonel Taverner, to step down.

The little boy appeared very keen to take in his surroundings, and it occurred to Mister Walton that Bird had never seen this place by daylight. The portly fellow put a gentle hand on the child's head and ruffled his soft hair. "You know, son," said the man, "you don't have to stay if this place troubles you or makes you afraid."

Bird's expression was serious as he searched Mister Walton's bespectacled eyes. "I'm not afraid," he said, and it was more than any of them had heard from him since he was brought aboard the *Nellie G.*

"Mr. Pembleton," said the sheriff carefully, "kept some things hidden somewheres about, didn't he?"

Without hesitation, Bird pointed toward the southern extremity of the fort's ramparts. "They took a stiff man over there," he said.

This statement occasioned some glances between them. Mister Walton took a nod from the sheriff as a sign that he should pursue this thought. He scooched down so that he was almost at eye level with the little fellow. "Mr. Pembleton and Tom Bull took a man to the hiding place?"

"A stiff man," said the child, his face indicating that he had been quite impressed by this anonymous figure.

"Good heavens," said Mister Walton quietly.

"Is it murder, do you suppose?" wondered Sundry Moss.

"After last night, I wouldn't put it past them," said Colonel Taverner.

"Are we all still game, gentlemen?" asked the sheriff.

Sundry, surprisingly enough, appeared the least so, but he said nothing as curiosity urged them to follow Bird down the slope of the fort grounds.

The character of the river grew more apparent as they descended the bank—the sound of the current against the shore, the cool air off the water, the increasing tang of salt. The Sheepscott had been dark and enigmatic the night before; today it glistened in the sun, blue as a Fourth of July remnant. Not simply caught in a separate mood, it was a different river; it was difficult to fathom that such danger had been experienced upon her.

On Clough Point, across the Sheepscott, three brawny maples burned orange in the fall light.

Bird stopped when he came to the rocky bulwark that formed the southern bastion of the fortification, and here he leaned over the wall and said, "It's down there."

Colonel Taverner was the first to look over the side; the tide was nearing its low point, hurrying out to sea, and a further bank of weedy, barnacled rock was revealed below the stonework of the bastion itself. "What are we to make of that?" Taverner asked the sheriff doubtfully.

"I know what Seth would say if he were here," said the sheriff.

"The old tunnels beneath the fort," said Sundry.

"Are there?" asked Mister Walton.

"That's the story," said Piper, "though I've never given it much credence. "Can you show us?" the sheriff asked the little boy.

To Bird, the entire business was utterly lacking in mystery. He nodded.

Sundry sat at the edge of the bastion and dropped down to the kelpy bank, where he secured his footing and reached up for the boy. He hadn't even gotten Bird on his feet before the child tapped a large stone in the wall and said, "It's there."

Sundry gave the rock, which was as broad as his shoulders and half a foot tall, a push and felt it give. Cool air exhaled from the crack above it, and the growl of stone on stone sounded behind the wall, as from an empty room. "I think there *is* something behind here," he said.

The sheriff joined them, the boy was lifted back out of harm's way, and together the two men managed to muscle several rocks out of place. They peered into the dark hole, and dank air greeted them from the shadows. "There are lamps and rope in the carriage," said Sheriff Piper.

*   *   *

"There have always been stories about tunnels beneath the fort, but I always assumed they were so many old lies," the sheriff was saying. By the time Mister Walton and Colonel Taverner had retrieved the equipage, Sundry and the sheriff had pulled more stones from the wall.

"This is why Pembleton needed Tom Bull, I'd guess," said Sundry, arching his back. "I wish we had him."

Standing in the mouth of the tunnel, Colonel Taverner lit the lamps. The floor of the opening was damp with the high tide. A crab scuttled from beneath a brick. None of them had forgotten the implication of Bird's "stiff man," and they each found occasion to touch the little boy's shoulder or ruffle his hair as a gesture of comfort and companionship. Even the colonel stood for a moment with his arm resting on Bird's shoulder, saying, "You've done well, lad," the light of the lamps shining in his one good eye.

The gloom within was all the more obscure for the brilliance of the day left behind. They formed something of a cordon around the boy, with the colonel and the sheriff in the lead. The light of the lanterns glistened from wet walls, and a draft of cold air touched their faces. The tunnel rose slightly, vaguely following the contour of the banks above them. The sheriff considered the bricks of the wall and wondered aloud how secure they were.

"It's a very handy piece of work," said the colonel.

When they did speak, it was in whispers that yet sounded loud and hollow within that close space. The sounds from the river behind them were strange and unnatural, the cry of a bird hardly recognizable. A train was approaching Wiscasset from the southwest, its whistle mournful and lonely as it echoed after them.

"It must have been built as a means to secretly man boats from the fort," posited the sheriff.

"Or man the fort from boats," said Sundry.

"Or to move contraband," said the colonel.

With a lantern in hand, the sheriff led them further. "There's something up ahead," he said.

The tunnel widened into a large room. The lamplight spilled into the shadowy expanse, dissipating itself in a pale attempt to fill the chamber. Sundry looked back at the mouth of the tunnel, a small, blinding light against the dark hole they had entered.

Colonel Taverner went first, his lamp raised, his head bent forward. A clutter of objects rose out of the darkness as the light of the lantern progressed into the room; chairs, a table, a set of drawers without a bureau or cabinet in sight, stacks of rotting papers; a mirror glinting back the colonel's reflection. Heaps of refuse deteriorating in the damp air.

Almost in the same instant, the three men behind the colonel caught sight of the figure, and Sheriff Piper, who carried a sidearm, called out a startled warning as he pulled the pistol from its holster. Taverner's head came around, and he saw the raised hand and the axe.

"Stop!" shouted the sheriff, even as Taverner took two or three steps back and reached into his coat for his own pistol.

There was the echo of Piper's shout, then silence, and each could hear another's breath, like the reverberation of his own. The figure remained in its threatening stance, the axe raised, the back tensed with latent force.

"It's the stiff man," said Bird.

The colonel let out a low chuckle. The lamplight gleamed off the dark brow and caught the wild whites of the eyes. Beneath the moccasin-clad feet was the bold legend Wawenock Rum-Soaked Cigars!

The wooden Indian stared fiercely at them. Mister Walton and Sundry Moss thought of old John Neptune and could find nothing in this fantastic work that remotely resembled their friend. They were a little embarrassed by it as it glared from the shadows.

"He's not real," said Bird.

"No," said Mister Walton. He laid a gentle hand on the child's head. "He's not, is he."

With the lanterns raised, the confines of the room became apparent to their gloom-adjusted eyes. Clearly, there was booty from several sources lying about the chamber, but the furniture, the mirror, a stack of frames leaning against one damp wall, might have come from a common origin, as if some large estate had been ransacked. There were even clothes heaped in one corner, damp with rot and suspicious with vermin. Bird stood in the midst of it all, more interested in the curiosity and activity of the men than the objects of their curiosity.

"Pembleton has been a busy fellow," said Sundry. He stopped to paw through a heap of diverse objects in one of the drawers. There were hat pins and jewelry and ribbons and buttons.

Taverner inspected a pair of chairs, like a rapacious buccaneer with his black patch; he fingered the carving around the mirror. "These were fine pieces," he said, "before they sat in here for more than a day or so."

Beside the colonel, Mister Walton pulled one of the frames away from its stack and turned it around. It was a large, hand-colored photograph of a tomb, covered with flowers. A banner hung over the flowers that said "In Memory." He put this aside and turned the next frame. Here was the picture of a prize cow before a large barn. The next was a smaller frame holding a lithograph from a magazine, the image of a barefoot boy fishing by a stream.

A walnut frame, ornately carved, came next; Mister Walton pulled it out from the wall and rested it, face out, against the others. He peered through the half-light, and realization slowly occupied his face, one feature at a time. "My word," he said quietly, his voice like a sigh in the dark.

The light upon the picture grew as Colonel Taverner came over, and that which had so taken Mister Walton was more apparent still. The colonel made a sound that indicated surprise. Sundry and the sheriff joined them, and finally, Bird took several steps toward Mister Walton.

It was the portrait of a young woman with dark hair cascading over one shoulder and large brown eyes cast slightly to one side and downward. The smallest, gentlest smile touched her mouth. She was seated, her hands resting in her lap, her dress a lovely pale green that disappeared into the background of the painting. "She's beautiful," said Sundry, hardly knowing that he had voiced the thought.

Mister Walton turned to the little boy. "Bird, do you know who this woman is?" The child came forward. He looked at the portrait—not at the woman *in* the picture exactly but at the picture *of* the woman—as if it were an old friend. "Do you know who she is?" Mister Walton asked again.

Gravely, the little boy shook his head. He looked upon the portrait with pleasure, perhaps even affection, but he had no name to attach to it. He did not know who she was.

But looking from Bird to the face in the frame, from the dark hair and the wide brown eyes of the child to those of the young woman, Mister Walton knew. And slowly Sundry understood; and the sheriff and Colonel Taverner.

Mister Walton felt a chill pass over him. He thought, for a moment, that he caught the scent of lily of the valley.

"She's very pretty," said the boy.

65. <u>Nom de Plume</u>
(October 19, 1896)

"I'LL NEVER SUGGEST SOMEONE IS EARLY with *any*thing again!" growled Fritz Corbel when Mollie stepped into his office. She wasn't sure how he even knew who she was, since he hadn't looked up; in fact, she could barely see him for the stack of papers and books on his desk. The familiar billow of smoke hovered over his balding pate, however, and she was almost warmed to see it.

"A situation arose that required my attention," she said.

"A bee got in your bonnet that required your hieing off after that kid!"

"I see there is no need to explain," she said, "since you know everything already." She was a little shocked at herself for sounding so flippant under these circumstances.

"Finally! Another body realizes!" The editor straightened in his chair and looked over the stacks before him. Mollie was decked out for the occasion, which didn't hurt his feelings. She had on a black-and-gold velvet jacket that sported long stays buttoned across the bust; the frills of her white blouse spilled out like a corsage, a striking contrast to her black hair, done up beneath a feathered hat and those fine dark eyes. "The only thing I *don't* know or, rather, don't understand is what you were thinking when you left me to pen two installments of the social column."

"How did they turn out?" she asked, trying to envision the irascible man at some grand event or elegant *soirée*.

"Oh, I just copied something you wrote a year or so ago," he muttered.

"I do have a story," she ventured after a moment's silence.

"The one I told you to leave to Peter Mall," he stated flatly.

She looked to one side rather than level her exasperation upon him.

"The story I told you to stay away from," he continued.

"There was a personal connection to the matter," she said, "and since I *was* there, I thought you might like a very exciting story of kidnapping, smuggling, missing persons, and a gunfight on the Sheepscott River."

"Yes, I heard something about it," said the editor without commitment. He seemed to have found something of interest before him.

"Well?" she said when she thought she had waited long enough.

"What?" he snapped. "Do you have your next column?"

"The story!" she demanded.

"What story?"

"The story I was telling you about?"

Fritz Corbel leaned back in his chair. He took his cigar and looked at it as if he weren't sure what he had plucked from his mouth. "Miss Peer," he said, "this is the sort of thing that Peter Mall can write with his hands tied behind his back."

Mollie was shocked to find her eyes misting with anger. Her mouth took on a determined set; her jaw stood out. "Mr. Corbel," she said. "I *am* Peter Mall."

He was still looking at his cigar. He put it in his mouth. He leaned to one side to look past Mollie, through the open door to his office and into the hall. "I know," he said. "And that out-of-work actor you had posing for you wasn't worth whatever you were paying him." Corbel leaned forward again and perused the sheaf of papers before him.

Mollie was stunned—first, that she had blurted out the secret that she had kept so long, and second, that it had been no secret at all. "Why didn't you say something?" she asked.

"A good lot of our readers would not find Peter Mall's stories proper for a woman to be reporting," said the man without looking up. He appeared unsure of himself for a brief moment and repeated this sentence to himself silently, as if wondering whether it had come out correctly.

"What should I do?" she asked.

"Do you have a column ready?"

"No."

"Then I suggest you go home and write one. Check Charlie for the mail, make something up, go ask Horace McQuinn! I don't care! Just save me from having to write that tripe again."

Mollie felt at sea, momentarily lost, as she turned to the door.

"In the future," said Corbel, "I will have Peter Mall's salary put in your envelope, and it's up to you to see that he gets it." He muttered to himself, "At least I won't have to mail the blamed thing!"

"I'll have a column for you tomorrow," said Mollie. She knew better than to turn around and left the editor's office without another word.

"Do that," said editor Corbel.

66. O'Hearn Farm
(October 28, 1896)

WYCK WAS GLAD that the brown calf was to be raised as a milk cow. The creature, barely a month old, kicked up its hind legs and gamboled alongside the fence; Bird ran along the other side, rarely laughing but always smiling. Wyck had had to scold the boy twice for getting in with the animal, but he was glad the kid had *some*one to run with.

Wyck's mother's black dog, plump as a sausage, stood up on the back porch and woofed. "Easy, Skinny," said Wyckford. "What is it?"

The dog woofed again, then dropped off the end of the porch and disappeared around the side of the farmhouse. Wyck shifted in his chair, then wished he hadn't. Sweat stood out on his forehead, and he felt ill for a moment. He had been trying to look through the kitchen window. He thought he could see his mother and his sister moving there, fixing lunch. He didn't know how they kept up with everything—with him to tend— even if he did refuse help for everything but the impossible.

"Someone's here," he called, and regretted that as well. It seemed that even his vocal cords were attached to his shoulder.

Bird looked up from the fence. Wyck closed his eyes. *The kid is safe*, he said to himself. It was what he always told himself whenever the pain threatened to overcome him or whenever he began to feel sorry for himself. *The kid is safe.* One night he had dreamed that Bird hit his head, down in Pembleton's lair, and never woke up; in the dream, Wyck was standing in Mrs. Barter's kitchen, holding him. Fortunately, Wyck *had* awakened quickly.

The pain dulled again to the moderate constant he had known the past few days. He felt a little cold suddenly but thought he would look silly with a blanket over him, like an old lady.

Skinny was barking on the other side of the house, and Wyck heard the clop of a horse and the rumble of carriage wheels, then the door as his mother went out to greet the arrivals. *Please, not Aunt Deb!* he thought.

Bird was leaning on the middle rail of the fence now, peering beneath the top rail, maybe whispering to the calf. The animal watched the boy with its liquid brown eyes.

Wyck could hear conversation in the house. His mother's voice raised cheerfully, his sister's with a certain amount of excitement. The back door opened, and Mrs. O'Hearn, surprisingly small (considering the size of her son), with gray hair tied up in a bun and a workaday housedress, stepped onto the porch. "Wyckford," she said.

"Yes, Ma," he replied, turning his head a little to see who was there. Mrs. Barter showed herself, looking tentative and sad. *I must look terrible*, he thought. Then, seemingly after some hesitation, Mollie Peer stepped onto the porch. "Mrs. Barter," said Wyck, half in question. "Miss . . . Mollie."

"Wyckford O'Hearn," said the landlady, as if to chastise him for letting such a thing happen to him.

Mollie said nothing but smiled a little wanly.

They didn't even see Bird hurrying from the fence; he was simply standing at the foot of the porch steps, looking up at Mollie as if he wanted to soak the sight of her in before she disappeared.

"I knew a haircut would do wonders for you!" declared Mrs. Barter. She looked as if she wanted to go down and hug the boy.

"Let's get some chairs over by Wyck, if it isn't too cold for you ladies," said Mrs. O'Hearn. "Emmy is putting on the coffee." She was already pulling a chair over near her son. "Bird helped me make gingerbread this morning, and it will still be warm."

Mollie leaned something against the back of her chair when she sat. She was holding a copy of the *Eastern Argus*. Bird pulled a chair up beside her and sat. The statuesque woman looked a little uncertain how to take this compliment, but she smiled and asked the little boy how he was.

"Very well, thank you," he said, just as Mrs. O'Hearn had taught him.

"This looks like a nice place for a young boy," said Mrs. Barter. She turned to Wyck. "How are you, Wyckford?"

"I'm getting better, thank you, Mrs. Barter."

"I'm glad," she said. She smiled softly, knowing the inadequacy of anything she could say. Wyckford had been her tenant for three years, and she had watched him play ball for three summers with nearly as much pride and excitement as if he had been her son. Above all, she understood what the game meant to him.

Mollie covered the awkward silence by unfolding the newspaper and setting it, front page out, in Wyckford's lap. *A Mysterious Portrait*, read a headline in the right-hand column, and below this it read:

The Search for a Kidnapped Child

Gunfight on the Sheepscott

New Mystery!

Readers Are Asked to Help!
by Peter Mall

Beneath these headlines was an engraving based on the portrait that had been discovered beneath Fort Edgecomb. Wyck glanced from the picture to Bird and back again.

"It's not a very *good* likeness," said Mollie. "Mister Walton had it done over three times at his own expense, but it still doesn't look like her."

Mister Walton had done quite a lot at his own expense, Wyckford knew, including shipping Wyck home by rail in a special car while he was still on his back. Wyckford knew they must find the boy's mother, but he had mixed feelings about it. He read some of the article, which took up three-quarters of the column and was continued on another page.

"This Peter Mall has got most of his facts straight," he said, sounding surprised.

"Yes," agreed Mollie. "He seems to have talked to the right people."

Wyckford felt awkward sitting there, looking at Mollie. She was so strong and so striking—that hint of Irishness in her nose and on her brow, the Latin cast to her large dark eyes, the fullness of her mouth—and he knew he was, at best, a big lug with fire-red hair, an open-faced Irish laborer; at worst, as at that very moment, he must appear ashen and old.

Mollie was thinking of that moment when she broke through the crowd at Brunswick and saw the Hibernian Titan make contact with the white sphere hurled in his direction. It was not the act of strength or power that had taken her so, nor the act of a sharp eye or a talent or an innate instinct; it was the act of sheer joy, like the right word in the right sentence. There was something in the sight that had made her heart, for one brief instant, leap as it seldom had. "I brought you something, Wyckford," she said.

"Bird?" said Mrs. O'Hearn. "Come help me get the gingerbread, now. And hold the door for Emmy when she brings out the coffee things."

Bird had been kneeling in his chair, looking at the object behind Mollie; he seemed eager to please Mrs. O'Hearn, however (though it may have been the prospect of warm gingerbread), and he leaped up at her command.

A table was placed among them, and Mollie and Mrs. Barter helped Wyck's sister arrange things. Emmy took advantage of this business to steal a closer look at Mollie.

"Years ago," Mollie said when they began to settle, "when I was young, my father was kicked in the leg by a horse, and it shattered his knee. Dad was hobbling around on a crutch for months after that, and it severely curtailed his work. There were some lean times, and for a while he thought he would never walk again. Eventually, he could limp along on his bad leg, but he had a terrible time bending his knee, which made everything difficult.

"So he bought a bicycle. He said that the problem was that he *could* walk on his bad leg. He *could* walk without bending that knee. But he couldn't ride a bicycle without bending it, and we thought it was the funniest thing at first, till we saw how hard it was for him to work the pedals.

"He rode everywhere. And when he had no work, he rode from one end of town to the other, and he used that knee till it gave in and bent because he wouldn't let it alone until it did!" Mollie was sitting straight now, her cup balanced on her knee. The story came faster as she told it, and the pride and the remembrance of her father's accomplishment infused her voice.

Wyck was a little astonished by this display. He had never heard Mollie go on so long about anything. She was quick with a witty reply or a sharp observation, but this was something he had never seen. She looked, for a moment, like a little girl bragging about her father, and he thought he had never liked her so much.

When she spoke again, her voice quavered. Wyck thought she had tears in her eyes, and he looked down at his hands. "So I have been thinking," she said, "what is very much like swinging a bat? It's not good enough just swinging in the air at nothing. You need a goal, like Father had a place to go every time he got on his bicycle." She reached behind her and produced an axe with a polished handle and a red blade. "When you can get up and about and the pain has gotten better, perhaps you can teach your shoulder to move properly again."

Mollie leaned the axe within reach of his good arm, then took interest in her coffee and a piece of gingerbread. She couldn't look at him.

Wyckford laughed softly. His mother shot him a look of warning; it was a well-known fact in their family that above everything, he hated to chop wood. "Maybe I can earn my keep, Mum," he said.

Mollie did not take his laughter unkindly but smiled when she looked at him.

You can't spill what you don't hold, Mrs. Barter was thinking, but Wyck thanked Mollie, and for the remainder of their visit there was little else said between them.

"There is something for you on the kitchen table," Mollie said to Bird when they were leaving. She reached out and brushed at his hair. They had said good-bye to Wyck and were in the front yard, where a single maple had loosed its leaves, and Wyck's brother-in-law had raked a pile of them for Bird to play in.

Mrs. Barter insisted on hugging the little boy now, saying, "You come visit me."

Mrs. O'Hearn thanked them profusely for coming and watched, as they left, with a pang of regret. She thought she would not see them again.

"He looked well, considering," said Mrs. Barter as the carriage took them to the station at Veazie.

Mollie said nothing.

"There's an old song," the older woman said wryly. " '*I went to the sea and shoveled sand, I gave an axe to a one-armed man.*' "

"Wyck isn't one-armed," said Mollie, looking out the window.

"No," said Mrs. Barter. "No, he isn't."

Bird came out on the back porch with the mechanical bear that they had first seen at Quentin McQuinn's, and he and Wyck watched it walk and stand on its head, and they even laughed a little together.

But both of them, quietly and in their own way, were thinking about Mollie Peer.

67. The Unsigned Verse
(October 30, 1896)

LATELY, IT SEEMED TO MOLLIE that she was bound to be surprised whenever she entered Mr. Corbel's office, and this time it was seeing Mister Walton, Sundry Moss, and the members of the Moosepath League crowding whatever small bit of floor that was not occupied by the editor's vast desk or stacks of paper, cigar boxes, and books. There was an incongruity, just seeing Mister Walton and her irascible boss in the same room together; but if anyone could quell the fuming smokestack behind the cluttered desk, she had faith that it was the chairman of the Moosepath League.

In fact, Mr. Corbel seemed in good humor as (per request of Christopher Eagleton) Sundry Moss explained how, three decades ago tomorrow, a weather-predicting milk cow had obtained a ticket for the night train from Wiscasset.

"What was her name?" asked the editor around the fiery stub of a cigar.

"Edith," said Sundry without blinking, "after my uncle's first wife."

"Miss Peer!" said Mister Walton, who was the first to notice her standing in the doorway. There was an immediate shift in the room as they turned their attention to the young woman. "We have just come by," said the chairman, "to see if there were any more letters here for us."

It had been decided that the editor's office would be the central location in the search for the woman in the portrait, but though certain helpful people had offered solutions to the problem, none of them had (in Sundry's words) panned out.

"Why don't you ever bring me stories like that?" demanded Mr. Corbel. He had taken the cigar out of his mouth and was looking at it as if he weren't sure how it got there.

"I didn't hear it all, I'm sorry," she said.

"The cow predicted the weather," said the editor.

"Certainly if I hear anything like it at Mrs. Tookey's benefit concert this weekend, I will report it to you."

"Mr. Corbel thought you might be able to introduce us to Mr. Mall, Miss Peer," said Ephram.

"Oh?" Mollie was a little startled.

"We were quite fascinated with his account of the adventure on the Sheepscott!" enthused Eagleton.

"It was a fair bit of reporting," admitted Mister Walton. Mollie looked carefully but could detect no irony in the man's face.

"One would have thought he'd been there himself!" said Thump.

"It is all in asking the right questions," she explained. She took a breath, then said, "After all, he *is* one of the best writers on the paper."

"Nothing you couldn't have written yourself, Miss Peer," said Mr. Corbel, dismissing this praise for Peter Mall with a wave of his hand.

"I was surprised not to see Miss Peer's name on the story, since she was there," said Mister Walton.

"Maybe next time," said the editor.

"And have you received any more letters?" asked Mollie.

"We did, actually," said the portly fellow. He reached into his jacket pocket and produced a single sheet of paper. On it was the following verse.

> Once more the League has proved its mettle
> And waiting for the dust to settle
> A missing sight might now be seen
> Upon the docks near Halloween.

It was unsigned, the only clue as to the author's identity being a tobacco-stained thumbprint.

They hesitated to quit Miss Peer's company, but after much hat-raising and well-wishing, the Moosepath League followed their leader out the door.

Thump was the last out, and he turned in the doorway with a look of concern occupying his bearded face. He thought, perhaps, that Miss Peer would appreciate a clarification. "We think it came from Mr. McQuinn," he said.

"Ah!" said Mollie. "Very likely. I wish you a good day, Mr. Thump, down at the waterfront."

Thump was a little thunderstruck by the melodious warmth in Mollie's voice and the sincere smile in her eyes. She was handing Mr. Corbel her latest column when they heard him run into the outer door.

Outside the offices of the *Eastern Argus*, Officer Samuel Skillings caught up with Mollie. She had been dreading this meeting and hoped, if she stayed in a crowd of people, she could postpone it longer still. But he was not to be put off any longer; he walked alongside as she hurried across the street, into a crowded portion of the sidewalk, and he was not cautious about pushing people out of the way. "Miss Peer!" he was saying. "Miss Peer!"

"Officer Skillings!" she said, as if surprised to see him, and more surprised still that he had any desire to speak to her.

"*Sam*, please," he insisted. "Miss Peer, I've been wanting to talk to you for the longest time."

"Yes . . . Sam." She had not stopped moving.

"I'm sorry to be so resolute, but if it wasn't the most intimate—"

"Excuse me," she said to a passing man she had nearly knocked over.

The man gave Mollie a hard stare, then flinched at a similar look from the policeman. Skillings took several long strides to catch up with her. "It's just that I have been wanting to ask—" He cast an embarrassed glance at those within hearing. It seemed he had to shout to make Miss Peer hear him. "I just wanted to ask—"

Mollie took a deep breath and stopped. She turned so quickly that Sam came near to running her over. Mollie pulled her head back and stepped away. "Sam," she said. "I have to say—"

"If you would just let me ask you—"

"—you are a very nice fellow—"

"I certainly wouldn't expect—"

"—and you have been a wonderful help to me with my researches—"

"Miss Peer."

"—and you were very sweet that day you came to the house so worried about me, although there wasn't anything to be concerned about and—"

"Miss Peer!"

She stopped.

"Please!"

He almost broke her heart, he looked so lovesick. "Yes, Sam," she said.

"I simply was hoping that . . . that you would introduce me to Miss Greenwood."

"I beg your pardon?"

"Miss Greenwood?" he said.

"Hilda?"

"I don't feel I have the right to use her name like that," he asserted demurely.

"What did you ask me?"

Sam Skillings gave her a look of concern, as if there might be something wrong with her that he hadn't realized. "I was hoping you might introduce me to your friend Miss Greenwood. *And* perhaps put in a good word for me."

"Hilda."

"Miss Greenwood, yes."

"Well, of course I would," she said.

A look of such complete relief and joy so brightened his face that she felt a little of its light, though she was still somewhat flummoxed.

"Oh, Miss Peer, I can't tell you how happy you make me!" he said.

A middle-aged woman passed by, and misunderstanding the scene (and Sam's words), she smiled at the young people.

"Please, call me Mollie, Sam." She put her hand out. "After all, we may become very good friends."

The policeman took Mollie's hand and gave it a short but sincere grip. "Do you really think so? Oh, thank you, Mollie!"

"Hilda did mention you the other night," she said carelessly.

"Miss Greenwood did?"

"She was rather disappointed that you couldn't stay for dinner the night you came by to inquire after me."

The officer had no idea that he had been invited. "Oh, my goodness, Miss Peer! You don't suppose she thinks that I have any attachment to you?"

"Don't say a word!"

Sam laughed at the notion. "She spoke of me?" he asked, but just then an altercation of sorts occurred between the drivers of two wagons down the street, and the official demeanor of the police officer took over. "Excuse me," he said to Mollie, and strode purposefully toward the dispute. "Now, what's going on here!" he shouted in his sternest law-enforcing tone.

Mollie continued down the street, blessedly relieved that she had not had the opportunity to disabuse the young man of his lovemaking when he had no intention of tendering it. She wondered, however, if she didn't feel a little offended. *Won't Hilda just shout*, she thought.

Mollie wondered then if she should have watched what happened between the drivers; there might have been an item for Peter Mall's pen. She shrugged. She wanted to go home.

Stranger things have happened!

The members of the club decided that they would walk to the waterfront, it being a grand fall day—almost the last of October, and it was not an odd thing that they would speak of recent events as they strolled down the Exchange. The day was crisp and sunny, and the rattle of the traffic and the clop of the horses were loud and invigorating.

"I am eager to renew our acquaintance with Mr. McQuinn's brother," said Ephram, who had thought often of Quentin McQuinn's clock shop.

The name of Amos Guernsey arose, and it was generously conceded between Ephram, Eagleton, and Thump that the actor had committed an error (or a series of errors, perhaps) in judgment; they sympathized with the man, since he must be feeling terrible about his brief tenure as their leader. "I think doing the opposite of what we intended was not successful," said Eagleton.

"It must be a very difficult thing to do," conjectured Ephram.

"I don't advise it," said Eagleton. "What do you think, Thump?"

"Hmm?" said Thump.

Mister Walton and Sundry had their own ideas about Amos Guernsey (they feared for the man's life if Wyckford O'Hearn or Mollie Peer ever caught up with him), but they thought it unnecessary to disabuse their fellow Moosepathians of their charitable notions.

"There are moments when a person does the opposite of what he plans quite by accident," said Thump, having considered Eagleton's question. "We were searching for Mr. Planke, and though I was the only one to find him, I did not succeed in bringing him in."

"Ah, Thump," said Ephram with a surprising dash of humor, "you came closer than I, who spent some time talking to a bush and a tree. I was never sure who I saw at the top of the slope."

"It may have been me looking for you," suggested Sundry.

"Whereas *I* occupied several minutes on my back," said Eagleton. "I was quite pleased when you fellows arrived and coaxed him off me."

"He was a very large animal," said Thump, "but I think I tumbled over him because he was so extremely black."

"He was a nice dog," said Eagleton, "but difficult to see."

"I was moving fairly rapidly," admitted Thump, who had been so startled by Ducky Planke.

"It is too bad we weren't able to find what he did with your hat," said Ephram. Eagleton, of course, had a *new* hat—a very handsome black topper.

Mister Walton brought them to a halt when they came to Commercial Street. "Ah, gentlemen!" he sighed. "Is there a bluer sky to be seen outside the fall of the year?"

Looking over the roofs that lined the waterfront, they *were* astounded by an excruciatingly blue sky, which was made the more intense by a few fleece-white clouds. The sky was to the color blue what the lush explosion of leaves in late May was to the color green; the very definition of a hue. The trees along the Portland streets were mostly bare now; only a few elms still clung to their yellow leaves, and one of these giants stood at the end of the next street, its crown like a ball of fire in the long light of the fall sun. The Moosepathians were loath to move, knowing they were looking upon something as ephemeral as a rainbow. Someone spoke:

> *"In Fall the breath comes wild and sweet,*
> *The heart is swiftly drumming;*
> *And birds who stay will oft' repeat,*
> *Old Winter soon is coming.*
>
> *"A certain corner of the heart,*
> *Crisp Fall with joy encroaches;*
> *Though Summer's blooms must now depart,*
> *And Winter fast approaches.*
>
> *"No other season ever knows*
> *Such joy and melancholy,*
> *As beauty in the eye swift flows*
> *From bloom, to leaf, to holly."*

It was Mister Walton.

"How very nice," said Eagleton, who had his notebook out in an instant. "Who wrote that?"

Mister Walton recalled something that Horace McQuinn once had said. "Nobody yet," quoted the portly fellow with a wink and a smile.

Eagleton was busy rectifying this situation, scribbling in his notebook as they continued on their way.

"It *is* a magnificent day," said Sundry. "Have you heard back from Miss McCannon?"

"Yes, in fact," Mister Walton said with a sigh. "She has shown great patience with my sudden parting. But she has been called to the sickbed of a relative in Orland, so I'm not sure when I will see her again."

"Ah, well," said Sundry. "It has been a fine month, all in all—"

"November is expected to open with fine weather," said Eagleton, quoting from his *Farmer's Almanac*. "Tomorrow, in fact, promises continued fair, with light winds in the southwest."

"High tide at thirty-three minutes past six o'clock," said Thump.

"It is now eleven minutes past one o'clock," said Ephram.

"—but I still wish I knew who those men were in Hallowell," continued Sundry.

A distinguished-looking gentleman stood at the northeast corner of Exchange and Commercial. He had a blue Hubbard squash under one arm. He heard their announcements and prognostications as the Moose-path League passed him by and wished he could hear more of this conver-sation, since (while the Moosepathians waited for a break in the traffic on Commercial Street) Sundry said, "Do you suppose we shall ever find the boy's mother? Or even discover who she was?" and Mister Walton said to him, "In its season, perhaps."

Then they were hurrying across the street, and the sight of them was swallowed up by the busy waterfront.

❖

IN THE FINAL YEARS of the nineteenth century, in the town of Hiram, Maine, near the western border of the state, Halloween was not greatly celebrated or even very widely recognized. Those children, therefore— particularly the boys—who felt that some activity should honor the season's mysteries were more often than not drawn to the old Linnett mansion, which had been left unoccupied since the winter of 1893.

The old pines that lined the carriage drive had a wakeful presence on such a night, when the wind ripped clouds across a field of stars. The hedges nearer the house had not been trimmed, and they wore the remains of previous seasons like unkempt beards.

The house itself was imposing, seated on a knoll in the midst of its overgrown yards; tall windows watched darkly, and the front columns were yet resolute. Approaching the old house by night, on foot, through the pines and past the hedges, the boys would often decide that Halloween was not such a demanding holiday, after all.

Jamie Huber and his best friend, Paul Leuve, were themselves hesitant as the house loomed above them, but several of their cronies were watching from the last twist in the carriage drive, and Jamie and Paul had promised these onlookers that they would flash a lantern from the front porch.

It was strange how the pointlessness of their mission seemed to increase the closer they got to the brick façade. The night was clear, but without a moon they were beholden to the faint glimmer of the Milky Way to keep them upon the dirt track.

Pride is a powerful thing, and boys must learn somehow the possible outcome of bold talk; after an agonizingly slow advance and much too soon, they stood at the front steps to the Linnett mansion.

Paul opened the lantern and flashed it at the boys behind them. After a moment, another lantern flashed back. "Let's go," suggested Paul. Now that they had arrived, however, Jamie regained a little of his bravado, and he proposed that they peer through some of the windows.

This was more easily said than done, since most of the windows were heavily curtained. They crept together, hardly breathing, from one casement to the next, almost fearing to look inside but sincerely disappointed whenever they found themselves blinded by dark drapery.

One curtain *had* partially fallen, though, and they were able to catch a glimpse of one end of a room, a chair or two, and a large, ornate mantelpiece. Paul shone the light past the break in the curtain, and they shielded their eyes against the glare in the glass.

There was little else to see, but they felt vaguely triumphant, having come this far—further than any of their friends had ever ventured.

"Look," said Paul, "above the fireplace."

Jamie did look but could see nothing.

"That's just it," said Paul when Jamie remarked at the lack of anything to see. "The wallpaper is faded except for that spot above the mantel."

Jamie looked again and realized that his friend's sharp eyes had discovered the place where a framed picture used to be. "I wonder what it was?" he said just as something in the room moved past his line of sight.

Paul saw it, too—a shadow, not cast by their lantern, gliding across the wall—and he scrambled to close the shutter to his lamp. Jamie hovered by his friend, torn between staying close to his comrade and flying with the wild fear that thrilled up his back.

Their feet hardly touched the front steps to the house, and they made no more sound than a light rain on the dirt track as they flitted through the darkness, past the hedges and the dark pines and the bend in the drive where their waiting friends gladly caught their fear and disappeared from the grounds of the Linnett mansion without a note of teasing or a word of explanation till they had covered the mile and a half to the center of town.

AUTHOR'S NOTE

TO THIS DAY, few figures engender such controversy in Moosepathian circles as that of Amos Guernsey, and several monographs have been published that attempt to resurrect his character and put the kindest light upon his motives and actions. Readers will come to their own conclusions.

Beyond his involvement with Mollie Peer and the Moosepath League, not much is known about the actor. His name does come up in a handful of theatrical reviews from about 1891 to 1894, none of which reflect very kindly upon his talents. "*As President Washington,*" wrote one critic, "*Amos Guernsey distinguished himself by remembering his lines.*"

Amos's journey from the wharves of Portland to his capture off Westport by Adam Tweed is fairly easy to trace, but after the flight from Winnegance, there seems to be no further record of him.

Though no mention is made in the relevant annals, Brownlow Davies was almost certainly the same personage as "Blackjack" Davies, who was a suspected highwayman on the roads outside of Augusta as early as 1882. This Davies did indeed make a short career in the Portland theater district in the early 1890s (generally playing stalwart heroes), and here a connection might be made with Amos. Davies spent only three months in jail and never revealed the identity of Henry Echo's persecutor. Suspicion, if not proof, did eventually fall upon Echo's dissolute brother-in-law.

This passage in the history of the Moosepath League is much discussed in the official chronicles, and it says something, I think, about the Moosepathian state of mind that, though sometimes spoken of as "the Adventure Underground," it has also been given the enigmatic title of "the Adventure of the Wooden Indian."

Brunswick's singular conclave of *Quibblers* has not met in many years.

Stories of the Merrymeeting persist, even to the present era. There are striking similarities between the stories concerning this institution and the faery-hills of England and Scotland. More than one dilatory husband or wife has laid claim to losing a day or even a week at the Merrymeeting. It continues to be well thought of in some circles.

The mystery of Bird and his identity was not yet solved by the end of October 1896, though New Year's Eve of 1897 would find the riddle mostly solved, partly as the result of the perception and kindness of the country lawyer Daniel Plainway.

These subsequent events, most of which occurred during December 1896, included the League's first involvement with two other Portland societies (which are not to be confused with one another), the Broumnage Club and the Dash-It-All Boys. There were also, during that period, the uproarious "Battle of the Smoking Pine!" and the initiation of a sixth Moosepathian. The circumstances of December 1896 have been variously dubbed "the Adventure of the Holiday Haunting," "the Adventure of the Three Legacies," and "the Adventure of the Mother's Eyes."

Someday it may be told.

Readers may wish to know what is unreservedly historical in this tale. To that end:

Fort Edgecomb stands to this day, and many are the "friends" that belong to its worthy society. Visit it and you may find the spreads of modern picnickers or the tents and pickets of Revolutionary War reenactors. On any day, however, it provides a beautiful view of the Sheepscott River. Tales concerning tunnels below the fort have been perpetuated by generations of storytellers.

Within a few years of the events recorded here, Cliff Cottage and the Tontine Hotel were both lost to fire.

The newspaper items from the *Eastern Argus* concerning the fate of the *Loala* are taken almost verbatim from the papers of the day, including the story of Captain Amey's solo journey from Portsmouth. (I have it from a coaster veteran that, if not common or entirely advisable, such a solo journey was not unheard of.)

Tales of John Neptune abound; he is not simply a historical personage but *several*. A long line of these Penobscot shamans and chiefs have proved their courage, wisdom, and ofttimes humor throughout the history of the state of Maine. It is sometimes difficult to separate them by their deeds; certain feats are variously ascribed among them.

Portland did indeed win the contract for the Atlantic and St. Lawrence Railroad, a business deal that proved an extraordinary asset to the port for many years. The race to Montreal, however, is shadowed in myth and legend. To this day, there are no statues to John Neptune and Isherwood Tolly.

Louis Sockalexis's story is a less happy one. He might have been an athlete for the ages—spoken of in the same breath with Jesse Owens and Babe Didrikson—if his comet had not burned out so quickly and completely.

Even so, Sockalexis cut a terrific swath through Holy Cross and Notre Dame, and it was his honor to inspire the name of the Cleveland Indians. With courage, gallantry, and wit, Sockalexis conquered poverty and prejudice, but found his downfall in drink. Wyckford O'Hearn met Sockalexis when he was at the height of his powers. Just fourteen years later, Sockalexis would be found dead of a heart attack, a yellowed newspaper clipping from his great days folded into a shirt pocket. His triumphs outweighed his downfall, I believe, and he is a hero to this writer.

The list of people to whom I am in debt for their kindness, wisdom, and support grows longer with every day. Some of the people I most want to thank are the many booksellers who have made me feel welcome, and who have shown their support along the front lines of the business: so here is to Darrilyn Peters and Georgina at Thomaston Books & Prints; Allan Schmid and Sandy at Books Etc. in Portland; Marc Berlin of BookMarc's in Bangor; Michael Herrmann of Gibson's Bookstore in Concord, New Hampshire; André Cinquina at Lauriat's in Concord, New Hampshire; Lola Furber of Bookland in Brunswick; Audrey & Jeff Curtis and Rosemary Nadeau of Sherman's in Boothbay and Freeport; Paul & Carol & Bret Lerner, Lisa Cummings, and Ed Shindel of the Owl and the Turtle in Camden; the folks at Sherman's in Bar Harbor; Richard & Ellen Chasse, and Paula Ayers of Kennebunk Book Port; Andrea Stark of Borders in Bangor; Kathleen O'Brien and Craig Elliot of Borders in Portland; Rosiland Lewis and Marilyn Mays at Port in a Storm in Somesville; and Becky Batchelor. Also Gretchen Moore at Bangor's B. Dalton; and Ruth E. Volpe and Sylvia Sarnacchiaro at Portland's Waldens.

My appreciation and regard go to Dwight Currie, Michael Kohlmann, Mitzi Hakey, Janis Kranza of the Misty Valley Bookshop, as well as the Unitarian Church, and the Fullerton Inn—all in the lovely town of Chester, Vermont, where a wonderful time was had by everyone at the fifth annual "New Voices for a New Year."

Regards to Mary Ann Betke and the Round Top Reading Group and also to the Ladies of the Georgetown Book Club.

Most especially, thanks to Jane and Mark Biscoe, Susan and Barnaby Porter, Penny and Ewing Walker, Pat and Clark Boynton, Joanne Cotton, Devon Sherman, Johanna Rice, Frank Slack, Hester Stuhlman, and all my friends at the Maine Coast Book Shop in Damariscotta. And continued good luck to Liz Padgett, Jesse Kirchner, and Helen Sampson.

Thanks to Jim Morris of WABI TV, Bangor; Scott Jones of WCLZ Radio in Brunswick; Marnie Maclean of WGAN TV, Portland; and Jim Crocker of WCSH TV, Portland.

Thanks to Dave Hurley and Larry and Sherry Schneider of King Eider's Pub in Damariscotta. I will always remember the fun of that first reading.

I wish I had the room to name everyone who sent their encouragement and laughter by post and telephone, and all the new acquaintances by mail who wrote to register their thoughts concerning Mister Walton and his associates. A special hello, however, to Jennifer Jackson, who felt something in common with the redheaded and feisty Cordelia Underwood—and rightly so, now that I think of it!

Thanks to Carol Brightman for her continued enthusiasm. Thanks to Nick Dean for his selfless help and his dedication to the truth about that magnificent era of ships and sailing.

To Michael Uhl, friend and mentor, my continued gratitude, as well as to my agent, Barbara Hogenson, her assistant Sarah Feider, and my editor at Viking, Carolyn Carlson. Thanks to Michael Driscoll and Lucia Watson.

Thank you, Jim Nelson, for your camaraderie and advice.

Thanks, of course, to my parents, my brother and sisters, cousins Stanley and Claudia Coffin, Aunt Edie, and Aunt Jean, and friends Kathleen Creamer, Les Harris, Karol and Gordon Clark, Barbara and J. D. Neeson, Brian and Rosa Redonnett, Ron and Patty Aho, Pat Ginaty, and David and Susan Morse.

Thanks to my wonderful in-laws, including Marjorie Hunter, to whom this book is dedicated.

Finally to my wife, Margaret Hunter—Maggie—who has helped to navigate every word and steered me clear of many a dark narrative headland. Without her this work would never have been. So to Maggie and our children, Hunter and Mary, thank you for blessing my life and constantly reminding me that the kindness, goodness, and laughter exemplified by Mister Walton, Sundry Moss, and the honorable members of the *Moosepath League* are not mere whims to be found only between the covers of a book.

Journey back to a snowy, nineteenth-century
Maine Christmas in Van Reid's new novel

DANIEL PLAINWAY

 OR

THE

HOLIDAY HAUNTING

of the

MOOSEPATH LEAGUE

❧ PROLOGUE ❧

November 27–December 2, 1896

1. The Empty House
Thanksgiving 1896

It had snowed for an hour or so that morning, and the large, wet flakes still coated the windward side of trees, lined the bare branches of oak and maple, and formed a speckled fleece over the evergreens that guarded the carriage drive to the Linnett house.

On the way home from Fryeburg, Daniel Plainway pulled the horse and trap up before the stone columns at the end of the drive. He and his sister had been celebrating Thanksgiving with friends, and the snow had actually made it safe to leave later than they had planned, as the road glowed in the dusk, and the tracks of other wheels and horses described the way in dark lines and pockmarks before them.

Martha Bailey complained just a bit (in a wordless groan) when her brother stopped before the Linnett property. They had just crossed the town line into Hiram, and she looked forward to a fire in her own hearth; but to tell the truth, she was snugly wrapped in several throws, and the soapstones, warmed in their host's kitchen oven, still radiated comfortingly beneath the quilts at their feet.

"Do you mind if I take a turn up?" asked Daniel. The expression on his face was almost childlike, though not untouched by a self-realizing humor.

"No," she said. "You've been thinking about it since we came the other way this morning."

His chuckle was almost unheard as he shook the reins and the brown mare turned her head between the tilting columns.

The house itself was not visible from the road, and the ancient pines lining the drive hid the gray sky and darkened the atmosphere beneath so that one trusted to the instincts of the horse. There were several turns in the way, and one dip over a tiny running brook before they came to the first row of hedges and the manse itself rising out of the knoll ahead of them, amorphous in the shadows. Not half a mile away was Clemons Pond, glazed with ice, a dark presence in the fields beyond and below.

As they neared the house, a small breeze stirred the hedges.

"Oh, hurry," said Martha. "This place gives me the chills."

He passed her the reins, untangled himself from the throws, and climbed down. The wet snow gathered on his boots and crunched in the stiffened, uncut grass. Martha could see footprints appearing behind the man more easily than she could see the man himself, giving her the shuddery impression of an invisible being approaching the house.

The steps to the porch complained of Daniel's progress; the key sounded dully as he turned it. The air within, when he opened the door, was colder than the November evening. He had known the people here, had handled many small legal businesses for the Linnetts in his capacity as a lawyer, but had spent most of his time among these walls as a guest and a friend.

Daniel stopped in the hall and peered into the gloom of the parlor, remembering the lights and the voices. Nell often played the piano in the evening when they gathered here, and everyone but Linnett himself sang, he being too concerned for his local fame as an old grouch. It had been an undeserved reputation for the most part, until the last year or so, and even then his great rage was the product of a broken heart.

Daniel Plainway was not sure that he believed in ghosts, but he didn't think he would be frightened if he met one here. *There's more to be feared from the living than the dead*, his parents had told him more than once. He looked up the dusty stairway and thought of Nell descending there: a child, a young woman. She had been dear to Daniel's heart, like a lovely cousin who brings the holiday with her.

The holidays he remembered best of all: the grand Thanksgiving feasts, the Christmas candles throughout the house, filling the rooms with light on the eve before like the very grotto at Bethlehem. Old Ian Linnett never tired of his annual Yuletide jest: On the night of the winter solstice (Doubter's Day, he called it) he would arrive with a tiny spruce—barely three feet high—and teased everybody by announcing that *this* was the tree; as soon as he had cajoled the laughing and complaining crowd to decorate the whimsical thing, the real tree would make its entrance upon the backs of sturdy men, and Linnett was never satisfied unless it scraped the ceiling in the front hall.

Daniel craned his head back to look at the ceiling where daylight might have revealed the scars left by the topmost branches of long-forgotten trees.

Standing in the door to the front room, across from the parlor, he did not need a light to discern the shapes of furniture covered in sheets and throws or to remember that Nell's portrait was missing from its place above the hearth. Other things were missing from the house these past three years. He was pretty sure he knew who had taken them. "If I had just seen it all coming," he said aloud, and he shivered to think that perhaps his voice was unwelcome there.

Then he heard it again, a soft sound like a young woman's voice, but as from some irrevocable distance, and almost the notes of a simple melody; no doubt the wind was in a chimney or playing against a cracked eave.

Daniel closed the front door and locked it, feeling a small regret for having come here again. He stood on the porch and thought, *It's almost as if I still believe they'll all be here.* After the gloom of the house the strange patterns of snow on the lawn seemed to give off a light of their own. He could see Martha, waiting patiently in the carriage. It was important that he not appear melancholy when he returned, which meant just a moment more to regain his bearings.

He stepped around the corner of the house and looked over the pond. Everything seemed frozen, pitched in a single moment of discovery, and the sensation was so strong within him that he was startled to see the footprints leading from the back of the house.

The kids have been up here again, he thought as he walked the side lawn. *Well, as long as they don't harm anything.*

But there was something about the footprints that did not suggest a youngster had made them. There was only the one set, for one thing, closely spaced and weaving slightly, and they came from the house, and stopped at the edge of the pond. Daniel had thought that he would be fearless in the face of a phantom, but the prints touched him with an apprehension that rose to a vague dread as he followed the tracks to a place overlooking the water. The impress of a body marked the snow.

Old man Linnett had come from the back of the house with that same halting, weaving gait. He had collapsed and died in this place more than three years ago; Daniel could almost vouch for the exact spot.

"Is there anything the matter?" asked Martha when he returned to the carriage.

How could she know in this dark? he wondered. "I only wish they were still here," he said.

"*I* wish you wouldn't come."

"It's all right," he said, patting her knee through the throws wrapped about her. He covered himself up as well as he could and shook the reins, hoping that he didn't appear to be in a hurry. "Something hot when we get home," he suggested.

She looked at him in the dark but could see nothing of his expression.

The horse, surefooted and undaunted by the prospect of ghosts, pulled them past the hedges and through the guardian pines to the road home.

2. A Voice Before Dawn
November 28, 1896

Lydia O'Hearn was not too proud to half dress herself beneath the covers, a practice she had observed, on cold mornings, since her husband first brought her to his farm in Veazie. Sean O'Hearn used to laugh and make her laugh whenever she hauled her things on in bed, sometimes with the blankets over her head. These days, without her husband to help warm the sheets (a warming pan was not the same thing by any stretch), there was all the more reason to snatch her clothes and scramble into them beneath the covers on a morning like this. It was dark, with the curtains closed against the chill, but when she did climb out of bed, she could see her breath in the room.

She hadn't been too avid about farm life, or country life for that matter, when she arrived with Sean thirty years ago; she hadn't been too avid about the life when he died twenty-two years later, but she stayed, and she ran things with the help of her daughter, Emmy, and son-in-law, Ephias Ostertag, and somehow had developed some fierce feelings for it all. Her other children—those who survived the rigors of life to become adults—had separated like geese that fold away in flight to light upon their own fields or ponds. One of these, her son Wyckford, had returned for a time, and she was glad to know, rising that morning, that he was there to help fill the house again.

Once dressed and on the landing above the front hall stairs, she looked out the octagonal window that Sean had put in for her as a birthday present the year before he died. It faced east and was often her first view of the day. A hint of dawn shone through the single frosty pane this morning, with what Lydia considered to be a lack of conviction.

She didn't know why, but it occurred to her that she should write to Mister Walton. Then she remembered that she had dreamed of this man she had never met and that he had been telling her about Bird's mother.

Once she had said good morning to the dog, Skinny (a fat black animal of amiable disposition), it did not take her long to shake up the coals in the kitchen stove and get some kindling blazing; with two large sticks of wood and the flues and drafts open she had the firebox roaring and the oven ticking. She put the kettle on and rattled some pans so that everyone would know that Mother was up. Closing the damper, she could feel the heat from the stove almost immediately. There was paper, pen, and ink in the cupboard drawer, and she arranged these on the table, set a chair by the stove, and opened the oven door. The light in the kitchen was yet pretty dim, but she could see to compose a letter.

Dear Mister Walton, she wrote. He was all but a stranger to her, and yet because of everything he had done, particularly what he had done for her son Wyckford and for Bird, she had no difficulty addressing him as *Dear Mister Walton* with all sincerity. She paused only to wet her pen, before continuing.

> You will be pleased, I know, to read that Wyckford has improved greatly since I wrote you last. The cold weather gets into his wound, and he still has difficulty moving his arm more than an inch or two, but he is not in such constant pain and is able to face the day with more hope.

Hope was the important notion here. Wyckford had been shot in the shoulder last October, and the bullet had done untold damage. Lydia's hope was that her son would be able to work again; she knew that a man unable to wield some sort of tool to make a living was not much valued by society and soon despised by himself. Wyck's own hopes were more specific, and less likely. For several years, during the warmer months, he had played semiprofessional baseball in Portland, and uppermost in his mind was the fear that he would never again be able to swing a bat.

Lydia heard small footsteps on the stairs, and she put down her pen to wait for the attendant feet to enter the kitchen. After a quiet interval a head of brown hair and a pair of brown eyes, three feet or so from the floor, peered around the jamb. There was the look of humor in those eyes, a little mischief even, which pleased her. "I hope you're not in your bare feet," she said, knowing that he was.

The little boy, known to them only as Bird, showed himself and his bare feet. Here was the object of Wyckford's efforts, and the efforts of

Mister Walton and many others, the single small life that had precipitated a kidnapping, mortal chase, and her son's near loss of life. She had quickly grown to love the child.

"You get over here!" she said in mock anger.

He grinned as he hurried, socks and shoes in his hands, to the table, where she pulled out another chair. He sat down, and she grabbed up his sweet, scarred little feet and began to rub them vigorously.

"Oh, they're like ice!" she declared, which pleased him more.

This had become a ritual with them, and no one could have guessed who looked forward to it most. When she had chafed his feet warm and dressed them, she got up and washed her hands under the pump—an icy reminder of the day—then pulled down some plates from the cupboard. The kettle was already rumbling. Something occurred to her then, and she said, "I was just about to write Mister Walton about you." With a thought of what to write next, she sat back down and took up her composition once more.

Bird seems to enjoy the farm more and more, and even Ephias doesn't mind him following about while he does the morning chores.

It was true. Though Ephias Ostertag was the unfortunate picture of a taciturn Yankee (what Emmy saw in the man, Lydia would never know) and though he seemed as stony as a New England field, he had warmed to Bird considerably and hardly growled when the boy accompanied him as he fed the creatures in the barn and milked the cows. But once Lydia's son was up and about, moving stiffly after another wakeful night with his splintered shoulder, the little boy was Wyckford's constant companion.

You will understand, I think, Mister Walton, when I confess to you that it will be difficult to see the boy go, if ever his mother is found.

Emmy appeared in the kitchen, exchanged good mornings with her mother, and informed the boy that her husband had decided to lie abed and let Bird do the chores. Bird looked game. Ephias was not long behind her, though, and he had overheard his wife's quip. "He's already milked some and gathered eggs," said the man, and this intelligence was meant as praise, despite the growl in which it was couched. The man sat down and stretched an arm toward the dog. Skinny made a grunting noise while Ephias stroked her head.

Emmy returned from the pantry with a slab of bacon, and soon thick slices of the stuff were snapping in the pan and scenting the air with smoke and spice. Ephias sat at the table and packed his pipe, which would hardly leave his mouth the rest of the day.

"What does an owl in the night mean?" wondered Emmy.

"Probably that there is an owl nearabouts," returned her mother.

"Granny used to say something about an owl at night," insisted Emmy.

"A dog howling after dark is not considered fortunate. It's all superstition."

"No, I'm sure it was an owl she used to go on about."

"You would hardly hear one during the day, I think."

"I've heard one three nights in a row," said Emmy. "He woke me up last night. It's a strange sound when you're half asleep."

"It's sitting in the apple tree by your window," said Lydia. She was surprised that an owl would take up residence at this time of year but said nothing.

Wyckford came down the stairs. His tread was the heaviest in the house, the more so since his wounded side had thrown off his gait. He was a man of some altitude, though no longer the splendid "Hybernian Titan" who had spent so much ink in Portland's sporting press. He looked gaunt and drawn these days and older than his thirty years. There were strands of gray in his bright red hair. He was uncomfortable with his function (or, more aptly put, his *lack* of function) in the household.

Ephias, who said nothing about Wyckford's presence, was nearly as discomfited as Wyck. Ephias, it was suspected, had always considered Wyckford to be capricious and unreliable; playing baseball, it would seem, was no way for a man to make a living, even for some fraction of the year. The adventure that had led Wyckford to rescuing Bird and coming to physical grief was only a symptom of an irresponsible nature.

But Wyckford had labored in his time—as a line tender for the railroad and demolishing old buildings to make room for the Portland sugar refinery—and the inactivity of the past month and a half had told upon him as much as the wound that had caused it.

He might have left, if not for Bird. There was a powerful bond between the redheaded giant and the little boy that had been immediate and hard to explain, but if Bird had unintentionally led him to these straits, his presence was helping to lead him out of them.

This morning, however, Wyckford did not linger on Bird, who was sneaking a piece of bacon to Skinny. "Where's that ax?" Wyck asked his mother, by way of good morning. Someone had given him an ax, hoping that the use of it would duplicate the swing of a bat and bring his arm back to life. Of all the chores that Wyck hated, while growing up on the farm, none had been so onerous to him as chopping and splitting wood. He had spent many an hour contemplating that ax and (not insignificantly) the person (that is, the young woman) who had given it to him.

"It's in the shed, I think," said Lydia. She didn't think Wyckford should be swinging an ax. It had been too soon since he'd been wounded, and she feared he would do more damage to his shoulder, not to mention the danger of chopping off a toe. Nothing else was said. Ephias didn't look any happier, lighting his pipe. Emmy did not turn around from the stove. But when breakfast was on the table, Wyck put some food into him.

He needed help getting a warm coat on, and Lydia couldn't see how chucking an ax was practical or even very smart. Bird was ready to join him and forgo the morning chores, but Wyckford clearly needed to approach this test alone.

Lydia touched Bird's shoulder and without a word shook her head.

Wyckford trundled out into the cold morning, looking ungainly but determined. They did not watch him, except for the little boy. As he stood below the kitchen steps, the man's breath came in great puffs of steam. Beyond him the backyard was bleak with frost.

"Ephias," said Lydia when the door was closed, but Ephias had his coat on already.

"I can see the woodpile from the barn," was all Ephias said. He gave a reverse nod to Bird, which was as much invitation as the little fellow had ever gotten from the flinty man. Bird hurried with his coat and hat and followed him out.

Perhaps it wasn't so strange that Bird could enjoy the morning chores with Ephias, neither of them ever said very much. Ephias's lack of words, however, was the weight of rocky fields and broken fences; Bird's silences were bright, the silences of someone who truly listens, like that of a man in a bird-filled wood. Bird followed Ephias, and Skinny waddled after Bird; they were an odd trio.

When they were gone, Lydia said to her daughter, "That was nice of Ephias."

Emmy was thinking she would cook an apple pie for her husband. "He'll surprise even himself some days."

Lydia didn't like to think of Wyck swinging an ax with his broken shoulder but knew somehow that it was necessary. She thought of the person who had given the ax to Wyckford and decided to ask Mister Walton if he had heard from her.

"Who are you writing?" asked Emmy. She had the dishes in the sink and was working the pump handle.

"Mister Walton." Lydia dipped her pen and considered the letter. The sound of her writing was large in the kitchen.

Emmy poured some hot water from the kettle in after and nearly had the dishes done before she spoke again. "Tell Mister Walton," she said, "that the boy is spoken for."

FOR MORE VAN REID TITLES THAT WILL ENCHANT AND AMUSE, LOOK FOR THE

CORDELIA UNDERWOOD
Or the Marvelous Beginnings of the Moosepath League
ISBN 0-14-028010-3

A *New York Times* Notable Book

"An amiable, richly populated first novel . . . Diffuse and leisurely, the novel seems designed for long afternoons in a hammock . . . Reid's gazillion characters sparkle."
—*The New York Times Book Review*

"Reminiscent of John Irving at his hilarious best . . . A charming, old-fashioned romp through Victorian New England."
—*Boston Herald*

In 1896 Portland, Maine, the young and beautiful Cordelia Underwood and the Moosepath League join forces to uncover a two-century-old family secret. Together, they set out on an entertaining and audacious quest fraught with Cupid's arrows, apparitions, a kidnapping, smuggling, and thievery—as well as wonderment and romance. *Cordelia Underwood* is a splendid yarn of the old fashioned variety.

And new from Viking

DANIEL PLAINWAY
Or the Holiday Haunting of the Moosepath League
ISBN 0-670-89171-1

Journey back to a snowy, nineteenth-century Maine Christmas in Van Reid's new novel *Daniel Plainway*. As the Moosepath League embarks on an adventure studded with unforgettable characters, country lawyer Daniel Plainway begins his own mission to find a deceased friend's long-lost son.

FOR THE BEST IN PAPERBACKS, LOOK FOR THE

In every corner of the world, on every subject under the sun, Penguin represents quality and variety—the very best in publishing today.

For complete information about books available from Penguin—including Puffins, Penguin Classics, and Arkana—and how to order them, write to us at the appropriate address below. Please note that for copyright reasons the selection of books varies from country to country.

In the United Kingdom: Please write to *Dept. EP, Penguin Books Ltd, Bath Road, Harmondsworth, West Drayton, Middlesex UB7 0DA.*

In the United States: Please write to *Penguin Putnam Inc., P.O. Box 12289 Dept. B, Newark, New Jersey 07101-5289* or call 1-800-788-6262.

In Canada: Please write to *Penguin Books Canada Ltd, 10 Alcorn Avenue, Suite 300, Toronto, Ontario M4V 3B2.*

In Australia: Please write to *Penguin Books Australia Ltd, P.O. Box 257, Ringwood, Victoria 3134.*

In New Zealand: Please write to *Penguin Books (NZ) Ltd, Private Bag 102902, North Shore Mail Centre, Auckland 10.*

In India: Please write to *Penguin Books India Pvt Ltd, 11 Panchsheel Shopping Centre, Panchsheel Park, New Delhi 110 017.*

In the Netherlands: Please write to *Penguin Books Netherlands bv, Postbus 3507, NL-1001 AH Amsterdam.*

In Germany: Please write to *Penguin Books Deutschland GmbH, Metzlerstrasse 26, 60594 Frankfurt am Main.*

In Spain: Please write to *Penguin Books S. A., Bravo Murillo 19, 1° B, 28015 Madrid.*

In Italy: Please write to *Penguin Italia s.r.l., Via Benedetto Croce 2, 20094 Corsico, Milano.*

In France: Please write to *Penguin France, Le Carré Wilson, 62 rue Benjamin Baillaud, 31500 Toulouse.*

In Japan: Please write to *Penguin Books Japan Ltd, Kaneko Building, 2-3-25 Koraku, Bunkyo-Ku, Tokyo 112.*

In South Africa: Please write to *Penguin Books South Africa (Pty) Ltd, Private Bag X14, Parkview, 2122 Johannesburg.*